CAPTIVATING KISS

Desperate to find her father, Alisha soundlessly dropped out the cabin's window, eager to get away from Black Wolf. But before she had taken even a step, a hand suddenly snaked out and strong fingers wrapped about her ankle.

Frustrated and angry, she tried to pull free, but his hold on her merely tightened. "Let me go!" she spat.

Her Indian captor let her loose—then grabbed her hand and pulled her roughly onto his bedroll. Before she could cry out, Black Wolf's lips had descended upon hers, claiming her with a breathtaking kiss.

Alisha's common sense told her not to respond, but as his mouth continued to take possession of hers, her self-restraint fled. Soft moans escaped her as she entwined her fingers in his black, flowing hair, encouraging his fervent fondling.

Black Wolf was now aroused beyond his control, and his vow to remain emotionally detached from this white slave was completely forgotten as passion swept him like wildfire and he proceeded to ravish her as he had no other woman in his life. . . .

SAVAGE CARESS

ROCHELLE WAYNE

ZEBRA BOOKS
KENSINGTON PUBLISHING CORP.

ZEBRA BOOKS

are published by

Kensington Publishing Corp.
475 Park Avenue South
New York, NY 10016

Third printing: May, 1992

Printed in the United States of America

For Jean, who knows first impressions are not necessarily lasting ones. And for Jan, who always knows if we're having fun.

Prologue

The rays from the cresting sun slanted luminously across the handsome Sioux warrior as he sat quietly beside the riverbank. The brave, dressed only in a loincloth, was seated cross-legged, his black eyes staring somberly into space.

The meandering river flowed placidly a short distance from the Sioux campsite, and as the azure sky lightened with the ensuing dawn, people began emerging from their tepees to start their morning activities.

The sounds coming from the awakening village reached the lone warrior's ears, but he paid no attention. Absently, he wiped at his perspiring brow, and as he continued to recall his vision, his strong body tensed. Visions were not uncommon for Running Horse; he'd often experienced the uncanny ability to foresee the future: these prophecies came to him in his dreams.

Running Horse's visions were usually uplifting and had often left him feeling exhilarated. However, the one he'd had only minutes before had given him cause to be deeply troubled. He wished he could believe that this particular dream would never come true. His glimpse into the future had him upset, and he questioned whether it was the spirits' way of punishing him for marrying a white woman.

Concentrating intently, he wondered whether he had somehow misinterpreted his dream. After several minutes of deep thought, he had to reluctantly admit that his vision hadn't been misread.

The warrior's folded shirt and leggings were on the ground close to his side. Reaching beneath them, he picked up his sheathed knife, and removing the weapon from its covering, he placed the sharp blade against his muscular forearm. Then, carefully, he cut himself several times, and blood immediately oozed from the multiple slashes.

Running Horse welcomed the pain, for only through physical punishment would the spirits grant him release from his troublesome vision.

Hearing someone approaching, he turned and glanced over his shoulder. Seeing his father, he smiled tentatively.

The older man went to his son and sat down. He didn't question Running Horse about his bleeding cuts, for it was the Sioux way not to pry. If his son wanted him to know why he had inflicted pain upon himself, he would tell him.

Running Horse had been awaiting his child's birth, and because it was custom for the arrival to be announced to a male relative of the father's, Running Horse asked, "Has my child been born?"

"Yes, the child is here," Swift Elk answered.

"I have a son," Running Horse stated with certainty.

Swift Elk smiled. "Why are you so sure that you don't have a daughter?"

"My vision foretold a son."

His father held his silence, hoping Running Horse would reveal his dream. Then, when it became apparent that the young man had no intentions of doing so, he asked, "This vision, did it leave you troubled?"

"Yes, Father." His eyes were distressed.

Swift Elk loved his son dearly, and his obvious sorrow had him worried. Still, he held his silence.

Running Horse rose to his feet and slipped on his leggings and his long-sleeved shirt, which hid his fresh cuts. Then, leaving his father, he headed into the Indian village to see his wife and newborn child.

As Swift Elk watched his son's departure, his eyes clouded with worry. He was a Sioux chief and his tribe was large. Chief Swift Elk was a fearsome warrior and a skillful hunter. He knew that someday his leadership would fall to Running Horse, for he had no other living sons. Once he had hoped that the spirits would grant Running Horse many sons, but he now felt different. His son had taken himself a white wife, and Swift Elk had been against the marriage. The chief harbored much hate for the whites who were invading this land which belonged to the Sioux.

Swift Elk gazed into the distance. He had a feeling that Running Horse's last vision was related somehow to his newborn son. The child's mother was white, and when the child became a man, where would his loyalties lie—with the Sioux, or with his mother's people? Had that been Running Horse's vision? Someday would the son of Running Horse leave the Sioux?

Entering the tepee, Running Horse found his wife

and child alone. They were lying on a bed made of soft buffalo rugs, and going to them, he knelt. His black eyes met the woman's blue ones, and for a moment he was mesmerized by her loving gaze.

Peeling the blanket away from the infant's face, she murmured, "Running Horse, meet your son."

He tore his gaze from hers and lowered his eyes upon the child. Gently, he placed his large hand against the baby's cheek and rubbed his fingers over the infant's smooth skin. Then, sitting, Running Horse announced quietly, "He will be called Black Wolf."

His wife agreed: "Black Wolf will be his Sioux name."

Running Horse looked at her questioningly. "His Sioux name?" he asked.

"Yes, but his white name will be Charles, after my father."

The warrior frowned. It was no wonder his vision had foretold of his son's mixed loyalties. Running Horse knew that his wife would teach their son the ways of the whites, embedding her people into his very soul!

It was on the tip of his tongue to forbid her to give the child a white name or to even speak to him about his white heritage. But he bit back the retort, for he had once promised her the right to teach their children the ways of the whites. For a moment he was angry with himself. Why had he relented and given in to this woman? Why was he always so weak where his white wife was concerned?

He turned his gaze to the woman's pretty face. He had loved her upon first sight. His thoughts drifting into the past, he remembered the day he had accidently come across her. She had wandered a distance from her parents' homestead to go swimming in the nearby river.

Hiding himself in the surrounding shrubbery, Running Horse had watched the beautiful woman. When she had emerged from the water and her bared beauty had been revealed to him, he had felt compelled to make her his own. Driven by an uncontrollable need for the young white woman, he had abducted her, forcing her to accompany him on the long journey to his father's village. It had taken the handsome warrior a long time to finally win her love. However, in order to do so, he had been forced to learn to compromise.

Now, as his eyes beheld her beauty, he once again relented. "Our son's white name will be Charles."

She smiled her thanks. "I'll call him Chuck."

Running Horse frowned. "You must not use that name publicly. My father and his people do not know that you have not fully adopted our ways."

She reached for her husband's hand and squeezed it affectionately. "I'll not shame you, Running Horse."

He brought her hand up to his lips, kissing her palm. "I love you, and I thank you for giving me a son."

"I love you, my husband," she whispered, her blue eyes shining sincerely, for she truly did love the powerful warrior. Then, detecting a hint of worry on his face, she asked, "Running Horse, is something wrong?"

"I had another vision," he said gravely.

"When?"

"When my son was being born."

"Tell me about this vision. Did it have anything to do with our child?"

"It foretold his future." Running Horse lifted the baby and cradled him gently in his strong arms. For a long moment, he stared at his son, his dark eyes shaded with sorrow. "I named our son Black Wolf because of my vision," he murmured somberly, his gaze now on his wife.

Carefully, he placed the baby beside its mother. Speaking softly and with feeling, he began to explain his vision. "I dreamt of a pack of wild dogs, and among them was one that was a cross between a wolf and a dog. He looked more wolf than dog, and he was black. Although he loved his clan, he nonetheless was always restless to know the wolves. Their blood flowed through his veins, and it was instinct for him to feel drawn to them. But he also felt a deep love for the dogs who had raised him and protected him all his life. His mother was a wolf; it had been his father who had brought her to live among the wild dogs."

Running Horse paused, concentrating intently on his vision before continuing. "Wolf packs began to move into the land belonging to the dogs, causing conflict and war to erupt. Often, at night, this half-dog, half-wolf would wander to the top of a high ridge, where he would listen to the howling of the wolves. For many years, his love for the dogs kept him from returning the wolves' constant, drawn-out howls; but, finally, his natural instincts prevailed. One night, when the moon was full, he climbed up onto the ridge. He did not wait to hear the sounds of the howling wolves. Instead, he lifted his head and cried one long, baleful wail, identical to that of the wolves'. Then he turned and looked down at the pack of dogs who were the only family he had ever known. His eyes filled with tears, and they spilled freely, falling onto the rocky terrain and rolling down the steep hillside. These tears flowed to where his father stood watching. The dog dipped his head and licked up his son's tears, then when he returned his gaze to the high ridge, he found it empty. He knew his son had gone to live with the wolves. The tears he had licked from the ground mingled with his own, and bowing his head, he shed not only his own tears, but also those of his son."

"What does this dream mean, Running Horse?" his wife asked.

"Someday, our son will leave the Sioux to live with the white man," he replied sadly.

She reached up and gently wiped away a tear that had fallen from the corner of her husband's eye.

Chapter One

Wyoming Territory
1868

When Todd Miller asked Alisha Stevens to walk out onto the veranda with him, she agreed reluctantly. If there had been a convenient way for her to avoid being alone with Todd, she'd have grasped the opportunity. However, the young woman hadn't been able to conjure up a plausible excuse, which left her no alternative but to accompany him to the front porch.

Now, stepping to the intricately designed railing, Alisha presented her back to the man as she watched the darkness of night fall like a blanket across her father's ranch.

Pausing behind her, Todd placed his hands on her shoulders and turned her so that she was facing him. His dark eyes, smoldering with passion, admired her exquisite beauty. Her long, platinum-blond hair and deep brown eyes made a striking, lovely contrast which never failed to amaze him.

"Alisha," he began seriously, "I have a very important question to ask you."

She sensed a marriage proposal, which had been her reason for wishing to avoid this tête-à-tête. She wasn't

14

in love with Todd Miller and had no desire to marry him. Two years ago, he had purchased the ranch that was located close to her father's. She had known for a long time that he was attracted to her, and although he was quite handsome, she couldn't return his affections. She had always sensed something in Todd Miller that she didn't like. He had never given her a tangible reason for disliking him, it was just a feeling. However, her father and brothers were friends with Miller, so he was often invited to the Stevens' home.

This evening when Todd had arrived, he had spoken alone with her father before asking to see her, and she strongly suspected that he had asked for her hand.

He was still holding her shoulders, and increasing his grip, he drew her closer. "Alisha, will you marry me? I have already spoken to your father, and we have his permission."

She sighed heavily, then moving away from his touch, took a couple of steps backwards. "I'm sorry, Todd," she murmured gently, "I can't marry you."

"But why?" he asked.

"I'm not in love with you," she answered candidly.

"Alisha," he said, frowning impatiently, "there aren't very many eligible bachelors in these parts, and you're already twenty-three years old. Are you planning on becoming a spinster?"

Amused, she smiled. "I have no wish to remain single, Todd, but I'll not marry just for the sake of marriage."

"Are you waiting for your knight in shining armor to come and sweep you off your feet?"

"Something like that, I suppose."

"Then you are living in a fantasy world." He was angry. "Life is not like a romantic novel. For most women, love comes after marriage."

She lifted her small chin and eyed him firmly. "You

15

might think I am a foolish romantic, but I'll hold onto my principles. I'll not marry a man unless I love him with all my heart."

He smiled confidently. "When you hear what I have to say about Johnny, I think you'll change your mind about marrying me."

"Oh?" she questioned, wondering what point he was making. Alisha had two brothers; Clint, four years older, and Johnny, two years older.

"Johnny is deeply in debt," Todd disclosed.

She asked testily, "Has he been gambling again?"

"Yes," he replied calmly. "Last week, he was playing cards at the Golden Horseshoe and lost quite a lot of money to Joel Carson. The man accepted his note, of course." He shrugged. "Although your father has the money to pay off Johnny's debt, the sum is large, and I'm sure it would be a financial strain." He smiled cunningly. "But Joel and I are good friends, and he owes me a couple of favors. If I were Johnny's brother-in-law, I'm sure I could convince Joel to tear up Johnny's note."

He stepped close to her and again placed his hands on her shoulders. "If you force your father to pay off this debt, it'll leave him with very little ready cash. As you know, it's quite difficult to run a ranch this size without ample funds."

Grasping his hands and flinging them from her shoulders, she said angrily, "Your marriage proposal is beginning to sound like blackmail!"

"Call it whatever you wish, but I will resort to any means to get you to marry me."

Her brown eyes shot daggers at him. "Now I understand why I haven't fallen in love with you! Somehow, I sensed you were a scoundrel!"

He chuckled. "Don't judge me too harshly, my love. All's fair in love and war. Besides, when we're married,

I promise you that I'll be a very considerate and loving husband."

"When we're married?" she challenged. "You sound very sure of yourself, Todd Miller!"

"I not only have confidence in myself, but also in you. I'm sure after serious thought you'll decide to marry me. I'll give you one week to think about it."

"Does Johnny know about this proposition you are offering me?"

"I implied that I'd personally see to it his debt was dissolved if you agreed to marry me."

Todd had pitched his hat on the porch swing when he and Alisha had walked outside, and now he moved over, picked up his hat, and put it on. Turning back to Alisha, he touched the wide brim, bade her good night, went to his horse, and rode away.

Lethargically, Alisha moved to the swing and sat down. She didn't find it hard to believe that Johnny was in debt to Joel Carson, who owned the saloon in town. She had always known about her brother's compulsive gambling. But she had a feeling that this time he'd gone further into debt than ever before. For a moment she was tempted to go to her other brother, Clint, and tell him what she had learned, but she quickly discarded the idea. There was nothing Clint could do about it, and it would only worry him if he knew.

Alisha groaned softly. Should she marry Todd and dissolve Johnny's debt? Could she bring herself to wed a man she didn't love?

She was deep in thought when her father suddenly came out onto the porch. Sitting beside his daughter he asked, "Did Todd leave?"

"Yes," she answered.

Raising his eyebrows, he prodded, "Well?"

She looked at him with a bemused expression.

"Didn't Todd ask you to marry him?"

She simply nodded.

"What did you say?"

"I told him I had to think about it."

Taking her hand into his, he squeezed it gently. "Honey, you could do a lot worse than Todd Miller."

"Do you like Todd?" she asked.

"He's a gentleman, and if you marry him, I'm sure he'd be a good and caring husband."

At the age of forty-nine, Jack Stevens was an exceptionally handsome man. His tall build was muscular, and his reddish-blond hair was thick and curly. Alisha's mother had been dead for twenty years, and Alisha had often wondered why her father had never remarried. But he had seemed perfectly content to raise his two sons and daughter without a wife's help.

Jack stretched tiredly, then grasping his daughter's arm, he brought them both to their feet. "Well, it's getting late. I guess we'd better turn in for the night."

Kissing his cheek, she murmured, "Good night, Papa." She hurried inside the house and to her room.

Although Alisha went straight to bed, it was a long time before she was able to fall asleep.

The next morning Jack Stevens and his sons were already at the breakfast table when Alisha joined them. Bidding a good morning to the three men, she sat down and poured herself a cup of coffee.

Studying his daughter closely, Jack noticed that she appeared tired. "Didn't you sleep well?" he asked her.

"Not especially," she whispered. As she sipped her coffee, Alisha's gaze centered on Johnny, who sat directly across from her. He was picking at his food and seemed nervous and on edge. She wondered if he was worrying about his debt to Joel Carson.

Finishing his meal, Jack leaned back in his chair. Thoughtfully he regarded his children. First, he looked at Clint, who was seated at the far end of the table. He was proud of his oldest son. Clint's tall and muscular build was identical to his father's, and he had also inherited Jack's reddish-blond hair. At twenty-seven, Clint Stevens was a stable and compassionate man, and the kind of son that a father could depend on.

Slowly Jack turned his gaze to his other son. Johnny was a big disappointment to his father. Unlike Clint, he was selfish and totally undependable. Jack was perfectly aware that his youngest son had little interest in ranching, preferring gambling and carousing to honest work. Johnny Stevens was extremely handsome. Taking after his mother's side of the family, his build was slim and his eyes and hair were dark.

Then Jack's gaze fell upon his daughter. Alisha was her father's pride and joy. She had inherited her platinum-blond hair from Jack's Swedish mother. Alisha's paternal grandmother had been a classic beauty, and the young woman was just as beautiful. Alisha was of average height, her frame graceful and well-endowed.

"Pa?" Clint said, gaining his father's attention.

Drawing his gaze from Alisha, Jack regarded his oldest son.

Clint continued, "When I went into town yesterday, I saw the Wyatt brothers."

Jack frowned angrily. "I told them to get the hell out of Wyoming!"

"I asked them when they planned to leave, but they said they'd leave in their own good time."

The three Wyatt brothers had worked a short time for Jack, but when he'd caught them stealing from him, he'd given them a choice: either leave Wyoming, or he'd turn them over to the sheriff. They had quickly chosen

19

the first alternative.

Pushing aside a nearly full plate, Johnny remarked, "I saw them yesterday too, and they told me they were leaving today."

"Good!" Jack declared. Deciding to change the subject to something more pleasant, he turned to Alisha and asked, "What are your plans for the day?"

"I thought I'd ride into town and visit Loretta Ingalls."

"Loretta Ingalls?" Jack pondered, then placing the woman, he remarked, "The new schoolmarm. I didn't know you two were friends."

"I met her last week at Todd's barbeque, and she invited me to have lunch with her today."

"I remember seeing her there," Johnny spoke up. "She isn't a bad-looking woman, for an old maid."

"Why must you place people in categories?" Alisha hissed.

Johnny smiled. "If you aren't careful, Alisha, you're going to become an old maid yourself."

"You're as bad as Todd," she replied, frowning.

His interest piqued, Johnny asked, "What do you mean? Has Todd asked you to marry him?"

She looked at him cunningly. "You'd be very happy if I married Todd, wouldn't you? Or should I say, relieved?"

"What's going on between you two?" Jack demanded.

"Nothing important," Alisha answered, getting to her feet. She began to stack the plates. "I'll help Mary with the dishes and housework, then ride into town."

Mary Cummings had been the Stevens' cook and housekeeper for ten years, and although it wasn't Alisha's job to help the woman, she never minded offering her assistance.

As Alisha cleaned up, her father and brothers

ambled out of the dining room to start their day's work. When she was alone, Alisha returned to her chair. She wondered how much money Johnny owed Joel Carson. Was the amount truly so large that paying it off would be a burden on her father's finances? Or had Todd exaggerated? Well, there was only one way to learn the truth; she'd personally visit Mr. Carson and ask him the extent of Johnny's debt.

Alisha's brow furrowed with consternation. Joel Carson had living quarters above his saloon, which meant she'd have to enter the Golden Horseshoe in order to see him. Although she felt pangs of anxiety, she lifted her chin and her eyes shone with determination. She'd go through with her decision and speak with Joel Carson. But never in her life had Alisha Stevens been inside a saloon.

As Alisha rode into the small town of Backwater, she was totally unaware of the striking picture she presented. Her long, flaxen hair fell gracefully from beneath a wide-brimmed hat, and the fringed hem of her riding skirt touched the tops of her western boots. She wore a long-sleeved yellow blouse, and around her slender neck she had loosely tied a colorful bandanna.

She was an experienced rider and controlled her magnificent white stallion with an air of assurance. Alisha Stevens and her impressive steed were indeed a fetching sight as they traveled slowly down the dusty street toward Loretta Ingalls' home, which was at the end of town beside the rustic one-room schoolhouse.

Loretta, working in her small flower garden, caught sight of her approaching visitor, and shading her eyes with her hands, she watched Alisha as she came closer.

Envy shone in the woman's eyes, for she admired Alisha's beauty and elegance. Although she was

21

twenty-eight years old, Loretta Ingalls was terribly shy and unsure of herself as a woman; but as a teacher she had every confidence in her abilities. With children she was never timid, but when she found herself in the presence of an eligible bachelor, all semblance of confidence deserted her, leaving her tongue-tied and withdrawn.

A whitewashed picket fence circled the house, and pulling up her horse, Alisha dismounted and looped the reins over a fence post.

Smiling warmly, Loretta said, "Alisha, I'm so glad you were able to come for lunch."

"So am I," she replied. "And I thank you for asking me."

Gesturing toward the front door, Loretta suggested, "Let's go inside, shall we?"

Alisha followed her friend into the house, where she was shown into the neat and modestly furnished parlor.

A little timidly, Loretta asked, "Would you like to chat awhile before lunch?"

Noting the woman's uneasiness, Alisha replied with a genuine smile, "Let's have a girl-to-girl talk."

When they were seated on the sofa, Alisha asked, "When does school begin?"

"In two weeks. I certainly hope the children will like me."

"I'm sure they will," Alisha assured her.

Loretta had only recently moved to Backwater, and since it was summer, school wasn't yet in session.

For a moment, Alisha studied the woman, whose auburn hair was pulled back into a severe bun, and she tried to imagine how the new school teacher would look were she to arrange her hair into a more flattering style. Alisha realized that Loretta could be very attractive if she didn't hide her appeal behind matronly

22

dresses and unbecoming hairdo.

Alisha's warm personality soon drew the other woman into an easy conversation. Relaxed and perfectly at ease, Loretta began to thoroughly enjoy her friend's company.

It wasn't until after they'd had lunch and had returned to the parlor that Alisha announced her intentions to visit the Golden Horseshoe.

Aghast, Loretta exclaimed, "You can't go into a saloon!"

"I must see Joel Carson," Alisha explained.

"Then why don't you send a note to Mr. Carson and ask him to meet you? If you want, you can have him meet you here."

"Thanks for the offer, but I think I'll just pay him a surprise visit."

"Why is it so important for you to talk to that man?"

"Last night, I learned that my brother, Johnny, owes Mr. Carson a considerable sum of money, and I intend to find out the exact amount. But my father doesn't know about this debt, so please don't mention it to anyone."

Sincerely, Loretta replied, "Oh I would never breathe a word of it!"

Alisha headed toward the front door. "Thank you for lunch and for the company."

Hastening to follow her, Loretta decided, "I'll go with you."

"I don't think that's wise, Loretta. If you are seen entering the Golden Horseshoe, you might lose your job."

The woman hesitated, but only for a moment. "No, I insist that you let me accompany you. Does Mr. Carson have quarters above his saloon?"

"Yes, he does."

"Then he'll probably talk to you there, and you

wouldn't want to be alone with a man like him."

"A man like him?" Alisha questioned.

Loretta smiled at what she considered Alisha's innocence. "He's a saloon owner and a gambler. Why, I'm sure no woman is safe alone with him. Especially a woman as beautiful as you are."

Alisha laughed goodnaturedly. "Very well, Loretta. You may come with me, but I sure hope no one sees you."

The other woman grew thoughtful. "Is there a back entrance?"

"I think so," Alisha replied.

"Then we'll slip in the back way."

Her brown eyes gleaming, Alisha remarked cheerfully, "Why, Loretta Ingalls, I didn't know you could be so cunning!"

Opening the door, she replied, "Not cunning, but probably reckless. If we are seen, our reputations might be ruined."

"We'll be careful," Alisha answered.

Then, together, the two women left, both hoping fervently that there would be no repercussions.

Chapter Two

Seeking shade, David Hunter sauntered to the covered wagon and sat down, the white canvas top blocking the sun's glowing rays. He drew up his knees and crossed his arms over them as he gazed dreamily into the distance. At the age of thirteen, David was a good-looking lad. His sable-brown hair was thick and unruly, causing a curly lock to fall insistently across his high forehead. His emerald-green eyes, framed by dark brows and long lashes, were beautiful, though the boy thought them too feminine, which caused him to despise what was in fact his best feature.

The sudden sound of a bottle falling against the floor of the wagon made David grimace, and his face hardened with a bitter frown. As usual, his father was in a drunken stupor and had fallen asleep and dropped his whiskey bottle. The boy ran his fingers through his hair, a gesture he always made when he was upset. Sighing deeply, he leaned his head back against the wagon, and closing his eyes, he thought about their small farm in Kansas. Envisioning the log cabin that had been the only home he had ever known, he could see his mother sitting on the porch, churning butter.

A wistful look crossed his face as he realized that

every time he remembered his mother, she was working. But then, he couldn't recall her ever having had time for leisure; it seemed she had labored from dawn until bedtime. His eyes grew misty, for he had loved his mother and wished she was still alive.

A loud, constant snore from inside the wagon told David that his father was now sleeping soundly. Unlike his mother, the boy couldn't remember his father ever overexerting himself with work. Whiskey and foolish dreams were the extent of the man's energies.

David considered this journey into the Black Hills his father's biggest folly. "There's gold in those hills," the man had sworn to his son. "It's just sittin' there, waitin' for us to come and get it!" Sensibly, David had reminded his father that there were also hostile Indians in the Black Hills.

However, the man was not about to be dissuaded, and against his son's advice, he had sold their homestead and embarked on this quest he was sure would make them rich.

David glanced about the countryside and wondered how much farther they would have to travel before locating the gold his father was so positive they'd find. Yesterday they had penetrated the Hills and they were now in land that rightfully belonged to the Sioux.

Standing, David stepped to the back of the wagon, reached inside, and withdrew one of his books. Walking to the shade of a tree, he sat down, opened the book, and began to read.

The boy's unquenchable thirst for knowledge annoyed his father, who was always complaining about him having his nose in a book. But David's mother had been proud of her son's intelligence and had encouraged his reading. Because his father considered education unimportant, he'd had no qualms about taking David out of school to accompany him on this

26

journey into the Black Hills.

Now David was deeply enthralled by a history of the American Revolution when a horse's whinny caused him to look up. The awesome sight confronting him made his face pale and a chill prickled the back of his neck.

In the near distance, eight Sioux warriors sat on their ponies. They were poised leisurely, as though they had no intentions of advancing, but had merely stopped to stare curiously.

To the lad they were a threatening sight, and for a moment, fear rendered him numb. His eyes, wide with disbelief, stared at the Indians, who were now eyeing him with hostility.

The small raiding party, led by the radical young chief, Two Moons, had left their village in search of plunder. Now, finding this lone wagon, they could hardly believe their good fortune.

Regaining his momentum, David bolted to his feet, and as he was rushing toward the wagon, the Indians broke their ponies into a run. Charging, they quickly covered the ground between them and the white intruders.

"Pa! . . . Pa!" David cried. Clutching the back of the wagon, he tried to climb inside and grab his rifle, but the chief, Two Moons, rode up behind him, causing the boy to spin around.

The chief and his companions pulled up their horses, then dismounted swiftly and agilely. The leader stepped to David, grasped his shirt and slung him roughly to the ground. Immediately, three warriors jumped inside the wagon and dragged the white man outside.

David struggled to sit up, but the chief's moccasined foot landed on his shoulder, pinning him to the ground. Helplessly, the boy looked on as his father was forced

27

to his knees. The man, shocked into sobriety, glanced at his son and was relieved to find him alive.

Removing his foothold, Two Moons moved toward the kneeling man. Slowly he slipped his knife from its sheath, then sneering with hate, he entwined his fingers into his prisoner's hair and jerked his head backwards. Placing the sharp weapon against the man's throat, he ended his victim's life with one swift slash.

David turned away, and as bile rose into his throat, he vomited onto the ground. He didn't need to look back to know that the chief was now scalping his father.

Showing no interest in the boy, the Indians began exploring the contents of the wagon, and when they found the white man's ample supply of whiskey, their mood became jovial.

Holding one of the bottles in his hand, the leader stepped back to David and gestured for him to stand up. Obeying, he got shakily to his feet. Turning, Two Moons spoke to one of his companions, and following the chief's instructions, he fetched some rope. Then, moving to David, he drew the boy's arms behind his back and tied his hands. The lad was then forced to return to the tree where he had earlier been reading and was shoved down to the ground.

Bracing himself against the tree's trunk, David watched the Indians as they continued to explore the wagon's contents, but finding little of value, they gave the bottles of whiskey their full attention.

Drawing up his knees, David leaned forward and rested his head. He was still nauseated, and had to swallow back fresh bile. He wondered why the Indians hadn't killed him. Were they planning on torturing him so his death would be slow and merciless? Finding his impending destiny too frightening to imagine, he turned his frantic thoughts to his father. David had never especially respected the man, but he had loved him. Tears filled his eyes, but with effort he forced them back. He wouldn't cry! He would not give these Indians the satisfaction of seeing him break down. He'd remain strong, regardless of what they did to him. He'd face it like a man!

The small town of Backwater, Wyoming, was located approximately seventy-five miles from the region known as the Black Hills. At the same time that David Hunter was bravely awaiting his fate, Alisha Stevens and Loretta Ingalls were slipping into the rear door of the Golden Horseshoe.

Joel Carson, ensconced in his suite, had been awake for just a short time. Because of his late schedule, he always slept until past noon, and when most people were having lunch, he was having breakfast.

He had just finished eating when a couple of loud raps sounded on his door. "Come in," he called.

He glanced toward the open portal, but the sight of his bartender ushering two ladies into the room sent him bounding to his feet.

"Sorry to disturb you, Boss, but I found these women slipping in the back door."

The bartender had a firm grip on each woman's arm. Casting the man an angry glare, Alisha pulled away from his bruising grasp. Then, looking at Joel, she said collectedly, "Mr. Carson, I need to talk to you."

The suave gambler smiled wryly. He wasn't personally acquainted with Jack Stevens' daughter, but he knew who she was. Then, regarding Alisha's companion, he tried to place the woman, but couldn't recall having seen her before.

Bowing elegantly, Joel inquired, "What can I do for you, Miss Stevens?"

She nodded toward the bartender. "I want to speak to you privately."

He dismissed his employee before asking, "Would you ladies like a cup of coffee?" He gestured toward the set table. "I have plenty left."

"No, thank you," Alisha answered.

He looked questioningly at Loretta. "Ma'am?"

Stammering, she mumbled, "No . . . no thanks." Standing a step behind Alisha, Loretta surreptitiously scanned Mr. Carson's quarters. She quickly noticed that the room had been decorated to suit a man's taste. Lifting her curious gaze, she saw the large framed picture hanging conspicuously on the wall behind the sofa. It was a painting of a nude woman poised provocatively on a bearskin rug. Blushing profusely, Loretta quickly looked away and returned her attention to Joel Carson.

He gave her a discerning smile. "Do you consider my art in bad taste, ma'am?"

Her embarrassment deepened. "I . . . I find it a little shocking."

Joel chuckled with obvious amusement. Dressed impeccably in a white linen suit and tailored brown shirt, he was quite handsome. His full moustache, which matched his sandy-colored hair, tapered to the edges of his sensual lips. As he continued to observe Loretta Ingalls' blushing cheeks, a bright twinkle shone in his hazel eyes.

"Mr. Carson," Alisha began, "I'd like you to meet Miss Ingalls. She's the new schoolteacher."

"How do you do, Miss Ingalls," he said, his eyes still glimmering.

Loretta, quickly becoming enthralled with the dashing gambler, wished she could respond with an air of sophistication; however, as usual, her shyness prevailed and she simply lowered her gaze to the carpeted floor and said nothing.

Alisha continued, "We came in the back door because we preferred not to be seen."

"I understand completely," he said warmly. "What can I do for you, Miss Stevens?"

"I was told that Johnny owes you money, and I need to know the exact amount."

Cocking a brow inquisitively, he asked, "Do you intend to take care of your brother's debt?"

"No," she replied.

"Did Johnny tell you about his loss?"

"Todd Miller told me," she answered, seeing no reason to avoid total honesty.

"Ah yes, Todd Miller," he answered, suddenly appraising the situation. "He came to me yesterday afternoon and asked me if I'd tear up Johnny's note if he were to request it. I wanted to know why he was so concerned about somebody else's debt, and he informed me that he planned to become related to the Stevens' family."

"Related?" Alisha repeated.

"Yes, by marriage." He regarded her soberly. "Miss Stevens, is Todd trying to compromise you into marrying him?"

"Maybe," she murmured.

"Ladies," he remarked, looking from one to the other, "I admit that I am a rogue and not a gentleman. However, even a rogue like myself has certain standards."

He moved away from them and walked to the oak desk located against the far wall. Opening a drawer, he withdrew a slip of paper. Returning, he handed it to Alisha. "This is your brother's note. Feel free, my dear, to rip it to shreds."

Astonished, Alisha exclaimed, "Mr. Carson, I don't know what to say!"

His grin askew, he replied, "Just say thank you, then tear up the note."

"Oh, I do thank you!" she declared, before thoroughly ripping the paper. She gave him the shredded remains. "Contrary to what you say, Mr. Carson, you are indeed a gentleman."

He pitched the scraps into a wastepaper basket, then going to the door, opened it and stepped out to the hall. Loudly, so his bartender would hear, he called, "Bill, come up here!"

The man hastened up the stairs and to his boss. "Yes, sir?"

"Escort the ladies downstairs and to the rear entrance." He moved back, and standing in the open doorway, motioned for the woman to accompany the bartender.

Bidding him a good day, they followed the other man, and the moment they were shown out the back door, Loretta exclaimed, "Isn't Mr. Carson extremely charming?"

"Yes, he's very charming," Alisha agreed. They walked away from the back of the building.

"How old do you suppose he is?" Loretta asked.

"Early forties?" she surmised.

Her friend concurred. "That would be my guess, too."

As the two women headed in the direction of Loretta's house, they didn't notice the three men who were lounging in front of the Golden Horseshoe.

The Wyatt brothers had recognized Alisha, and they

kept her in their sights as she and her companion strolled away from the saloon. The siblings, with their unkempt beards and unwashed bodies, were an odious threesome.

Walter, the youngest, muttered flatly, "I'd sure like to stick it to that Stevens bitch."

Although Joe eagerly replied that he'd also like to have her, Jesse, who was the oldest, remarked thoughtfully, "I just figured out how we can make ourselves some money and get even with Jack Stevens at the same time."

Enthused, his brothers asked, "How's that?"

"Let's follow Miss Stevens and see if she's in town alone. If she is, we'll kidnap her on her way back to the ranch. Her pa will pay a lot of money to get her back."

"Ain't that kind of dangerous?" Walter asked.

The Wyatts stepped into the street, and while following Alisha from a distance, Jesse replied, "It won't be all that dangerous, 'cause while you two hold the woman prisoner, I'll contact her old man. He can't do nothin' to me, 'cause he'll know if he does, you two will kill his daughter. I'll tell him to get us some money out of his safe, then I'll take him to his daughter. Naturally, I'll make it clear that we ain't to be followed. We'll have the girl hidden about two days' ride from here. That's so's there won't be no way the Stevens brothers or any of the cowhands can trail the old man and me without me a-knowin' it. Then, when we reach the place where you two are keepin' the woman, we'll kill her and her pa. After that, we'll head for Mexico."

"Where are we gonna hide her out?" asked Joe.

"Remember that cave at the foot of the Hills? That'll be the perfect place to keep her hidden."

Walter grinned with lewd anticipation. "Jesse, while

33

we're holdin' her prisoner, can we stick it to her?"

His brother laughed boisterously. "Yeah, but save some of it for me, 'cause before I kill her, I'd like to sample her goods."

As the Wyatts envisioned themselves assaulting Jack Stevens' beautiful daughter, they became anxious to set their hastily laid plans in motion.

Chapter Three

As Alisha rode out of town, she was totally unaware of the danger that lurked close behind. The two Wyatt brothers who followed her kept their horses at a reasonable distance, giving the impression that they just happened to be traveling in the same direction.

Although Alisha soon realized that she and the men were covering the same ground, she wasn't overly alarmed, for she had no reason to suspect foul play. But taking a quick glance over her shoulder, she noticed the twosome were now steadily shortening the distance, and this began to make her uneasy. Deciding to let them pass, she pulled up her white stallion.

Reaching her, the brothers nodded politely. "Good afternoon, ma'am," Jesse nodded, smiling congenially.

They brought their horses to a halt, and before Alisha had time to realize what was happening, they were on either side of her.

Moving speedily, Walter's arm shot out and slipped her rifle from its scabbard.

Her eyes narrowing angrily, Alisha asked Jesse, "What's the meaning of this, Mr. Wyatt?"

His smile widened. "Miss Stevens, you're gonna take a ride with my brothers, while I visit your old man."

She was beginning to feel frightened. "I . . . I don't understand."

"You've heard of kidnappin', ain't ya?" Walter baited, his beady eyes traveling openly over her tempting curves.

"Kidnapping!" Alisha exclaimed. "If you try something so foolish, my father and brothers will kill you!"

It was Jesse who responded to her threat. "If there's any killin' done, it'll be the Wyatts killin' the Stevens."

"Why are you doing this?" Alisha demanded.

"We need the money," Jesse answered. "Besides, your old man owes us. He fired us without payin' us our wages."

"He should've turned you over to the sheriff!" she cried.

Hearing a rider approaching, Jesse looked back and was relieved to see that it was Joe. Abducting Miss Stevens on open ground was making him nervous. Also, they were still too close to town, and so far they had been extremely lucky that no one had passed by.

As Joe drew up, Jesse asked quickly, "Did you get the supplies?"

"Yeah, I got everything we'll need," he replied.

"You two take the woman and start for the Hills. I'll bide my time till sundown, then I'll go see Stevens. By then, he ought to be good and worried about his missin' daughter." He eyed Walter, his stern face unyielding. "You got to travel fast and use caution, which means you got to leave the woman alone until you're safely hidden in the cave. So don't be tryin' to get between her legs till then."

Alisha gasped, and her face paled noticeably. Dear God, she'd rather they killed her than . . . *than what?* The prospects were terrifying.

"Don't worry, Jesse," his youngest brother assured him. "I ain't gonna play around with her while we're

36

travelin'.'" He turned his gaze upon Alisha and added lustfully, "But when I get her to the cave, I'm gonna spread them pretty legs and get right in between 'em."

Alisha had never fainted in her life, but now, as a feeling of weakness came over her, she came dangerously close to passing out. Taking a deep breath, she fought back her dizziness. Her composure restored, she began to contemplate escape. It was her only chance! But how? *How?*

Her powerful stallion began to prance restlessly, causing Alisha to pull back on the reins. *Her horse, of course!* she suddenly realized. He was her means for escape! Her quick appraisal told her that the animals the Wyatts were riding couldn't possibly catch her stallion.

Putting her plan into action, Alisha, moving with incredible speed, jabbed her boots into the steed's sides as she simultaneously slapped the reins against his neck.

Bolting, the strong stallion bounded forward, his huge body pushing its way past the men's smaller horses.

The stallion's unexpected flight took the Wyatts by surprise, and for a moment, they were too stunned to react. Then, regaining his senses, Jesse swiftly drew his rifle. Taking perfect aim, he pointed the barrel of the gun at the fleeing horse.

Meanwhile, Alisha didn't dare look back to see if they were giving chase; instead she concentrated on guiding the horse and keeping him at a full run.

At the same moment that the rifle shot exploded, the beautiful, sleek stallion plunged head first onto the ground. The bullet had sunk deeply into the horse's flank, and the animal screeched shrilly as his rider was thrown forward.

Alisha landed solidly against the hard earth and

37

excruciating pain coursed through her body. The collision had knocked the breath from her lungs, and stunned, she came very close to losing consciousness. However, her stallion's cry of agony brought her back to awareness.

She tried to sit up, but the effort was too painful. Managing to heft herself to her hands and knees, she crawled pathetically to her injured horse.

The animal was on his side, trying vainly to get back up, but the fall had broken his right foreleg. Reaching the frightened stallion, Alisha spoke gently to him. Sitting, she lifted his large head and placed it on her lap. Soothed, the horse quietened somewhat as he allowed his owner to stroke his face.

Alisha loved her horse, and tears streamed from her eyes as she petted her faithful friend. He would die, and it was all her fault! Oh, why had she attempted such a foolish escape? She should have known one of the Wyatts would shoot her horse!

The three men rode to the young woman, and, dismounting, Jesse stepped to Alisha, gripped her arm and forcefully jerked her to her feet. Lifting her struggling form into his brawny arms, he carried her to his youngest brother. Walter reached for Alisha, and in spite of her attempts to stop them, they managed to place her on Walter's saddle. She was sitting in front, and the young man's arms went about her, pinning her against his hard chest.

Her tears still flowing copiously, Alisha stole a loving glance at her stallion. "Don't let him suffer!" she pleaded to Jesse. "Please, don't let him suffer!"

"Get the hell out of here and head straight for the cave!" the oldest Wyatt commanded, offering no response to Alisha's plea.

Obeying, Walter and Joe spurred their horses into action. For a little while, Jesse watched their departure, then drawing his pistol, he stepped over to the injured stallion.

Alisha and her captors had only traveled a short distance, when a shot rang out.

Leaning forward, Walter placed his lips next to his captive's cheek, and finding the man's touch repulsive, she cringed. His fetid breath fell across her face as he murmured, "Your horse is out of his misery."

Avoiding his intimacy, she turned her head sharply to one side. Laughing, he made no further attempts to nuzzle her; instead, he moved a hand to her breast and cupped her firmly.

Grabbing him, she strove fruitlessly to remove his hand, but realizing her strength pitted against his was no contest, she finally gave up.

Controlling her tears, she declared resentfully, "My father will kill you for putting your dirty, slimy hands on me!" Then, to herself, she swore fervently, *If I don't kill you first!*

With the dead stallion lying on the road leading into Backwater, Jesse knew he couldn't wait until sundown before visiting the Bar-S Ranch. It was only a matter of minutes before someone would ride by, recognize Miss Stevens' horse, and notify her father that his daughter's stallion had been shot. Jack Stevens would immediately set out to search for her.

Stepping to his own horse, Jesse mounted with haste and began galloping toward the Stevens' ranch. He was worried over this unexpected turn of events. Was it a bad omen, a sign that his and his brothers' plans were doomed?

Jesse was so deeply involved in his thoughts of failure that he didn't spot the lone rider advancing in his direction. Suddenly aware of him, Jesse pulled up his mount. As the man came closer, he saw that it was Johnny Stevens. Pleased, the oldest Wyatt smiled. He'd tell him about his sister, and then he'd demand that Johnny give him a safe escort onto the Bar-S spread.

Arriving, young Stevens reined in his horse and stopped beside Jesse. His countenance hard, Johnny asked gruffly, "Why in the hell aren't you and your brothers on your way out of Wyoming?"

The other man smirked coldly, "Don't get uppity with me, Stevens!"

"Where are your brothers?" he demanded.

Watching Johnny closely, he answered, "They're with your pretty little sister."

"Goddamn it, Wyatt! What are you trying to tell me?"

"My brothers and me, we've kidnapped Miss Stevens. If you don't believe me, look back yonder and you'll see her dead horse."

Peering into the distance, Johnny spotted the white stallion. His dark eyes bulging with rage, he threatened, "If my sister has been harmed, I'll blow off your worthless head!"

Jesse grinned confidently. "Stevens, you ain't in no position to be makin' threats. Now, I want you to take me to your father. Him and me, we got some talkin' to do."

But Johnny didn't comply, for his thoughts were racing dangerously. Using poor judgment, he decided to force Wyatt into telling him where Alisha had been taken.

Johnny reached for his holstered pistol, and seeing his intent, Jesse's hand lurched for his own weapon.

The men drew in unison, but Johnny was a fraction quicker, and his pistol fired. He had meant to merely wound Wyatt, for he certainly didn't want the man dead. However, Johnny's aim was off target and the shot was fatal.

Jesse Wyatt's body dropped from his horse and onto the ground. Dismounting, Johnny hurried to his victim, hoping desperately to find him still alive. When he saw that the man was dead, he groaned with remorse. Now, how in the hell would they learn Alisha's whereabouts? As his thoughts turned to his father, Johnny's slender frame tensed and perspiration beaded his brow. He could well imagine the lecture he'd receive from Jack Stevens. He knew the man would be boiling mad at him for killing Jesse Wyatt. But, damn it, he'd had no other choice! Johnny sighed heavily, for he was sure that his father wouldn't see it that way. Alisha was God only knows where, and he had just killed the only man who could've told them where she was.

Going to his horse, Johnny mounted. A bitter snicker crossed his face. If it had been Clint who had come upon Jesse, he probably would've handled the situation much differently. In fact, he most likely would've extracted a confession from Wyatt, rescued Alisha, and brought her safely back home before their father even knew anything was amiss.

Although Johnny Stevens loved his sister, he loved himself more, and putting himself first, he decided simply not to tell his father what had happened. When Wyatt's body was found, no one would know who killed him; furthermore, no one would give a damn. Soon, though, someone would come upon Alisha's dead horse and report it to Jack. A search for his sister would inevitably come about. Of course, if he were to go to his father right now and tell him the truth, the search would start much sooner.

For a moment Johnny fought with his conscience, then decided it wasn't imperative that he confess his blunder. The two Wyatt brothers wouldn't harm Alisha; they had to keep her alive for ransom. Relieved with his decision, he exhaled deeply. This way, his father would never know that he had killed Jesse and foolishly silenced the only man who could take them straight to Alisha.

Sparing himself a reprimand, he turned his horse around and headed for home, where he planned to silently await whoever would come to the Bar-S and report finding Alisha's horse.

The Wyatt brothers kept their horses at an even canter, the unvarying pace stretching out the miles between them and the area where they'd abducted their prisoner.

Alisha was finding the journey almost unbearable; if Walter wasn't fondling her breasts, he was whispering obscenities in her ear. She despised the repulsive man and his closeness nauseated her.

A heavy cloud cover began moving in from the west, and taking note of the approaching weather, Alisha hoped it wouldn't storm. The falling rain would completely wash away their tracks, making it impossible for anyone to trail them. Alisha knew her father very well and was aware that he'd order Clint and the ranch hands to try and pick up her trail, while giving Jesse the false impression that he alone would accompany him to this cave where she was to be imprisoned. Familiar with her father's tactics, Alisha was positive that the moment Jack Stevens rode away with Jesse Wyatt, Clint and the others would set out to find her.

The clouds were dark and threatening, and as she watched them swirling about in the sky, Alisha's hopes plunged. It was going to storm; there was no longer any doubt in her mind.

Walter, also aware of the foreboding weather, yelled to his brother, "You reckon we ought to stop? It's beginning to look like we're in for a downpour."

As a streak of lightning zigzagged overhead, Joe replied, "Yeah, I reckon we'd better."

A loud clap of thunder roared loudly, and glancing about, Walter tried to find a place that would offer some type of shelter. The rocky terrain was interspersed with sagebrush and scattered boulders, but rolling hills beckoned in the distance. Pointing toward them, Walter decided, "Let's head for them hills. Maybe we can find some kind of coverin' there."

Urging their horses into a full run, the riders made a beeline for their destination. When they reached the area, the storm had yet to unleash its fury. Although it remained threatening, and lightning continuously lit up the sky, the dark clouds had yet to burst.

Spotting an indentation in the bluff, shaded by a shrubbery overhang, Walter and his brother drew up their horses. Dismounting, the young Wyatt grabbed Alisha around the waist and lifted her from the saddle. The moment her feet touched ground, she pushed away from him, spun about and walked swiftly to the partial shelter that nature had afforded.

As Walter followed his captive, Joe securely tethered the horses, then he quickly joined his brother, who was now standing beside Alisha, eyeing her greedily.

"Joe," he began, his voice husky with anticipation, "since we got to hole up here till the storm passes, don't you reckon we ought to get us some lovin'?"

"Yeah, I sure do," Joe agreed, his own eyes traveling hungrily over the young woman's seductive beauty.

Alisha knew she'd rather risk death than give in meekly to her captors. Taking them off guard, she shoved past the two men and made a frantic dash for

43

the horses, where she hoped to grab one of the rifles.

It was Walter who took off after her, and his long strides easily caught up with hers. Tackling her at the waist, he sent them both crashing to the ground. Frantically she struggled against his strength, and as her arms flayed wildly, her hand brushed against his holstered pistol. Her calmness suddenly restored, Alisha clutched the gun's handle, and in a trice she had the weapon drawn.

Realizing she had stolen his pistol, Walter grasped her wrist, but as he tried to wrest the gun free, it went off. The bullet plunged deep into his chest, killing him on impact. His body dropped limply atop Alisha, and, as she frantically attempted to push him off, Joe arrived. Kneeling, he pried the pistol from her hand, then carefully shoved Walter's body to the side. The sight of his dead brother made him gasp sharply. Rising to a standing position, he glared murderously down into Alisha's frightened face.

"You goddamn bitch!" he raved. "You killed my baby brother!" He still had Walter's pistol, and slowly, he raised the gun and aimed it at the helpless woman. "I'm gonna kill you for what you done!" he rasped, his grief driving him nearly insane.

Suddenly, picking up a strange scent, the two tethered horses began to whinny and prance nervously. Reacting, Joe spun about, his eyes cautiously scanning his surroundings.

Taking advantage of the moment, Alisha scrambled to her feet. Joe's back was still turned, so taking him by surprise, she lurched for the pistol in his hand.

Her desperate attack was in vain, and powerfully her captor's swinging arm landed against her side, sending her sprawling to the earth, rolling down the embankment. Joe fired his gun, but his aim went awry and the bullet lodged into Alisha's shoulder. Having only wounded her, he was about to shoot a second time when out of nowhere a rifle shot thundered.

Alisha gasped with astonishment as her opponent reeled forward, landing face-down onto the ground. Joe's lifeless body came to rest mere inches from his brother's.

She longed to sit up and see who had saved her, but her wound had rendered her motionless. She had never felt such agonizing discomfort. The pain was so intense that her injured shoulder burned as if a dozen branding irons were pressing into her torn flesh.

She glanced at her wound and was alarmed to see that she was bleeding heavily. Loss of blood was making her woozy, and on the brink of passing out, she was finding it an effort to keep her eyes open. Vaguely she detected footsteps, and she knew whoever had rescued her was hurrying to her side. She hoped she could remain conscious long enough to express her thanks.

As Alisha turned her head to see her rescuer, a blinding flash of lightning illuminated the tall, handsome Sioux warrior who was kneeling at her side.

Staring into the brave's somber face, Alisha caught her breath with renewed fright, but rumbling thunder roaring across the landscape drowned out her gasp. Slowly, the approaching blackness of unconsciousness began to creep over her, and, as the warrior's face faded from her vision, she sank into oblivion.

Chapter Four

Jack Stevens stood at the study window and somberly watched the heavy precipitation. The dark clouds were releasing sheets of rain, the downpour falling so thickly that the earth was muddy and filled with intermittent puddles.

The three men seated in the large room were watching Jack as he remained poised at the window. Clint, sitting behind the oak desk, glanced at Johnny and Todd Miller. They were on the sofa, each with a glass of bourbon in their hands.

It had been Todd who had come to the Bar-S and announced that Alisha's dead stallion had been found. Miller's foreman had come upon the horse and Wyatt's body and had reported them to his boss, who had immediately ridden to the Stevens' ranch with the upsetting news. Now the three men were waiting anxiously for the rain to let up so they could set out to search for Alisha.

"Will this blasted rain ever quit?" Jack grumbled, whirling away from the window.

Clint's sigh was one of disappointment. "If there were any tracks, they've washed away."

Pacing, Jack mumbled, "None of this makes any

46

sense. Why in the hell has Alisha disappeared, and why was Jesse Wyatt's body found only a couple of yards from the stallion? And where in the hell are the other two Wyatts?"

"Maybe she's been kidnapped," Johnny spoke up, offering his speculation as though it had suddenly occurred.

"Kidnapped by whom?" Clint asked.

"The Wyatts," Johnny replied.

Todd Miller frowned impatiently. "If the Wyatts are behind her disappearance, then why was Jesse shot?"

"I . . . I don't know," he stammered. Feigning deep concentration, he suggested, "Jesse might have been on his way here to see Pa, when someone came upon him. Maybe they argued, and then this person killed Wyatt."

Jack eyed his youngest son keenly. "Johnny, do you know something you aren't telling us?"

Quickly, he assured him, "No, Pa. Damn, what makes you think that?"

"I'm sorry," he apologized, chastising himself for thinking Johnny might be hiding something. But he had caught his youngest son in lies so many times that he often had trouble trusting him. Now he believed his suspicions were totally unfounded: Johnny wouldn't hold back information that could help locate his sister.

Rising from his chair, Clint moved over to stand beside his father. Placing a hand on the man's shoulder, he said confidently, "We'll find her, Pa."

Jack leaned into his son's embrace. "Dear God, please keep her safe!" For a moment, Jack gave in to his fear, then withdrawing from Clint's arms, he was once again collected. Peering out the window, he remarked hopefully, "It looks like the rain is beginning to let up." Then, speaking to Johnny, he ordered crisply, "Son, go to the bunkhouse and tell the men to get ready to pull out. To hell with the rain. I'm not waiting any longer. Have ample supplies packed because, damn it, we aren't coming back until we find Alisha!"

As Johnny left to carry out his father's instructions, Todd stood and offered, "If you don't mind, I'd like to ride with you."

"Of course, I don't mind," Jack answered.

"We'll stop by my ranch and pick up my men."

"Good," Clint declared. "When we reach the area where Alisha's horse was found, we'll split up and search in different directions."

"Clint," Jack began hesitantly, "do you think Johnny's guess might be right? Do you suppose the Wyatt's kidnapped Alisha?"

The man shook his head. "It just doesn't add up, Pa. If the Wyatts abducted Alisha, why was Jesse killed? Johnny's speculation that someone just happened to kill him is too farfetched."

"Then where are Joe and Walter?" Jack questioned.

"Maybe they're somewhere in town," Clint answered.

Jack turned to Todd. "Has any of this been reported to the sheriff?"

"My foreman came straight to me, but before coming here, I sent him to town to report everything to the sheriff."

Heading for the door, Clint remarked, "I'm going to ride into town and see if the sheriff has learned anything, then I'll meet you where the stallion was found."

"All right," Jack agreed. Alisha's strange disappearance had him totally baffled. He wondered gravely if he'd ever see her again. This countryside was vast, and without tracks, finding her might very well be impossible. God, why had he allowed her to ride alone?

48

But then, she had often gone into town by herself and nothing had ever happened to her. He had become so accustomed to her independence that he'd grown lax where her safety was concerned. He had failed his daughter, and if she were dead, he was to blame!

David Hunter's captors had him tied securely to the tree, and any thoughts he'd had of escape were now dashed. The rope, which was stretched across his chest and arms, was looped about the large trunk. He was bound in a standing position, and his legs were beginning to tire. The overhanging limbs blocked most of the falling rain, keeping the lad relatively dry. The Indians had sought shelter inside the covered wagon, where they were still thoroughly enjoying the confiscated whiskey.

As a flash of lightning lit up the dismal sky, David cringed. He knew that standing beneath a tree during an electrical storm was highly dangerous. He'd probably be struck by lightning. His brow furrowed thoughtfully. Dying by lightning might be a blessing in disguise, for it would most likely be a quicker and more merciful death than what the warriors had in mind.

His father's body was still lying beside the wagon, and David purposefully kept his eyes turned away from the gruesome sight.

The boy strained against the binding rope. He was uncomfortable, thirsty and needed pressingly to relieve himself. But with his arms bound to his side, it was impossible for him to unbutton his trousers. Although he was determined to be brave, his courage was beginning to waver. Tears kept stinging his eyes, and he was constantly forcing them back. This weakness made him angry at himself. When the Indians decided to kill him, would he become a coward and beg them to spare his life? *No! . . . No!* he swore to himself. *I won't grovel! I'll face my death like a man! I will! Damn it, I will!*

Alisha had remained unconscious as the Sioux warrior successfully removed the bullet from her shoulder and bandaged the wound. He had carried her to the shelter where the Wyatts had intended to hole up through the storm.

Now, as he finished tending to her injury, he replaced the gauze and antiseptic inside an army-issue medical kit. Then, returning his knife to the sheath tied about his waist, he moved out from beneath the shrubbery overhang.

The rain had slowed to a steady drizzle, and the small drops splashed lightly against the tall warrior as he walked to the spot where he had left his horses. He took the reins to his saddled pinto, then moving to the young black stallion, he also grasped its reins. Moving quickly, he led the animals to the Wyatts' tethered geldings. Leaving the pinto free, he tied the other horses together.

Then, he stepped back to the pinto and patted him affectionately. The horse was getting on in years, and as he examined the steed, his experienced eye reminded him that it was time to retire the animal. He glanced over at the young stallion, who would be the pinto's replacement. As soon as he had the other horse properly trained, he intended to put the pinto out to pasture. "Don't worry, old man," he said, speaking perfect English. "Retirement won't be so bad. I'll see that you're surrounded by beautiful fillies."

Remaining beside the horse, the man's thoughts drifted to the woman he had saved. He wondered who she was and why she had been with those two men. Had she been abducted? That was the most logical explanation, and he was sure that when she awoke, she would want him to take her home. His handsome face grew worried. Backwater was the closest town, and she probably lived there or on one of the nearby ranches.

However, he didn't have time to take her home. While he had been at Fort Laramie visiting his friend Major Landon, he'd received word that his father was gravely ill. If he took this woman to Backwater, the white sheriff would insist on a thorough investigation. The sheriff was certain to hold him prisoner until he could send and then receive confirmation from Fort Laramie. Furthermore, he was Sioux, and the Sioux were supposed to remain in the Black Hills. He was now in territory that whites considered their own, and off limits to Indians. Major Landon would of course confirm his story, and he would then be set free. But it would take at least two days or more for everything to be settled, and he couldn't waste such valuable time, not with his father ailing.

Leaving the horses, the warrior returned to Alisha. Kneeling beside the sleeping woman, he studied her closely. Her blouse had been ruined, and he'd replaced it with one of his extra shirts. The suede garment was much too big for her, causing the hem to fall past her hips.

As he watched her, he began to think. He couldn't very well leave her here alone. In her weakened condition, she couldn't make it home by herself. If she had been abducted, there might be a posse searching for her. However, there was no guarantee that they'd find her.

He groaned inwardly as he resigned himself to taking the woman with him. Traveling alone, it would've taken him at least a week to reach his father's village, which was located deep in the Hills. Now, with an injured woman accompanying him, it'd be at least ten days or more before he reached home. It was now the last week of August, and if his father's illness lingered, he would have to wait until spring before returning the woman to her home. Winter came early in the Dakotas, and to travel through the region after the first snowfall was dangerous.

Considering the possibility, he smiled with mild amusement and tried to imagine how this lovely young woman would behave when she learned that she might spend the winter in a Sioux camp.

Knowing there were still a few hours of daylight left, he decided to move on. Opening the medical kit, he reached inside and removed a bottle of smelling salts. Before awakening his patient, he allowed himself a moment of luxury as his eyes surveyed her with appreciation. Admiring her full, sensuous lips, he was tempted to lean over and kiss them, but resisting the temptation, he uncapped the bottle and waved the strong scent beneath her nose.

As the ammonia scent brought her back to consciousness, Alisha coughed and her hand moved to the bottle to brush it aside.

Replacing the smelling salts in the kit, the warrior waited expectantly for the woman to open her eyes.

Slowly her eyelids fluttered; then, as her vision cleared and the Indian's face came into full focus, she tensed rigidly. Her sudden tautness sent a sharp pain coursing through her wounded shoulder. Grimacing, she attempted to grab at the bandage, but the warrior's hand quickly clutched hers.

His firm grasp was frightening, and she stared warily into his face. When he released his hold, she began to relax somewhat. Now, as her initial fear dwindled, she took a closer look at this man who had saved her from

Joe Wyatt. His vivid blue eyes, which contrasted against his dark skin, added to his striking good looks. He must be a half-breed, she decided. His straight black hair was shoulder-length, and he wore a plain leather band about his high forehead. His build was powerful, and his buckskin shirt fit snugly across the wide breadth of his shoulders. She noticed the way his tan leggings hugged his hard thighs and long, muscular legs.

Taking her eyes from the impressive warrior, she glanced at her shoulder. Pushing aside the suede tunic, she saw that she had been bandaged. Why, this Indian must've removed the bullet! If he had meant her harm, he wouldn't have doctored her! Hoping he could speak her language, she looked at him and asked eagerly, "Do you understand English?"

He came close to answering, but then decided it would be better to let her believe that he didn't speak English. If she knew he could speak her language, she would start pleading with him to take her home. Deciding he'd just as soon spare himself the scene, he remained noncommital.

"English," she repeated. "Do you understand what I'm saying?"

Feigning ignorance, he picked up the medical kit. Leaving her, he went to one of the Wyatt horses and placed the kit inside the saddlebags. Returning, he once again knelt at Alisha's side. She was lying on a blanket, and slipping his arms beneath her, he lifted her and the blanket together.

As he carried her toward the horses, she asked pressingly, "Where are you taking me?"

Again, she received no answer.

Knowing she was too weak to sit a horse alone, the warrior placed her gently on his pinto. Easing his moccasined foot into the stirrup, he mounted behind her. He had her sitting sidesaddle, and encircling one arm about her, he lifted the reins. Then, guiding the pinto to the other three horses, he grabbed the lead rein with his free hand.

Fear returning, Alisha begged, *"Please* let me go!"

The drizzling rain was beginning to fall heavier, and wrapping the pinto's reins about the saddle horn, the warrior arranged the woman's blanket so that it kept the rain from her face.

Alisha had lost a lot of blood, and she was too weak to struggle. Feeling a little faint, she leaned against the man's wide chest. If only she knew where he was taking her! Were they going to his village, where he planned to make her his slave? Growing up in the Wyoming territory, she'd heard horrible stories about whites who had been enslaved by Indians. As she recalled some of those tales she shuddered. If she had her strength, perhaps she could manage to flee, but she knew she was too frail to make the attempt. She began to hope desperately that their trip was a relatively long one, for in another day or two she might be strong enough to escape.

Growing drowsy, Alisha gave in to her weakened condition and closed her eyes. Her last thought before falling asleep was of escaping.

Realizing that the woman was no longer awake, the warrior smiled tenderly as he looked down into her lovely face. He knew she had to be frightened, yet she was showing a lot of courage. Remembering how he had accidently come across her and her attacker, his admiration for Alisha grew even stronger. It had taken him a moment to retrieve his rifle and take aim, during which time he'd seen how she had daringly tried to grab the pistol from the man's hands. When the pistol had been fired, he'd been afraid that he was too late to save her.

54

A small smile curved his lips as he wondered what his father, Running Horse, would have to say about his bringing this white woman home with him. His grin widened. He couldn't say too much about it; after all, his father had once done the same thing. Running Horse had married his white captive, but unlike his father, Black Wolf had no intention of following suit. He had promised himself a long time ago that he would never marry a white woman. Not even one as beautiful and as brave as this woman that fate had brought unexpectedly into his life.

Worrying about his father's bad health, and growing anxious to see him, Black Wolf urged the horses into a faster canter.

The rain had dissipated and the sky was clearing as the afternoon light gradually gave way to the advancing shadows of dusk. The sun, a brilliant orange, sank radiantly into the west as its fading glow fell across the secluded area where Black Wolf had chosen to camp for the night. The site was well hidden by dense shrubbery and a few scattered pines and spruces; these trees were indigenous to the region and farther up in the Hills they grew in great numbers.

Alisha was still sleeping, but as Black Wolf pulled up the pinto, she awoke. Stirring, she moved her head from his chest and sat upright. She was a little surprised to find that it was now so late. Her brow furrowed as she wondered how long she had slept. Becoming aware of the warrior's close proximity, she observed him through half-lowered eyes and found herself admiring his finely-sculptured features.

I've never seen a man so handsome, Alisha suddenly realized. His lips were mere inches from hers, and when he favored her with a half-smile, she noticed that his grin was slightly crooked, but filled with such sensuality that it sent her pulse racing.

Moving lithely, Black Wolf dismounted, then using extreme care, he reached for Alisha and lifted her from the horse. Careful not to hurt her shoulder, he carried her to a towering tree, and kneeling, he eased her down upon a soft bed of pine needles. Placing her in a sitting position, he urged her to make herself comfortable by leaning back against the tree's broad trunk.

His considerate ministrations renewed Alisha's hopes that she might be able to convince him to set her free. He started to return to the horses, but she grasped his arm. Her large brown eyes looking directly into his blue ones, she spoke slowly and with emphasis, "Please try to understand what I'm saying. I want to go home."

She waited, hoping desperately that he'd respond to her words.

The pleading in her beautiful eyes touched Black Wolf deeply, and he came very close to letting her know that he could speak her language; however, as his ailing father came to mind, he decided against communication with his lovely companion. Initially, she'd plead with him to take her home or free her, then when that failed, she'd begin to demand his cooperation. Even if he explained why he didn't have time to escort her home, and told her why it was too dangerous for her to travel alone, he was quite certain that she'd not relent. They had a long, arduous journey facing them, and he'd just as soon not spend it arguing with this woman who he sensed was not only stubborn but also determined.

Keeping his expression impassive, Black Wolf drew away from her tenacious grip and sprang gracefully to his feet.

Her hopes dashed, Alisha sighed with disappointment as she watched the warrior tend to the horses, then set about making camp. Her attention remaining solely on the attractive Indian, she noticed how his every motion expressed an innate dignity as he moved with incredible grace. His moccasined feet stepped noiselessly as he gathered fallen twigs and branches for the fire. His blue eyes were always watchful, and nothing escaped his observation.

Black Wolf had his supplies stored on the young stallion, and going to the horse, he removed his bundled provisions. He soon had a fire blazing and their supper cooking over the open flames.

Alisha had continued her unwavering scrutiny, and realizing the salt pork and beans that were to be their meal had come from a white man's store, she wondered if the warrior had purchased them, or if the goods had belonged to the Wyatts. Then, remembering the medical supplies, she became curious as to how he had acquired the army-issue first-aid kit. She turned to the saddle placed close to the pinto, and squinting so she could see it more clearly, she recognized it as the same kind of saddle that white men used. Her curiosity deepened. Why did this Indian, who apparently didn't speak one word of English, have possessions belonging to the whites? Had he stolen them, perhaps even murdered for them?

Black Wolf poured her a cup of coffee, then dished up her dinner. He brought her the food and drink. As she accepted the proffered fare, she came close to thanking him, but believing he wouldn't understand, she kept silent. She watched as he whirled about, returned to the campfire and began eating his own dinner.

The meal was tasty, and Alisha was so hungry that she had no trouble finishing her supper. Placing the empty tin plate at her side, she once again leaned back against the trunk. Although she was growing drowsy, a more pressing urge was plaguing her. She needed a moment of privacy, but how in the world was she to let this warrior understand?

Well, she thought firmly, there are some things that can't be put off indefinitely, and this is one of them! She would venture into the surrounding shrubbery, and if he tried to stop her, she'd simply find a way to make him understand.

Her mind made up, Alisha managed to get to her feet, the movement sending a dull, aching throb pounding in her wounded shoulder. Grimacing, she used her good arm to cradle the other; then, casting the warrior a wary glance, she headed uncertainly into the bushes. She was expecting him to come after her at any moment. When it became apparent that he wasn't going to deter her, she breathed a big sigh of relief.

She took care of her needs quickly, and, as she returned to the campsite, she gave the warrior a sidelong glance. He was watching her every move, but his face was inscrutable, and she wasn't sure if he was her friend or foe.

Stepping to her place beneath the tree, Alisha sat back down, but the effort caused another pain to course through her shoulder. This time it was so severe that she couldn't hold back from crying out.

Aware of her discomfort, Black Wolf leapt to his feet, hurried to the medical kit and brought it to Alisha's side. Kneeling, he reached for her shirt to peel it away from her shoulder.

Her first impulse was to brush his hand aside, but her better judgment prevailed. Her wound needed tending to, and she couldn't very well manage it alone.

The warrior's strong hands were very gentle as he cleaned and re-bandaged Alisha's injury. She tried to remain indifferent to his tender touch and extreme closeness, but against her own volition, his presence provoked a feverish response. His virility was over-whelming, and afraid he might sense her feelings, she was relieved when he drew the sleeve of her shirt up over her injury. Finished, he picked up her dishes and the medical kit and went back to the campfire.

Black Wolf kept his eyes turned away from the darting flames, for the fire's brightness caused night blindness, and his vision must stay sharp in case a predator might come into their midst. Staring off into the distance, he thought about the woman in his care. He had been acutely aware of her response to his presence, and although he'd been tempted to take her in his arms and kiss her, he'd nonetheless resisted. She was a white woman, and he mustn't let himself become emotionally involved. But as he recalled her alluring beauty, he began to wonder just how far he could stretch his will-power.

He decided not to dwell on this. It was late and time to get some sleep. His blue eyes sparkled as he wondered about the woman's reaction when she learned that he planned for them to share the same bedroll. However, as his musings continued, the glint left his eyes. To lie beside such a beautiful creature all night and not make love to her was going to be pure agony.

Chapter Five

The night was chilly, and David Hunter shivered as a gust of wind suddenly ruffled his hair. Although it was still summer, David had read enough about the Dakotas to know that cold weather struck early in this northern region and was not surprised that the day's rain had left a chill in the night.

Still bound to the tree, David was on the verge of exhaustion, but the rope about his chest and arms kept him on his feet. He looked over at the covered wagon, where the drunken voices of his captors were now less jubilant. David knew their consumption of whiskey would soon have them sleeping soundly. David struggled vainly. If only he weren't tied so securely he might be able to break free and escape. However, the rope was knotted tight. Giving up, the boy ceased squirming.

Catching sight of one of the warriors leaving the wagon, David tensed expectantly. When the man drew closer, he saw that it was the leader. His strides, which swayed drunkenly, brought the Indian closer and closer to his prisoner.

Two Moons was indeed a threatening sight, and to the thirteen-year-old boy, he appeared as evil as the devil himself. The chief's long black hair was worn in two braids, and his shirt and leggings were made of leather that fit his hard, masculine body like a second skin.

Pausing in front of David, Two Moons leered maliciously into the boy's watching eyes. A sardonic, taunting smile spread across his face. Slowly he assessed David's youthful, healthy body.

"You make good slave. You young, and you work many years for Two Moons."

David gasped, and his eyes widened with surprise. "You speak English!" he exclaimed.

"I speak white man's tongue," Two Moons mumbled. The whiskey caused his words to slur.

Although David came very close to begging the man to set him free, he refrained from doing so. His knowledge of Indians was limited, but he did know that they respected courage.

Two Moon nodded toward the dead body still sprawled on the ground. "Was man your father?"

Meeting the warrior's eyes with a boldness he wasn't sure he truly possessed, David answered, "Yes, he was my father."

"Why you here? This land belong to Sioux."

"My father was searching for gold."

Two Moons frowned. "White man's yellow gold!" He spit onto the ground. "This gold, get all white men killed. But for now I let you live. You be Two Moons' slave. You not die until I work you to death." He laughed evilly.

Swallowing his fear, David continued to eye the warrior intrepidly.

Although the boy's courage impressed Two Moons, the warrior had very little compassion; furthermore, for whites he had no compassion whatsoever.

Moving with lightning speed, Two Moons reached

out and grabbed a handful of David's hair. Shoving his head downwards, he snarled, "First lesson; you no look me in eyes. You slave, you lower than dog, you keep eyes to ground when I talk to you."

Releasing his hold on the boy's hair, he took a step backwards, then as he laughed cruelly, he kicked his captive in the stomach.

If David hadn't been tied to the tree, the powerful blow would've sent him to his knees. His stomach revolted and sent bile rising into his throat. He tried to vomit onto the rain-drenched earth, but most of it landed on his clothes.

Two Moons would have enjoyed staying and inflicting more torture upon his prisoner, but all the whiskey he had consumed was making him sleepy. Leaving the boy alone, he returned to the wagon.

Heaving, David coughed up the last of the bile. He was in considerable pain, but he knew the pain he had suffered tonight was probably mild compared to what he'd endure in the days to come.

Remaining true to his vow, the lad was still determined to face his fate like a man. He'd stay strong, regardless of what happened to him. This Indian called Two Moons could torture him, even threaten to kill him, but he wouldn't let the man break his spirit. When his death finally came, he'd die with his dignity still intact!

"I swear it!" David vowed solemnly, mustering his will power. Although his stomach still ached terribly, the lad remained dry-eyed. Facing his destiny with the courage of a man, he left his boyhood behind.

Jack Stevens, along with his ranch hands, his sons, and the sheriff, were camped at the area where Joe and Walter had been shot. Two men had been sent back to town with the bodies, and they were supposed to locate Todd Miller and tell him where he could find the others. The search party had split into two different directions, Jack leading one group and Todd leading the other.

Now, sitting by the campfire, Clint told his father, "If Todd rides throughout the night, he and his men should be here by dawn."

"If he isn't here when we pull out, I'm sure he'll catch up to us," Jack replied. He looked to the sheriff. "What do you make of this?"

Sheriff Davis shrugged. "I'm not sure." He was a big man, and though in his late fifties, his build was still solid and strong. "A few of the townspeople saw the Wyatts leave town soon after Alisha left. I think they all came upon a small band of Sioux. Jesse probably tried to escape and was shot. Then, for some reason, when they reached this place, the other two Wyatts were killed. These Indians are most likely heading for the Hills." He shrugged again. "Of course, this is speculation. The rain washed away all tracks, so there's no way to know if Indian ponies were in the vicinity."

"Your idea makes a lot of sense to me," Johnny agreed. He was sure the sheriff's story was partially true. Alisha, Joe and Walter probably were attacked by Sioux, but not until they had reached this area.

"I find your speculation a little hard to believe," Clint said, speaking to Sheriff Davis. "A Sioux raiding party might wander down from the Hills and steal a couple of steers, but I don't think they'd abduct Alisha and the Wyatts. We haven't had serious problems with the Sioux for many years. They simply want to live peacefully in the Hills and be left alone. They're no longer at war with us, unless we trespass on their territory."

Johnny declared bitterly, "Damn it, Clint, you're

always sticking up for those dirty savages!"

Jack groaned. "God, if a band of warriors are responsible for Alisha's disappearance, they'll probably. . . ." His voice caught in his throat. "They'll rape her time and time again, maybe even kill her!"

Quickly Clint said, "Pa, we don't know that she's with a band of Sioux."

"Then who the hell has her?" Jack cried.

Carrying his bedroll, Black Wolf ambled to the tree where Alisha sat watching him. She wished she could look at him with indifference, but she couldn't help admiring his superb build and handsome features. Noticing the single bedroll, she mistakenly believed he intended it for her. When he was within reach, she expected him to hand her the blankets, and she lifted her good arm to receive them. But he made no move to give her the blankets, and she let her arm drop to her side.

Kneeling, Black Wolf prepared their bed, then motioned for her to take her place on the bottom blanket.

Alisha smiled gratefully and wished she could make him understand how much she appreciated his making the bed for her. Favoring her wounded shoulder, she lay down on the blanket. The night air was nippy, and she pulled up the top covering. Snuggling into her bed, she once again smiled at the warrior. Although she believed he wouldn't understand, she nonetheless murmured a gentle thank you.

Black Wolf found her smile lovely and innocently seductive. He had to restrain himself from leaning over and kissing her tempting lips. Looking away, he put the temptation from his mind, then lifting the top blanket, he slipped beneath it.

Sitting up with a bolt that sent a stinging pain through her shoulder, Alisha demanded, "What do you think you're doing? You can't sleep with me!" Suddenly, she frowned impatiently. "Why am I spouting words you can't even understand?" Using her good arm, she tried to shove him away.

His hand shot out in a flash and caught her wrist. His grip was firm, and his blue eyes were unyielding. Easily, he urged her to lie back, and placing one leg over hers, he had her pinned. She made an attempt to struggle, but the effort caused her wound to throb uncomfortably. Relenting, she submitted, but the warrior kept his leg where it was, and she was held fast.

Black Wolf took no pleasure in imprisoning her, but he was afraid if he didn't keep her beside him, when he fell asleep, she'd try to run away. For her own safety, he knew he must keep her from escaping.

Seeing that he had no intention of removing his leg, Alisha realized it would be a waste of energy to try to resist his strength. Besides, in the struggle, she might very well do more injury to her shoulder and that might spoil her chance for escape.

Surrendering to his dominance, Alisha gradually became aware of the intimacy involved in their closeness. With his leg resting on hers, his maleness was pressed against her thigh. She wanted to move her hips away from his touch, but the feel of him was awakening a longing in her that she'd never before experienced. He began to grow hard, and aware of this change, she gasped deeply. Unsure now of her feelings, she tried to move away, but his leg tightened over hers, drawing her thigh flush to his hardness.

Slowly, rhythmically, he rubbed up against her, and the stimulating friction made Alisha long to turn toward him and welcome his stiff maleness between her thighs. She was confused and somewhat frightened of this overwhelming need to feel him pressed against her in such an intimate fashion. Fighting against this desire, she told herself to roll to her other side and present him her back. She almost carried out her own instructions, but in order to turn away from him, she'd have to lie on her wounded shoulder. She was left no choice except to remain lying on her back, or else lie facing him. She quickly decided her present position was by far the safest.

Calling upon all the will power he could muster, Black Wolf moved so that his hardness was no longer touching her. He must remain emotionally detached and avoid her tempting charms. There was no place in his life for a white woman.

Alisha was relieved that she could no longer feel him so intimately. This mysterious man had a magnetism that drew her like a moth to a flame. She couldn't fathom why she was so attracted to him. My goodness, they didn't even speak the same langauge! Besides which they were from two entirely different cultures. A look of petulance crossed her face. Why was she thinking of him as a romantic suitor? She was his prisoner, not his date for the evening! He probably had a wife, or wives, and when they reached his village, he'd hand her over to these women so she could take over their more strenuous chores. How could she have allowed this man's closeness to send her thoughts swirling so recklessly? He was her enemy, and she mustn't let herself forget that for one moment. She had to keep her wits about her and give the prospect of escape her full concentration.

Bolstered by her resolve, Alisha decided the quickest way to regain her strength was through rest. She closed her eyes and waited patiently for sleep to overcome her. Maybe in another day or two she'd be recovered enough to manage a way to escape. Somehow she would flee from this warrior and return home. Silently, she swore to herself that she'd succeed or die trying!

Alisha Stevens was not alone in her thoughts of escape; thirty miles north of where she lay waiting for sleep, David Hunter was contemplating his own chances to flee.

By now the boy's legs were so tired that they could barely support him; but when he let them weaken, his weight caused the rope bound about his chest to cut roughly through his shirt and into his flesh. He had no choice but to force himself to stand.

His years growing up on a farm and taking care of most of the chores had toughened the lady's young body. Although he was uncomfortable, tired, and miserable, he was also stout and healthy, which now gave him the strength to endure.

Fear gripped David, and a foreboding chill crept up his spine when he spotted two drunken warriors emerging from the back of the wagon. Talking to each other in loud, slurred voices, they stopped to relieve themselves, making the boy even more conscious of his own need to do likewise. Then the two Indians staggered over to intimidate him.

The warriors, Straight Lance and Black Feather, bore a hatred of whites as powerful and as evil as their chief's.

Pausing in front of the boy, they exchanged a few words in their own language. Although David couldn't understand exactly what they were saying, he sensed correctly that they were deciding how to torture him without causing lasting injury.

Laughing demonically, Black Feather stumbled drunkenly back to the wagon. Returning with a container of matches, he held them up in front of

David's face.

Oh God! the boy prayed frantically. *Help me be brave! Please don't let me turn into a coward!*

Black Feather struck a match. Its bright flame was reflected in the warrior's eyes, making them dance with an eerie, wicked glint.

Holding the flaming match, he stepped behind the tree, where David's hands were tied together. The boy could feel an intense heat drawing closer and closer to his fingers. Determined to show no outward pain, he braced himself against the trunk and waited courageously.

When the burning flame licked mercilessly across his fingertips, David had to bite into his bottom lip to keep from crying out. The match quickly burned out, and Black Feather immediately struck another and held it to the boy's fingers.

But soon the drunken warrior tired of his cruel game, and beckoning to his companion, they went back to the wagon to sleep off their drunk.

David was now alone, and if he were to give in to the tears stinging his eyes, no one would know; yet the boy still would not weaken. The tips of his fingers were burning with pain and tender blisters were forming.

I must close my mind to the pain and concentrate wholly on something else, he thought. If I don't, I'll start crying like a babbling kid! And I'm not a kid; not any longer!

Blocking out the pain, David set his mind on escape. Somehow, he'd get away from these Indians!

Chapter Six

The sun rose brilliantly, casting a golden glow over the landscape, and as the sun's warmth fell across Black Wolf's face, he came alertly awake. Aware of the woman snuggled against his side, he turned to see her face. Her eyes were closed, and he noticed the way her long lashes curled. He admired her platinum tresses; he'd never seen hair so blond it was almost white. Cautiously he touched a stray lock and rubbed its silken softness between his fingers. Then, releasing the strand, he lowered his vision to her mouth. Admiring the sensual shape of her lips, he was again struck with a compelling need to kiss her. Deciding one little kiss was harmless, he leaned over and placed his lips softly against hers.

His gentle touch roused Alisha, and somewhere between sleep and consciousness, she parted her lips and responded. The mouth caressing hers was causing a pleasant sensation to build within her, and her body arched instinctively to his caress.

Carefully Black Wolf moved to lie between her thighs. Her legs, submissive, seemed to open of their own accord, and her divided skirt made it easy for him to press his rising hardness against the most tender part

69

of her body.

His lips were still on hers, and as his passion began to soar, his kiss grew with intensity. His tongue darted between her teeth, tasting, relishing the sweetness of her mouth.

Now fully awake, Alisha came to her senses and tried to turn away from the mouth that possessed hers so ardently.

Aware that she was no longer responding, Black Wolf ended their kiss, and then with the litheness of a wild animal, he sprang to his feet. Looking down at her with an expression she couldn't discern, he motioned for her to get up.

Obeying, she left the bedroll and stood in front of him. His passionate kiss had left her shaken, but showing no outward sign of how she felt, she met his unwavering stare with one of her own.

He was the first to look away, and, kneeling, he quickly rolled up the blankets. Without giving her a backward glance, he carried the bedroll toward the horses.

She watched him for a moment before moving to the dead campfire. Deciding she preferred not to remain idle, she set about starting the fire and filling the coffee pot. Because of her wounded shoulder, the task she had undertaken was difficult and awkward; but with unaltering determination, she was successful and finally had the coffee brewing over the open flames.

As Alisha prepared the morning brew, Black Wolf tended to the horses. Finishing, he walked over to the campfire and sat down.

Looking up at her companion, Alisha was puzzled to see that he held her yellow blouse in his hands. When he began to rip the garment into shreds, her puzzlement deepened even more.

Keeping one of the long strips of material, Black

Wolf stood and gestured tersely for her to come to him. She was beginning to find his motions and gestures perturbing, and she chose to ignore this one. If he wanted her for something, then he could come to her! Did he expect her to jump every time he snapped his fingers?

Reading her defiant thoughts, Black Wolf suppressed a smile. Feigning an angry scowl, he once again signaled for her to come closer.

As before, she refused to budge.

Enjoying this game he played with her, Black Wolf hardened his eyes, making them glare with a murderous rage. He was curious as to how long she'd remain stubborn before her better sense prevailed.

Eyeing him with a level stare, she said coolly, "I'm not scared of you. I don't care if you do give me to your wives. I won't bow to you or anyone else!" She sighed impatiently. Why was she wasting her breath talking to a man who couldn't understand a word she was saying?

Black Wolf raised an eyebrow imperceptibly. Give her to his wives? Is that what she thought he planned to do with her? Moving a hand to his mouth, he pretended to cough so she wouldn't see the smile he had failed to suppress.

Alisha lifted her chin petulantly. Even though he couldn't comprehend her words, it made her feel better to express how she felt. Continuing her defiance, she snapped, "And I don't give a damn *how* many times you gesture for me to do your bidding, I'll not humble myself before you. I'm a Stevens, I come from strong stock, and you'll not destroy my spirit. I don't care what you do to me; you can work me, abuse me, and even torture me, but you'll never make me surrender." *There,* she thought, *I guess I told him!* A tiny smile emerged. *Thank goodness he didn't understand one word I said.* For although Alisha had spoken quite

71

bravely, she wasn't so sure she had the grit to live up to her statements.

Masking his amusement, Black Wolf slipped his knife from its leather sheath. Using the weapon he gestured for her to join him.

Warily, Alisha regarded the knife's blade, which reflected the sun's brightness and flashed ominously. Meeting his steely gaze, she submitted, "All right, this time I'll relent." Walking toward him, she continued, "It's a shame you can't speak English. If you weren't a savage brute, I could let you know that my father would pay you handsomely for escorting me safely home."

Placing a hand on her shoulder, he turned her so that her back was facing him. Then using the torn remnant from her blouse, he formed a loop. He slipped it over her head and carefully eased her arm into the makeshift sling. He cut off the excess cloth with his knife, then returned the weapon to its sheath before tying the material into a loose knot behind her back.

With her arm cradled, the pain in her shoulder was immediately alleviated, and Alisha started to smile her thanks, but before she could, the Indian moved away to the fire. She watched him as he knelt and poured himself a cup of coffee. Slowly, she went to his side and joined him. He poured another cup of the warm brew and handed it to her.

As she sipped the coffee, she tried to study him without being too obvious. This handsome warrior piqued her curiosity. She had always heard that Sioux men treated their women captives cruelly and harshly. Strange, she thought, that he has shown me only kindness and tender care. Why was he showing her such compassion? When they reached his village, would he still be so considerate? She seriously doubted that he would; he probably just wanted her to get well

72

quickly so that when he gave her to his wife or wives, she'd be able to start working without delay.

Black Wolf looked up at the sun, and taking note of its ascent, decided it was time to move on. Skipping his own breakfast, he gave Alisha a strip of jerky and motioned for her to take it with her. Then he poured the remainder of the coffee over the flames, dousing the fire.

Swiftly, as Alisha looked on, he began to break camp. She watched as he gathered up what was left of her ripped blouse and placed it in the saddle bag draped across Walter's horse.

Standing beside the animals, he signaled for her to come to him. She complied, even though his constant gesturing still grated on her nerves.

Leading her to Joe's horse, Black Wolf helped her into the saddle. Alisha was glad that he had apparently decided she could ride alone. She had dreaded sharing the pinto with him, for his closeness provoked a desire within her that she preferred to avoid.

As he remained beside her horse she looked down into his face. His azure eyes watched her closely. She tried to read his thoughts but could not. Her scrutiny grew intense, and her gaze left his eyes to travel downward to his full lips. Recalling their morning kiss, and how his mouth on hers had stirred her passion, a flush warmed her cheeks.

Moving away abruptly, Black Wolf went to the pinto and mounted. His brain raced, for he too remembered the stirring kiss that he and Alisha had shared. He shook his head as though to clear the white woman from his mind. He must force himself to be indifferent and think of her only as someone in need of his care. There was no permanent place in his life for this beautiful lady whose path had crossed his.

Black Wolf took the reins to the extra horses, then

turning to Alisha, he gestured with his head for her to follow. As they urged their mounts forward, he quickly decided it would be best to keep the woman at his side. Bringing up the rear and beyond his view, she might try to escape. For a moment he considered letting her make a run for it. She seemed much stronger now, and with luck and fortitude, she had a chance of making it home. But Black Wolf was fully aware of the many dangers that could befall a woman traveling alone, and his concern for her safety overcame his need to be free of her. Looking over his shoulder, he motioned for her to move her horse up alongside his.

Alisha decided to obey, but when she noticed that he was no longer watching her, an idea suddenly occurred. As she came abreast of Walter's horse, her good arm shot out, and with the deftness of a pickpocket, she removed what was left of her blouse from the saddlebag. Her eyes now glued to the warrior's back, she stealthily dropped the material onto the ground, then with an air of calm, guided her horse alongside the pinto.

She was sure that Clint and the others were searching for her, and now she hoped they would come upon this area and find her torn blouse. At least then they would know they were on the right track. Then, too, Alisha worried about her father. Had he left the ranch with Jesse Wyatt, and had they found Joe's and Walter's bodies. Was her father by now with Clint and the others? Or was he still accompanying Jesse? *Dear God,* she prayed, *please let Papa be alive and well!*

Chief Two Moons and his men were late rising, for the large amount of whiskey they had consumed the night before had caused them all to slip into a drunken stupor. They had fallen asleep inside the wagon, and, awakening, Two Moons groaned as he sat up to look around. His companions were as bad off as he and moaning with hangovers. Silently he cursed their weakness for the white man's firewater. His head pounded in pain, and his stomach churned as he crawled to the wagon's opening and clambered to the ground. The sun's brightness shone mercilessly into his bloodshot eyes, and squinting against the glare, he stumbled to the side of the wagon, where he bent over and vomited completely onto the white man's dead body.

Chief Two Moons was within his young captive's vision, and the boy quickly shut his eyes to black out the horrible sight. David himself would have vomited if his stomach hadn't already been empty.

Straightening up, Two Moons looked over at his prisoner. Seeing that the boy had his eyes closed, the heartless warrior guffawed; but in his morbid humor his head throbbed painfully, and his laughter quickly ceased.

Wondering why the Indian had suddenly become silent, David opened his eyes and turned cautiously toward the warrior. He was afraid he'd see the man advancing, and so when Two Moons stepped to the back of the wagon and began issuing orders to his men, David sighed gratefully. Within a short time, Two Moons had his companions out of the wagon and preparing to leave.

Looking on, David wondered if the leader still planned to keep him as a slave. Could he have changed his mind? Had he decided to kill him? The boy was so tired, thirsty, and uncomfortable that he wasn't sure if he cared anymore about his fate. He had been tied in a standing position now for over twelve hours, and his legs ached so badly that if it weren't for the rope binding him to the tree, he was sure he'd collapse.

Ready to leave, Two Moons hastened to his prisoner, and taking out his knife, severed the rope.

David's legs buckled, and he dropped to his knees. Sneering, Two Moons kicked the boy in the rear, sending him face down onto the muddy earth. Grasping him by the shirt collar, the warrior jerked him to his feet. David's face was covered with mud, patches of it so thick that it clung to his long lashes.

Glaring coldly into the youngster's eyes, the chief growled, "You walk or I kill you!"

Forcing strength back into his wobbly legs, David pulled away from Two Moons' firm hold. Then, with a defiant whirl, he spun about and unbuttoned his trousers. If the Indian wanted to punish him for relieving himself, David didn't care; he wasn't about to wait so long that he'd end up wetting his pants!

To David's surprise, Two Moons made no move to punish him and waited until the boy was through before shoving him toward the others, who were already mounted on their ponies.

The Indians had commandeered the two horses used to draw the wagon, and David thought Two Moons would tell him to ride one of them. Instead, the man tied a long rope around the boy's wrists, mounted his own pony, and forced his prisoner to walk behind.

Placing one tired leg in front of the other, David inwardly cursed the cruel warrior. Sensing correctly that Two Moons would drag him if he were to trip and fall, he lowered his eyes to the ground and kept a close watch on his feet. The terrain was rough in places, and it would be easy to stumble.

The lad's mouth was extremely dry, and it was becoming difficult for him to swallow. He longed to

76

ask Two Moons for a drink, but he had a feeling his request would go ungranted. Somehow, David seemed to know that his only hope for water was not to ask for it. Two Moons would offer him a drink, but not until the boy had earned his respect by being silently obedient.

Chapter Seven

Dusk was falling as Black Wolf and Alisha neared an old abandoned shack at the foot of the Black Hills. The log cabin was in fairly good shape, considering that no one had lived in it for a long time.

The couple had traveled practically nonstop since early morning, and Alisha was not only bone-tired, but her shoulder ached terribly. Guessing that Black Wolf intended for them to spend the night at the cabin, relief enveloped her. She could hardly wait to dismount, spread out a blanket, and lie down. She felt as though she could skip supper and simply sleep away the rest of the day and night.

Towering spruces and pines surrounded the lonely shack, their sweeping branches shading the building's partially dilapidated roof. A radiant sunset descended behind the tall trees, and for a moment Alisha forgot her discomfort as she admired the natural beauty of the evening. As the sun set she guided her horse to the shack and dismounted.

Quickly Black Wolf swung down from his pinto, and stepping to Alisha's side, he took her arm and led her inside the cabin.

Alisha found the cabin unfurnished. She turned to

her companion to try and make him understand that she wanted a blanket, but before she could attempt to do so, he walked back outside.

Left alone, Alisha moved slowly to the fireplace and sat down. The wooden floor was covered with dust, adding even more grime to her skirt. Fleetingly she wondered if the garment would ever wash clean. Thinking of clean made her conscious of herself, and she desperately longed for a bath. She smiled as she envisioned herself sinking into a large tub of hot water. Oh, a bath would be so heavenly!

Detecting the warrior's return, she turned to look at him. He was carrying a blanket, and when he reached her side, he spread it out for her.

"You must've read my mind," she murmured. Lying on the blanket, she rolled to her side.

She waited until he had crossed the floor and had gone back outdoors before closing her eyes. Within a short time, she was sleeping soundly.

Chief Two Moons and his men stopped in a wooded area to camp for the night. They were now three day's ride from their village and were growing anxious to return home. Their raiding excursion had been a success. The cooking utensils, firearms, ammunition, and other odds and ends were articles the Indians could use. They had also acquired two horses and a young slave. Yes, the raid had indeed been a profitable one!

Once again David was tied to a tree, this time in a sitting position. The rope stretched across his chest and arms and was secured behind the broad trunk, and a rope looped about his ankles, tying his feet together.

Two Moons had forced his prisoner to go all day without a drink, and the boy was becoming dangerously dehydrated. Although his throat was terribly parched and he desperately needed water, David had refrained from asking for a drink. Defeated, miserable, and fearing the days to come, he sometimes felt as though he'd just as soon die of thirst.

Leaning his head back against the trunk of the tree, he tried not to think about water or about the pain shooting through his tired feet. He wondered how many miles he had walked or run today. Most of the time, Two Moons had kept the pace slow enough for David to walk, but there were moments when he'd speed up his horse, forcing the boy to run in order to keep up.

Hearing someone approaching, David stiffened. Seeing Two Moons carrying a canteen, his urgent need for life-giving water almost made him greet the warrior with a smile. However, remaining still and showing no emotion, David's face was impassive as Two Moons knelt in front of him.

Opening the canteen, he placed it to his captive's dry, cracked lips. He then tilted it upwards, and David greedily accepted the water, gulping each swallow as though it would be his last.

Removing the canteen and capping it, Two Moons regarded his prisoner with a certain degree of respect. Taken with the boy's fortitude, he came close to wishing the lad was younger so that he could adopt him. But the boy was now too old to forget the ways of the white man, and his loyalties would undoubtedly remain with his own kind.

"You brave," Two Moons mumbled. "If you Sioux, you grow into fearless warrior and take many scalps. Too bad you white and must die as all whites will die!"

Bounding to his feet, Two Moons walked swiftly away from his prisoner and rejoined his companions sitting around the campfire. Three rabbits were roasting over the open flames, and looking at Straight

Lance, Two Moons ordered gruffly, "When the food is cooked, take the boy something to eat."

"You should make him go hungry for another day," Straight Lance argued.

His black eyes flashing angrily, Two Moons spat, "Don't tell me how to take care of my slave!" Although Two Moons harbored much hate for his white enemies, some of them had won his respect; his young prisoner was now among their number. But though respectful, Two Moons had no compassion for whites, and he still intended to make the boy his slave.

Loretta Ingalls was dressed for bed and preparing to retire when a couple of firm knocks sounded on her front door. Slipping on her robe and leaving the bedroom, she hurried to see who would be calling so late.

At the closed door she asked loudly, "Who's there?"

"Joel Carson," came the reply.

Surprised but pleased, Loretta pivoted quickly toward the mirror hanging on the wall. She hastily examined her reflection. She thought she looked a little pale and pinched her cheeks to make them rosy. Turning back to the door, she opened it and said, "Mr. Carson, please come in."

He doffed his hat. "Excuse me for calling at this late hour, but I need to talk to you for a moment."

Showing him into the parlor, she replied sincerely, "Please don't feel bad. It's really not all that late." She lit a lamp, then faced her caller, waiting for him to explain his unexpected visit.

"I suppose you know about Miss Stevens's disappearance," he began.

"Yes, I do."

"I was wondering if maybe you've heard anything

81

new. Has she been found?"

"Not that I know of."

"A couple of Stevens's ranch hands showed up in town with two dead bodies—Joe and Walter Wyatt. I thought one of the hands might have stopped here to let you know if they had found Miss Stevens."

She shook her head. "No, I haven't heard anything." Pausing hesitantly, she asked, "Mr. Carson, would you like a cup of coffee?"

"No, thank you, ma'am."

Without being too obvious, she looked him over carefully, finding him dashingly handsome in his dark suit and white ruffled shirt. She glanced down at her own clothes, a cotton gown and her robe, old and threadbare. She was sure she must look quite dreadful. Self-conscious, she kept her eyes downcast.

Watching her, a warm smile spread over Joel's face. He had an eye for beauty and was aware that the new schoolmarm was a very attractive woman. He wondered why she camouflaged her loveliness with matronly dresses and an unflattering hairstyle. Tonight, however, her hair was in two braids, and he tried to imagine how the long tresses would look cascading freely. The longer he studied Loretta, the more curious he became about her. Deciding to get to know the woman better, he said, "On second thought, I think I'd like a cup of coffee. That is, if it isn't too much trouble."

Her eyes darting happily to his, she declared, "Oh, it's no trouble at all. Please have a seat, and I'll go to the kitchen and prepare the coffee."

"I'll go with you," he offered. "There's no reason for me to sit in here alone when I can be talking to you."

Flattered, Loretta replied a little breathlessly, "Very well, Mr. Carson."

Following her to the kitchen, he said, "Please call me Joel."

Blushing, she mumbled, "My name is Loretta."

Carson sat at the kitchen table. He watched Loretta as she rekindled the wood stove. "Where did you live before coming to Backwater?" he asked.

"I was living at Fort Sill, Oklahoma. My father was a missionary doctor and he took care of the Indians on the reservations; I was their schoolteacher. My mother died when I was a small child. Then, last year, my father took ill and passed away. Losing him was very hard on me, and I thought maybe a change of scenery would help. I telegraphed my qualifications as a teacher to quite a few papers in the west, and when I received an answer from Backwater, I decided to take the position here."

Loretta turned away from the stove and filled the coffee pot. She was amazed to find herself talking so easily with Joel Carson. She'd always been so unsure and timid around men, but there was something about this man's manner that put her perfectly at ease.

Placing the pot on the stove, she asked, "How long have you lived in Backwater?"

"A little over a year."

"Was there a special reason why you chose to settle here?"

"My wife and I were traveling by wagon train to San Francisco." He paused and swallowed heavily before continuing. "My wife was killed by the Sioux. We were moving to San Francisco because she had family out there. After I lost her, I saw no reason to continue the journey. I left the wagon train and wandered here to Backwater. Before I was married, I was a professional gambler. After I became a widower, I decided to slip back into my old ways. I won the Golden Horseshoe from the proprietor in a poker game. The former owner is now my bartender."

Stepping to the table, Loretta sat down. "Your wife

83

must've been a very good influence on you."

"Yes, she was. I loved her very much, and I would've done anything for her. Her uncle in San Francisco was going to give me a partnership in his lumber business. I had every intention of living a respectable life, and was even looking forward to doing so."

"How long were you married?"

"Six months," he answered somberly.

Loretta was silent for a long moment as her thoughts drifted to Alisha. Then, her gaze sweeping to his, she asked intensely, "Do you think Alisha has been kidnapped by Indians?"

Thinking of his dead wife, and the way in which she was tortured before dying, he mumbled gravely, "God, I pray that Miss Stevens is not at the mercy of the Sioux!"

Kneeling beside Alisha, Black Wolf gently shook her good shoulder to awaken her.

Drowsily she opened her eyes, but as soon as she detected the delicious aroma of food cooking, she came awake quickly. Sitting up, she was surprised to see the fireplace glowing and supper simmering over the flames. She could hardly believe that she had slept so soundly. The savory aromas made her acutely aware of her hunger. Leaning forward and looking inside the iron pot, she exclaimed, "Rabbit stew!" Apparently while she had slept, this warrior had hunted a rabbit, cleaned it, and even prepared the meal. My goodness, how long had she been asleep? Looking at the only window, she saw that it was pitch dark.

Black Wolf dished up her supper and handed it to her. Accepting the bowl, she said softly, "I wish you could understand me, so I could thank you."

Black Wolf had already eaten, and moving away, he

hurried across the room and outside. He had placed his bedroll on the rickety porch, halfway between the front door and the window. To escape, the woman would have to use one of the two exits, and he intended to sleep between them so she couldn't leave without waking him.

He sat down on the bedroll, then leaned back against the cabin. Sleeping beside the woman last night had been pure torture for Black Wolf, and he wasn't about to put himself through that again. His willpower could be stretched only so far, and where his lovely companion was concerned, his self-restraint had reached its limit.

Meanwhile, inside the cabin, Alisha's thoughts were racing intently as she ate her supper. Did the warrior plan to sleep outdoors? If so, should she try to escape later tonight? Was she strong enough to make it back home? Her shoulder still ached terribly. But then, this might be her last chance. They were at the foot of the Hills, and tomorrow they'd be traveling through Sioux territory. Even if her family were searching for her, it'd be suicidal for them to venture into the Black Hills. No, if she allowed this warrior to take her into the Hills, she might be lost to her own people forever. The terrifying thought of never seeing her father or brothers again made up her mind. She would escape tonight!

Chapter Eight

Alisha had no problem staying awake, for the long sleep she'd had earlier had been sufficient rest. She knew she must be patient and give the warrior time to fall asleep before attempting to escape. She didn't know exactly where he had placed his bedroll. She'd been tempted to go to the door and peek out; but fearing he might spot her and guess her motive, she'd decided not to take the chance.

Now, sitting on her pallet, she looked closely at the open window as she tried to judge if it was wide enough for her to slip through. Yes, she was sure she could manage it. The window was probably her best bet, for the warrior was more than likely sleeping in front of the door.

Alisha's brow furrowed as she wondered where the Indian had put the horses for the night. They had to be close by, and she was certain that finding the animals would be easy. She hoped frantically that the horses wouldn't whinny as she approached them. She didn't doubt that her companion was a light sleeper, for she already knew him well enough to sense that his instincts were as alert as a wild animal's.

Alisha eased her arm from the makeshift sling. She'd

need the use of both arms to crawl through the window. Soundlessly, she stood and rolled up the blanket. Suddenly, she was taken aback. Supplies! She'd need supplies. The warrior kept them bundled on his black stallion, and she hoped they would be wherever the horses were. She felt no animosity toward the Indian, so she'd only take what she needed and leave him the rest.

Deciding it was now late enough to make her break, Alisha stepped furtively to the window and she peered cautiously outside. The night was overcast, and she could barely see two feet in front of her. Leaning out the window, she looked downward, praying she wouldn't see the warrior sleeping there. Finding the spot beneath the window bare, she sighed with relief. Carefully she dropped the blanket onto the porch, and favoring her injured arm, she managed to crawl through the window. Quickly, she bent over to pick up the blanket, but before she was able to grasp it, a hand suddenly snaked out and strong fingers wrapped about her ankle.

Gasping, Alisha's eyes widened as she made out the warrior. His bedroll had been placed so close to the window that he could reach her by stretching. It hadn't even been necessary for him to stand up to capture her.

Frustrated as well as angry, she tried to pull free, but his hold on her ankle merely tightened. "Let me go!" she demanded.

He turned her loose, and she was about to storm back into the cabin when, with no warning, he grabbed her hand and pulled her roughly down onto his bed. His harsh treatment was painful to her injury, causing her to cry out.

Black Wolf hadn't wanted to hurt her, but she'd brought the pain upon herself. Didn't this defiant little vixen realize how dangerous it was for her to travel alone? He wondered if he should talk to her and assure her that he wasn't going to harm her, or make her his slave.

If she understood the circumstances, maybe she'd quit trying to escape. As he mulled over the possibility, he gazed down into her large brown eyes. She was watching him guardedly, but he couldn't discern any fear on her face. Apparently she wasn't frightened. He was quite taken with her dark eyes and light hair, finding the contrast beautiful. She was indeed a prize, this lovely spitfire that fate had brought into his life. Smiling to himself, he tried to imagine how she'd react if he let her know he could speak English fluently. He didn't hesitate to believe that she'd be quite upset, not to mention embarrassed. Weighing the pros and cons, he decided to wait a little longer before letting her know that he could communicate with her. However, he wasn't looking forward to that moment. She would probably turn on him with the viciousness of a wildcat.

Alisha wished she could read his thoughts. He didn't appear angry, so obviously he wasn't considering punishing her. Assured that he meant her no harm, she relaxed. As her eyes lingered on his features, she once again became aware of how handsome he was. His shoulder-length black hair fell about his bronzed face, making his vivid blue eyes prominent. She had never seen a man with such a finely sculptured visage, and as though her hand had a will of its own, she raised it to his face, tracing his features with her fingertips.

For a moment he permitted the caress, then, slowly, his hand moved to grasp hers and moved it to his lips. Turning her palm upward, he placed a light kiss upon it.

The touch of his lips sent a thrill through Alisha that startled her. Why was she so strongly attracted to this warrior? How was it possible for her to desire a man with whom she couldn't even communicate? She mustn't let this strange desire weaken her defenses. Although he had saved her life, he was still her enemy and was holding her against her will. God only knew what he planned to do with her once they reached his village.

Black Wolf was still holding her hand, and as Alisha tried to pull free, he moved lithely and wrapped an arm around her waist. Lifting her against him, he then rolled over her, pinning her beneath him. Firmly he pressed his thighs to hers as his mouth came down and claimed hers in a breathtaking kiss.

Common sense told Alisha not to respond, but as his mouth continued to take possession of hers, her self-restraint deserted her. Swiftly she lifted her arms around his neck as her lips parted to accept his probing tongue.

Aroused, Black Wolf shoved his hardness against her, and even through his buckskins, she could feel how badly he wanted her.

Never had Alisha been so intimate with a man, and although the feel of his stiff manhood was new to her, it was also so stimulating that she instinctively arched against him. His undulating hips made his hardness rub up and down between her thighs, and as a fiery longing ruled her senses, she began to match his rhythm.

Black Wolf broke their passionate kiss and moved his lips to her neck, where his tongue flickered teasingly against her flesh before coming to rest at the hollow of her throat.

Soft moans escaped as Alisha entwined her fingers in his black, flowing hair, encouraging his fervent fondling.

Black Wolf was now aroused beyond his control, and his vow to remain emotionally detached was completely overwhelmed as his hand went to her breasts, caressing first one and then the other.

Alisha was also beyond reason, for now she was conscious of nothing save this man who was making her feel so alive, so ecstatically on fire!

This beautiful, uncontrolled desire between Black Wolf and Alisha would have totally consumed them, making them as one—if at that moment the horses hadn't begun to whinny nervously.

Heedful, Black Wolf leapt to his feet and grabbed his rifle. Cocking the weapon, he started toward the tied horses when, out of the dark shadows, a mountain lion suddenly sprang forward. The wild predator had an innate fear of man, and catching the scent of humans, he turned away and darted away into the brush.

Knowing the cat wouldn't return, Black Wolf didn't fire. Holding the rifle loosely at his side, he turned around to see if Alisha was frightened. He was surprised to find her gone. He hurried to the cabin door and opened it. Looking inside, he saw to his relief that she was spreading her blanket in front of the fireplace. Quietly he closed the door and returned to his bed. He was wide awake and knew it would be a long time before he'd be able to fall back asleep. His manhood ached for release, but although he was uncomfortable, he nonetheless sighed gratefully. If it hadn't been for the mountain lion's intrusion, he'd have made love to the white woman. Black Wolf unquestioningly believed it would've proven to be a big mistake. He must not let himself fall in love with a white woman, for if he did, she'd insist that he leave the Sioux and live in the white man's world. He was bound and determined never to leave his father or his father's people. Running Horse had told his son about his dream which had predicted that someday Black Wolf would leave the Sioux to live with the whites. But Black Wolf was set on proving his father's dream wrong. His loyalties lay with the Sioux, and unlike Running Horse's vision, he would not leave the wild dogs to live with the wolves!

As Black Wolf pondered the situation, Alisha had thoughts of her own. The moment she had seen the mountain lion, she had darted inside the cabin. She hadn't hurried indoors because she feared the cat, but because she feared her overwhelming desire for the mysterious warrior who had come so unexpectedly into her life. His kisses and caresses had left her shaken, and she breathed deeply, trying to calm herself.

Finally, when her heartbeat had slowed to normal, she became more determined than ever to escape. But now her reason for leaving was coupled with a stronger compulsion than simply to go home; she must flee from this handsome warrior who had such control over her emotions, such power over her body!

The next day's journey was uneventful, and although Alisha made no further attempts to escape, she remained hopeful that an opportunity to flee would present itself. However, as they traveled farther into the Black Hills, the dangers for Alisha of riding alone increased. Aware of this, she knew if she didn't soon find the chance to get away, the odds against her reaching home safely were minimal. The Hills were full of Sioux who greatly resented whites intruding on their territory. She had heard tales of whites who had entered this region never to be heard from again.

Traveling with a man who didn't speak English was tedious to Alisha. She didn't understand why she had no fear of the warrior, but for some inexplicable reason, she wasn't frightened of him. She *did* dread reaching his home, for she still believed that he planned to make her a slave. Furthermore, she was sure the people in his village would treat her with hostility.

The sun was just beginning to make its descent over the horizon when unexpectedly Black Wolf grabbed the reins from Alisha's hands, bringing their horses to a sudden halt.

Thinking he may have heard something, Alisha glanced about hoping desperately to spot Clint and the others. The surrounding terrain was covered with heavy vegetation, and she could see nothing except trees and shrubbery. Disappointed, she sighed and turned back to the warrior. Her eyes widened with anxiety when he drew his rifle and cocked the weapon. He *had* heard something! Her heart beat rapidly; she tried not to let her expectations run away with her; but against her will they soared. Was she about to be rescued? Would she soon be home with her family?

Detecting the sounds of approaching horses, Alisha stiffened. Expecting to see a search party breaking through the shrubbery, she slipped her arm from the sling. Then moving swiftly, and taking Black Wolf off guard she lurched for his rifle. Grabbing it, she tried wildly to pull the weapon from his hands.

Moving the rifle to his side, Black Wolf used his other hand to trap her wrists. His grip was painful, causing her to grimace. He released her quickly, urged his pinto forward, and rode into the thicket.

Left alone, Alisha was uncertain whether to make a run for it. She was about to turn her horse and flee, but before she could, Black Wolf returned. The eight Sioux warriors accompanying him sent a chill down her spine. Had her companion been expecting these men? Had she been wrong to think he was taking her to his village? Dear God, what did he and these other Indians plan to do with her? The possibilities were terrifying!

As the riders pulled up, Alisha suddenly noticed they had a white captive with them. Looking closely, she saw that their prisoner was a young boy. He was standing behind one warrior's pony, and a long rope bound his wrists. Upon closer examination she could see that his captor was holding the other end of the rope. Her heart went out to the lad. Good Lord, the warrior was leading him around like a captured animal! The youngster looked so tired, filthy, and defeated that Alisha wanted to dismount, run to him, and take him into her arms.

Meanwhile, David Hunter hadn't looked in Alisha's direction; instead he was staring down at the ground. Sensing that someone was watching him, he slowly lifted his gaze. The sight of a white woman hit him unexpectedly. He wondered if she was also a prisoner, or if she was traveling with this warrior of her own free will.

The boy's and the woman's eyes met as each tried to read the other's thoughts. But when Black Wolf and Two Moons dismounted and began talking, the prisoners turned their attention solely to the warriors.

The men spoke in their own language, and although Alisha and David listened intently, neither could understand what was being said.

"Where did you find the boy?" Black Wolf asked Two Moons.

"The boy and his father were searching for the white man's yellow gold."

Black Wolf's eyes bore into the other man's. "Did you kill his father?"

"His scalp now hangs on my lance."

"What do you plan to do with the boy?" Black Wolf's face showed no emotion. Although he had never liked Two Moons, he had no personal grievances against him.

"He will be my slave."

Black Wolf tore his gaze from Two Moons' and looked thoughtfully at the lad. He knew he couldn't leave the boy at the young chief's mercy. He had to find a way to save him. Turning back to face Two Moons, he asked, "Will you trade him?"

The man smiled, looked away and appraised Alisha. Finding her desirable, he bartered, "I will trade him for the white woman."

"She isn't a slave to be traded or sold," Black Wolf stated firmly.

Two Moons arched his dark brows. "Have you taken yourself a white wife?"

"I don't intend to discuss the woman."

"But if you will not give me the woman, what do you have to offer me for the boy?"

Moving, Black Wolf walked to the young stallion, took the reins, and led him back to Two Moons. The horse had been given to him by his good friend Major Landon. This was a superb animal, and although Black Wolf regretted giving him up, the boy's life was more important to him.

Admiration shone in the chief's eyes as he expertly evaluated the black stallion. "The horse is worth more than a boy slave."

"Give me your prisoner, and the horse is yours."

Thinking Black Wolf a fool for making such a trade, Two Moons laughed gleefully as he stepped to his captive. Removing his knife, he cut the rope that tied David's wrists. Then, roughly, he shoved him toward Black Wolf.

Losing his balance, David stumbled and fell to his knees. Two Moons started to kick him, but hesitated when Black Wolf cried out, "If you injure him, the deal is off. I have a long way to travel, and the boy must be able to keep up."

Not wanting to take a chance on losing the stallion,

Two Moons assisted the boy to his feet, then placing a hand on his arm, led him to Black Wolf.

Black Wolf gave the stallion's reins to Two Moons and the exchange was complete.

Poised beside his new owner, David didn't have to be told that he'd just been traded for a horse. It hadn't been necessary to understand the language to comprehend what was taking place. He prayed that this warrior would be kinder than Two Moons.

Alisha had also noted the trade and was grateful for the exchange. Surely, working together, she and the boy could manage a successful escape!

Chapter Nine

"What is your name?" Alisha asked David. They were riding side by side as Black Wolf rode close behind. The boy had been given Walter's horse. As soon as Two Moons and his men had left, Black Wolf had decided to move onward and cover a few more miles before night set in. He could easily overhear his companions' discussion, and he listened attentively.

"My name's David Hunter," the boy now answered. "What's yours?"

"Alisha Stevens."

Alisha, Black Wolf thought, silently savoring the name. A beautiful name for a beautiful lady.

David's face hardened with animosity as he asked, "Why are you traveling with a dirty, lowdown, murdering Indian?" Suddenly afraid that the warrior understood English, David feared he might have blundered. With a curt nod in Black Wolf's direction, he asked, "Does he speak English?"

David had lowered his voice; nonetheless Black Wolf's acute hearing picked up his query.

"No, he doesn't understand," Alisha assured him. Then, as quickly as possible, she explained why she was accompanying Black Wolf.

When she had finished, David told her what had happened to his father and how he himself had been treated by Two Moons and his comrades.

"I'm sorry about your father," Alisha said sincerely.

The boy swallowed the lump in his throat. "He wasn't even buried. His body is still beside the wagon where it's exposed to wild animals and vultures." David felt a violent rage consuming him. He had never hated anyone, but he now hated Indians with a passion. "These savages aren't even human!" he fumed.

"No, David, you're wrong," Alisha disagreed. "You can't judge all Sioux by Two Moons. I think this warrior traded his horse for you to save you from Two Moons' brutal treatment."

Black Wolf was pleased to hear Alisha stand up for him.

David conceded with reluctance. "Maybe you're right." Then his voice became excited. "But regardless of his reasons for saving either one of us, we're still his prisoners, and we've got to find a way to escape!"

Alisha was in total agreement. "Do you have a way in mind?" she asked anxiously.

Sounding more confident than he truly felt, David answered, "Well, there's only one of him and two of us. We'll have to wait for the right moment to jump him."

"The right moment?" she repeated, somewhat dubious.

"Sooner or later, he'll make a careless move, and when he does, we'll make the most of it."

Alisha couldn't imagine the skillful warrior ever making a careless move. Aloud she said, "David, I don't think this man will do anything careless."

Black Wolf was flattered; apparently, she held him in high regard.

"You better hope he does," David mumbled, "because it's the only chance we have." He was silent a moment before asking, "What do you think he plans to do with us?"

"I suppose he'll take us to his village and make us slaves."

"Do you think there's a search party looking for you?"

"Yes—I'm sure of it."

"Will they follow you into the Hills?"

Alisha shrugged. "I don't know . . . but as badly as I want to be rescued, I hope they don't come into the Hills. The Sioux consider this territory their own, which it rightfully is. The Fort Laramie Treaty gave them the land in the Dakotas. The Sioux hold this region sacred and are hostile to all white intruders."

"Are you saying that if this Indian takes us deep into the Dakotas, we may never be rescued?"

"Quite a few of our people have been abducted by the Sioux, taken into these Hills, and never heard from again."

David gasped in disbelief. "Why doesn't the Army search for them?"

"The Black Hills are vast, the Sioux villages numerous, and the cavalry doesn't have the manpower to cover so much territory and search every village along the way. But Papa believes that the cavalry will grow in size, and someday the soldiers will outnumber the Sioux. He says it's only a matter of time until the Sioux nation is wiped out or placed on reservations. When that happens, all the white captives who are still alive will be accounted for."

Still listening, Black Wolf emitted a long sigh. He knew Alisha's prophecy would come to pass. Someday the mighty Sioux nation would cease to exist. The thought was emotionally painful. Although Black Wolf loved his father's people, his mother's blood also flowed through his veins, and his feelings were often

98

mixed. If only the Sioux and the whites could avoid conflict. But Black Wolf knew that a full-fledged war was inevitable. When that time came, would he choose sides, or try to remain neutral?

Suddenly, feeling the pinto's muscles tense, Black Wolf cleared his mind to give his surroundings his undivided attention. His instincts told him he and his captives were being trailed. His pony had sensed a close presence, and if Black Wolf hadn't been preoccupied, the danger wouldn't have escaped his notice. He became attuned to the pinto's reflexes. The horse wasn't unduly alarmed, which meant the scents he'd detected weren't too unfamiliar. Two Moons! Black Wolf moaned inwardly, now certain that the brutal warrior and his men were following.

Jack Stevens held the torn remnant from his daughter's yellow blouse as he stood in front of the abandoned cabin. Gazing thoughtfully into the distance, his vision became fixed on the rolling hills edged against the horizon; their towering peaks reaching upwards to caress the clouds.

"Are you all right, Pa?" Clint inquired, moving to stand beside him.

Shaking his head, Jack looked down at the material in his hands. They had come upon the torn blouse the day before, and finding it had given Jack hope. They were on the right track, and with luck, they might find Alisha before it was too late. He groaned solemnly, then returned his gaze to the majestic hills. "She's been taken into Sioux territory."

Clint concurred silently. He wondered if he'd ever see his sister again.

Straightening his posture and speaking strongly, Jack declared, "We're going in the Hills after her!"

"Pa, that's suicidal!" Clint argued.

"Since finding Alisha's blouse, we've tracked only one Indian pony, which means she's been abducted by a lone warrior. One Indian doesn't make our mission overwhelmingly risky."

"You aren't thinking rationally. The Hills are rife with Indians, and once we trespass on their land, we won't have only one of them to worry about."

Approaching, Sheriff Davis had overheard Clint's last remark. "He's right, Jack. It's foolhardy to even consider riding into the Black Hills."

Desperate, Alisha's father cried, "What am I supposed to do? Give up, and let the Indians have my daughter?" His voice quivered with grief. "My God, I can't just let her go!"

The sheriff was sympathetic. "I can understand how you feel. But getting yourself and others killed isn't going to help Alisha. And if you enter Sioux land without the proper authorities, you'll probably all be massacred."

Todd and Johnny had now arrived. Todd asked the sheriff, "What do you suggest?"

The law officer thought for a moment. "Contact the army," he advised. He looked at Jack. "Ride to Fort Laramie and ask for a military escort to take you into the Hills."

"But that will take days!" Jack exclaimed.

"That's true, but it's the only logical choice you have."

Undecided, Stevens turned to his oldest son. "What do you think?"

"Pa, I want to find Alisha as badly as you do, but I think the only chance we have of ever seeing her again is to ask the Army for assistance."

In spite of his anxieties, Jack's better judgment held. "All right, we'll go to Fort Laramie." He planned to take both sons with him, but he knew his foreman could run the ranch.

"The trip will be shorter if you leave from here," Sheriff Davis said.

"Yes, I know," Jack replied. "I wasn't planning to go back to the ranch." He glanced from Clint to Johnny. "I'll send the men home, then we'll head for the fort."

Clint nodded agreeably, but Johnny was against the idea. Although the youngest Stevens wanted his sister found, he didn't see why it was necessary for him to accompany his brother and father. They certainly didn't need his help in reaching Fort Laramie, and when they ventured into the Hills, they'd have an armed escort, so they wouldn't be needing his gun. Preferring to return to the ranch, and to partake of the good times to be had in town, he said to Jack, "Pa, maybe I should stay and run things at home."

"Nonsense," his father rebuked. "The ranch will operate just fine without you." Considering the subject closed, Jack offered Todd his hand. "Thank you for coming this far with us."

Accepting the handshake, Miller answered, "You're more than welcome. I'll pray that you find Alisha safe and unharmed."

As Jack turned his attention to the sheriff, Todd walked away from the gathering and over to his horse. Resting an arm across the saddle, he leaned against the animal. His final words to Jack came back to torture his mind. "I'll pray that you find Alisha safe and unharmed." Well, he might find her safe, but Todd seriously doubted that she'd be unharmed. This Indian who had stolen her had probably already raped her time and time again. When he grew tired of her, he'd most likely give her to other warriors. By the time Jack could locate his daughter, she would no longer be fit for a white man. Envisioning the wild savages abusing her

101

lovely flesh made his stomach constrict, and, for a moment, he thought he might actually vomit. He breathed in deeply and the nausea passed. Thank God he and Alisha were not officially engaged, for the Stevenses would've expected him to honor the wedding arrangement. Alisha had turned down his marriage proposal, so he was not obligated. He released a sigh of relief, for he found the thought of marrying a woman who had been raped by Indians repulsive.

Black Wolf was perfectly aware that his companions were watching him like hawks, waiting for him to make a careless mistake. They were standing close by, their eyes glued to his every movement as he set up camp. He had his back turned in their direction and they didn't see his thoughtful expression as he decided it was time to let them know he could speak English. With Two Moons following, they must be warned not to escape. Black Wolf believed Alisha and David were safe as long as they stayed with him, but if they were to run away, Two Moons wouldn't hesitate to grab them. The boy was a valuable slave, and Alisha's beauty was a temptation to any man.

As Black Wolf was considering revealing the truth, David had decided it was time for him and Alisha to attempt an escape. The warrior's back was turned, his rifle proppped against a tree. If they could move fast enough to take the man unawares, they might reach him before he managed to retrieve the gun. There was no reason for them to try for one of the rifles which had belonged to the Wyatts; those were unloaded, and their ammunition was stored on the pinto.

In a lowered voice, David told Alisha, "While I rush him, you go for the rifle."

Having second thoughts, she whispered, "But,

102

David, he has a knife. What if he . . . ?"

Interrupting, he said softly but forcefully, "If he goes for his knife, shoot him. You do know how to use a rifle, don't you?"

Her answer was a simple nod. Shoot him? Could she bring herself to kill the man who had not only saved her life, but had also taken such good care of her? She suddenly remembered the wonderful feel of his lips and the exciting sensation she had felt when his muscular body was pressed intimately to hers. No, she couldn't shoot him; however, she kept this to herself, hoping desperately that it wouldn't come to such a showdown.

Nudging her with his elbow, David ordered, "Let's go; I'll charge him and you run for the gun."

Obeying, she ran for the rifle as David flew toward the warrior's turned back.

Black Wolf knew the boy was attacking and waited for just the right moment; then spinning about, his foot caught David below the knees, sending the lad falling headlong onto the ground. Next, pivoting smoothly, Black Wolf dived for the rifle and grabbed it just seconds before Alisha arrived.

However, Alisha was running so fast that her strides carried her straight into Black Wolf. She crashed solidly against his hard frame and the collision knocked her backward. Losing her balance, she fell heavily to the ground, landing quite painfully on her rear.

When she heard his amused laughter, she glared murderously up at him as she got back to her feet. Rubbing her sore bottom, she lashed out, "You pompous bully! And to think I had decided not to shoot you! Oh, if I had it to do all over again, I'd beat you to that rifle, and then I'd shoot that silly grin right off your face!"

"Is that anyway to talk to a man who saved your

life?" Black Wolf asked lightly. "Besides, I didn't make you fall, you fell on your lovely derrière without any help from me."

Alisha was flabbergasted to hear him speak English, and as David came to stand at her side, he also stared with wonder.

It was David who first found his voice. "I thought you said he didn't speak English," he muttered to Alisha.

When she offered no reply, the boy swept his gaze from the warrior and to Alisha. Detecting the violent rage within her, he took a couple of steps to the side.

Black Wolf, also aware of her erupting anger, braced himself for the confrontation that was about to explode.

Placing her hands on her hips and eyeing him furiously, she ranted, "You contemptible . . . lying . . . smug . . ."

In a trice, Black Wolf was at her side with his hand clamped over her mouth. "Shh . . . shh," he whispered. "There's someone coming."

Wrestling free, she yelled, "Good! I hope it's my family, and when my father finds out . . ."

Again, before she could stop him, Black Wolf covered her mouth. With his hand muffling her tirade, he looked at David. "I have reason to believe Two Moons is close by," he said. Then, turning Alisha so that he could see her face, he stared down into her angry eyes. Keeping his hand on her mouth, he urged, "Two Moons may be planning on rushing *us,* so for your own sake, shut up and do as I say."

Her fear of Two Moons was stronger than her anger, and at his warning she nodded.

Cautiously he removed his hand. When she remained silent, he began to issue orders, "David, get my rifle and take Alisha into the shrubbery and stay hidden."

Without question, David and Alisha obeyed, and as they darted into the thicket, Black Wolf headed for the pinto. Quickly, he had one of the Wyatts' rifles loaded.

From behind a heavy bush, David and Alisha watched the warrior take cover behind a tree. The dark silence of night hovered eerily as they waited, both wondering fearfully if Two Moons was about to make an appearance.

Alisha gasped softly as a lone rider materialized. Slowly his horse broke through the surrounding vegetation. When he was in clear sight, Black Wolf put down his rifle and stepped swiftly out from behind the tree. Alisha, looking closer, saw that the visitor was an Indian boy.

As he dismounted, Black Wolf yelled to his traveling companions.

Taking Alisha's arm, David assisted her to the campsite. Pausing in front of the Indian boy and Black Wolf, they both eyed them with a certain degree of hostility.

Now that the fear of Two Moons no longer existed, Alisha's resentment had returned, causing her to stare peevishly at Black Wolf. Oh, she still had so many things to say to him! How dare he pretend not to speak English!

Meanwhile, as her anger continued to build, David's eyes were locked in a heated gaze with the Indian boy's. They were the same age, their builds identical. And as each proceeded to measure the other, both decided immediately that they didn't like what they saw.

Black Wolf, aware of everybody's animosity, felt a sense of dread. They still had a long way to travel before reaching his father's village. The Indian boy,

Flying Hawk, was one of Running Horse's people and would now be journeying with them. Black Wolf worried as he wondered how he could keep peace between David and Flying Hawk. The way in which the two boys regarded each other made it quite apparent that they'd soon be at each other's throats. Carefully Black Wolf turned his attention to Alisha and was met by an expression even more hostile than the ones he had just encountered.

He folded his arms across his chest and shook his head slightly. It was going to be a very, very long trip.

Chapter Ten

Seated at the campfire, Alisha and David stared distrustfully across the flames at the two Indians who, in turn, regarded them with misgivings.

The tension caused Black Wolf no end of grief. He wished he could simply set David and Alisha free, for he dreaded the journey ahead. However, with Two Moons following, letting the boy and woman leave was out of the question. He was quite certain that they would remain safe as long as they were under his protection, but if they were on their own, Two Moons would have no qualms about capturing them and taking them to his village. For their own safety, Black Wolf had no choice but to keep them with him.

A pot of coffee was brewing over the fire. Taking a cup, Black Wolf filled it to the rim. He took a sip before speaking to Alisha and David. "First, let me assure you both that you won't be slaves in my father's village; on the contrary, you'll be guests and treated well."

He paused to take another drink, and Alisha studied him with astonishment. She was awestruck by his flawless English and the ease with which the language came to him. He spoke it as though it were his native tongue.

Black Wolf continued. "Second, I'm quite sure that Two Moons is trailing us, hoping you two will head out on your own. If you do, I've no doubt that he'll capture you, but as long as you stay with me, I don't think Two Moons will try anything."

Interrupting, David asked, "How do we know you're telling the truth about Two Moons following?"

"You don't," Black Wolf muttered flatly. "You must take my word for it."

The lad smirked. "You're probably just telling us that to keep us from escaping." He still had Black Wolf's rifle, and he drew the weapon closer, his eyes daring the warrior to take the gun away from him.

Black Wolf smiled. "You and Alisha are free to leave anytime you please. I have warned you of the danger. If you choose not to believe me, then by all means, leave."

David looked anxiously at Alisha. "Let's go!"

She shook her head. "David, let's not act in haste. If what he says about Two Moons is true, then we mustn't leave."

Regarding her, Black Wolf's admiration for Alisha deepened. He respected her for not panicking, for not making a rash decision. His eyes meeting hers, Black Wolf offered, "Why don't we take a ride and see if Two Moons is camped close by?"

"What will he do if he catches us spying on him?" she questioned.

Black Wolf answered evenly. "We won't be caught if you do as I say."

Alisha hesitated, but only for a moment. "All right, I'll go with you. But if we don't find Two Moons, then David and I are leaving."

Offering no comment, Black Wolf finished his coffee, then turning to Flying Hawk, he spoke the Sioux language. "While we're gone, keep a close watch on the boy." There was no reason for him to explain his conversation with Alisha and David, for Flying Hawk understood English.

Rising, Black Wolf went to David's side, bent over, and picked up his rifle. The lad considered trying to stop him, but the hard warning in the man's eyes quickly dissuaded him from doing so. Black Wolf gestured for Alisha to follow, then headed toward the pinto.

Hurrying, Alisha caught up to him. The horse was still saddled, and Black Wolf helped her mount before slipping his rifle into the leather sheath. Then he swung up behind her.

"Why are we taking only one horse?" she asked.

"The pinto is trained to move quietly, and our mission must be carried out in total silence."

There was something in his tone that made her wonder if he was only pretending to be serious. She frowned. She had a feeling that this devious warrior really had no fear of Two Moons at all.

As Black Wolf urged the pinto forward, Alisha said what was on her mind. "You aren't worried that Two Moons will catch us spying."

He chuckled. "He's no threat to me or to Flying Hawk." His tone became cautious. "But he poses a threat to you and David. Make no mistake, Madam, if Two Moons is given the opportunity to capture you two, he'll do so. I don't suppose I have to tell you what he and his men will do to you."

The mere thought made her shudder. "No, you don't have to explain."

He leaned closer, placing his lips next to her ear. "I know you have a lot of questions to ask, but I must insist that you refrain from doing so. Later, you can ask as many questions as you please, and if my answers anger you, you can feel free to throw your temper tantrums. Now, it's imperative that we both remain

quiet. If Two Moons is following, his camp is close by."
She could feel his warm breath against her ear, and a
tingling sensation swept through her. "Can I trust you
to be silent?"

She moved her head, trying to avoid the feverish
feeling that his lips and breath provoked. "Yes, you can
trust me," she murmured. Then, lifting her chin and
stiffening her back, she added peevishly, "And I don't
throw temper tantrums!"

"That remains to be seen," he said, smiling.

Alisha and Black Wolf had been gone for quite some
time, yet David and Flying Hawk had continued sitting
at the campfire, silently glaring at each other.

Trying to judge his opponent's strength, David
wondered if he could take him in hand-to-hand
combat. The strenuous chores he'd handled on the
farm back home had toughened his muscles, and David
had confidence in his ability to fight. He knew he was
exceptionally strong for his age and build. The longer
he studied the Indian boy, the more certain he was that
he could whip him.

Meanwhile, as David's confidence was soaring,
Flying Hawk had no doubts that he could beat this
white boy were they to get into a fight. Certain he'd be
victorious, a pleased smile spread across his face.

"What in the hell are you grinnin' about?" David
sneered, believing his words wasted, for he was sure the
Indian couldn't speak English.

"I see myself beating you until you cry like a girl and
beg me to stop."

David smirked. "I'm sure glad you speak English, so
we'll have no problem understanding each other." His
eyes narrowed angrily. "You'll never see me cry like a
girl! And if you call me a coward again, you're gonna

110

find my fists in your face!"

Flying Hawk laughed carelessly. "You're soft, like all white boys. I could beat you with one arm tied behind me."

"Oh yeah?" David returned. "I kinda suspected you were dumb. Now I know it!"

Enraged, Flying Hawk cried, "You speak words that can get you killed. Soon your scalp could hang on my lance."

"That'll be the day!" David laughed sarcastically.

The other boy's black eyes shot daggers. "If not for Black Wolf, I would kill you now! Lucky for you, he wants you to live!"

Leaping to his feet, David egged him on. "Well, don't let Black Wolf stop you. Get up, damn you, and I'll give you a one-way ticket to your happy hunting ground!"

Accepting the challenge, Flying Hawk rose swiftly. Edging his way around the fire, he moved toward his opponent. Vigilantly, they began to circle, each waiting for the right moment to attack. However, at that moment, Black Wolf's and Alisha's sudden return brought their confrontation to an abrupt halt.

Reading the situation, Black Wolf wondered if perhaps he should let the boys have their fight and get it over with. But worried that one of them might seriously hurt the other, he decided against it.

Flying Hawk and David returned to their places at the fire, their expressions promising each other that the brawl had merely been postponed.

Joining them, Alisha helped herself to a cup of coffee. She was also aware that the boys had been about to fight. Sitting beside David, she told him calmly, "We located Two Moons' camp."

"Then he's following us?" he asked.

"Yes," Alisha answered. She regarded the boy sternly. "David, for our own safety we mustn't be alone. Which means that you and Flying Hawk must learn to get along with each other."

Taking a stance beside Flying Hawk, Black Wolf reinforced Alisha's words. "There will be no fighting."

The Indian boy's face hardened in resentment. Although he wanted very much to prove himself the stronger, he would nonetheless obey Black Wolf's command. He had been taught obedience from an early age, and to defy a direct order from an elder was beyond comprehension.

Pressuring David, Alisha insisted, "I want you to promise me that you won't fight."

He gave in reluctantly. "All right, I promise."

Black Wolf said to Alisha, "Come with me; we have a few things to talk about."

"Where are we going?"

"Not far," he answered, offering his hand.

Alisha allowed him to help her to her feet, but as they headed away from the fire, she quickly withdrew her hand from his.

They walked in silence until they were a good distance from the boys. Pausing, Black Wolf leaned casually against a tree trunk. The night was partially overcast, and as the half-moon peeked out from behind a cloud, its silver rays shone down on Alisha. Bathed in soft moonlight, she was breathtakingly beautiful.

"Who are you?" she demanded. "You aren't your everyday, run-of-the-mill Indian."

He laughed good-naturedly. "Everyday, run-of-the-mill?" Amused, he arched his eyebrows.

"You know what I mean," she spat.

"My name is Black Wolf, and my father is Chief Running Horse. Have you heard of him?"

She thought for a moment. "No, I don't think so."

"Well, he isn't too renowned. He has always tried to live in peace with his fellow man, regardless of race or creed. Which is probably why you aren't familiar with his name. Chiefs like Red Cloud who have proclaimed war on whites are much better known than my father."

"How is it that you speak English so flawlessly?"

"I speak it as it was taught to me."

"Who was your teacher?"

"My mother. She was white."

Her curiosity remained, but deciding that the mysteries surrounding this warrior could wait, she turned to the subject that interested her the most. "Why didn't you let me know you could speak English?"

"Because I knew you'd insist that I escort you home, and I preferred not to do so."

"But why?" she cried.

"My father is seriously ill. I was at Fort Laramie when I received word of his grave condition. A runner was sent from my village to the nearest Sioux camp, and from there another runner was sent. This pattern was repeated until the message was delivered to the village closest to Fort Laramie. A runner from that village came and notified me. With Running Horse ill, I couldn't waste the time it would've taken for me to escort you home. I'm sure I'd have been locked behind bars until the sheriff could confirm my story. The Sioux might consider the Hills as their own, but your people consider all other land exclusively theirs."

"If you didn't want to escort me, then why didn't you simply set me free?"

"You were too weak; furthermore, this region is too dangerous for a woman to travel through alone."

"But if it wasn't for Two Moons' presence, you'd now let me go?"

"Yes, but I'd do so with reservations. Even with the boy accompanying you, you might make it out of this wilderness, but I seriously doubt it."

She knew he was right and didn't argue. "Why were

you at Fort Laramie?" Her curiosity concerning the fearless warrior had returned.

"Because I speak English fluently, the Army often uses me as a translator. But this time, I wasn't at the fort on business. I was visiting my good friends, Major Landon and his wife."

She glanced back toward the campfire, where the two boys were still seated. She nodded toward Flying Hawk as she asked, "Are you two related?"

"No, but he lives in my father's village. He knew I was on my way home, so he decided to meet me. The boy and I are very close."

"Why is he so hostile to David?"

He grinned easily. "I'd say the hostility is a mutual one. David hasn't been exactly cordial."

"I'm sure when David was telling me what happened to him and his father, you were listening to every word. So you know why David is unfriendly. Can you blame him for feeling the way he does?"

"No, but neither do I blame Flying Hawk. David's father was killed by Sioux, but Flying Hawk's parents were murdered by white soldiers. He has sworn to avenge their deaths, and someday he will."

She frowned disapprovingly. "You sound as though you agree with him."

Showing no emotion, he replied, "Flying Hawk is proud, and whether or not I agree, I'll not try to take away his pride."

She sighed impatiently. The conversation had drifted onto a course that was not to her liking. Avoiding further talk of violence, she inquired, "When can you take me home?"

"I'm not sure," he hesitated.

Her brow became puzzled. "What do you mean, you aren't sure?"

"It all depends on my father's condition. I won't

leave him as long as he's seriously ill. Hopefully, when we reach my village, his health will be considerably improved. If so, then I'll take you home as soon as possible."

"If his health hasn't improved?" she questioned, tensing.

"Then you and David will remain my guests for an extended period of time." He watched her closely, adding, "It may even be necessary for you and David to spend the winter in my father's village."

"What!" she cried, incredulous. "I can't stay there all winter!"

"You'll have no other choice," he replied levelly.

Perturbed, she moved to place her hands on her hips, but the sudden movement sent a sharp pain through her shoulder. Grimacing, she clutched at it.

Sternly, Black Wolf remarked, "You should use the sling I made for you."

"I left it on my horse." The pain began to lessen, and her eyes were unyielding as she continued, "I refuse to spend the winter at your father's village. You must take me home, or find someone who will. Surely you can ask one or more of your fellow warriors to give me and David an escort."

"I could," he replied. "But I won't."

"Why not?"

"You two aren't their responsibility; you're mine. I won't ask them to leave their homes to guide you and David safely out of these hills."

Resenting his attitude, she said heatedly, "I am not your responsibility!"

A sensual smile played across his lips, and amusement shone in his brilliant blue eyes. "Like it or not, as long as you're under my protection, you're not only my responsibility, but also my property."

"Property!" she fumed. "You speak as though I'm

115

your slave!"

Tolerantly he replied, "I've already told you that you'll be my guest, not my slave. But you must realize that I'm taking you to a Sioux village. You have to know that there is much distrust and resentment between my people and yours."

She became even more petulant. "Will you stop treating me like an Eastern greenhorn! I was raised in these parts, and I'm fully aware of the conflict between your people and mine."

"Then you must realize why it's imperative for you and David to be my property. The people in my village will honor and respect what belongs to me."

Stepping forward, he reached for her hand, but she drew back. However, Black Wolf was not about to be denied, and moving quickly, he grabbed her hand and held it firmly. "Pay close attention to what I'm saying. If it becomes necessary for you and the boy to stay through the winter, your visit can be quite pleasant so long as you do as I tell you." He grinned disarmingly. "You might even find the experience rewarding, and someday you can tell your children and grandchildren all about your adventure."

She lifted her chin indignantly. "I doubt if it'll be an experience I'd care to remember. Living in a tepee and sleeping on buffalo rugs isn't exactly my idea of a perfect way to spend the winter. I'd much rather be home on my ranch."

He released her hand, turned back to the tree, and once again leaned casually against the trunk. "Believe me, Madam, you don't wish you were home any more than I do. But unless you want to take your chances with Two Moons, you're stuck with me. I suggest that you make the best of it."

Contrite, she answered, "Please don't get the wrong impression. I'm very thankful to you for all your help."

Her voice took on a note of pleading. "But surely you understand my feelings. The thought of spending the winter in a Sioux village is unnerving."

Reassuringly he told her, "You have nothing to fear."

She studied him guardedly. Nothing to fear? Didn't he know her greatest fear was Black Wolf himself? If she were to spend an entire winter in his company, how could she possibly fight this strong desire that he could awaken so easily within her?

His eyes met hers, and in their depths he could read her thoughts, for his thoughts were the same. Softly, he advised, "Let's just take it one day at a time. This is all conjecture. By now, my father may be completely well, and soon you'll be back home." He looked hopeful. "More than likely, you'll be spending the winter with your family."

She continued to study him. His long black hair, dark complexion, and Indian garb made him appear Sioux, but his blue eyes and features denied his father's blood. Apparently he bore a strong resemblance to his white mother. Envisioning him with shorter hair and western clothes, she knew his likeness to the Sioux would be hardly noticeable. Then too, his flawless English and his manners were as polished as her brothers'. This impressive warrior was indeed an enigma, and Alisha wondered how well they'd come to know each other. She contemplated the prospect. If they spent the winter together, she had a strong feeling they would become intimate. The possibility was at once thrilling and upsetting. What if she were to fall in love with him? Could she give up her way of life for his? The Sioux and the whites were now upholding a semblance of peace, but she knew it was only temporary. Someday war was sure to erupt, and if she were living with Black Wolf, could she continue to do so, knowing his people and hers were fighting?

Alisha sighed and thrust these dark possibilities from her mind. She was letting her imagination run away with her. In all likelihood, Running Horse would be recovered, Black Wolf would then take her home, and they'd never see each other again.

"We'll be leaving at daybreak," Black Wolf remarked, his voice bringing her out of her troubled thoughts. "So you'd better start supper so we can eat and then turn in for the night."

She knitted her brow. "I don't mind preparing our meal, but I do resent being ordered to do so."

He chuckled pleasantly. "You have a lot of spunk, Miss Stevens; but though I admire your spirit, I insist that you learn to obey my orders."

Suddenly finding her irresistible, he moved with incredible speed and his arm encircled her small waist. Pulling her close, he bent his head, and suddenly his lips were on hers, kissing her passionately, almost savagely.

He let her go without warning, and Alisha stumbled backward. Her lips still tingled from his passionate assault, and she rubbed her fingers over them gingerly.

Giving her a firm pat on her rounded posterior, he urged her toward the campfire. "I suggest you leave and start supper; otherwise, I'll feast thoroughly on your lovely attributes and totally relish every nibble."

Responding to his lighthearted mood, she smiled saucily and favored him with a mock salute. "Yes, sir!" she quipped. Heading for the fire, she smiled radiantly. Placing her hand over her heart, which was still racing from his exciting kiss, she wondered if she was falling in love with Black Wolf. He's so handsome and impressive, she mused, how could any woman help but become hopelessly enamored.

All at once, her smile vanished and was replaced with

a worried grimace. Could he possibly be married?

Whirling around, she called back anxiously, "Black Wolf, do you have a wife?"

"No," he answered. "I don't have a wife—or wives."

She smiled once again before hurrying to the campfire, for she was now more than willing to cook supper.

Chapter Eleven

Loretta Ingalls was still amazed that she could converse so easily with Joel Carson. She had always been timid and self-conscious in any gentleman's presence, but for some reason she was perfectly at ease with the dashing gambler. When he had asked her to have dinner with him at the hotel, she had happily accepted the date. She had been afraid that her shyness would return and she'd be poor company; however, Joel's friendly manner had erased her apprehensions, and she had been a most charming dinner companion.

Now, as Joel walked her home, Loretta was feeling light-headed, for she had enjoyed quite a few glasses of wine. She wasn't used to drinking alcoholic beverages and actually was a little tipsy.

Her steps were unsteady, and noticing this, Joel placed a supportive hand on her arm. Smiling warmly, he asked, "Are you all right?"

Flushed, she replied weakly, "I shouldn't have had so many glasses of wine."

He smiled at her innocence. "You'll grow accustomed to wine, for I intend to take you to dinner often. That is, with your permission."

Thrilled, she answered quickly, "Permission granted."

He removed his hand from her arm, and she immediately missed his touch. Then, slowly, he took her hand into his. His hold was firm and her fingers interlocked with his. She had never before strolled hand-in-hand with a suitor, and she felt as giddy as a schoolgirl.

Carefully, he guided their steps into the nearby deserted street and toward her home which was at the edge of town. Earlier, the evening sky had been partially overcast, but now it was clear and dotted with clusters of twinkling stars. The moon cast a soft glow upon them as they walked side-by-side, hand-in-hand.

Joel's eyes swept thoughtfully over Loretta as he wondered if, in time, he could grow to love her. He found her very attractive even though she concealed her beauty with unbecoming dresses and a severe hairdo. But he had every intention of encouraging her to change her way of dressing and to ask her to rearrange her hair into a more flattering style. He supposed her mode of dress was due to her upbringing, since her father had been a missionary. Shrugging off her present appearance as insignificant, he turned his thoughts exclusively to her inner charms. She had a pleasing personality and was very intelligent. She was a genuine lady, and that appealed to a side of him which he thought had died along with his wife. Yes, she was a good influence on him, and the kind of woman who made a man think about marrying, settling down, and raising children. Joel Carson didn't try to delude himself. He knew he could never love Loretta as much as he had loved his wife; that kind of love came around but once in a lifetime.

Loretta was lost in her own musings. To her it seemed incredible that a man as dashing as Joel Carson could be interested in her. She was sure he could have his choice of any of the unmarried ladies in and around

Backwater, so why had he chosen to date someone as uninteresting as herself? But then, maybe she was misinterpreting his motives. He might not think of her in a romantic way, but merely as a friend. He was probably still grieving for his wife and wanted their relationship to be a platonic one. Becoming curious about his marriage, she asked, "Joel, does it bother you to talk about your wife?"

"No," he answered. "Why do you ask?"

"No special reason," she murmured evasively.

He smiled knowingly. "Loretta, if you're curious about my wife, feel free to ask about her. If you were a widow, I'd want to know about your husband."

"You would?" she questioned, surprised. Had she been wrong to think he wanted only a friendly relationship?

"Of course I would," he replied. His hazel eyes regarding her tenderly, he suggested, "Shall I tell you about my marriage?"

"Yes, please do."

"My wife and I were both southerners. I fought for the Confederacy, and it wasn't until after the war that I met Bonnie Sue. Her brother and I were in the same regiment, and when I traveled to Memphis to visit him, he introduced me to his sister. Their family had been planters, but they lost everything during the war. Soon after we met, her father died. Her mother had passed away a couple of years before. I was eighteen years older than Bonnie Sue, but our ages were never a factor. I guess you could say we fell in love at first sight. After we married, her brother moved to Missouri, where he had friends, and Bonnie Sue and I decided to travel by wagon train to San Francisco. That's when her uncle offered to make me a partner in his lumber business."

They had arrived at Loretta's house, and stopping at

122

the picket gate, Joel released her hand, reached into his jacket pocket, removed a cheroot, and lit it before continuing. "The wagon master had warned everyone that his scout had found evidence which proved that a band of Sioux were somewhere close by. The wagon master didn't believe they posed a threat, but he did give explicit orders for everyone to stay close to the wagons."

He paused to take a long drag from his smoke. "Bonnie Sue was an immaculate young lady. She hated going days without a full bath. Washing from a basin never made her feel clean. Late one afternoon, the wagon train camped close to the river. The order to stay close to the wagons was still being enforced. A meeting had been called, and every man was expected to be there. When I left to attend the meeting, I never dreamed that Bonnie Sue would leave the safety of the wagons and go down to the river. When I returned and found her gone, I thought she was probably visiting with one of the women. I searched throughout the camp, but no one had seen her. The fear that she might have gone to the river to bathe hit me suddenly, and I rushed to the riverbank to look for her. By this time, the scout heard about her disappearance, and he came down to the river. Searching, we soon found her clean clothes, towel, and soap. Reading the tracks left in the damp earth, the scout saw that she'd been abducted by Indians—he estimated it was four or five warriors. We hurried back to camp and notified the wagon master, who quickly asked for volunteers and soon had a search party organized. We rode through the night, and it was dawn when we came upon Bonnie Sue's body."

Joel looked at his cheroot, then dropping it, he squashed it with the heel of his boot. His voice was now tinged with grief. "The Indians had burned her at a

123

stake. She had been burned so thoroughly that her body was beyond recognition. Before killing her, they had stripped her, and her blue dress and underthings had been left scattered nearby." He paused and then went on. "I'm sure she was raped and tortured. As the men were removing her body from the stake, her wedding ring fell from her finger. I saw it fall, and I knelt to pick it up. Until that moment, I'd been in shock. But when I picked up her ring, the numbness wore off and I went berserk. I thought I was losing my mind."

Loretta interrupted gently, "Please, Joel. Don't talk about it anymore. The memory is too painful."

He was silent for a time, then murmured somberly, "I buried the ring with her."

Touching his arm, she said sympathetically, "I'm so sorry."

Deep in thought, he said, "Bonnie Sue was as beautiful as an angel, and I always told her that her golden hair was her shining halo." His voice broke. "My God, she was so small and fragile . . . and those savages . . ."

"Joel, don't think about it!" Loretta urged.

He sighed heavily. "I'm sorry."

"Don't be sorry," she replied. "I shouldn't have asked you to talk about her. Such painful memories should be put to rest."

"I'm trying to forget," he admitted, shaken. He took both her hands into his. "I think you can help me start over again, Loretta."

She smiled tenderly. "Oh Joel, I'll help you in any way I can."

"May I kiss you?" he asked so quietly that she barely heard his request.

"Yes," she whispered.

Slowly, he drew her into his embrace. His lips

descended to hers, and at first, his touch was extremely gentle; but as a fiery need surged, his kiss deepened.

Responding, Loretta clung tightly, and when his tongue sought entrance, she willingly parted her lips. She had never been passionately kissed, but her inexperience didn't prevent her from returning his ardor freely.

Joel relinquished her hesitantly. His passion was aroused, but he didn't want to rush her, or risk their relationship. "May I see you again soon?" he asked.

"Yes, of course," she answered faintly, for his kiss had left her quite breathless.

Touching her arm, he helped her through the open gate and said, "I'll walk you to the door."

When she had the door unlocked, he gave her a light kiss on the cheek; then, as soon as she was inside, he turned and headed toward his saloon.

Shortly before dawn, Joel and his bartender had the saloon closed and secured. It had been a busy night and Joel was tired as he climbed the stairs to his quarters. Opening the door to his rooms, he moved slowly to his liquor cabinet and poured himself a nightcap. With the glass of brandy, he went behind his desk and slumped into the soft, leatherbound chair. Leaning back against the plush upholstery, he sipped his drink.

Sadness shadowed his face as his thoughts drifted to Bonnie Sue. God, how much I loved her! he exclaimed to himself. Tears emerged, blurring his vision, and he wiped a hand across his eyes. Then, hesitating, he opened a desk drawer and withdrew a framed picture of his wife. Placing it on the desktop, he stared solemnly at her lovely image. For a moment he wondered if he should try to locate an artist and have a portrait painted from the daguerreotype, but he quickly dismissed the idea. With only his description to go on, how could an artist correctly capture the true color of her golden hair, the exact shade of blue in her eyes? A perfect duplication would be impossible.

A wistful smile appeared as he continued to gaze at his wife's image. Talking about Bonnie Sue with Loretta had been a mistake, for it had awakened too many memories. Minutes passed as he sat silently, his eyes glued to the picture. Finally, he opened the drawer and put the picture away.

He went to the other room and prepared for bed. Undressed, he drew back the covers and lay down. But it was a long time before Joel fell asleep, and when he did, his dreams were filled with memories of Bonnie Sue.

The early morning sun shone brightly upon the awakening Sioux village. Most of the families were still inside their tepees, and only a few people had ventured outside when the bedraggled woman emerged from her wigwam. Pausing, she looked up at the rising sun, but its brightness caused her to look away. Another day, she thought depressingly. She frowned bitterly. Another day to be abused and humiliated! If only she had the courage to commit suicide, then all her tribulations would be over. Maybe I do have the courage to die! she suddenly decided. But her better judgment intervened. I mustn't give up! I could still be rescued! Surely someday soldiers, or maybe white trappers, will come here to Chief Bear Claw's village and ransom me! Dear God, I must hold dearly to that hope, or else I'll lose my mind!

She needed urgently to relieve herself, and tossing her unwashed hair back from her dirt-smudged face, she began to walk toward the thick shrubbery bordering the village. She allowed herself a moment of weakness as she thought of how heavenly it would be to take a bath and wash away all the grime coating her body. But, as a slave, she was not entitled to such luxuries.

The woman had walked only a short way when she was deterred by a sharp, gruff voice, "Golden Hair, come back!"

She turned about, and keeping her eyes downcast, she started back to the wigwam.

The warrior waiting for her return was a threatening and unattractive figure. His beady eyes narrowed hatefully as he watched his white slave's sluggish approach.

Reaching her master, the woman stood with head bowed, as she had been taught. The man smelled strongly of bear grease and foul perspiration; the odors were overwhelming. Even if she was rescued and taken back to civilization, the woman seriously doubted if she'd ever be free of the offensive smell of this man. The odors would probably linger in her nostrils forever.

"When Strong Fox tells you come, you move fast!" he growled. Then, to add emphasis to his demand, he slapped her powerfully across the face.

The unmistakable sound of flesh striking flesh brought the man's wife outside. Seeing that her husband was reprimanding their slave, Warm Blanket smirked, "Golden Hair make poor slave. I tell her fetch stick, so I can beat her." Warm Blanket was a big, heavy woman with a strength that matched her build.

The white woman remained outwardly unemotional. She knew Warm Blanket had spoken English so she would understand and be frightened. She also knew that she should show fear, for her courage annoyed the Indian woman. She had been the couple's slave now for over a year and she knew their ways.

Strong Fox, deciding to let his wife deal with Golden Hair, left the two women to tend to his horses. Warm Blanket was about to order her slave to find a long, sturdy stick when suddenly an Indian woman hurried over to them. Her words flowing with excitement, she told Warm Blanket that a baby was about to be born. Wanting to witness the birth, Warm Blanket forgot about punishing her slave and left quickly with the other woman.

Alone, Golden Hair turned to head for the shrubbery, but the child stepping out of the tepee caused her to halt. She welcomed the girl with a smile. It was hard for the white woman to believe that Little Star was the daughter of Strong Fox and Warm Blanket. Whereas her parents were cruel, Little Star was compassionate. In fact, the child was Golden Hair's only friend.

Little Star had heard her father slap the woman, and she asked in English, "Did Father hurt you?"

She moved her hand to her cheek, which still stung from the blow. "Yes," she replied, "but I'll be all right."

Gingerly, the child reached for Golden Hair's hand and squeezed it softly. Her caring gesture touched the woman profoundly, bringing a sudden surge of tears to her eyes.

Seeing the woman's tears roll down her cheeks, etching a path down her dirt-encrusted face, Little Star called Golden Hair by her white name; "Please don't cry, Bonnie Sue."

Chapter Twelve

Standing in the distance, Black Wolf watched the boys and Alisha breaking camp. Although David and Flying Hawk worked swiftly and silently, they kept casting heated glares at each other. This friction had Black Wolf on edge. Knowing Flying Hawk, he didn't doubt that the Indian boy would make David's stay at Running Horse's village a difficult one.

Continuing to look at David, Black Wolf studied the lad's soiled clothes and the grime which covered his face and arms. Tonight they'd camp beside the river, and David could wash his clothes and take a bath. Black Wolf also saw that Alisha's clothes were not much cleaner than David's. He was sure they'd both find the river a welcome sight.

He had heard David telling Alisha about the ways in which Two Moons and his men had tortured him, and deciding to check the boy's burned fingers, Black Wolf strode over to him.

David, rolling up his bedroll, saw the warrior coming, and standing rigid, he waited somewhat apprehensively. Although this man seemed to be quite friendly, the boy still had his doubts. In his opinion, Indians were not to be trusted.

"Let me see your fingers," Black Wolf said.

"What for?" David asked warily.

Black Wolf had little patience with the boy's distrust, and grasping David's hands, he turned the palms upward so he could have a clear view. Examining the blisters, he saw that they were red and puffed. "Bring me the medicine kit," he called to Flying Hawk.

Resentfully, David pulled away his hands and grumbled, "I don't need your help."

Sternly, Black Wolf remarked, "Those burns are infected. I have some salve that will heal them." Realizing that the boy had been through a terrible ordeal, Black Wolf's heart softened. "Don't be so hostile, son."

"I'm not your son!" he bellowed. The anger he had kept repressed since his father's murder and his own capture surfaced irrationally. "One of these days, I'm gonna get even with all you damned Indians!"

Aware of David's outburst, Alisha wondered if she should try to reason with him, but then decided it would be best to let Black Wolf handle the boy's anger without her interference.

Bringing Black Wolf the medicine kit, Flying Hawk eyed David scornfully. He was about to rile the boy even more, but Black Wolf's sharp command deterred him. "Hand me the kit, then go tend to the horses."

Black Wolf waited until Flying Hawk was gone before telling David, "I'm growing impatient with your hostility. The four of us are stuck with each other, and it's important that we learn to get along." He opened the medical kit and removed the salve. "Now give me your hands."

Obeying, David let the warrior tend to his burns, but the moment Black Wolf was finished, the boy hurried over to Alisha.

Joining her, he mumbled, "I don't trust Black Wolf. I

think he's only pretending to be our friend. When we reach his village, I bet he'll change his tune."

"Why do you think that?" Alisha asked.

"He's a damned Indian, isn't he?"

"David," she sighed, "you're as bad as Flying Hawk. He hates all whites because his parents were murdered by soldiers. Now, you intend to hate all Indians because Two Moons killed your father."

His expression remained unyielding, but before she could continue reasoning, Black Wolf called to her.

Leaving David, she walked over to the warrior. Gesturing for her to come closer, he said, "I need to check your wound."

She still wore Black Wolf's shirt, and because the garment fit loosely, she simply eased the material off her shoulder.

Carefully, Black Wolf removed the bandage. "There's no further use for this," he said, throwing the bandage onto the smoldering campfire. Smiling, he added, "You're healing very well, and there's no sign of infection."

She returned his smile. "I had a good doctor."

Gazing into her upturned face, he was suddenly mesmerized by her sweet smile. But reminding himself to remain emotionally detached, he quickly looked away and headed toward the horses.

Walking up to Flying Hawk, and lapsing into the Sioux language, Black Wolf said, "David's father was killed by Two Moons. I doubt if the boy can find his way back to the area where Two Moons found them. When you were on your way to meet me, did you run across a wagon and a dead body?"

A bitter scowl came to the boy's face. Apparently, Black Wolf was considering burying David's father. Flying Hawk believed the white man's body should be left to the wild animals and the elements, but lies were never spoken by the Sioux, so he answered truthfully, "Yes. I saw the wagon and the dead man."

"How far are they from here?"

"A half a day's ride to the north."

They were heading north, and Black Wolf remarked, "Good, it won't be out of the way."

"Why waste time burying the man?" Flying Hawk mumbled.

Black Wolf was peeved with his young charge. "Don't let your hate become an obsession. A good warrior learns to put revenge in its proper perspective."

Flying Hawk made no reply, but his face remained hard.

Black Wolf didn't tell David and Alisha where they were going until they were almost upon the wagon. Then, giving the order to pull up, he guided the pinto alongside David. They had crested a small hill, and nodding in the direction of the incline, he said gently, "Your wagon is at the bottom. I think you should stay here with Alisha, while Flying Hawk and I . . ."

Before Black Wolf could finish, David, reacting impulsively, slapped the reins against his horse and disappeared down the side of the hill. Telling Flying Hawk and Alisha to remain, Black Wolf took out after him.

Reaching the wagon, David drew to a stop, dismounted, and rushed toward his father's body, which lay still sprawled on the ground.

Meanwhile, the speeding pinto had caught up to the boy, and leaning over, Black Wolf's arm encircled David at the waist. Lifting the struggling boy, the warrior held onto him as he urged his horse toward the cluster of trees that grew in the near distance.

Reining in, Black Wolf released the boy, then swung

down from the saddle. David made a frantic attempt to run back to the wagon, but the warrior's strong hands on his shoulders stopped him.

"Let me go, damn you!" David yelled, fighting vainly against the man's superior strength.

His temper flaring, Black Wolf shook his opponent roughly, his treatment causing the boy's head to jerk back and forth. "Listen to me!" he shouted. "For your own sake, don't look at your father! Good God, son, his body has been exposed for days!"

His senses returning, David ceased his struggles, and as his body grew limp, he fell against Black Wolf.

The man put his arms around the boy, drawing him closer.

David's grief became overpowering; nonetheless, he was determined not to cry. Pushing away, he took a step backwards, and feeling tears emerging, he wiped quickly at his eyes.

Understanding, Black Wolf said tenderly, "Crying over your father will not make you any less a man. It only makes you human."

"I won't cry!" David insisted stubbornly. His chin began to quiver, and he could no longer control the tears that flowed freely in spite of his words.

It took only a small gesture on Black Wolf's part for the boy to lean into his embrace. Against his will, David released his bottled-up grief, and his body was racked with hard sobs.

Black Wolf's arms remained around the boy until his sobs quieted. Then, slowly, he let him go.

Ashamed, David mumbled, "I guess you think I'm a crybaby."

Black Wolf responded compassionately, "No, of course not. I would have thought less of you if you hadn't cried for your father."

The boy was a little skeptical. "I thought Indians

admired courage."

"We do, but tears are not always a sign of weakness. Don't you think we cry over our loved ones? Where did you get the notion that Indians don't have the same feelings as whites?"

"From books, and from my personal experiences," he grumbled.

"Don't be so quick to pass judgment, David. A wise man never draws conclusions hastily."

David wasn't convinced, but keeping his doubts to himself, he asked hesitantly, "Are you gonna tell Flying Hawk that I cried?"

Gently Black Wolf replied, "No, I won't tell him." He stepped to the pinto. "I'll have Flying Hawk bring Alisha here, then he and I will see about burying your father."

"There's two shovels tied to the side of the wagon. Two Moons didn't take them."

Black Wolf mounted and was about to leave when David made a request. "After you have his body covered, I want to help dig the grave. I don't want Flying Hawk doing anything for me or my kin."

"All right," Black Wolf agreed.

The warrior rode away, and David sat down beneath the shade of a tree. As he absently brushed back the stray lock that insistently fell across his forehead, he wished he hadn't broken down in front of Black Wolf. However, he had to begrudgingly admit that the man's sympathy had seemed genuine. Had he been mistaken about Black Wolf? Was the man truly his friend? Although David was beginning to trust the warrior, he did so with caution.

The river was a welcome sight to Alisha and David, and anxious to wash, they both dismounted hastily.

Running to the bank, Alisha knelt, and cupping the cool water in her hands, she splashed her face and arms.

Joining her, David asked, "Would you like to borrow a pair of my trousers and a shirt?" Two Moons hadn't bothered to take the boy's clothes, and after the burial, David had gone inside the wagon and gathered up his belongings, including some of his favorite books. He had wanted to take them all, but knowing he had no room to carry them, he had chosen a select few.

Glancing down at her dust-coated apparel, she replied gratefully, "Thank you, David." Her eyes swept over him fleetingly as she wondered how well his clothes would fit.

Reading her thoughts, David replied, "They should be about the right size."

As David was leaving to fetch the clothes, Black Wolf walked up to Alisha, took her hand and drew her to a standing position. "Are you planning on taking a bath?"

"Yes, of course," she answered, wondering why he had asked.

"Wait here and I'll get a bar of soap, and then we'll go farther downstream and take our baths."

"We'll do what?" she exclaimed.

"Take our baths," he repeated innocently.

Astonished, she replied, "If you think for one minute that I intend to bathe with you, then you are badly mistaken!"

Grinning, he replied evenly, "Madam, the way I see it, you have two choices. You can either bathe with me, or with Two Moons. If you go downstream alone, he'll most assuredly find you."

"I'm not going to bathe with either one of you!" she cried, detecting the mischievousness in his eyes.

Raising a brow, he queried, "Oh?"

135

"While I bathe, you're going to stand guard and protect me from Two Moons!"

He chuckled slyly, "But who will protect you from me?"

Playing along with his teasing, she said daringly, "If you try anything, you might be the one in need of protection."

Laughing heartily, he remarked, "I'll be on my guard."

Catching sight of David, she cast the warrior a saucy smile and remarked, "This might prove to be a most interesting bath." However, Alisha was embarrassed by her own provocative implication, causing her cheeks to redden.

Seeing her blatant blush, Black Wolf's laughter deepened as he left to get the soap, plus clean clothes for himself.

Returning momentarily, he took Alisha's hand, and before leaving, he warned the boys against fighting. He had his belongings under one arm and his rifle held loosely at his side.

Alisha kept her hand enclosed in his as they strolled farther downstream. With a sidelong glance, she studied him secretively. A gentle wind was blowing, and its soft force ruffled the warrior's long hair, giving him a handsomely savage look that sent Alisha's heart racing. His virile good looks moved her so profoundly that she actually felt a fiery longing surge through her body; its intensity pinpointed between her thighs.

Reaching a secluded area, Black Wolf stopped, and nodding toward the cool water, he said smoothly, "Your bath awaits."

"You will be a gentleman and keep your back turned, won't you?"

He raised a brow. "Gentleman? If I remember correctly, you once told me I was a savage brute."

"That still remains to be seen," she replied pertly. She grew uncomfortable recalling the morning she had spouted her tirade, but of course, she had believed he couldn't understand a word she was saying.

Gazing deeply into her large brown eyes, Black Wolf longed to take her in his arms, but resisting the temptation, he said firmly, "It's getting late. You'd better take your bath." He handed her the bar of soap, then moved away to take a protective stance in the close distance. Propping his rifle against a pine tree, he turned his back, giving Alisha privacy.

Worry was etched on Black Wolf's face. He was letting this white woman penetrate his emotions, and if he wasn't careful, she'd soon be in his heart. It would be so easy to fall in love with her, for she was everything he wanted in a woman. No, not everything, he reminded himself. She isn't Sioux!

Black Wolf had heard Alisha telling David about her family and the Bar-S. Her father was a wealthy rancher, and he couldn't imagine Alisha giving up her pampered lifestyle to marry him and live in a Sioux village. He believed it would be terribly unfair of him even to ask her to make such a sacrifice. At present, his people were living well, for game was plentiful in the Hills, but he knew these bountiful days were numbered. Someday, the U.S. Army would terminate the Fort Laramie Treaty and there would be much bloodshed on both sides.

Lost in his thoughts, Black Wolf wasn't aware that Alisha had finished bathing until he heard her light footsteps. Turning, he watched her as she came to stand at his side, noticing the way in which David's trousers clung tightly to her womanly hips and shapely legs. She had left the two top buttons of the plaid shirt undone, and he could see the deep cleavage between her full breasts. Her beauty was fetching, and once again Black Wolf had to call upon his will power to keep from embracing her.

Alisha wished she knew what he was thinking. She could see that he seemed troubled, but she failed to connect his present mood to herself. She supposed he was worried about his father's health. Offering him the bar of soap, she said softly, "It's getting dark; you should hurry and take your bath."

He didn't take the soap; he was too enthralled with this lovely vision standing before him. He regarded her long, damp tresses. Then he reached over and touched a tendril, curling the flaxen-colored lock around his finger. "I've never seen hair so blond," he murmured.

"My grandmother had hair the same color," she whispered, now very conscious of his closeness.

Letting the strand fall free, he stepped back and mustered a semblance of aloofness. "You'd better return to camp. By now, David and Flying Hawk might be trying to kill each other."

She didn't want to be dismissed; she wanted him to take her in his arms. Well, she decided boldly, if he won't kiss me, then I'll kiss him!

Dropping the bar of soap, and taking Black Wolf by surprise, Alisha placed her arms around his neck, bringing her lips up to his. Remembering the thrill of his body against hers, she thrust against him, longing to feel his hardness.

With passion overpowering his convictions, Black Wolf slipped his arm around her waist, drawing her tightly against him. Entwining his fingers in her hair, he pressed her mouth ever closer; and when her tongue darted between his teeth, a low murmur sounded deep in his throat.

His defenses vulnerable, Black Wolf surrendered to Alisha's charms, but the sudden snap of a twig sounded close by. Turning her loose abruptly, he started to grab

138

his rifle when, out of the corner of his eye, he caught sight of a rabbit darting into the shrubbery. Realizing the furry creature had been the intruder, he smiled.

Alisha had also seen the rabbit, and thinking Black Wolf would now take her back in his arms, she waited for him to resume their embrace.

However, he had quickly taken control of his passion, and deeming the rabbit's intrusion fortunate, he said curtly, "Go back to camp." He saw the hurt that came to her eyes, and it made him feel like a cad. Nonetheless, his convictions had returned. For both of their sakes, he decided he must cool their relationship.

Holding back tears, Alisha went to the bank, picked up her dirty clothes, and without a backward glance, headed toward camp.

She had walked only a short way when all at once she stopped, turned about, and began retracing her steps. She knew Black Wolf wanted her; she could feel it in his kisses and in the way he held her. Why was he so insistent on fighting against their mutual passion? Determined to make him open up and confide in her, she strode steadily toward the bank.

Seeing that he was bathing, she went to the water's edge and sat down, placing her bundle at her side.

Aware of her presence, Black Wolf called, "Why did you come back?"

Her expression set, she replied firmly, "I want to know why you keep fighting our love." He was standing waist-deep, and the soft glow of twilight falling across the water made it easy for her to see the powerful muscles in his chest and arms.

"Our love?" he queried, as though the term was absurd.

She lifted her chin stubbornly. "I intend to stay right here until you tell me what I want to know."

He confronted her. "Alisha, have you ever seen a

139

naked man?"

"No . . . no, I haven't," she stammered.

"Well, unless you leave right now, you are about to see one, for I have finished with my bath."

She swallowed nervously. Should she leave? For a moment, she considered doing so, but her desire for Black Wolf intervened, keeping her riveted to the spot. Her heart began to beat rapidly as she anticipated seeing this man's handsome physique.

Black Wolf had thought she'd leave, and he was surprised when she didn't budge. Well, so much for my convictions, he thought flippantly as he began to move through the water and toward the bank. This time, the teasing little woman had gone too far and there would be no turning back.

Smiling devilishly, Black Wolf told her, "Beautiful lady, you're about to get more than you bargained for."

Chapter Thirteen

Sitting close to the campfire, David had an open book in his lap and was reading intently when Flying Hawk walked up to him.

Aware of the Indian boy's presence, David looked up from his book to ask irritably, "What do you want?"

Frowning, Flying Hawk muttered, "Why you waste time reading words?"

"It's not a waste of time," David said.

Flying Hawk stared curiously at the book. "What words say?"

"I'm reading about the Alamo," he replied. "I don't suppose you've ever heard of it?"

Flying Hawk's intelligence was sharp, and he was always more than willing to acquire more knowledge. He had seen books in Black Wolf's tepee, and a few times the warrior had read to him. Now, his interest piqued, Flying Hawk asked, "What is this Alamo?"

"Well, the Alamo was founded in 1718 as the chapel of the Mission of San Antonio de Valero. On March 6, 1836, a great battle took place there."

"Battle," Flying Hawk repeated, taking a seat beside David. Tales of war never failed to enthrall him. "Read to me about this battle."

"All right," David answered evenly, although he was surprised by the request. Returning his attention to the book, he began to read aloud, "The United States claimed Texas along with the Louisiana Purchase in 1803, and then in 1819 gave the area to Spain in exchange for Florida. Mexico won the area two years later, when it gained independence from Spain."

Fascinated, Flying Hawk listened intently. As David read about Jim Bowie, Colonel William Travis, and Davy Crockett, the young Indian found the three men impressive. When David began to describe the final battle, he could well envision the carnage, and in his mind he could see these brave defenders who, when they had no time to reload, had wielded their rifles like clubs.

Finishing, David looked over at his lone audience and asked, "Well, what do you think?"

"Read again Colonel Travis's words."

David turned back to the correct page. "To the people of Texas and all the Americans in the world. I shall never surrender or retreat. I call on you in the name of liberty, of patriotism and everything dear to the American character to come to our aid . . . If this call is neglected, I am determined to sustain myself as long as possible and die like a soldier who never forgets what is due to his own honor or that of his country . . . Victory or Death."

"I shall never surrender. Victory or Death," Flying Hawk mumbled thoughtfully. "Travis was brave like Sioux warrior. Someday, I will say same words to white soldiers."

Closing the book, and placing it at his side, David answered shortly, "Then your fate will be the same as the colonel's."

Flying Hawk scowled. "If Bluecoats come on Sioux land, they will die."

"If?" David questioned impatiently. "You can bank on it. Someday, this land will be opened to white settlers."

Leaping to his feet, Flying Hawk snapped, "No! We will never let your people have our land!"

"We'll take it, just like we finally took Texas," David remarked.

Sneering, Flying Hawk replied, "Maybe someday, we will face each other across a battlefield."

David laughed brusquely. "It's a day to which I look forward."

For a moment, the boys eyed each other unwaveringly, then whirling about, Flying Hawk stalked to his bedroll, lay down and turned his back.

As the handsome warrior moved through the water and toward the bank, Alisha was spellbound. She knew she should get up and leave, but she was frozen in place and could only stare with wonder as the man's superb body was revealed. Considering his powerful build, she was amazed that he moved so lithely. Although she was tempted to lower her vision to his maleness, she nonetheless kept her eyes above his waist.

Stepping out of the water, Black Wolf leaned over, grasped her hand, and drew her swiftly into his arms. Imprisoning her, he uttered hoarsely, "You shouldn't have come back."

Apprehensive, Alisha sighed. "I wanted you to tell me why you keep resisting this attraction between us." Conscious of his hardness pressed against her, she mumbled nervously, "I didn't mean for this to happen."

He grinned roguishly. "You didn't mean for what to happen, Alisha?"

"You . . . you know," she stuttered, blushing.

He released her abruptly, bent over, and picked up his discarded clothes. Watching him, Alisha's feelings were mixed. A part of her was relieved, for she wasn't sure if she wanted their relationship to deepen. However, another part of her was disappointed, for she wanted this man with every fiber of her being. She sighed resolutely. Well, apparently Black Wolf had made the choice for her, sparing her a confrontation with her emotions.

Carrying his clothes, he walked swiftly to the surrounding shrubbery, and now left alone, Alisha decided to return to camp. She wondered if Black Wolf was angry and thought her a tease.

She was about to pick up her bundle of clothes when, forcefully, a pair of strong arms grabbed her from behind. Lifting her, and carrying her back toward the bushes, Black Wolf gazed down into her face and murmured, "I've wanted you from the first moment I laid eyes on you, but I tried to fight it."

Warily, she asked, "Why did you decide to quit fighting?"

"Why do you think?" he returned, somewhat gruffly.

"I . . . I'm not sure," she stammered.

Taking her into the shrubbery, he knelt and laid her down upon his spread clothes. "I wish I could offer you a soft, comfortable bed, but this is the best I can do."

Looking up into his eyes and seeing their determination, Alisha grew uneasy. Vainly, she made a feeble attempt to hold onto her innocence. "Black Wolf, please let me go back to camp."

He lay beside her, drew her into his arms, then claimed her lips with his. Alisha's better judgment warned her not to respond, but she had no defense against the handsome warrior and was soon returning his passionate kiss with a fervor of her own.

With his lips still on hers, Black Wolf's hand moved

downward to deftly unbutton her shirt. Pushing aside the material, his lips left hers to caress her bare breasts.

Alisha gasped, for she had never before been so intimate with a man. A little frightened, she started to move away, but sensing this, Black Wolf rolled on top of her. Now pinned beneath his powerful frame, she was trapped. Continuing to kiss and suckle her breasts, Black Wolf soon had her writhing and moaning with awakening passion.

Entwining her fingers in his dark hair, she pressed his mouth closer, loving the feel of his lips and tongue caressing one breast and then the other.

"Oh, darling," she moaned wantonly. Needing to feel his hardness pressed between her thighs, she arched her hips; and as his erect organ slipped snugly against her, an exciting tremor ran throughout her body.

"Alisha," he whispered thickly, before once again kissing her demandingly.

Returning his kiss, Alisha questioned if she was falling in love with Black Wolf. She must be; otherwise, she'd have the strength to refuse him. Dear Lord, she thought desperately, I'm about to give myself to a man who isn't my husband!

Aware of her feelings, Black Wolf raised himself up on an elbow, and gazing into her watching eyes, he said evenly, "I can't promise you marriage, so if you want to save your virginity for your husband, you'd better leave now."

"Would it be so easy for you to let me go?" she asked timorously.

"No," he sighed. "But, nonetheless, I wouldn't try to stop you."

"What do you want me to do?" she whispered. Her emotions were swirling.

"I want you to tell me to make love to you," he said hoarsely, aching for release.

Surrendering, Alisha replied in a quivering voice, "Make love to me."

"Sweetheart," he whispered, kissing her deeply. Rising to his knees, he quickly removed her boots, then undoing her trousers, he slipped them down her hips and past her slender legs. She wore nothing underneath.

The warrior's passion deepened even more as his gaze traveled over Alisha's lovely body. Gently, his hand moved over her smooth stomach, and his touch caused Alisha to gasp softly. He leaned over and his lips met hers as his hand now roamed downward to cup the blond triangle between her delicate thighs.

His finger probed, entering her slowly, and his invasion sent Alisha's need soaring. Holding tightly, she squirmed beneath his magic touch, and when he began to probe rhythmically, her hips moved up and down, welcoming his exciting caress.

"Oh, Black Wolf! . . . Black Wolf!" she cried fervently, never imagining that a man's touch could feel so heavenly, so wonderfully ecstatic!

Carefully, so he wouldn't hurt her wounded shoulder, he slipped her small frame beneath his powerful one. With his knee, he parted her legs, then resting his weight on one arm, he wrapped the other around her waist, bringing her hips up to his.

Gazing deeply into her eyes, he murmured, "There will be a moment of pain."

"Yes, I know," she whispered in a voice so weak it was almost inaudible.

Alisha was a little frightened, and seeing this, Black Wolf said tenderly, "Don't be afraid. You're about to experience a pleasure beyond words."

She smiled hesitantly. "Darling, if it makes me feel just half as good as I feel right now, then my pleasure will be immeasurable."

146

His blue eyes filled with love as he moaned, "Alisha! Oh God, how much I want you!"

He pressed his hardness against her, and, as he penetrated, his strong frame trembled with need. Suddenly, lunging forward, he entered her completely.

Alisha whimpered as Black Wolf took her innocence, and for a moment, she grew taut and pushed against him. But, slowly her discomfort began to fade, supplanted by a feeling so excitingly intense that her arms were suddenly around him, drawing him closer.

Aroused by her response, Black Wolf's hips moved rapidly, driving him in and out of her; and equaling his passion, Alisha met each hard thrust.

Now lost in their passionate union, they were oblivious to everything except each other as they glided blissfully into their own erotic paradise.

Bathed in soft moonlight, Black Wolf and Alisha lay side by side as they enjoyed the evening breeze drifting refreshingly across their naked flesh.

Turning and placing an arm across her lover's chest, Alisha murmured, "Black Wolf?"

"Yes?" he whispered.

Alisha was uneasy, for she feared the answer to the question she was about to ask. "Why can't you promise me marriage?"

He sighed heavily. "Before we even discuss marriage, don't you think you should find out what it's like to live in a Sioux village?"

Quickly sitting up, she looked anxiously into his eyes. "But, Black Wolf, we wouldn't have to live with the Sioux. My father promised me that if I married a man who didn't own property, he'd build us a house and give us a large portion of good grazing land."

His expression resentful, he asked irritably, "Is that

what you want, Alisha? To live on your father's ranch?"

She was puzzled by his anger. "Black Wolf," she began pressingly, "it's not as though you'd have any problems adjusting to my way of life. You act more white than Indian."

"Do I?" he snapped, sitting up and reaching for his clothes. "If what you say is true, then I must change my ways, for I don't claim my white heritage. I'm proud to be Sioux."

He began to dress, and following suit, she questioned impatiently, "Why aren't you also proud of your white blood?"

"Alisha, I was raised as a Sioux, so naturally my father's blood predominates." Standing, he slipped on his leggings, then his moccasins. Alisha was dressed but still seated, and looking down at her, he said harshly, "I've always been afraid that if I became involved with a white woman, she'd want me to leave my people and live in her world." He cocked a brow, and his expression was hard. "Well, Madam, you have proved my fear justifiable."

He reached for her hand and drew her quickly to her feet. His blue eyes unyielding, he remarked, "We'll have to take measures to make sure what happened tonight doesn't happen again. We live in two separate worlds, and you don't want to leave yours anymore than I want to leave mine." When she offered no reply, he insisted gruffly, "Isn't that true?"

Alisha longed to dispute his words, but how could she deny the truth? She didn't want to give up her way of life to live with the Sioux. How could she possibly adjust to such a drastic change? Unable to admit he was right, she remained noncommittal; however, her silence confirmed his words.

As Black Wolf continued to watch her, a look of tenderness shadowed his face. He didn't blame her for the way she felt. Her eyes were downcast, and placing a hand beneath her chin, he tilted her face upwards. "I'm sorry, Alisha," he whispered. "What happened tonight was all my fault. I took advantage of your innocence."

Feeling desperate, she pleaded, "Why did you make love to me, when you knew all along that there is no future for us?"

Tolerantly, he answered, "A man's sex drive can be very strong, and don't forget I told you that I couldn't promise marriage."

She felt as though her dignity had been crushed and her heart broken. Reacting irrationally, she blurted out, "A man's sex drive! Is that all I am to you?" She was hurting, and wanting to hurt him in return, she continued angrily, "I don't want or need your marriage proposal! Besides, I already have a fiancé. His name is Todd Miller and he owns a large, prosperous ranch!" This untruth brought Alisha a pang of guilt, but she cast it aside. Black Wolf had merely used her to satisfy his male lust, and she wasn't about to let him think she was desperate for a man's affections!

Showing no outward response to her declaration, Black Wolf said tersely, "It's time to go back to camp."

He reached for her hand, but brushing past him, Alisha hurried to the riverbank and picked up her bundle of clothes. Without looking back to see if he was following, she began walking swiftly toward camp.

Black Wolf stood beside the shrubbery and watched her hasty retreat. He was angry with himself, causing a deep frown to harden his features. He had been a fool to succumb to Alisha's alluring charms. There was no place in his life for Alisha, and although he knew there could be a place in her life for him, he stubbornly held onto his convictions. He'd not leave his father or his father's people!

His thoughts turned to Alisha's fiancé, and against

149

his will, he was struck with a moment of intense jealousy. Quickly, he buried this feeling and told himself that her engagement to Todd Miller was for the best.

Black Wolf, believing his and Alisha's worlds could never be united, swore henceforth to keep a safe distance between himself and the white woman. But he didn't try to delude himself. He knew resisting his feelings for Alisha would not be easy, for he had fallen in love with her.

Meanwhile, as Black Wolf remained alone with his thoughts, Alisha had returned to camp and was kneeling beside the river, washing her clothes. Tears continued to threaten, and she had to blink repeatedly in an effort to hold them back, for she was determined not to cry. She wanted to hate Black Wolf, but she couldn't. She couldn't even blame him for what had happened. He hadn't made a fool of her; she had made a fool of herself. He had been completely honest and told her beforehand that he wasn't promising marriage. Why? Why had she surrendered so easily to a man who had wanted nothing more than to release his sexual urge? Determined to wait for the man she would love and marry, she had always held on dearly to her virginity. Then, with astonishing ease, Black Wolf had melted her defenses and taken her innocence.

Laying out her clothes to dry, Alisha stood and moved to the glowing campfire. David had supper cooking over the flames, and hearing her approach, he asked, "Are you hungry?"

"Not especially," she mumbled. Going to her bedroll, she lay down and gazed up at the brilliant stars dotting the heavens. She sighed disconsolately, for she knew why she had given in to Black Wolf. She loved him . . . she loved him with all her heart.

150

Chapter Fourteen

"What!" Jack Stevens bellowed, glaring at the young lieutenant with disbelief.

"You heard me," Lieutenant Wilkinson replied. Seated behind his desk, he watched the three men standing before him. Although he was sympathetic, at present he could offer no help.

As despair washed over him, Jack eased himself into a chair. Leaning forward, he rested his elbows on his knees, then cradled his head in his hands. Dear God, he and his sons had traveled practically nonstop to Fort Laramie, never once thinking that the Army wouldn't offer them immediate assistance.

Placing his hand on his father's bowed shoulders, Clint asked, "Are you all right, Pa?"

Defeated, he moaned, "I don't know."

Clint turned to the officer, and his expression seemed questioning, so Lieutenant Wilkinson repeated everything he had said earlier, "I wish I had the authority to give you an escort into the Hills, but such an order must come from Colonel Johnson or Major Landon. I'm sorry that they are both at Fort Fetterman, but they are expected to return early next week."

"Can't you send a wire to the fort, asking for their permission to help us find my sister?" Clint questioned anxiously.

The lieutenant shook his head. "A decision as important as this would never be granted by telegram. I advise you to wait for the colonel's and the major's return."

Sitting upright, Jack said with a choke in his voice, "Each day my daughter is gone increases the chance that we'll never find her."

"I'm sorry," Wilkinson murmured. He was sincerely apologetic, but there was nothing he could do. "We have a hotel here at the fort. It certainly isn't elaborate, but it's clean and fairly comfortable. You're more than welcome to stay there."

"Let's go to the hotel, Pa," Johnny whined. He was miserable and tired and longed for a bath.

"All right," Jack sighed, deciding they had no other choice but to wait for the two officers. Standing slowly, he looked at the lieutenant. "Do you think the colonel and the major will give us an escort?"

"The final decision will rest with Colonel Johnson, but if the major requests it, permission will most likely be granted."

Rising, Lieutenant Wilkinson showed the three men to the door, and as he was bidding them good day, a woman and her young daughter suddenly arrived.

Stepping through the open doorway, the lieutenant nodded politely. "Good afternoon, Suzanne," he said, smiling. Then, making introductions, he gave her the names of the three visitors. Speaking exclusively to Jack, he proceeded, "This is Mrs. Landon, and her daughter Kara."

"You must be married to Major Landon," Jack said.

"Yes, I am," she answered.

Somberly, he replied, "Ma'am, I certainly hope your

husband isn't delayed, for my daughter's life may very well depend on how soon he returns." Without further elaboration, he motioned for Clint and Johnny to follow, then headed toward the fort's hotel.

Jack had been too worried about Alisha to notice Mrs. Landon's astounding beauty, but her loveliness hadn't escaped his sons' notice, especially Johnny's.

Clint and his brother were walking a short way behind Jack, and Johnny kept glancing over his shoulder so he could continue admiring the major's wife. "She sure is a good-looking woman, isn't she?" he asked Clint.

"Yes, but she's married, and don't you forget it," Clint urged. "While we're guests on this fort, you watch your conduct."

Johnny frowned. "Damn, to hear you talk, you'd think a woman wasn't safe in my presence. Besides, I don't fool around with married women." His expression growing puzzled, he added, "The major's daughter looked like a half-breed, didn't she?"

"I don't know, I didn't really look at her," Clint answered.

"Well, I noticed her, and I'd be willing to bet my last dollar that she's got Indian blood. Why do you suppose an officer and his wife would want a damned half-breed for a daughter?" He chuckled slyly. "Or maybe the girl's the major's little bastard by a Sioux squaw."

Clint was disgusted. "Johnny, do me a favor, will you?"

"Sure, what do you want me to do?"

"Shut up," he snapped.

Meantime, as the three Stevenses were heading for the hotel, Lieutenant Wilkinson told Suzanne why the men had come to the fort.

"For their sakes, I hope my husband and the colonel aren't late returning." She sighed regretfully. "It's too

153

bad that Black Wolf isn't still here. He'd be the ideal man to find Mr. Stevens's daughter."

Alisha sat a distance away from the camp. Black Wolf and the boys were around the fire, but wanting a moment to herself, she had left the others. Wandering to a towering spruce, she had decided to sit beneath it. Now, alone with her thoughts, she gazed back toward camp. She could barely make out the flickering flames or the three people gathered beside the fire's warmth. Feeling chilly, she crossed her arms over her chest and hugged herself. The farther north they traveled, the colder the nights became.

As usual, her mind was on Black Wolf. Three days had passed since they had made love, during which time they had been successful in their attempts to avoid close contact. Clearing Black Wolf from her thoughts, she began to worry about her father. What had happened between him and Jesse Wyatt? Her deep concern for Jack made her wonder if she and David shouldn't take their chances with Two Moons and try to make it back home. But as she conjured up an image of the threatening warrior, a foreboding chill ran up her spine. The terrifying possibility that she and David could be captured by Two Moons persuaded her to remain in Black Wolf's protection.

Catching sight of Black Wolf leaving the camp and walking in her direction, caused Alisha to tense. Why was he seeking her? As far as she was concerned, they had nothing to discuss. He had made it apparent that he had no intentions of leaving the Sioux, and she was against giving up her way of life to join him in his. He was stubborn, but she could be just as stubborn!

Joining her, Black Wolf sat down. Placing his rifle at his side, he said, "You shouldn't wander this far from

154

camp. It isn't safe."

She felt like telling him there seemed to be no place that was safe; after all, it was in his very presence that she had lost her innocence.

The night was clear, and the landscape was enshrouded in moonlight. Black Wolf could easily see Alisha's face, and taking note of her sullenness, he asked gently, "What's wrong?"

Evading the full truth, she murmured, "I'm worried about my father."

"I understand," he whispered. Encouragingly, he continued, "Maybe Running Horse will be all right, and I'll soon be taking you home."

Thoughtfully, she questioned, "I wonder what will happen to David? He told me that he doesn't have any close kin." Her expression lightened. "I'm sure Papa will offer him a home at the Bar-S."

His eyes twinkling with esteem, Black Wolf remarked, "I admire David. If I ever have a son, I wouldn't mind having one with David's qualities."

Impulsively, she queried, "Why aren't you married? You must be almost thirty. I thought Indians married at a young age. By now, you should already have sons."

"Our women marry quite young, but it's not all that rare for a man in his thirties still to be a bachelor. It takes years to learn how to be a good warrior and a skillful hunter. And a man must master these capabilities before he can adequately take care of a wife and children."

Unable to repress her curiosity, she asked, "Is there someone special in your life?"

"Special in what way?" he questioned, smiling wryly.

"You know what I mean," she answered testily. "Are you in love with an Indian maiden?"

"It seems, Madam, that I'm not as fortunate as you are. I don't have a fiancée."

155

Alisha came close to telling him that she had fibbed about having a fiancé. However, she quickly chose not to do so. Admitting to the lie would be too embarrassing; furthermore, what difference would it make? There could never be a future between Black Wolf and herself anyway.

"I suppose he's very worried about you," Black Wolf said quietly.

Her dishonesty made her uncomfortable. "Wh . . . what?" she stammered.

"Miller. I'm sure he's worried."

"Yes, of course he is," she mumbled. Changing the subject, she requested with genuine interest, "Will you tell me about your village?"

"What exactly do you want to know?"

"Honestly, Black Wolf," she complained. "You have an exasperating habit of answering my questions with a question. Why do you make it so difficult for me to get information from you?"

"Do I?" he asked.

"You're doing it again!" she fussed.

"Alisha, you needn't concern yourself with my home, for I'm sure your stay there will be an incredibly short one."

Carefully, she cautioned, "Black Wolf, you shouldn't get your hopes up too high that your father will be well. You should prepare yourself for whatever you might find."

"Yes, I know," he admitted soberly. Touched by her concern, he said, "Alisha, you're a very wonderful and compassionate lady. I only wish . . ."

"What do you wish?" she asked, watching him closely.

"I wish we didn't live in two separate worlds," he groaned.

She smiled ruefully. "So do I, Black Wolf."

Fighting the need to take her into his arms, Black Wolf leaned over and offered her his hand. Helping her up, he said brusquely, "It's late. You'd better go back to camp and get some sleep."

"Aren't you coming?" she asked.

"Tonight Flying Hawk is taking the second watch, and I'm taking the first. So I'm going to have a look around."

"Do you plan to look for Two Moons' camp?"

"He's no longer following us."

"Since when?" she asked, surprised.

"Since yesterday," Black Wolf answered. He watched her carefully.

"Then David and I are free to . . . ?"

"Free to leave?" he concluded. "Alisha, do you honestly believe that you and David can find your way out of these Hills? More importantly, what chance do you think you two would have in this wilderness? You not only have the Sioux to worry about, but there are also unsavory characters in these Hills who wouldn't hesitate to kill the boy and rape you."

Alisha knew that he was right. She and David would have little chance of reaching home safely. Although she wanted desperately to learn if her father was well, her only logical choice was to stay with Black Wolf until he could take her home. It would be foolhardy to try and leave these Hills without Black Wolf's protection. If she were to try and attempt such a foolish feat, she'd probably not live to see her father again.

Conceding wisely, she murmured, "David and I will stay with you. I only hope . . ."

"What do you hope?" he prodded gently.

"That our stay at your village will be a short one. I'm anxious to return home because I'm worried about my father."

"I understand," he replied.

157

"How much farther is it to your village?"

"Four, maybe five days." Turning away from her, he reached down and picked up his rifle.

Alisha let her eyes roam over the warrior's handsome physique. His buckskins clung snugly to his muscular frame, and as she admired his strong build, she longed to fling herself into his embrace and feel his arms holding her close. She raised her vision to his shoulder-length black hair, and to the plain leather band he wore about his head.

He was now aware of her attention, and when she looked into his face, his blue eyes met her dark ones. Black Wolf, finding her as desirable as she found him, said determinedly, "Alisha, go back to camp. Let's not start something that can only end with unhappiness."

"Hasn't it already started?" she countered.

"You're right," he agreed. "So we must end what we foolishly started."

She concurred, although it was painful to do so. She turned to leave, but there was a question she needed to ask. Turning back, she said, "Black Wolf, there is something that has been gnawing at me."

"What's that?"

"Are there white slaves at your village?"

"No," he replied.

"Thank goodness. I was worried that I might see my own people in bondage." Leaving, she began walking back to camp. She was greatly relieved that she wouldn't be forced to see white slaves. She'd heard numerous stories about the cruel ways in which the Sioux treated their white captives. Thank God, she wouldn't be a witness to such brutal degradation!

Bonnie Sue sat alone on the riverbank, her back turned toward Chief Bear Claw's village. The intermittent sounds of dogs barking, babies crying, and the soft neighing of horses sounded throughout the site, but the camp was relatively quiet and most of its inhabitants were asleep.

As the young woman stared vacantly, tears rolled down her cheeks. For a short time, she allowed them to fall unhindered, then leaning forward, she cupped a handful of water and splashed the cool wetness over her face. The moonlight shone on the river and Bonnie Sue could see her reflection. Her pathetically thin body tensed as she stared at her own image. The woman's gaunt face made her high cheek bones protrude and her chin recede. As she continued to stare at her reflection, the eyes that stared back were glazed with despair, and her long golden hair fell about her face in wild disarray.

I look like a heathen, she thought dully, sitting upright. She was wearing a ragged pair of tan leggings, and drawing up her knees, she rested her arms across them.

I will soon kill myself, she mused calmly, as though she were considering something of mild importance. She thought about the baby growing in her womb. Strong Fox's child! If this child were to make Strong Fox and his wife treat her more gently, and if the baby were to be accepted with kindness, then Bonnie Sue would go through with her pregnancy, but Warm Blanket had already informed her that the child would make no difference.

Bonnie Sue was barely showing, but Warm Blanket's sharp eyes had seen the slight bulge across her slave's stomach. Bonnie Sue sensed correctly that Strong Fox's wife hated the unborn child. Since the day her husband had brought the white woman to their tepee, he had practically stopped bedding her, preferring their skinny slave to his own wife. Although Warm Blanket harbored much resentment for Bonnie Sue, she resented the child even more. She herself hadn't been able to conceive since Little Star, and she begrudged Bonnie Sue the ability to conceive from Strong Fox's seed.

Straightening her legs, Bonnie Sue looked down at her stomach. Placing a hand across her abdomen, she murmured despondently, "I don't hate you, little baby. In fact, I'm your mother and I love you. But it's because I care that I've decided not to let you be born. You won't go alone, for I'll go with you. You'll never suffer Warm Blanket's cruelty. I can bear what she does to me, but I could never bear seeing her mistreat you."

Detecting footsteps, Bonnie Sue glanced over her shoulder, and spotting Warm Blanket, she got quickly to her feet.

Arriving, the big woman drew back her arm, then slapped her slave across the face. "Why you not in tepee? Strong Fox wake up and want to share your bed." Sheer hate radiated in Warm Blanket's beady eyes as her gaze became fixed on Bonnie Sue's stomach. Sneering, she threatened, "Maybe I kill baby when it born."

The Indian woman waited expectantly for her slave to plead for the child's life, but when Bonnie Sue showed no emotion, Warm Blanket ordered harshly, "Hurry to tepee. Strong Fox not like to wait."

Obeying, Bonnie Sue took long, anxious strides which belied her feelings. She despised submitting to Strong Fox, but it gave her a vindictive pleasure to make Warm Blanket think that she was willing.

Reaching the tepee, Bonnie Sue paused. Taking a deep breath she tried to conjure up the will power to enter. She dreaded the evil man's hands bruising her flesh and his hard organ pumping in and out of her. The impending certainty caused a violent shudder to shake her thin frame. Then, suddenly, against her own

160

volition, Joel Carson's image flashed before her. His memory made tears smart in her eyes, and an emotional pain cut sharply into her heart. Oh Joel! . . . Joel! she cried inwardly. I still love you so much! Dearest God, how dearly I love you!

"Golden Hair!" Strong Fox bellowed from inside the tepee.

The man's harsh voice startled Bonnie Sue, causing Joel's image to disappear. Bracing herself for the degrading ordeal which awaited, the young woman pushed aside the leather flap and entered the tepee.

Chapter Fifteen

Alisha hadn't imagined that Running Horse's village would be quite so large, and as she and the others rode through the encampment, she was surprised by the number of tepees she saw. Groups of women and children left their activities to follow Black Wolf, Flying Hawk, and their two guests as they headed slowly toward the chief's home. The old men and warriors were just as curious as the women and children; however, they were less conspicuous and trailed at a distance, giving the impression that they were only mildly interested.

Growing up in Wyoming Territory, Alisha had often seen Indians, but never had she been in the midst of so many. She noticed that quite a few of them were eyeing her hostilely, and she urged her horse closer to Black Wolf's.

Reaching the conical tepee located in the center of the village, Black Wolf pulled up and dismounted. Glancing at Alisha and David, he said tersely, "Stay mounted until I tell you otherwise."

Both nodded silently. Their eyes were glued to the tepee as they wondered who would be coming out to greet them.

For a moment, David turned his vision from the tent's opening to view the dwelling's construction. Looking closely, he saw that it was held up by a circular framework of poles brought together at the top in such a manner that the poles crossed and supported each other. He supposed the covering was made from soft-tanned buffalo skins. Suddenly, the leather flap was pushed aside, and the warrior stepping through caught David's attention. He appeared middle-aged, and his stock build was obtrusively strong. His long black hair was braided, and he wore a beaded head band adorned with an eagle feather. The man's fringed buckskins, embellished with beads of different colors, was a striking costume.

David and Alisha looked on as the warrior and Black Wolf exchanged greetings before embracing. Then Flying Hawk quickly dismounted and was welcomed in the same manner.

"How is my father?" Black Wolf asked.

"He grows worse," he answered gravely.

The men had spoken in their own language, and turning back to David and Alisha, Black Wolf explained, "Running Horse is very ill." Still speaking English, he introduced his two companions to the warrior. "Kicking Buffalo, this is Alisha and David."

The Indian didn't verbally acknowledge the pair, but merely stared at them with an expression that was far from cordial.

"Kicking Buffalo is my uncle, Running Horse's younger brother," Black Wolf told them.

The two whites were uneasy under the warrior's hard scrutiny, and noticing this, Black Wolf gained his uncle's attention. "Where is my father?"

The question had been spoken in English, and Kicking Buffalo answered in suit. "He is inside." Gesturing toward the open flap, he proceeded, "Come;

Running Horse awaits his son."

Without excusing himself, Black Wolf ducked inside the tepee with his uncle close on his heels.

The moment Black Wolf disappeared from sight, Alisha's and David's uneasiness became more intense. The two were surrounded by Running Horses people, and the majority of faces staring at the two intruders were unfriendly.

"I don't think we're welcome here," David said quietly. He attempted to sound unconcerned.

"I think you're right," Alisha replied, also feigning and air of nonchalance.

Overhearing their remarks, Flying Hawk laughed resentfully before leaving. They watched him until he reached a nearby tepee, then glancing back, he cast David and evil look before bending over and entering the dwelling.

The minutes that passed as Alisha and David waited for Black Wolf's reappearance seemed interminable. When at last he stepped out of the tepee, they both sighed with relief.

Alisha started to speak to him, but the beautiful maiden following Black Wolf outside caused Alisha's words to die on her lips. Although the girl was quite curvaceous, Alisha guessed her to be around sixteen. She was exceptionally pretty, and as she caught sight of the white woman, her extraordinary large eyes widened with admiration.

Unknown to Alisha, the girl was finding her unbelievably lovely and was totally amazed by the white woman's platinum-blond tresses. She had never dreamed that anyone could have such light-colored hair.

The Indian girl was standing a step behind Black Wolf, and taking her hand, he drew her forward. Their

164

hands remained clasped, and their affectionate familiarity sent a twinge of jealousy through Alisha.

Black Wolf waited for Kicking Buffalo to join them before saying to David, "Son, it has been decided that you'll stay with Kicking Buffalo and his family." He glanced at the girl beside him. "This is Spotted Fawn. She's Kicking Buffalo's daughter."

Alisha brightened. If the girl was Kicking Buffalo's daughter, then that meant she was Black Wolf's cousin. Her jealousy was almost eliminated until, suddenly, she wondered if the Sioux married their cousins.

David wasn't eager to live with Kicking Buffalo and his family, but knowing he was in no position to make demands, he was willing to submit. However, Black Wolf's next words were to provoke an outburst.

"Flying Hawk is Kicking Buffalo's adopted son, so you'll also be living with him."

"No!" David shouted. "I won't share a tepee with Flying Hawk! I won't, damn it! And you can't make me!"

Releasing Spotted Fawn's hand, Black Wolf stalked to David's horse, reached up and jerked the boy to the ground. Grasping his arms in a viselike grip, he ordered harshly, "You'll do as I say!"

David tried to squirm free, but Black Wolf held on tenaciously. Ceasing his struggles, the boy asked pleadingly, "Why do you want me to stay with Flying Hawk?"

Setting him free, Black Wolf replied, "Someday, I hope you will find the answer to that question by yourself." Moving to Alisha's horse, Black Wolf helped her dismount.

"Where am I supposed to stay?" she asked, watching him anxiously.

"I'll tell you later. First, I want you to come with

David and me."

"Where are we goin'?" David grumbled. He was still perturbed.

"To Kicking Buffalo's home, where you'll get your first lesson on Sioux etiquette."

David looked doubtful, for he couldn't fathom Indians practicing any form of etiquette. Keeping his suspicions to himself, he accompanied Black Wolf and Alisha to the designated tepee.

"Wait here," Black Wolf told them. Then, announcing his presence, he went inside the dwelling. Alisha and David hadn't long to wait before Black Wolf reappeared with Flying Hawk and an Indian woman.

"David, this is Basket-Weaver. She's Kicking Buffalo's wife. She speaks English fairly well."

The woman smiled warmly as her eyes traveled over her new charge. She was impressed with the boy's handsome and healthy appearance, and she also sensed intuitively that he was brave.

Standing beside Basket-Weaver, Flying Hawk grumbled, "Why must white boy stay here?"

His patience thin, Black Wolf answered sharply, "Kicking Buffalo has ordered it so, and it's not your place to question his decision." Stepping back, he gestured for Alisha and David to enter the tepee.

They complied, and Black Wolf followed them inside. Poised close to the entrance, Alisha and David studied the tepee's interior. It resembled a hollow cone, and each lodge pole was covered with a lining of leather. Just forward of the center was the lodge fire, set in a little depression. An orderly circle of cobblestones outlined this cooking pit.

The beds were located on the north and south sides of the lodge. They had a headpiece made from willow rods which were laid parallel and woven together with strips of leather. The beds, padded with dry grass and pelts, were covered with old blankets. However, over this were placed better blankets and also pillows stuffed with feathers.

"The bed on the south side belongs to Kicking Buffalo and Basket-Weaver," Black Wolf began. Although he was speaking to David, he expected Alisha to pay close attention. "Their children, Spotted Fawn and Flying Hawk, also have their beds on this side. Guests, such as yourself, are expected to sleep on the opposite side. During the day you are supposed to keep your place in the lodge, unless moving about in pursuit of some duty. You are to store your personal belongings behind your bed, and nothing is to be left scattered about."

Black Wolf stalled his lesson to see if David was paying attention. Convinced that he was, Black Wolf continued, "Lodge etiquette requires that visitors and others never pass between the master and the fire, or furthermore, in front of anyone. You will always pass behind the others; they in turn will show courtesy by giving you room to do so."

David made no comment, but he seriously doubted he'd receive any acts of courtesy from Flying Hawk.

Black Wolf proceeded. "Every day two meals will be cooked, breakfast and supper. You will always be on time and gather with the others around the lodge fire. Before anyone touches the food, Kicking Buffalo will take a small portion and cast it into the fire in recognition of the belief that all food comes through the goodness of the unseen power. Basket-Weaver will serve you your food, and at the end of the meal, you should remember to thank her for preparing a delicious fare."

"I'll remember everything you said," David replied. So far the instructions had seemed relatively simple, and he was sure he'd have no problems following them.

"Lessons are over for the present," Black Wolf remarked. "Basket-Weaver will show you where you'll sleep, then get your belongings and stash them behind your appointed bed." He turned to Alisha and took her arm. "Come with me."

As he ushered her outside, she asked, "Where are you taking me?"

"To my own lodge, which is located beside my father's."

Black Wolf had a firm lock on her arm, and she tried to pull away, but his grip was too firm. "Surely you aren't planning for us to share the same tepee," she uttered warily.

He made no reply until they reached his lodge, then throwing aside the flap, he said strongly, "We'll talk inside."

Before she could argue, he urged her through the opening and into the tepee. Giving the interior a superficial glance, she saw that it was similar to the one she had just left.

Black Wolf closed the leather flap, then turning to face her, he explained their circumstances. "Kicking Buffalo has insisted that we live here together. Due to my father's illness, he's now acting as chief, and I have no alternative but to obey his orders."

"But you're Running Horse's son! Why aren't you acting as chief?"

"I wasn't here when Running Horse took ill, so the council decided on Kicking Buffalo. My return won't make them change their choice."

"Why does Kicking Buffalo want us to live together?"

"Alisha, you're a strikingly beautiful woman, and if you were unattached you'd become a very big temptation to our unmarried braves. My uncle believes

168

that we must avoid these complications. If the men believe you belong solely to me, they won't try to pursue you in any way."

Kicking Buffalo's reasoning made sense, and Alisha didn't disagree with the acting chief's decision. Moving away from Black Wolf, she walked over to stand beside the unlit fire lodge. Wringing her hands apprehensively, she murmured, "But if we are to share this tepee, how can we possibly avoid close contact?"

Black Wolf sighed audibly. "We can't," he whispered.

Desperate, Alisha cried, "Black Wolf, I'm very attracted to you, but except for that one time, I've been able to keep it under control. If right now we were to go our separate ways, I could get over you. But if our relationship is given a chance to deepen, I don't know if I could stand losing you! We both know we have no lasting future together. Our final parting is inevitable!"

Black Wolf was tempted to sweep her into his arms and tell her that if they were truly in love, they'd find a way to remain together. However, knowing he'd doubt the certainty of his own words, he made no move to embrace her. Instead, he said hopefully, "There's still a chance that my father will get better, and then I can take you home." He didn't make foolish remarks about them curbing their desires as they waited for Running Horse's recovery, for Black Wolf already knew the temptation would be too overpowering to resist.

"When you saw Running Horse, what did he say about David and me?"

"He was only able to stay awake for a few minutes, so I didn't have a chance to tell him about you two."

"Do you have any idea what is ailing him?"

"It's his lungs; consumption."

"Has he been seen by a white doctor?"

"No, he refuses to be treated by one."

"Can't you persuade him to change his mind?"

"Even if I could, there's little chance that I'd find a doctor who'd treat him. White physicians limit their patients to their own kind, unless they practice on reservations."

Alisha knew he was right, so she said no more.

Going to the flap and pushing it aside, Black Wolf remarked, "I need to tend to the horses and take care of other matters. So you won't be alone while I'm gone, I'll ask Spotted Fawn to stay with you. She speaks English fluently. I taught her myself."

Remembering the Indian girl's beauty, Alisha asked hesitantly, "Black Wolf, do Sioux marry their cousins?"

Understanding the reason behind her question, Black Wolf laughed heartily as he left the tepee.

Perturbed at him for not answering, she yelled to his departing back, "I don't need anyone to stay with me! I'm perfectly capable of being alone!"

A few minutes later, Spotted Fawn made her appearance. Alisha had taken a seat on Black Wolf's bed, but at the Indian girl's arrival, she got to her feet.

Motioning for her to sit back down, Spotted Fawn said affably, "Please, do not let me disturb you. Rest, while I make a fire."

Returning to the bed, Alisha watched the girl going about her chore. She noticed how Spotted Fawn's movements were flowing and graceful. Dressed in soft suede, which was decorated with different colored beads, the young woman presented a lovely picture.

When Spotted Fawn had the fire lodge glowing, she went over and sat beside Alisha. Her young eyes gleaming with curiosity, she asked, "Does my cousin, Black Wolf, love you?"

The question taking her off guard, Alisha stammered, "Why . . . why do you want to know?"

"Although many maidens have tried to win Black Wolf's heart, he has kept it locked away. I have often wondered what kind of woman it would take to finally steal it from him."

"Well, I don't have Black Wolf's heart," Alisha answered. "He isn't in love with me."

"But you are his woman!" Spotted Fawn exclaimed, as though that in itself meant she had won Black Wolf's love.

"Why do you think I'm his woman?"

"You share his lodge," she replied. "Then he must love you," Spotted Fawn declared firmly.

Seeing no reason to try and convince her otherwise, Alisha made no further reference to her relationship with Black Wolf. As fatigue washed over her, Alisha yawned tiredly.

"Maybe you should take a nap," Spotted Fawn suggested.

"I am awfully tired," Alisha murmured.

Rising, the Indian girl said briskly, "You sleep for a short time, then I'll wake you so you can start first lesson."

Perplexed, Alisha questioned, "First lesson?"

"Yes. Black Wolf told me to begin teaching you how to cook."

"Cook?" she repeated angrily. "I already know how to cook."

"You do not know how to cook Sioux-style."

Alisha was fuming. "How dare Black Wolf issue such an order! I have no intentions of attempting any style of cooking, except my own! And you can tell him I said so!"

Spotted Fawn repressed a grin. Apparently, this white woman was not afraid to defy Black Wolf. Her

171

cousin had finally met a woman who would stand up to him. Again telling Alisha to get some sleep, Spotted Fawn returned to the fire and sat down. Now, smiling openly, she tried to imagine Black Wolf's reaction when she told him what Alisha had said. He'd no doubt be very angry. The longer she thought about it, the more confident she became that Black Wolf's obstinacy would win out over Alisha's. The white woman might be stubborn and spirited, but Spotted Fawn believed it'd only be a matter of time before Black Wolf had Alisha doing his bidding.

When Running Horse awoke from his fitful sleep, he found Black Wolf sitting at his bedside. Seeing the concern on his son's face, he murmured weakly, "Do not worry so much. I am more than ready to go to the spirit world." His dark eyes took on a dreamy haze. "Your mother is there, waiting for me."

Suddenly, racked with a coughing spasm, Running Horse's frame heaved violently as he tried to clear his lungs.

Moving quickly, Black Wolf helped his father sit up, then when the coughing bout ended, he lowered him back down onto his bed.

Thoughtfully, Black Wolf studied the ailing man. Running Horse's build was still strong in spite of his illness, but his face was drawn and his eyes watery. Gravely, Black Wolf wondered if his father would survive the bitter winter that would soon be upon the land.

"Father, I have something important to tell you," Black Wolf began. "I didn't return alone."

Interrupting, Running Horse told him, "Yes, I know. Kicking Buffalo has already told me about the woman and the boy." He smiled approvingly. "Son, you had no choice but to bring them with you."

"I'm glad that you understand. As soon as you are better, I'll take them back to their own people."

"The woman," Running Horse murmured. "Is she beautiful?"

Taken aback by his father's inquiry, Black Wolf replied hesitantly, "Yes . . . yes, she's very beautiful."

"Do you love her?" he asked point-blank.

The younger man sighed dejectedly. "What difference does it make? You know my feelings about marrying a white woman."

Running Horse sensed that his son was indeed in love. "You are foolish to fight your love for this woman. She is part of your destiny. The spirits foretold your future the day you were born. You cannot alter what is to be. The spirits, in their wisdom, have sent the white woman to you. She will help shape your destiny!"

"No!" Black Wolf argued, guilt plaguing him. "I won't leave the Sioux!"

Understanding, Running Horse said quietly, "Your guilt is a burden you bring upon yourself. Son, a man must follow his destiny without question. The spirits have spoken. Why do you deny their wisdom?"

Black Wolf's reply was emotional, "Father, why do you keep insisting that I abandon the Sioux?"

Running Horse was tiring. "Abandon?" he whispered feebly. "Why do you choose such a word?"

His son started to answer, but before he could, the chief drifted back into sleep. For a long moment, Black Wolf remained beside his father, watching him with deep love.

Then, standing, he moved across the enclosure and to the entrance. Bending over, he stepped outside and paused to look about the village, and as his thoughts

173

ran fluidly, he recalled his father's words. "You are foolish to fight your love for this woman. She is part of your destiny."

Slowly, Black Wolf turned toward his own tepee, where he knew Alisha was waiting. With Running Horse's prediction still heavy on his mind, he headed toward his lodge.

Chapter Sixteen

Black Wolf entered and found Alisha asleep, with Spotted Fawn sitting by the fire. He said to his cousin, "Thanks for staying with Alisha."

Standing, Spotted Fawn began a little hesitantly, "I told the white woman that you wanted me to start teaching her to cook, but she refuses to learn."

Black Wolf was not surprised, for he had expected as much. He would have to reason with her.

Their voices roused her, and Alisha stretched gracefully before sitting up. Meeting Black Wolf's unwavering gaze, she asked irritably, "Why in the world do you want Spotted Fawn to teach me the Sioux way of cooking?"

"It's become necessary for you to learn," he answered evenly.

Alisha arched an eyebrow. "Oh? May I ask why?"

Moving in front of her, he stared down into her curious face. "I seriously doubt that Running Horse's health will improve in time for me to take you home within the near future. Which means that you and David will most likely be spending the winter here."

"What!" she gasped, leaping to her feet. She didn't want to live in this village for an entire winter, nor did she want to wait that long before seeing her father. "No!" she argued desperately. "I won't stay here for months on end!"

"Yes, you will!" he retorted impatiently.

"We'll see about that!" she threatened. "You can't tell me what I can or cannot do!" Her temper cooling, she tried to explain her feelings. "It was different when I thought there was a good chance that David and I would only be here a short time. I didn't really think it would come down to us living here all winter."

Black Wolf turned to Spotted Fawn. "Leave us alone."

Doing as her cousin requested, she left quickly.

Whirling around to face Alisha, Black Wolf uttered gruffly, "Alisha, you knew all along that you might have to stay here all winter."

"No, I didn't know for certain!" she snapped.

"Then you chose to block the possibility from your stubborn little mind, just as you are now blocking out your true reason for wanting to leave."

"True reason?" she queried. "I want to go home! Isn't that reason enough?"

"You want to run away from me!" he countered. "And away from the feelings we share."

She lifted her chin defiantly. "I told you my father would give us a house and land, but you don't want to live with me."

"I don't want to live on a ranch!" he argued. "I belong here with Running Horse and my people."

"Why do you deny your mother's blood?"

"I don't!" he remarked.

"The hell you don't!" she cried angrily.

He frowned disapprovingly. "Cursing doesn't become a lady."

"Don't you dare preach to me!" she spat.

Realizing their bickering was getting them nowhere,

176

Black Wolf moved away and took a seat beside the lodge fire.

Standing her ground, Alisha declared firmly, "I insist that you find someone to take me home."

Gazing into the hot coals, Black Wolf became inflexible. "You're staying right here, and if you try to leave, I'll come after you and drag you back."

"My first impression of you was right! You *are* a savage brute!"

"A moot point, my love," he murmured.

"I'm not your love! I hate you!" Exasperated, Alisha sat back down on the bed and stared at Black Wolf.

"I don't think you hate me," he said quietly, still looking at the smoldering coals. "You simply hate the idea of living with Indians."

She didn't dispute his words, for she knew they had a ring of truth. Her knowledge of Indians was limited to the stories she had heard, tales often told by those who were biased against the Sioux.

"If I'm prejudiced against your people, then you're just as prejudiced against mine," she replied evenly.

"As I said before, we live in two separate worlds," he remarked softly.

"And never the twain shall meet," she finished.

He turned and looked at her. "Alisha, regardless of our personal feelings, it'd be very foolish for you to leave here on your own. I won't impose on any of my father's warriors to give you an escort. As I've already told you, you are not their responsibility. If you want to live to see your father again, you'll stay here until I can take you home, whether it be days, weeks or months." Standing, he continued, "Furthermore, since we must live together, I think it will ease the tension between us if we avoid any talk of love or commitments. We both know where our loyalties lie, and there's no chance that either of us will change our minds."

Agreeing, she replied stoically, "So be it."

His attitude now impersonal, Black Wolf said briskly, "Cooking in an Indian lodge is different than cooking over the white man's stove. Since I don't plan to starve during your duration here, I must insist that you let Spotted Fawn teach you how to properly prepare our meals."

Alisha smiled shrewdly, remarking innocently, "But, Black Wolf, you promised that I'd be your guest. Guests aren't supposed to cook meals, so I should think it'd be your place to cook mine."

Amused, he grinned. "Touché, Miss Stevens. However, there is a valuable lesson you must learn."

"Oh?" she queried.

"A woman has certain duties, and cooking is one of them."

"That's a very convenient point-of-view."

He walked over, took her hands, and drew her to her feet. Then, releasing his hold, he stepped back and looked her directly in the eyes. "You will find, Madam, that I'm the master of my humble lodge. I'll expect you to do as I say."

"Besides cooking, what other duties will I be expected to perform?" She watched him with a certain degree of amusement.

"None beyond your capabilities," he answered.

Brushing past him, she went to the center of the lodge. Keeping her back turned, she said matter-of-factly, "Well, since I'm apparently the maid, I think my first job should be making up another bed. Your humble lodge has only one, and since there are two people living here, we are one bed short."

"One bed will suffice," he declared.

Whirling about, she exclaimed, "I don't think so! Only a few minutes ago, you said to ease the tension we

178

must avoid talk of love or commitments. Just how do you intend to avoid love when we are sharing the same bed?"

"Making love and pledging love is not the same thing," he came back.

"Your attitude is typically male!" she spat.

"And yours is typically female," he returned. "Only a woman would be so foolish as to think she could live with a man she desired and not sleep with him." Giving the interior a casual glance, he added, "Besides, this is a bachelor's lodge and too small for another bed. The subject is closed, and I don't want any further argument."

She glared at him. He was so pompous, so sure of himself! Did he intend for her to be his mistress and housekeeper and then, come Spring, bid her a fond farewell as though she were his hired help? Well, she had her pride to protect . . . and her heart! She didn't doubt that he'd take both as though they were of little value.

There was a small stack of blankets in the corner, and going to them, she picked up several. Taking them to the opposite side of Black Wolf's bed, she spread them out on the bear-skins that covered the earth floor.

"What do you think you're doing?" he asked, aggravated.

"I'm making myself a place to sleep," she remarked sharply.

Stretching out on his own bed, he said casually, "Your defiance is admirable, but in this case, it's a total waste of time and energy. You'll be sleeping with me tonight and every night that you're here."

Taking her place on the blankets, she retorted, "We'll see about that!"

Turning on his side so that he could see her, he questioned, "It's still daylight, not to mention that I haven't had my supper, so why are you lying down?"

"Why are you?" she asked querulously.

"I'm weak from hunger," he moaned, as though dangerously on the brink of starvation.

Alisha tried to suppress a smile, but failed. If only she could stay angry at him! Why did their bickering always end on an amusing note? Sitting up, she relented, "Black Wolf, I'd be quite willing to fix supper, but there's no food in your lodge."

Bounding to his feet, he told her, "That can easily be rectified. I'll borrow some food from Basket-Weaver." He headed for the entrance, but instead of leaving, he looked at Alisha and said with a smile, "I'll help you cook our meal."

She also smiled. "In return, I'll not let your masculine comrades know that you helped with woman's work."

He laughed. "I appreciate your consideration." Favoring her with a fond wink, he darted outside.

David was sitting on his bed reading a book when Flying Hawk entered the tepee. The Indian boy nodded to Basket-Weaver, who was cooking their supper, then he ambled casually to David. "My friends and I, we are playing games. Do you want to join us?"

David was immediately on his guard. "What kind of games?"

Flying Hawk eyed him challengingly. "Come outside and we will show you." He smirked. "If you are afraid, I will ask the girls to let you play their womanly games."

Closing his book with a bang and placing it behind his bed, David leapt to his feet. Accepting Flying Hawk's dare, he said abruptly, "I'm not scared to play your silly games!"

Pleased, Flying Hawk laughed. "We will see how

strong you are."

"I can whip you!" David said firmly, following his adversary outdoors.

As they emerged, Black Wolf arrived. "Where are you taking David?" he asked Flying Hawk.

He pointed toward his friends, who were standing in the distance. "We decided to invite our white visitor to join us in a game."

Black Wolf and Flying Hawk were speaking in their own language. Although David couldn't understand what they were saying, he knew he was the topic of their discussion.

Studying the Indian lad suspiciously, Black Wolf prodded, "Exactly what kind of game?"

"A wrestling match," he answered in truth.

Looking at David, Black Wolf asked, "Did you know Flying Hawk expects you to participate in a wrestling bout?"

"No," David replied. He squared his shoulders, and raised his chin obstinately. "But I'll gladly oblige him."

For a moment, Black Wolf's eyes flickered back and forth from one boy to the other. A shadow of a smile played about his lips as he said calmly, "You two have been itching for a fight since you first laid eyes on each other. So get on with it."

Flying Hawk's face actually beamed. He could hardly wait to prove to David that he was the better fighter.

Meanwhile, David was also looking quite satisfied, for he was anxious to win this fight and show Flying Hawk who was the better man.

As the boys hurried to the Indian lads who were gathered and waiting, Black Wolf decided to watch from a distance.

Observing Flying Hawk's dozen companions, David estimated their ages to range from ten to fourteen.

They, in turn, gave the white boy a close perusal.

Flying Hawk explained the rules to David. "Everyone wrestles at the same time, but each one of us will choose an opponent. If one of us sits down, he gives up and will be left alone. Whoever remains standing, is open for an attack. The game goes on until only one is left standing."

"Sounds simple enough," David muttered.

Feigning courtesy, Flying Hawk offered, "You are a guest, so you may have first choice. Who will be your opponent?"

David chuckled coldly. "Now who in the hell do you think?"

Hate radiating from his dark eyes, Flying Hawk threatened, "It will give me great pleasure to break your arms!"

"Not nearly as much pleasure as it's going to give me to break your head," David retorted.

Overhearing their violent remarks, Black Wolf began to question his own judgment in allowing this fight. He had hoped that physical combat might eventually cool their animosities. Sometimes, the only way to lose bottled-up anger was to release it by action.

Some of the people in the village soon came to realize that the white boy was going to participate in a wrestling bout, and curious, they left whatever they were doing to watch the event. Suddenly, Black Wolf was no longer alone, but was surrounded by other spectators.

As time passed, Alisha grew impatient waiting for Black Wolf's return. Surely it didn't take this long to borrow some food from Basket-Weaver. Her stomach began to churn with hunger, and losing what little patience she had left, Alisha decided to go out in search of Black Wolf.

Leaving the lodge, she noticed a large group of people gathered in a circle. She was not so much interested in whatever they were watching, but spotting Black Wolf among them, she headed in their direction.

Making her way past a couple of warriors and to Black Wolf's side, she started to question him, but the sight in front of her shocked her into silence.

Alisha's eyes widened with astonishment as she stared at David and Flying Hawk. The other boys had quit wrestling, and only these two had remained in combat. None of the spectators was finding this surprising; from the very beginning, the contest had been between Flying Hawk and David. It was exclusively their fight.

Both boys were badly battered and bruised, but neither was about to give up. Their strength and ability to fight was well-matched, and most of the people watching believed the battle would end in a draw.

Grabbing at Black Wolf's arm, and getting his attention, Alisha demanded, "Stop this fight!"

He pulled away from her grasp. "I can't," he remarked flatly.

"Why not?" she insisted.

"Their honor is at stake," he answered, as though that made everything all right.

"Honor be damned!" Alisha raged. "If you won't stop it, then I will. Just look at them, they're both bleeding!"

Kicking Buffalo, walking up behind Black Wolf, overheard Alisha's anger. "She is right," he said to his nephew, speaking English. "The fight must be stopped."

"I agree, but how can we stop it without wounding their honor? We don't want to belittle them in the eyes of their peers. If we break it up, the other boys will laugh at them."

Kicking Buffalo thought for a moment, then answered, "I will tell Basket-Weaver to stop the fight. Supper is ready, and it is time for her family to gather around the lodge fire. A contest is no excuse to be late."

As Kicking Buffalo was leaving to get his wife, Alisha tried to brush past Black Wolf, but he grabbed her wrist. "Where are you going?"

"To your lodge to get the medical kit. Their cuts will need doctoring."

"Basket-Weaver will tend to them," he said, keeping his fingers locked about her wrist.

Forcefully, she jerked free. "She can take care of Flying Hawk, but I'll tend to David!"

"All right," Black Wolf relented. "I'll bring David to the lodge; you go there and wait for us."

She cast one last worried glance at David, who was then on the receiving end of Flying Hawk's jabbing fist; then she hurried away, hoping frantically that Basket-Weaver would arrive in time to stop the fight before one of the boys was seriously injured.

Chapter Seventeen

While Alisha tended to David's cuts and abrasions, Black Wolf took it upon himself to fix their evening meal. Although he usually had his meals with Running Horse, meals which were prepared by his father's second wife, Black Wolf was nonetheless an adequate cook.

Dabbing antiseptic on a deep cut above David's left eye, Alisha said irritably, "It looks more like you were in a fist fight than a wrestling match."

The medicine stung. "Ow!" David complained, drawing back.

"You men!" Alisha fussed, dabbing on more antiseptic. "You pound on each other mercilessly to prove you're a man, then act like a little antiseptic is unbearable." Studying the gash, she continued worriedly, "I'm afraid this cut is deep enough to leave a scar."

"Good!" David remarked. "Now maybe people will notice my scar, instead of my eyes."

Baffled, Alisha questioned, "Why do you say that?"

"I despise my eyes," he grumbled. "They look too girlish!"

Alisha smiled. "David, you have beautiful eyes.

Their color is a perfect emerald-green, and your black lashes are so thick and long that they actually curl on the ends."

"That's why they look so damned sissified," David mumbled, obviously disgusted.

Alisha knew that someday his eyes would have the power to melt a woman's heart, but realizing this knowledge would bring him no comfort at his age, she dropped the subject.

Black Wolf, sitting at the fire and keeping a watch on supper, had overheard David's remarks. He regarded the boy thoughtfully as Alisha finished tending to his wounds. Black Wolf could see that David was not only going to be an extremely handsome man, but also a brave and intelligent one. He would grow into the kind of man that a father could be proud of. Again, Black Wolf hoped that if he had a son, he'd have David's admirable qualities.

Closing the medical kit, Alisha asked, "David, why did you let Flying Hawk persuade you to fight?"

"He didn't," David answered. "I wanted to fight just as badly as he did."

"But why?" she demanded.

"I wanted to show him I could fight," he remarked, as though his reply made everything crystal-clear.

"Alisha," Black Wolf spoke up. "It's important for a boy to learn how to fight. Then, when he becomes a man, he can defend himself."

She looked up at him doubtfully. "You men always resort to violence to settle disputes. Haven't you ever heard of diplomacy?"

Black Wolf chortled. "I'll remember that the next time I'm engaged in hand-to-hand combat. I'll see if I can whip my opponent with words."

Taking sides with Black Wolf, David also laughed.

"Maybe you can *talk* him into a state of unconsciousness."

Alisha didn't want to smile, but she couldn't help herself. "All right," she conceded. "You two made your point."

At that moment Flying Hawk's shadow fell across the kerosene-lit interior.

Seeing the boy standing at the open entrance, Black Wolf said, "Come in."

Entering, Flying Hawk's gaze went straight to David. "My mother waits to serve supper."

"You'd better leave," Black Wolf told David. "It's impolite to keep Basket-Weaver waiting."

David was reluctant. He dreaded returning to Kicking Buffalo's lodge. He supposed it wouldn't be so bad if Flying Hawk lived elsewhere. Slowly, he got to his feet, and as his eyes swept over the other boy's face, he was pleased to note that it was as battered as his own.

David went to the open flap, then turning, he bade Alisha and Black Wolf good night. Bending over, he stepped outside. Flying Hawk was directly behind him.

As the boys left, Alisha stood up and darted out of the tepee. Pausing, she watched David and Flying Hawk as they headed toward Kicking Buffalo's lodge. If they got into a fight, she was determined to break it up.

Keeping his strides even with David's, Flying Hawk mumbled, "The next time we fight, there will be no one to stop it."

David gave him a sidelong glance. "I'm ready for a rematch any time you are."

"When the time comes, we will leave the village. No one will know where to find us. Then we will fight until one gives up." He turned to look at David, who met his hard gaze. "Or, maybe, we will fight to the death!"

"You must want to die young," David retorted, undaunted.

Although Flying Hawk found the white boy's intrepid courage bothersome, he was nonetheless impressed. The Sioux respected bravery, even in their enemies. However, this admiration didn't discourage Flying Hawk from riling David. Grinning cunningly, he declared, "My friends and I, we have chosen a name for you."

"I already have a name," David replied.

"A white man's name!" Flying Hawk said with distaste. "A name should mean something. This David, what does it mean?"

"It's a Biblical name. And it's better than being called a flying hawk. Hawks are sneaky chicken eaters and should be shot."

Offended, Flying Hawk replied sharply, "It is an honor to be named for the hawk, and I bear my name proudly. How will you bear yours, Squaw Eyes?"

"What did you call me?" David shouted, stopping in his tracks and doubling his hands into fists.

"You are to be called Squaw Eyes," he said, laughing.

They were very close to their lodge, and, at that moment, Kicking Buffalo stepped outside. The warrior's presence brought their brewing fight to an abrupt halt.

"Come inside," Kicking Buffalo ordered gruffly, his tone brooking no argument.

Alisha, still standing in front of her tepee, was able to see the boys and Kicking Buffalo. When the boys went inside with the man close on their heels, she sighed gratefully. At least for now, there would be no more fighting.

Stepping outside to join her, Black Wolf said, "Are

you ready for dinner?"

"Yes, I'm starved," she answered.

He took her arm to lead her back inside, but an old man moving slowly past their tepee caught Alisha's attention. He was wearing the usual buckskins, and his long gray hair was braided, but it wasn't the man's appearance that had caught Alisha's eye so much as the strange way he was looking at her. The hard bitterness on his wrinkled face sent a chill up her spine. But when he glanced away from her to look at Black Wolf, the resentment faded and was replaced with a pleasant smile.

As the old man moved farther away, Alisha asked, "Who is he?"

Watching his departure, Black Wolf answered, "Chief Iron Kettle."

"If he's a chief, why is he here in Running Horse's village?"

"He's no longer a chief. It's now an honorary title. He once had his own village and it was quite large. Two Moons was one of his warriors. Because Iron Kettle agreed to the Fort Laramie Treaty and wanted to avoid warfare with the Army, Two Moons rebelled. He left Iron Kettle's village, inciting the majority of the warriors to leave with him."

"Why did Iron Kettle look at me as though he hated me?"

"His hate was not aimed at you personally. But you're white and he has a lot of animosity for your people. He tried relentlessly to keep peace with the cavalry, and in return, a battalion of soldiers butchered his village. Since he had lost most of his people to Two Moons, his warriors were badly outnumbered by the soldiers. Flying Hawk's parents were killed in that massacre."

"Why did the soldiers attack?"

189

"They were led by Captain Newcomb, who took it upon himself to butcher Iron Kettle's village. It was not an order from his superiors. He would've been court-martialed if he hadn't been killed in the attack."

"Who killed him?"

"Flying Hawk. He and his mother, Prairie Flower, were in the midst of action, and Captain Newcomb shot at them. He missed Flying Hawk but killed Prairie Flower. Flying Hawk had his father's rifle, and he shot the captain."

"Then Flying Hawk saw his mother die?"

"Yes, and after the massacre, he swore that someday he'd revenge his parents' deaths by proclaiming war on all soldiers."

"Why did this Captain Newcomb attack Iron Kettle's village?"

"He was a firm believer that the only good Indian is a dead one." Dismally, he added, "His belief was not unique but is shared by other army officers." His eyes, filled with sadness, swept over the peaceful Sioux village, and as an infant's cry sounded softly, Black Wolf whispered so quietly that Alisha barely heard his words. "Have you noticed that an Indian baby's cry is no different than a white baby's?"

"What point are you making?" she asked.

"We're all human, so why must we destroy each other?"

"Black Wolf, during the Civil War, brother killed brother. If men can kill their own kinsmen, they certainly won't draw the line with Indians. Men will always find reasons to kill each other. And the Sioux are no different. Haven't your people fought with other Indians?"

He answered wistfully, "Of course we have."

"War is a vicious circle, and there's nothing we can do about it, so let's eat, shall we?" She smiled, hoping to lighten his mood.

Responding, he grinned warmly, gestured for her to precede, then followed her inside.

Following dinner, Black Wolf took a bucket and went to the river which flowed placidly at the edge of the village. He filled the container, then returned to his lodge and placed the bucket beside the fire.

"You can heat this water if you want to wash up before going to bed," he told Alisha. Then turning to leave, he said with a disarming smile, "I'll make myself scarce so you can have privacy."

"Thank you," she replied.

Alone, Alisha quickly set about heating the water, then stripping, she enjoyed a sponge bath, scrubbing herself thoroughly. Having nothing to wear as a nightgown, she decided to sleep nude, and going to the blankets that she'd spread out earlier, she lay down and drew up the top cover.

Black Wolf entered so silently that she wasn't even aware of his presence until she suddenly found him kneeling at her side. Without uttering a word, he slipped his arms beneath her, lifting her and the top cover into his arms. Standing, he began carrying her to his bed.

"Black Wolf, take me back to my pallet!" she said petulantly.

Refusing, he continued his course, and when they reached his bed, he laid her down somewhat roughly. Moving with incredible speed, he jerked off her blanket and dropped it to the dirt floor. Quickly she tried to sit up, but reacting alertly, he fell over her, pinning her beneath him.

"Let me go!" she demanded desperately, knowing full well she'd not have the strength to refuse his advances.

Keeping her imprisoned under his powerful frame,

he raised up on one elbow and gazed down into her eyes. The golden glow from the lantern flickered softly, making it easy for him to see her. "Alisha, why are you fighting me? What are you trying to protect? You already lost your innocence, and you can only lose it once."

"Maybe I'm fighting for my pride," she declared, although she knew her pride had little to do with it. She was fighting for her heart, for she didn't doubt that Black Wolf would break it into little pieces.

"I don't want your pride," he answered evenly.

"Then what do you want?" she asked sharply.

"Your cooperation would be nice, but with or without it, I intend to make love to you."

"Surely you wouldn't stoop to force!" she gasped.

He raised a brow. "I'll merely be taking what belongs to me."

"I don't belong to you!" she argued.

His eyes twinkled teasingly. "When living with the Sioux, you must adapt to their ways. You are the woman who shares my lodge, which means you belong to me."

"Will you please stop teasing me with your Sioux customs to persuade me to do everything your way?" Perturbed, she lashed out, "Black Wolf, you heartless cad! You'd have no qualms about sleeping with me all winter, then, come Spring, dump me like unwanted goods!"

"Dump you?" he repeated questioningly, his mood now serious. "I'd marry you if I thought you'd be happy living in my world. However, I think you'd always long for the life to which you have grown accustomed." When she offered no response, he insisted firmly, "I'm right, aren't I?"

"I . . . I suppose so," she stammered, wishing she could tell him he was wrong. But her feelings were too confused for her to understand how she truly felt.

Speaking plainly, he continued, "Now that we have that settled, I have another point to make. If you think for one minute that I'm going to live with you for an entire winter and not make love to you, then you are either very stupid, or unbelievable naive."

She was piqued. "I'm not stupid or naive!"

"Good!" he remarked, sounding impatient. "Then let's stop all this wasted talk and make love."

Finding his attitude callous, she began squirming and tried vainly to push him aside. Her movements were stimulating to Black Wolf, and when her hips arched toward his, he shoved his mounting erection between her thighs. Simultaneously, he captured her lips with his, and when she attempted to turn her face away, he moved his hands to either side of her head. Holding her still, he intensified their kiss, his tongue probing in and out. As his passion soared, he interrupted their kiss to let his tongue flicker across her lips. Then, again, he kissed her demandingly, and so passionately that all her defenses were swept away.

Alisha's arms went around Black Wolf's neck as she returned his kiss with a fervor as eager as his own. Aware of his hardness pressed incitingly against the core of her passion, she opened her legs wider to welcome the feel of him.

Black Wolf's lips now left hers to trail downward to her full breasts. Cupping them in his hands, his mouth moved back and forth from one to the other as he suckled gently at their taut nipples.

Then, slowly, his lips dipped farther down her slender frame, etching a blazing path past her waist and stomach before pausing between her alabaster thighs.

Such intimacy caused Alisha to tense up, and sensing her uncertainty, Black Wolf murmured soothingly, "There are more ways than one to make love, my innocent. Relax, and let me love you completely."

She drew a nervous breath, but grew still as his hands slipped beneath her buttocks to elevate her thighs. Slowly, expertly, Black Wolf set Alisha's passion on fire, and she was soon moaning with intense pleasure. Her inhibitions forgotten, she entwined her fingers into his jet-black hair, encouraging his intimate, empassioned fondling.

Black Wolf was reluctant to stop, but his need was becoming too overpowering, and leaving the bed, he undressed with haste.

Watching, Alisha's love-glazed eyes traveled over his handsome physique with deep longing.

Leaning over the bed, Black Wolf's powerful frame hovered above hers. "Guide it in," he whispered, his tone husky.

Gingerly, she reached for him, touching him there for the first time. He was rock-hard and throbbing for release. Sliding her fingers around his maleness, she guided him to her, and as she felt his initial penetration, she removed her hand and wrapped her arms around his strong shoulders.

He lunged suddenly, entering her so demandingly that she cried out with surprise.

"Wrap your legs around my back," he instructed her.

His request seemed odd to Alisha, but obeying, she locked her ankles about him. When his hardness penetrated even farther inside her, she understood the reason for the position and wholeheartedly approved of it!

Responding to the wondrous thrills Black Wolf was awakening within her, Alisha drew her man closer within the circle of her arms and surrendered to the sensations that were now all-consuming.

*   *   *

Alisha was lying on her back, and gazing upwards through the open smoke flap, she could see a great number of twinkling stars shining brilliantly in the evening sky. The kerosene lamp had been extinguished, but the night was clear and its shadowy light filtered softly inside the tepee.

Black Wolf, turning to lie on his side, placed an arm across Alisha's waist and drew her closer. "What are you thinking about?" he asked, wondering why she was being so quiet.

"I was thinking about us, and how easily I always surrender to you," she whispered.

He sighed heavily. "Alisha, I never meant for any of this to happen. When I first realized how attracted I was to you, I tried to keep my feelings in check. That evening at the river, you were so beautiful and tempting that my will-power completely crumbled. However, I still believed I could restore my will power and avoid any more such situations. If Running Horse was well, and if Kicking Buffalo hadn't ordered us to live together . . ."

Interrupting, she said crisply, "Black Wolf, you don't need to explain. I understand that our relationship is controlled by circumstances and not by the fact that it's something we both wanted." Her crisp tone belied her true feelings, but she wanted Black Wolf to believe she could analyze their relationship with a composure as cool as his own. If she were to confess her confusion and torment, he'd probably tell her she was being naive.

Alisha's feigned coolness was successful, and Black Wolf believed her as composed as she sounded. He wasn't sure why he found her unemotional attitude painful. Did he want her to declare her love and convince him that she'd be happy sharing her life with him, regardless of where they lived? Angry with himself for letting this white woman torment him so, he swore to himself that he'd not fall more in love with her. When it came time to take her home, he'd make sure he could do so without any regrets.

"We'd better get some sleep," he remarked tonelessly. "The Sioux rise early."

She rolled to her side, turning her back to Black Wolf. Snuggling, he drew her against him, fitting his body to the contours of hers.

Alisha fought back emerging tears. He hadn't even bothered to kiss her good night. Apparently, his affections were limited to his sexual drive; once that was satisfied, he couldn't care less about making her feel desired . . . let alone loved!

Chapter Eighteen

Major Blade Landon was seated at his desk and talking to his head scout when the young sentry announced Jack Stevens and his sons. The major was expecting their visit and told the soldier to admit them.

As the three Stevenses walked into the office, Landon stood, offered his greetings, then gesturing to the chairs placed in front of his desk, suggested that they be seated.

The scout was poised beside the front window, his arms folded across his chest. Speaking to the visitors, Major Landon introduced the man. "This is Justin Smith. He's Fort Laramie's head scout."

Jack nodded toward Smith, then asked the major, "Did Lieutenant Wilkinson explain everything?"

Leaning back in his chair, the officer answered, "Yes, he told Colonel Johnson and myself about your daughter's abduction and your request for a military escort." For a moment, he thoughtfully studied the elder Stevens. Major Landon was a handsome man, his build tall and muscular. Absently, he brushed his fingers over his well-groomed mustache. Then, clearing his throat, he proceeded, "The colonel has agreed to give you the escort."

Alisha's father was so relieved that he couldn't stop from crying aloud, "Thank God!"

Continuing, the major explained, "Lieutenant Wilkinson and his men will accompany you, along with Mr. Smith. I must stress strongly that you are to follow the lieutenant's and Smith's instructions. If you refuse to do so, they have already been ordered to terminate this search and return to the fort."

Stepping away from the window and taking a stance beside the officer's desk, the scout remarked, "Mr. Stevens, believe me, we understand how anxious you are to find your daughter. But you're a rancher, not an Indian fighter. I kinda doubt you know much about the Sioux or the way they do things. The best chance you got of gettin' your daughter back is to do as I tell you."

Jack regarded the brawny scout. He was dressed in fringed buckskins and had a full black beard which perfectly matched his collar-length hair. Jack didn't doubt that Smith knew his business, and he intended to do exactly as the man said.

"You'll have my full cooperation," Jack assured him.

Now that the formalities had been taken care of, the major decided it was time to get down to business. "Mr. Stevens, you need to send a telegram telling your men to meet you at Luther's Trading Store with five steers and three good horses."

Jack was puzzled. "Why?"

"If you're fortunate enough to locate your daughter, you'll have to bargain for her release."

Sitting stiffly, Johnny blurted angrily, "Oh yeah? Well, when we find my sister, I'll take her back, and if the damned Sioux don't like it, they can go to hell!"

Justin Smith guffawed. "You plannin' on takin' on the whole Sioux nation by yourself, son?"

Johnny resented the scout's laughing at him, but before he could come back with a snide remark, Clint said firmly, "Johnny, if you can't say something worth hearing, keep quiet!"

As his youngest son was sulking, Jack spoke to the major. "If I have my men deliver the steers and horses, how much time will we lose riding to this trading post to get them?"

"If you send the wire immediately and tell your hands to move quickly, they should be able to have the livestock delivered within two days. In the morning, you and the others will leave, ride to the trading post, and wait for your men to arrive. From there, you'll head for the Hills and into Sioux territory."

"Very well," Jack agreed. "Although I hate losing any time whatsoever, I'm sure you know what's best."

"Also," the major continued, "you might consider buying a few goods at the trading store. Blankets, cooking utensils, and trinkets. To learn your daughter's whereabouts, you'll probably have to buy information in the villages you visit."

"These damned savages must be greedy bastards!" Johnny grumbled.

Letting Johnny's remark pass, Major Landon proceeded, "It's already September, and winter will soon be here. Because of the approaching weather, I can give you an escort for only six weeks. If your daughter hasn't been found by then, you'll have to postpone your search until Spring."

Jack nodded agreeably, inwardly praying that they'd find Alisha before their time ran out.

Getting to his feet, Jack said, "If you have nothing more to say, I'll see about sending that telegram."

Rising and stretching his arm across the desktop, the major offered Jack his hand. As they shook hands firmly, Landon said sincerely, "I hope you find your daughter, Mr. Stevens."

Jack returned his thanks, then he and his sons left the

major's office.

As the sentry closed the door behind the three men, Major Landon said to Justin, "I don't think it's necessary for you to take the Stevenses to Running Horse's village. He refuses to hold whites as captives; furthermore, the chief is too ill to receive visitors."

"But Black Wolf might be able to help us," Justin pointed out.

"With his father ill, we shouldn't impose on him. Besides, it's a long way to their village, and you have only six weeks. If the woman isn't found and Mr. Stevens decides to continue the search in the Spring, then we'll ask Black Wolf for his help."

"All right," Justin replied. He moseyed toward the door. "Well, since I'm gonna be leavin' in the mornin', I reckon I'll spend the rest of the day with my family." The scout had a wife and infant daughter, and they lived in a log cabin at the fort.

"Justin," the major remarked, "you'd better keep a close watch on Johnny Stevens. He's liable to cause you trouble."

Reaching the door, the scout turned and looked at Landon. "I already figured that out for myself," he drawled. "Don't worry, I don't trust him no farther than I can throw him."

There was no shade where Bonnie Sue was working, and the sun's hot rays shone down inexorably. Pausing, she wiped a hand across her perspiring brow. She supposed she wouldn't find her present chore quite so strenuous if it weren't for her condition. Her pregnancy made her tire easily, and she was often sick to her stomach.

She went back to scraping off the flesh, fat, and sinew from the animal skin draped across a wooden beam. The skin had been hung over a graining log, which was stuck obliquely into the ground so that its upper end was waist high. Using a steel blade, Bonnie Sue worked diligently until the skin was clean, then reversing it, she tried to remove the animal's hair, but in spite of her efforts, the hair remained stuck.

Telling herself that she didn't care if the cursed skin ever came clean, she dropped the blade, letting the valuable tool fall heavily to the ground.

Shading her eyes with her hand, Bonnie Sue gazed at the meandering river. It looked so cool and refreshing that she longed to wade into the water and splash its wetness over her sweat-drenched body.

Heaving a tired sigh, she sat down on the grass, crossed her legs, and resting her elbows on her knees, cupped her chin in her hands. She was only a few feet from Strong Fox's lodge, and she knew if Warm Blanket were to come outside and catch her loafing, she would be punished.

As she continued to stare vacuously at the river, Bonnie Sue's thoughts were strangely unemotional. I'll commit suicide tonight, she decided calmly. I'll wait until the village is asleep, and then I'll wade into the river and keep going until it's over my head. I can't swim a stroke, so I'll certainly drown. No one will try to save me because everyone will be asleep.

As usual, when her thoughts turned to suicide, her better judgment tried to intervene, but this time Bonnie Sue didn't listen. There would be no miracle, no rescue. If she kept waiting for soldiers or white trappers to visit Chief Bear Claw's village, then she'd wait in vain. She couldn't even hold onto the hope that Joel might be searching for her, for he believed her dead. When Strong Fox and the other warriors had abducted her, they had made certain that no one from the wagon train would give chase. The warriors had also captured a Kiowa squaw, and Bonnie Sue had watched as they stripped the woman and tied her at a stake. Then, Strong Fox had made Bonnie Sue remove her own clothes and put on the Indian woman's. When he had slipped off her wedding ring and placed it on the Kiowa squaw's finger, Bonnie Sue had understood his tactics. Joel and the others would believe that she was the one who had been killed. Bonnie Sue had then been forced to witness the woman's slow, painful death.

"Golden Hair!" Warm Blanket bellowed angrily. The woman had a voice that matched her huge body, and her bellow now echoed resoundingly.

Springing to her feet, Bonnie Sue tried to excuse her idleness. "I was only resting for a moment."

"You no rest, you work!" Warm Blanket yelled. "I teach you lesson you never forget!" She darted back inside the tepee, then returned quickly with a long, sturdy stick.

The woman had beaten her captive on several occasions, but Bonnie Sue had a foreboding that this time would be the worst.

Warm Blanket stepped toward her slave with long, determined strides. Grasping the stick securely, she drew back her arm, then swinging powerfully, she brought the wooden weapon down across Bonnie Sue's narrow shoulders.

The violent blow sent Bonnie Sue to her knees, and biting into her bottom lip, she held back a scream. Crawling, she tried to get away from her tormentor, but Warm Blanket was not about to weaken. She raised the stick over her head and it whizzed through the air as she sent it crashing against Bonnie Sue's back.

The Indian woman's arm flayed wildly as she struck her slave time and time again. The inflexible weapon dug into Bonnie Sue's flesh, leaving deep, jagged slashes.

Bonnie Sue could no longer hold back her screams, and her shrill cries could be heard throughout the camp. Although some of the people disapproved of Warm Blanket's cruelty, there was nothing they could do. The white woman was a slave and belonged body and soul to Strong Fox and his wife.

Warm Blanket's irrational hate for her slave had erupted into a fit of rage, and in all probability she might have killed the helpess woman if Little Star hadn't suddenly arrived. She'd been in the distance playing with friends. But she had heard Bonnie Sue's screams and had come running.

Grabbing at her mother and pulling her away from Bonnie Sue, Little Star pleaded, "Please don't hurt her anymore!"

Warm Blanket's anger began to soften, but not her resentment, and while casting aside the stick, she muttered bitterly, "Hereafter, Golden Hair will live outside!" She turned about awkwardly, folded her arms beneath her heavy bosom and marched to her tepee.

"Please, Mother!" Little Star begged. "Golden Hair must be seen by the Medicine Woman!"

"No!" she refused emphatically as she entered her lodge.

Kneeling beside Bonnie Sue, the girl cried, "Golden Hair, please don't die!" At the young age of ten, Little Star didn't know what to do for her friend.

Bonnie Sue, on the verge of hysterics, whispered desperately, "Joel . . . Joel, help me."

Joel laughed boisterously, and his chuckles were so hearty that they shook his shoulders.

Loretta smiled; she loved the sound of his laughter. But then, she loved everything about Joel Carson.

They were having a picnic in a grassy area a few miles from town and were enjoying wine with their meal. Joel had indulged in several glasses and the potent beverage was making his mood merry.

The food had been placed on a blanket spread between them, and now Joel reached over and took Loretta's hand. As he looked her up and down, he smiled approvingly. Taking Joel's tactful advice, Loretta had retired her matronly dresses and had made herself ones that were flattering and colorful. Her long auburn hair was unbound, and the silky tresses fell radiantly about her shoulders.

Squeezing her hand affectionately, Joel murmured, "Loretta, you're very beautiful."

A becoming blush warmed her cheeks. "Thank you," she whispered.

He gave her hand another squeeze before releasing it. Then taking a chicken leg from the picnic basket, he bit off a portion, and as he chewed it he studied Loretta thoughtfully. For the past couple of days, he'd seriously contemplated asking her to marry him. They hadn't known each other very long, but since their first date they had spent a lot of time together, and Joel felt as though he'd known her for years. Suddenly he reached a final decision, and he laid the piece of chicken on his plate and moved over to sit beside her.

Placing an arm around her shoulders, he said softly, "Loretta, I've fallen in love with you." He spoke the truth, for he did truly love her.

Thrilled, Loretta cried joyously, "Oh Joel, I love you too!"

Drawing her into his embrace, he kissed her with deep longing, and sliding her arms about his neck, she responded ardently.

"Darling," he murmured, "will you marry me?"

She could hardly believe that he wanted her to be his

wife! She had never dreamed that someday she'd have a husband as handsome and as suave as Joel Carson!

"Yes, of course I'll marry you," she replied, her voice ringing with happiness.

He kissed her again, sealing their engagement. Then, keeping her held loosely within his arms, he told her of the plans that he'd been mulling over for the last few days. "I don't want us to live here in Backwater. There's no future here for me. Besides, I want to be a family man, not a saloon owner. Selling the Golden Horseshoe is no problem, for the bartender wants to buy it back. After we're married, I think we should winter at Fort Laramie. That way, we'll be there when the first wagon train comes through. We can sign on with the train and travel to San Francisco. Now that I'm no longer Bonnie Sue's husband, I doubt if her uncle will offer me a partnership in his business, but I'm sure he'll give me a job."

His plans for their future sounded wonderful to Loretta. Nonetheless, she felt a certain obligation to her teaching position. When she had accepted the job, she'd given the impression that she planned to stay in Backwater for an extended period of time. It hadn't been deliberately misleading; at the time, she had believed it so.

Hesitantly she said, "Joel, we can't leave until another teacher can arrive to replace me."

He smiled. "I think fate has stepped in and taken care of that problem for us."

She sat up straight and looked at him questioningly.

Continuing, he explained, "I saw Todd Miller the other night, and he told me that his widowed aunt is moving to Backwater. She's a school teacher. I'm sure she'll be more than willing to replace you, because Todd said that although she plans to live with him, she'd rather be financially independent. Talking with

205

Todd, I got the feeling that he isn't looking forward to taking care of his aunt. This way, she'll not be a burden on him but will be given the house you're now using. Todd said that she's due to arrive next month."

Throwing her arms about him and hugging him enthusiastically, Loretta exclaimed, "I can't believe everything is working out so wonderfully!"

"Believe it, darling," he whispered in her ear. "Fate is on our side, and from this moment forward, we'll be together. Nothing and no one will ever come between us."

Warm Blanket held firmly to her decision to make Golden Hair stay outdoors. Although Little Star had pleaded with her mother to change her mind, the squaw remained determined. As far as she was concerned, the white woman could now live with the dogs.

Little Star, realizing her mother wouldn't relent, had gathered up a stack of blankets and had spread them beside the tepee so Bonnie Sue would have a place to sleep.

Now, as the sun was dipping over the horizon, Little Star sat close to her friend. The girl's face was troubled, and tears stung her eyes. She was afraid that Golden Hair was dying, for the woman was losing a lot of blood. Little Star was puzzled; the blood wasn't coming from Golden Hair's cuts, but was flowing from between her legs.

If Little Star had been older, she'd have known that Bonnie Sue was miscarrying. Although the girl didn't understand what was happening, she knew the bleeding had to be stopped. Leaving Bonnie Sue and defying her mother, Little Star rushed to the Medicine Woman's lodge. It took much pleading on the child's part for her to convince the healer to help Golden Hair.

The Medicine Woman went to Bonnie Sue, and although somewhat reluctant, she began to tend to her patient. As she did so, Warm Blanket came outside and would have stopped her if Strong Fox hadn't intervened. In his own way, the warrior could be cruel; however, his cruelty was not as deeply rooted as his wife's. Unlike Warm Blanket, Strong Fox could feel a certain compassion for whites even though he considered them to be his worst enemies.

Strong Fox ordered Warm Blanket back indoors, and the Medicine Woman was left in peace to continue her ministrations. When she was finished, she returned to her lodge, leaving Little Star to look after Bonnie Sue.

Dusk had fallen, bringing a chill to the air, and Little Star covered Bonnie Sue with blankets. If only her mother would change her mind and let Golden Hair stay inside. The child sighed plaintively, for she had never known her mother to change her mind about anything. She knew her father would not intervene again; he had defied his wife once and would not disgrace her a second time, not for a mere slave!

Bonnie Sue had drifted into unconsciousness, but now as she came awake, she was gripped with pain. There didn't seem to be a part of her body that didn't ache unbearably.

Opening her eyes, and seeing Little Star, Bonnie Sue asked weakly, "I lost the baby, didn't I?"

The girl looked surprised. Baby! Was that why Golden Hair had bled so much? She nodded, answering hesitantly, "I think so."

Showing no emotion, Bonnie Sue closed her eyes and hoped desperately for sleep to return. Sleep was an escape, but now that she didn't have her pregnancy to slow her down, sleep would be a temporary escape; for as she waited for deep repose to take over, Bonnie Sue decided that as soon as her health permitted, she'd run away. When she had first been brought here, she'd attempted escape a couple of times, but her attempts had been in vain. Both times, Strong Fox and his comrades had found her and brought her back to suffer Warm Blanket's severe punishments. She had soon come to believe that escape was impossible and had given up. Bonnie Sue supposed it was still unlikely that she'd succeed, nonetheless, she resolved to give it a try. This time she'd take a knife, and if Strong Fox and the others caught up to her, before they could capture her, she'd sink the knife's blade into her own heart!

Chapter Nineteen

Alisha worked with care as Spotted Fawn taught her to prepare the meat that would be the main course for Black Wolf's dinner. Although the fowl's head and wings had been removed, Spotted Fawn told her that its larger feathers were not to be plucked. She then showed Alisha the proper method for spreading a thick coat of clay over the bird, while taking care that no part of the fowl was uncovered. Then the clay-wrapped bird was placed in the embers and covered with ashes and glowing coals. As Alisha built a hot fire over the food, Spotted Fawn explained that the meat should cook for an hour or so.

When she left, Alisha tended to the rest of the dinner on her own. Sitting beside the lodge fire, Alisha wrinkled her nose with distaste as she thought of the cooking fowl. She couldn't imagine the dinner being very appetizing, not with the bird's feathers still attached. If Black Wolf preferred his meat with feathers, then, hereafter, he could cook his own meals!

Spotted Fawn had brought some berries and nuts to go with the fowl, and before showing Alisha how to cook the bird, she had explained the best way to prepare the rest of the food. The berries were simple;

Alisha had only to sweeten them with maple sugar, and she carried out this task with ease. However, the nuts were to be pounded in their shells, then cooked in boiling water until the shells were all skimmed off. She did this, and while they were still boiling, she wiped her hands together in a final gesture and mumbled, "Well, so much for dinner. If Black Wolf doesn't approve, then that's too bad."

Alisha remained idle for a long time, then moving away from the lodge fire, she went to the bed and sat down. Her disposition was somewhat testy, for Black Wolf had left this morning while she slept, and he hadn't yet returned. He hadn't even bothered to wake her to tell her when he'd be back, and she had spent the whole day expecting his return. It was now late afternoon, and he was still missing. Was it going to be like this for the entire duration of her stay? Would he take off every morning, leaving her alone? If it hadn't been for Spotted Fawn's visit, she would have gone all day without company, for David hadn't even paid her a call.

Alisha began to feel depressed as she thought about Black Wolf and David. She had believed her company meant as much to them as theirs did to her. But apparently she'd been mistaken; otherwise, they wouldn't have stayed away.

Sighing dejectedly, she gave in to her gloomy mood. She lowered her gaze to her lap and absently toyed with the beads that adorned her dress. Spotted Fawn had loaned Alisha some clothes, plus a comb, brush, and hand mirror.

Alisha was so absorbed in her thoughts that at first she wasn't aware of Black Wolf's quiet return. But catching a movement, she looked up quickly and saw him standing just inside the tepee.

Looking her over closely, Black Wolf found her very

desirable in her borrowed garb. As she got to her feet to greet him, the Indian dress, which barely fell past her knees, clung seductively to her soft curves. Continuing his observation, he saw that she wore a pair of brown, high-topped moccasins.

"Where have you been all day?" she asked, her irritation obvious.

He regarded her with amusement. "Is that any way to welcome your man home?"

"In the first place, don't take it for granted that you're my man, and in the second place, how dare you leave and not bother to let me know that you're going to be gone all day."

He was carrying his rifle, and moving farther into the lodge, he propped his weapon in the corner. "You were sleeping so soundly that I didn't have the heart to wake you." He looked at her and grinned wryly. "Besides, you need your sleep so you'll be well rested."

"Rested?" she repeated, eyeing him sternly.

"I don't want a tired woman sharing my bed," he remarked.

"Sex!" she spat. "Is that all you think about?"

"Winter will soon be upon us, and during the winter months, there's little else to think about."

"Well, it isn't winter yet," she replied firmly. "Furthermore, maybe Running Horse's health will improve considerably, and you'll still have time to take me home."

Her unpleasant mood began to worry him. "Alisha, what's bothering you?"

"Nothing," she mumbled evasively, sitting back down on the bed.

He walked over and sat beside her. Gently, he prodded, "I know something is wrong. Why don't you tell me about it?"

"I just feel . . . I feel . . ." she whispered hesitantly.

211

"Go on," he encouraged.

"I feel rejected," she admitted.

"Why?"

"You left me all day, and David didn't even bother to visit."

He smiled tenderly. "That's because David was with me. I took him hunting. Our trip was successful; we managed to get two deer. I left them outdoors; I'll clean them later."

"You two went hunting?"

"Yes," he answered. "Alisha, we can't expect Kicking Buffalo and Basket-Weaver to supply our food indefinitely."

She suddenly felt foolish. "I suppose you think I'm behaving very childishly."

"No, I don't," he said softly. "I know your surroundings are unfamiliar and perhaps a little unnerving. Tomorrow when I go hunting, I'll tell David to stay here with you."

"No, that won't be necessary," she answered. "I'm sure David would rather go with you."

Placing an arm around her waist, he drew her snugly against him, then lowering his lips to hers, kissed her endearingly.

"How's your shoulder?" he asked.

"It's almost as good as new. I didn't think it would heal so quickly."

"It was only a flesh wound, even though it did bleed a lot." Again, he kissed her, then asked, "How long until dinner?"

"Dinner!" she cried. She had forgotten all about it. As she rushed to the lodge fire, she hoped it wasn't ruined. Kneeling, she removed the boiling nuts, then took the roasting fowl from the embers. Remembering that Spotted Fawn had said to break the clay that had now hardened in the fire, she took a cooking utensil, broke the shell and pulled it off. As the feathers came away with the clay, Alisha gasped with surprise. Sampling the meat, she took a bite and found the fare delicious and fit for any epicure. Glad that her dinner had turned out so well, she looked at Black Wolf and said proudly, "Dinner is ready."

Seated on his bed, David watched Kicking Buffalo and his family. Basket-Weaver and Spotted Fawn were busy tidying up after dinner as Kicking Buffalo sat beside the lodge fire, talking quietly to Flying Hawk. Never in his life had David felt so out of place. Firmly, he had come to the decision that if there was one place where he definitely didn't belong, it was in a Sioux village. He had nothing in common with these people and wished he was back home on the farm. Although he felt sorrow for the loss of his father, he couldn't help wishing the man had never undertaken this senseless trip! Thinking of the farm made his heart heavy with homesickness.

When Black Wolf suddenly announced his presence and entered the lodge, David was so glad to see him that he smiled widely. He felt comfortable in Black Wolf's company, for the man acted more white than Indian. David had enjoyed their hunting trip, even though they hadn't spoken much. When stalking game, silence was an important factor.

Black Wolf paid his respects to Kicking Buffalo and his wife, then turning to look at David, he asked, "Do you mind giving me your assistance?"

"Of course not," David said instantly. Leaving the bed, he went to the warrior eagerly.

Black Wolf gestured for David to go first, then following him outside, he said, "I need some help cleaning the game we caught today."

"All right," the boy agreed. Growing up in the country, David had often cleaned game and knew he'd have no problem assisting Black Wolf with the chore. In fact, he was looking forward to the work, for he wanted to show Black Wolf that he was as capable as any man. Today, he had taken down one of the deer, and it had made him proud to prove that he could be a successful hunter.

The man and boy worked nonstop until they had the two deer cleaned and prepared; then deciding to go to the river and wash, they walked a short way from the village and downstream. It had been a long, tiring day for both of them, and as they undressed and went into the water, their movements were slow. Black Wolf had brought a bar of soap, plus a small bundle of clothes, and after sudsing himself thoroughly, he pitched the soap to David.

Rinsing off and wading out of the water, Black Wolf slipped into a breechcloth. Sitting on the bank, he watched as David quit his bath. Joining Black Wolf, the boy reached for his discarded clothes, wishing he'd thought to bring a clean change.

Pitching him a piece of material, Black Wolf said, "Here; wear this. You'll find it very practical and unrestricting."

It was a breechcloth, and David looked at it somewhat modestly. "It won't cover much," he mumbled.

"It'll cover all it needs to," the warrior answered, smiling.

Reluctantly David slipped into the Indian garb. Sitting beside Black Wolf, he complained, "I feel naked in this thing."

Laughing heartily, he replied, "You shouldn't be so modest."

"Ma would turn over in her grave if she knew how I was dressed. She'd think it's indecent."

"Sometimes, what is decent or indecent is strictly in the eyes of the beholder."

"I suppose you're right," he answered, not quite convinced.

"If the girls in this village could see you right now, their eyes would gleam with desire."

"Girls," David muttered, his tone uninterested.

Curious, Black Wolf asked, "What's the matter? Don't you like girls?"

"I've never been around them that much," he answered, wishing their discussion would take another turn. He'd had no experience in this field and didn't know what to say. If Black Wolf wanted to discuss things like history or hunting, then he'd be on more familiar turf.

"How old are you, son?"

"Going on fourteen," he replied.

"Then it's about time you started noticing the fairer sex." He grinned, sighing audibly. "Women, there's nothing like them."

David looked doubtful.

Seeing his skepticism, Black Wolf remarked, "Just wait; someday before too much longer, you'll understand what I'm talking about."

David still had his doubts, but keeping this suspicion to himself, he quickly changed the subject. "Do you think your father is getting better?"

"I don't know," Black Wolf answered somberly.

"Then Alisha and I might have to stay here all winter?" He sounded unhappy.

Concerned over the boy's feelings, Black Wolf asked, "Is living here that hard on you, David?"

He shrugged. "I guess it wouldn't be so bad if Flying Hawk lived elsewhere." He looked curiously at the man. "Yesterday when we arrived, I asked you why I had to stay in the same tepee with Flying Hawk, and you said that you hoped I'd find the answer by myself. Well, I haven't been able to find it."

"I'm hoping that living in close quarters will make you two boys learn to be friends."

"Friends?" David exclaimed angrily. "Flying Hawk and I will never like each other!"

Black Wolf was not entirely convinced; he still believed there was a chance for Flying Hawk and David to befriend each other. Knowing it would be useless to try and get David to even tentatively agree, he stood up and remarked, "It's time to turn in for the night. I plan to hunt again tomorrow. Do you want to go with me?"

Grabbing his clothes and getting to his feet, David answered without hesitation, "Sure, I'll go."

"We won't leave as early as we did this morning."

"Why not?"

Thinking of Alisha, and how she hated being alone, he replied, "I plan to have breakfast with a beautiful lady."

David smiled. "Alisha is very beautiful, isn't she?"

Black Wolf raised an eyebrow. "Son, it seems you've mislead me and are beginning to take notice of women. However, you're gonna have to find your own woman, for Alisha belongs to me."

The boy laughed. "Oh yeah? Well, if I were you, I wouldn't be so cocked sure. Knowing Alisha, she's liable to tell you that she belongs to no one but herself."

As Alisha waited for Black Wolf's return, she decided to look over the contents inside the lodge. After all, if this tepee was going to be her home for the winter, she might as well familiarize herself with its possessions. The cooking dishes and utensils were stored on the south side of the entrance, while Black

Wolf's riding gear was placed to the north. These articles didn't interest her, and she merely gave them a cursory glance. At the rear of the tepee Black Wolf kept his personal belongings. Although she moved across the lodge toward Black Wolf's stored items, she was hesitant to look them over. She shouldn't invade his privacy. She started to turn away when a stack of books suddenly caught her notice. She hadn't seen them earlier in the day, for they were stored behind other articles.

It's no wonder Black Wolf speaks such flawless English, she mused. He apparently spends a lot of time reading.

There was a Bible placed on top of these books, and she reached over and picked it up. Knowing marriages, births, and such were usually recorded in Bibles, she opened the book and thumbed through it until she located the right pages. Then, taking the Bible to the kerosene lamp, she sat down and began to read.

The first page was a marriage record. Alisha was sure that Black Wolf's mother had written the information. Her name was Abigal Lansing and she had married Running Horse in the spring of 1835. The month and date hadn't been recorded, and Alisha figured the woman hadn't known the exact dates. There were no calendars in a Sioux village. On the next page, births were recorded. She read outloud: "Black Wolf (Charles Lansing), born in the summer of 1838."

Alisha paused, gasping softly. Charles Lansing! She knew a man named Charles Lansing! He owned a ranch a few miles from the Bar-S, and he and her father were good friends. Could this man possibly have been kin to Abigal? Her father perhaps? No, of course not, Alisha thought hastily. I've known Charles all my life and he's never mentioned having a daughter abducted by Indians. Nor has Papa ever said anything about it,

217

and if it had happened, Papa would have known.

Deciding the names were coincidental, she continued to read. There were two girls born after Black Wolf's birth. They had both been born in the winter of 1848, so apparently they were twins. Although they had Indian names, Abigal had also given her daughters Christian names: Hannah and Rebecca. She wondered where Black Wolf's sisters were, and why he hadn't mentioned them.

Turning the page, she saw that she had now come to where deaths were recorded. The first two names were Hannah and Rebecca, who had died of pneumonia in their infancy. Alisha felt sorry for Abigal. How tragic and sad to lose two babies! She continued to read, but here the handwriting had changed. Abigal's had been flowing and graceful, but now the writing was bolder and more pronounced. She was certain it was Black Wolf's. He had recorded his mother's death, stating that Abigal had died of smallpox in the summer of 1863. She's only been dead five years, Alisha realized. She didn't know why she had supposed the woman had passed away a long time ago. Maybe she had come to that conclusion because Black Wolf seldom talked about his mother.

At that moment, Black Wolf entered the lodge, and glancing up to meet his gaze, Alisha nodded toward the Bible. "I hope you don't mind my reading it."

"Of course not," he answered. "Running Horse gave the Bible to my mother as a gift. He swapped furs for it at a trader's store."

For a moment her eyes moved over his physique, which his breechcloth barely concealed. He had never looked more Indian to her than he did right now, and his savage reflection caused her pulse to quicken with desire. Glancing away so she could restore her composure, she decided to tell him that she knew a man

218

named Charles Lansing; but before she could, he pitched his dirty clothes in the corner and announced flatly, "Tomorrow you need to wash clothes."

She placed the Bible at her side, and as the name of Lansing slipped her thoughts, she remarked petulantly, "Is that another one of my womanly duties?"

He smiled. "Only one of many." Sitting next to her, he continued, "I plan to leave in the morning to hunt, but I'll have breakfast with you first."

"Obviously you think you're talking to someone who gives a damn." She was piqued. Why must he go off again and leave her? She didn't like staying alone in a Sioux village. There was too much animosity between the Sioux and the whites, and she feared what might happen to her during his absence.

Draping an arm about her shoulders, he coaxed, "Come now, Alisha. Don't get all riled up. I have to go hunting if we're going to eat this winter."

"Then let me go with you!" she declared, her enthusiasm building.

Instantly, he sent her spirits plunging. "Absolutely not. Hunting isn't a woman's duty. I've already explained that while you're living here it's important that you . . ."

She interrupted. "I know, it's important that I adapt to the Sioux way of doing things." Lifting her chin defiantly, she remarked, "What if I were to refuse and do as I please?"

"Then I would have to beat you."

He had spoken lightly, but there was a promise in his eyes that made her wonder if he was serious.

Continuing as though he hadn't just threatened her with violence, he said, "David's going hunting with me. I think I'll go to Kicking Buffalo's lodge in the morning and ask David if he wants to have breakfast with us. I know it's hard on him living with Flying Hawk and

219

trying to adjust to his strange surroundings."

Alisha was somewhat perturbed. She felt Black Wolf wasn't nearly as concerned about her as he was about David.

"Well, let's go to bed," Black Wolf said, stretching tiredly.

Agreeing, Alisha picked up the Bible, stood, and carried it back to where it belonged. As she placed it on the stack of books, the name Charles Lansing once again crossed her mind. She turned about to discuss the name with Black Wolf; however, he had followed her, and before she could utter a word, he had swept her into his arms and was carrying her to their bed.

Laying her down with care, he stretched out beside her, and responding to his closeness, Alisha put her arms around his neck and urged his lips down to meet hers.

Their need for each other was strong, causing their passion to build quickly and fervently. Black Wolf soon had her undressed and his breechcloth removed. Then, placing his body over hers, he entered her powerfully.

Immediately, her legs were wrapped about his waist, drawing him in deeper. Black Wolf's hips began to move rapidly, and meeting his thrusts, her hips converged with his. Equaling him stroke for stroke, Alisha responded with such ardor that Black Wolf could barely control his urge to climax. Managing to maintain his erection, he continued to make love to her until, wonderously, Alisha's body was racked with tremors as she achieved complete satisfaction.

Surrendering to his own completion, Black Wolf drew her thighs snugly against his and released his seed deep within her.

He kissed her tenderly, then leaving the bed, went over and extinguished the lantern. Returning, he lay beside her and held her close.

Resting her head on his shoulder, Alisha snuggled intimately. I'm falling more and more in love with him, she thought somberly. In the Spring when it's time for me to go home, will I be able to leave him? Alisha sighed deeply because she knew it was still too soon for her to find the answer. Could she possibly live with the Sioux? If she chose to do so, she had no doubt that her decision would break her father's heart. Furthermore, this peace the Sioux was upholding with the soldiers and white settlers was merely superficial.

Her thoughts racing turbulently, Alisha turned to Black Wolf, hoping he might be able to soothe her worries. She was immediately disappointed, for his even breathing told her that he had fallen asleep. As usual, he had satisfied his lust and was now through with her!

Agitated, she rolled roughly to her side and faced the lodge wall.

Her heavy movement brought Black Wolf awake. Turning and placing his arm about her waist, he asked softly, "Is anything wrong?"

Alisha had lost her need to confide in him, and still upset, she remarked sarcastically, "What could possibly be wrong? I've always wished I could leave my comfortable home for an Indian wigwam!"

Black Wolf frowned. She'd never conform to his life, and he would be a fool if he was to ever hope that she might. "You can always try praying for a short winter," he said, resentment surfacing.

"Don't you think I already have?" she retorted, though it was an untruth. "Why don't you go back to sleep? Obviously you're too tired to keep your eyes open."

Understanding the reason behind her sour mood, Black Wolf suddenly smiled. "Alisha," he began tolerantly, "I was up this morning before dawn, then spent the whole day hunting. I'm sorry I fell asleep, but I'm just so very tired. Was there something you wanted to talk to me about?"

The need to confide hadn't returned, and she wasn't sure if it ever would. Besides, what difference did it make? Discussing their problems wouldn't make them go away. There was no happy medium; he wanted to live in his world, and she longed to stay in hers. "No," she mumbled. "There's nothing I want to talk about."

Unconvinced, but seeing no reason to pressure her, he answered, "Then in that case, I'll go back to sleep. Good night, Alisha."

"Good night," she whispered. Although she tried desperately, it was a long time before she could put her mind at rest and fall into a deep slumber.

Chapter Twenty

Alisha was sitting at the lodge fire drinking coffee when Black Wolf returned from Kicking Buffalo's tepee. Alisha had expected David to be with Black Wolf and she asked after him.

Black Wolf looked upset. "He and Flying Hawk slipped off sometime this morning. When Basket-Weaver got up to start breakfast, both boys were gone."

"Why would David leave with Flying Hawk? He knew you were expecting him to go hunting with you."

Sitting beside her, Black Wolf poured himself a cup of coffee. "I imagine Flying Hawk dared him to leave, and David felt as though he had to prove he wasn't afraid."

"Do you think they are planning to fight?" Alisha was worried.

"I'm sure that's their plan," he answered, sipping his coffee.

"You must find David and bring him back," she urged him.

Although Black Wolf shared her concern, he knew that hunting game was more crucial than searching for the boys. Furthermore, if they were given the chance to fight exhaustingly, maybe their animosities would run out of fuel and begin to cool. Finishing his coffee and putting down the empty cup, he remarked, "I'll keep an eye out for them while I'm hunting."

As he got to his feet, she asked, "Aren't you going to have breakfast?"

"If I have to look for the boys and hunt at the same time, I'd better not take time to eat."

Alisha also rose. Touching his arm, she murmured intensely, "I'm worried about David."

He smiled reassuringly. "I'm sure he'll be fine."

Alisha wasn't so sure, and returning Black Wolf's smile, she replied, "Be careful."

Bringing her into his arms, he kissed her long and hard, then stepping to where he kept his riding and hunting gear, he put together what he'd need.

She brought him a few strips of jerky. "Here; you'll need something to eat."

He kissed her again, then left. Standing at the open flap, Alisha watched him until he walked out of her line of vision. Then, turning, she went back to the lodge fire. Pouring herself a second cup of coffee, she sighed wearily, for she had a feeling it was going to be a long day.

By the time Flying Hawk and David approached the hill where they'd planned for their fight to take place, the sun had climbed high into the sky.

Pointing to the summit, Flying Hawk announced, "We will ride to the top, then dismount and find out who is the better man."

David was impatient. He couldn't understand why Flying Hawk had wanted to ride so far from the village. He had been looking forward to spending the day with Black Wolf, and now, thanks to Flying Hawk, his day had been ruined.

"Why don't we just dismount now and get it over with?" David asked irritably.

Flying Hawk cast him a scornful look. "Do not be so anxious to die, Squaw Eyes."

Before David could pull him from his horse and try to punch him in the nose, Flying Hawk sent his mount loping toward the foot of the hill. His face flushed with anger, David galloped behind him. Squaw Eyes! How he hated that name! Flying Hawk would pay dearly for using it!

The incline was steep, and in a few places a little precarious, causing the climb to be long and difficult.

Although David knew it was important to keep a close watch on the terrain and guide his horse carefully, the arduous trek couldn't hold his full concentration. Flying Hawk filled him with such hostility that it was hard for him to think about anything else. This morning, the Indian boy had awakened him before first light, daring him to slip away to a place where they could fight without interference. David had accepted the dare without a moment's hesitation. After he thoroughly whipped Flying Hawk, maybe the Indian would leave him alone.

Flying Hawk was also giving the trail less concentration than was wise, for his thought were racing as heatedly as David's. He had disliked the white boy at first sight, and David hadn't done anything since then to make Flying Hawk have a change of heart. In fact, the more the Indian boy was around Squaw Eyes, the deeper his resentment grew. For some reason which Flying Hawk couldn't understand, this white boy had won Black Wolf's affections. Flying Hawk admired Black Wolf and looked up to him more than to any other warrior, and Black Wolf's friendship with David galled him. Flying Hawk was jealous of their relationship, though he was not about to admit himself capable of such pettiness.

Luckily the boys reached the apex without a mishap. They dismounted without formalities, and stepping away from their horses, they stood across from each other.

"We will fight until one of us gives up," Flying Hawk declared.

"Or is disabled," David added.

Before they could launch their attack, the horses, having picked up a dangerous scent, suddenly began to whinny nervously and prance with excitement. Whirling about, the boys started to race to the animals to grab their reins and restrain them. But the horses had made such a quick turn that they fled back down the trail as though they were being chased by an unseen demon.

As the animals wisely made their escape, a low, vicious growl came from within the dense thicket that covered the right side of the summit. The other side was a steep drop off, and fearfully, the boys began backing toward this side as their eyes stared toward the full shrubbery. Once again the deep rumble sounded threateningly.

David had no idea what might emerge from the thicket, but Flying Hawk was familiar with the deadly growl, for he had heard it before. Flying Hawk was scared and with good reason.

The growl was now a continual roar, and as the dark brown animal lurched swiftly from the thick vegetation and onto the open ground, David gasped, "A damned grizzly!"

The words had barely passed his lips when the bear, moving incredibly fast for its build, darted toward Flying Hawk, raised up on its back legs, and before the boy could budge, swatted him with its huge paw. The

226

strong blow landed across Flying Hawk's chest, knocking him to the ground.

The bear's sharp claws had slashed into the boy's flesh, leaving long, deep cuts which had begun immediately to bleed profusely.

For a moment David was not only paralyzed with fear but even incapable of lucid thought. Then, as a movement caught his eye, he turned quickly toward the thicket, expecting to see another angry grizzly. He was relieved to find that it was only a cub. He turned back to the attacking bear. It was still standing on its hind legs, and David knew that any moment now it would drop to all fours, then pounce on Flying Hawk and tear him to pieces.

David had never had to think so quickly, and it would be a long time before he'd mull over his actions and be amazed by them. The fact that he had decided instantly to try and rescue Flying Hawk would astonish him even more than his fearless deed.

David, certain that the cub belonged to the grizzly, reached down and picked up a large stone. Taking careful aim, he threw the rock and it hit the cub's head, landing solidly behind its right ear. Startled more than hurt, the cub bellowed loudly. As David had hoped, the baby's cry caught his mother's attention. Protecting her young, the bear dropped to all fours and rushed to the cub with intentions of nosing him back into the thicket where he'd be safe.

As the grizzly was seeing to her cub, David hurried to Flying Hawk and knelt beside him. Before he could assist the other boy to his feet, the mother bear had sent the cub away and was ready to resume her attack. Reappearing from the thicket, she raced headlong toward her two victims.

David, realizing there was only one way out of her path, stood and grabbed Flying Hawk beneath his arms. He dragged him to the summit's edge and shoved him off the side. The bear was now so close that David could feel her hot breath on the back of his neck. He jumped over the edge just in the nick of time, for he had actually felt the wind in her swinging blow ruffle the back of his hair.

It was a long way down the hillside, and as David tumbled helplessly down the dangerous slope, he doubted if he'd survive the fall. His body, rolling uncontrollably, pounded roughly over rocks and against prickly shrubbery. The fall seemed endless to David, and as his body became bruised and battered, he felt certain that he was about to die.

David hit the bottom of the hillside so powerfully that the breath was knocked out of him. He was on the brink of passing out when suddenly he was able to breathe again. Wondering if he had any broken bones, he sat up gingerly. Although there wasn't a part of his body that didn't ache, he had survived the fall without serious injury.

All at once remembering Flying Hawk, he got to his feet and looked about. Spotting the boy lying only a few feet away, David hurried over to him.

Flying Hawk was conscious, and kneeling beside him, David asked, "How badly are you hurt?"

"I don't know," he moaned.

Blood was still flowing from the cuts on Flying Hawk's chest, and removing his own shirt, David said, "I need to wrap this around you. Can you sit up?"

He was able to comply, and David tied the shirt snugly, hoping it would staunch the constant flow of blood. Except for the slashes the bear had delivered, Flying Hawk seemed to be in fairly good condition; like David, he was visibly bruised and cut.

Flying Hawk remained sitting upright. If he was well enough to sit without assistance, David hoped he might even be able to travel.

"We've got to get out of here," David remarked. "Do you think you can walk?" Cautiously, he glanced over his shoulder and looked up at the hilltop. He couldn't see the bear. He prayed she wasn't trekking down the path, planning to confront them again.

The loss of blood was making Flying Hawk weak, and he muttered, "Leave me. I do not have the strength to walk all the way back to the village."

"I can't leave you!" David argued. "There isn't a wild animal from a mile around that won't pick up the scent of blood and come to investigate. When they find that the blood is on you, you're dead meat."

"If I go with you and one of these animals decide to attack, how can you protect either one of us? You have no weapons."

Mustering a sense of humor, he answered, "Well, I'm pretty good at throwing rocks. Or didn't you see me hit the cub?"

"I saw what you did," he answered. Although he had been in the face of death, he had been aware of David's strategy, and not even his own possible demise had prevented him from being shocked. "Why did you save my life?" he asked, puzzled.

"Maybe I didn't want the bear to cheat me out of the pleasure of whipping you." Thinking about their perilous fall down the hillside, he added, "It's a wonder I didn't kill us both."

Flying Hawk frowned. Owing his life to David was a bitter pill to swallow.

Seeing his scowl, David said, "What happened today doesn't change anything. As soon as your cuts are healed, we'll still have our fight." Standing up, he reached down and helped Flying Hawk to his feet. The Indian boy was so weak that he had to lean against David to keep from keeling over.

Flying Hawk placed an arm around David's shoulders, then as David grabbed him at the waist, they started forward.

As they moved slowly, David remarked hopefully, "Maybe we'll run across our horses."

"As scared as they were, they will keep running until they reach home."

"Yours might," David replied. "But the village isn't home to my horse, so maybe he'll lose his bearings and decide to stop and graze for awhile." David had ridden the horse that once belonged to Walter Wyatt. "What do you think? Do you suppose we'll find him grazing?"

Flying Hawk didn't answer. In his mind, he could see the white boy's horse trailing his own all the way back home. The chance of it stopping was so remote to Flying Hawk that he didn't think it deserved a reply.

"What about that bear?" David asked. "Do you think we'll run into her again?"

Flying Hawk tensed. He knew that this possibility was not a remote one. However, he offered no comment.

"Damn it, Flying Hawk!" David fussed, aggravated with his companion's silence. "That grizzly hit you on the chest, not across your mouth! You can talk, so why in the hell won't you answer my questions?"

"My answers would not ease your mind," he decided to reply.

"Then keep them to yourself," David mumbled.

"I thought that I was," he remarked. Flying Hawk smiled before he himself had realized it. Quickly, the smile disappeared. Why was he conversing with this white boy as though they were comrades? He mustn't forget his deeply rooted hate for all the whites. Squaw Eyes was his enemy, not his friend.

Studying the trees that were standing about them in abundance, David decided, "If we see that bear, we'll have to climb one of these trees." Exhaling deeply, he continued, "I've never seen an animal as big as that damned bear!"

He turned to look at Flying Hawk, and catching sight of the blood that had already soaked through the shirt, David grew gravely worried. He was afraid if those cuts weren't sewed up soon, the boy would bleed to death. Time had become of the utmost importance, and David tried to hurry them along, but Flying Hawk was too feeble to manage a quicker pace.

Realizing that he was slowing them down, Flying Hawk said again, "Leave me."

"I'll leave you just as soon as I get you to Kicking Buffalo's tepee," David promised.

Black Wolf heard the horses before he crested the small hill and spotted them running in the direction of home. Urging the pinto into a full gallop, he quickly shortened the distance between himself and the fleeing animals.

Aware of the man's presence, David's horse came to a stop, but Black Wolf rode on past him and caught up to the other one. Taking its reins, he led the horse back to where David's was waiting. Then, leading both of them, Black Wolf began to follow the tracks the horses had left behind.

When he reached the hill where the boys had planned to fight, the two horses remembered the bear's scent and began to balk. Although Black Wolf tugged harshly on their reins, they refused to budge. Giving up, he tied them securely to a tree and began his climb up the path leading to the hill's summit. The bear had left, but her scent still lingered, and picking it up, the pinto grew fidgety. Black Wolf knew his horse wouldn't get nervous without a good reason, and he drew his rifle and placed it across the front of his saddle.

They reached the apex, and Black Wolf dismounted. Taking his rifle with him, he moved away from the pinto and began checking the ground for signs. It didn't take long for him to ascertain what had taken place. He hurried to the edge and looked down but couldn't see if the boys were at the bottom.

Rushing back to the horse, he swung into the saddle, turned his mount around, and hurried back down the path. When he'd been studying the ground, he'd seen a patch of blood and knew that one of the boys was injured. Black Wolf knew that even one swat from a grizzly could be fatal. Worried, he sent the pinto into a faster pace. The pinto was obedient, as well as sure-footed, and he reached the bottom of the trail quickly and safely.

Untying and grasping the reins to the other two horses, Black Wolf went in search of the boys.

Flying Hawk continued to bleed heavily, causing him to grow weaker and weaker. Finally, his legs buckled, and he fell to the earth in spite of David's efforts to keep him upright.

Kneeling beside the fallen boy, David saw that he had passed out. Determined not to leave him behind, David managed to grasp him so that he could heft him over his shoulder. Flying Hawk's size was the same as David's, and his weight was almost more than David could lift.

It was a struggle to get back up on his feet, but successful, he shifted Flying Hawk so that his full weight rested on his shoulder and back. David began to walk, but his burden was awkward, causing him to stumble. Regaining his balance, he pushed onward. He didn't know how much farther he'd be able to carry Flying Hawk, for he was tiring quickly.

David's strength had just about reached its limit when Black Wolf rode into sight. Seeing him, David sighed gratefully; then kneeling, he eased Flying Hawk to the ground.

Pulling up, Black Wolf dismounted swiftly and went to David's side. Looking down at Flying Hawk, he asked, "How is he?"

"I'm not sure," David answered. "He passed out a short time ago. But that damned grizzly swatted him a good one."

Black Wolf lifted the unconscious boy, placing him across his shoulder so that he could mount his horse. Then, cradling him in one arm, he picked up his reins.

Meanwhile, David had gotten on his own horse and had taken the reins to Flying Hawk's pony. Flying Hawk looked dangerously pale, and David asked, "Is he going to live?"

"If he does, he'll have you to thank," Black Wolf replied.

Knowing there was no time to lose, they sent their horses into a run. Although Black Wolf was gravely worried about Flying Hawk, his worry didn't stop him from being proud of David. In his estimation, the boy was an exceptional lad, and he couldn't have been more pleased with him if David had been his own son.

Chapter Twenty-One

Jack Stevens and his party were two weeks into their journey when they came to Chief Rain Cloud's village. The travelers had visited several Sioux camps, but this one was much smaller than the others.

Justin Smith's instructions were always the same. When they rode into a village, the soldiers, as well as Clint and Johnny, were supposed to remain mounted. Then the lieutenant, Jack, and Justin would enter the chief's tepee for a conference. The five ranch hands who had brought the cattle and horses to the trading store had joined in the search party, but they stayed a distance from the village and kept watch over the livestock.

Now, as Clint waited impatiently for his father and the others to finish their business with the chief, he was beginning to feel discouraged. The fear that they might never find Alisha had always been with him, but as their journey continued with no results, his fear grew stronger. He didn't want to admit that she could be dead, but against his will, the possibility kept creeping into his thoughts. Johnny was mounted beside him, and turning to look at his brother, Clint asked, "Do you think we'll ever find Alisha?"

His question only registered vaguely with Johnny, for he was preoccupied with a pretty Indian girl who was openly staring at him. She was standing only a few feet away in the midst of other young maidens. Her large brown eyes were shining with admiration as she regarded the white visitor. She was totally enthralled with the young man, for she'd never seen anyone quite so handsome.

Johnny responded absently to Clint's inquiry, "I . . . I don't know if we'll ever find her."

The other maidens moved away, leaving the girl alone, and seeing this, Johnny dismounted.

"Where are you going?" Clint asked.

"Don't worry about it!" he snapped. "You aren't my keeper!"

"Smith said to remain mounted, and he's not going to like you disobeying."

"Justin Smith can go to hell! I don't like the man anyhow!" Anxious to talk to the Indian girl, Johnny turned and began heading in her direction.

He had taken only a couple of strides when Justin and the others stepped out of the chief's tepee. The scout caught sight of the young Stevens, and moving quickly, he blocked Johnny's path.

"What in the hell do you think you're doin'?" Justin demanded angrily.

Eyeing the rugged man resentfully, Johnny grumbled, "I intend to speak to that Indian gal."

"You do and you're liable to get your throat cut," he warned sternly.

At that moment, a threatening and powerfully strong warrior walked up to the Indian girl and took a protective stance at her side. His feral eyes glared at Johnny as though daring him to come any closer.

"Who's that?" the young Stevens asked Justin, nodding toward the watching warrior.

"He's probably her father, and I imagine he's just itchin' to slit your Adam's apple." Justin grabbed Johnny's arm, and his thick fingers held him in a viselike grip. Lowering his voice so that only Johnny could hear, the scout said viciously, "Now, you listen to me, you horny little toad, while we're on this search, don't you do anything to rile these Sioux. If you do, all of us are liable to pay for your mistake with our scalps."

Justin released his hold, and although Johnny cast him a bitter look, he wisely kept silent.

Jack, standing beside the lieutenant, watched his son and the scout. He began to question his judgment in bringing Johnny on this mission. He was perfectly aware that his youngest son was unruly.

The two men returned, and as Johnny was mounting, Jack announced, "Chief Rain Cloud said that he's heard of a white woman at Bear Claw's village. He doesn't know how long she's been there, and he's never seen her so he couldn't give us a description."

Clint was hopeful. "God, it could be Alisha!"

"Don't get your hopes up too high," Justin cautioned.

Clint nodded agreeably, but although he knew the scout was right, he was nonetheless optimistic.

Going to the pack horse, Jack removed several wrapped articles that he intended to give to the chief. The information about the white woman had not come free of cost.

"How far is it to Bear Claw's village?" Clint asked Justin.

"Two days' ride," he answered, then moved over to assist Jack with the chief's gifts.

It was midday when the search party reached Chief Bear Claw's village. They had been spotted when still

236

some distance from the camp and were now being escorted by dozens of warriors.

As they rode toward the chief's tepee, none of the visitors took notice of the little Indian girl who was following their progress. Several women and children were watching and tagging along, so there was no reason for this one child to capture anyone's attention.

As Little Star continued to keep the intruders within her vision, her heart pounded with excitement. She hoped desperately that these men were Golden Hair's kin and had come in search of her. Bonnie Sue hadn't recovered from her beating and miscarriage. It seemed to Little Star that the woman's health was faltering instead of improving. The child was afraid that her friend was dying, but if these men were looking for her, surely they could make her well!

Reaching Chief Bear Claw's lodge, Justin told everyone to stay mounted. Then, as the chief stepped outside, Justin got down from his horse.

The scout and Bear Claw conversed in Sioux for a few minutes. When they completed their short discussion, Justin turned to Jack and the lieutenant and told them to follow him inside the tepee.

Little Star, watching the proceedings, waited until the chief had entered his lodge with a few of his warriors, Strong Fox among them. Then she moved furtively closer to the two civilians who had remained mounted. She took no interest in the soldiers, for she knew that none of them would be kin to Golden Hair. Thoughtfully, she studied the two men.

Clint and Johnny soon became aware of the child's intense perusal and turned to look at her.

Johnny merely frowned, and finding her scrutiny rude, wished she'd go away.

Mistaking the girl's interest for curiosity, Clint smiled indulgently as he looked with kindness into her pretty face.

Clint's friendly smile made Little Star's decision for her, for she had been trying to decide which man she should approach. Carefully, she walked up to the side of Clint's horse, and gazing up imploringly, she whispered, "Please come with me."

"I'm sorry," he replied gently, somewhat surprised that the child spoke English. "But I'm not supposed to dismount."

"You please come!" she pleaded. "White woman die if you not help her!"

Clint tensed. "What did you say?" he exclaimed, although he had heard her correctly.

"White woman dying," Little Star cried, tears filling her eyes.

"Where is this woman?" he asked urgently. My God, was it Alisha?

"She sleeps beside tepee. My mother make her live outside with dogs." Her voice breaking with a sob, she groaned, "Please help her!"

Clint could hardly believe what he was hearing. Live outside with the dogs! It had stormed last night. Had this woman been left out in the heavy rain? Dearest God, was she Alisha?

Tugging at his pants leg, Little Star begged, "Please come!"

Pitching his reins to Johnny, Clint said hastily, "If Pa comes out before I return, tell him I'll be right back."

Thinking Clint had simply been humoring the child by doting on her, Johnny had paid no attention to their conversation. "Where are you going?" he now asked, vastly curious.

Clint didn't take time to explain. Instead he followed the child. Little Star was so anxious to take him to Golden Hair that her steps raced.

238

Bear Claw's people watched the girl and man with amazement. They knew of Little Star's fondness for the woman slave and were sure that she was taking this man to Golden Hair. Many of them shook their heads with sympathy for the child. Her parents would punish her severely for doing such a thing. They knew Strong Fox was with the chief, so they looked about in search of Warm Blanket. She was nowhere to be seen, which was just as well, for none of them wanted to witness the scene that would surely erupt if Warm Blanket saw what her daughter was doing.

Strong Fox's tepee was located at the edge of the village, and as they neared her home, Little Star cautioned, "We must be quiet. My mother inside and she must not hear us."

"All right," Clint agreed instantly.

"When I left, my mother sleeping. I think she still sleeps. If Warm Blanket awake, she come outside to stare at you and others."

The child slipped her small hand into Clint's and guided him to the south side of the tepee.

Bonnie Sue was lying on a bed of blankets, and the covers were drawn up around her head, which prevented Clint from knowing at first sight if she was Alisha.

Hurrying to the woman, and kneeling at her side, Clint whispered desperately, "Alisha?"

Bonnie Sue stirred in her sleep and the top cover slipped down past her head. As her face came into clear view. Clint sighed with heavy disappointment.

Little Star had heard Clint say Alisha, and going to his side, she said, "Golden Hair's white name is not the name you called."

"Yes, I know," he answered quietly. "I thought she might be my sister."

Little Star was worried that he wouldn't help Golden

Hair, for he was looking for someone else. "You still help Golden Hair?" she asked, holding her breath.

"Of course I will," he replied.

Although they were speaking softly, their tones had brought Bonnie Sue awake. As she left the darkness of sleep, she thought she must be delirious. It seemed she had heard a white man's voice, but it couldn't be possible. It had only been a dream! Her eyelids fluttered open, and as Clint's face came into focus, she was so afraid to believe her eyes that she told herself she was hallucinating.

Clint's heart was filled with pity for this helpless woman. Her face was so pale and drawn that it had the look of death upon it. Her tangled, filthy hair was soaking wet, and he knew that she had been forced to weather last night's storm with only blankets for protection. Feebly, she moved an arm out from beneath the cover, and he was shocked by how thin she was. Clint placed his hand over hers and her flesh was so hot that it startled him.

"She's burning up with fever," Clint told the child.

Oh dearest God! Bonnie Sue cried inwardly. I'm not imagining this man; he's truly here! She tried to speak, but her voice failed. I must talk to him! she thought desperately. I must ask him to help me! Again, she attempted to communicate, and although her voice was terribly weak, Clint was able to understand. "Help me . . . please help me," she whispered pathetically.

He smiled tenderly. "I promise I'll help you, Ma'am. You just rest easy, because you're going to be all right."

Grateful tears streamed down her face, but she was too weak to brush them aside. Clint took a clean handkerchief from his pocket and gently wiped at her heartrending tears. Speaking to Little Star, he asked, "How did she get so sick?"

"Warm Blanket beat her with stick, make Golden

Hair lose baby. Then Warm Blanket tell Golden Hair she live outside with dogs."

Clint looked to the near distance, where five mangy dogs were watching his every move. His eyes hardened with anger.

Following his heated gaze, Little Star explained, "The dogs lay with Golden Hair and keep her warm through night. But dogs could not keep her dry. When it rain last night, Golden Hair get very wet. Please do not be angry at dogs."

"It's not the dogs who should be shot, but Warm Blanket!" Then, realizing he had thoughtlessly insulted her mother, he apologized. "Forgive me. I shouldn't have said that."

Ashamed of her mother's cruelty, Little Star lowered her eyes and made no comment.

Jack's spirits fell as he walked slowly from Bear Claw's tepee. Chief Rain Cloud's information had been correct, there was indeed a white woman in this village, but she wasn't Alisha. Bear Claw had said that this woman had been a slave now for over a year, and the warrior Strong Fox had confirmed his word. Then Strong Fox had announced that this woman belonged to him, but knowing about the five steers and three horses, he was eager to tell Jack that he'd trade his slave for the livestock. However, Jack turned down the warrior's proposal, which angered Strong Fox. Anxious to keep the conference peaceful, Justin had then explained that the steers and horses were only to be traded for the white man's daughter. Jack, concerned for this white slave belonging to Strong Fox, had offered him odds and ends for her release, but Strong Fox had firmly refused.

Now, as Jack left the tepee with Justin, he asked the

scout, "Do you believe the woman has been here for as long as they said? How can we be sure she isn't Alisha?"

"They don't have any reason to lie. If they had your daughter, they'd be right glad to trade her for the livestock. Cattle and horses are more important than a slave."

"What can we do to help this woman?" Jack was hesitant to go off and leave her.

Justin shrugged. "There ain't nothin' you can do, unless you're willin' to give them those steers and horses."

"You know why I can't do that!" Jack remarked firmly. It was then that he noticed Clint's absence, and stepping quickly to Johnny, he asked, "Where's Clint?"

"Hell, if I know. He left with a little Indian girl, but he didn't take time to tell me where they were going."

"Here comes Clint," Justin declared, catching sight of the man walking swiftly in their direction. Little Star had stayed with Bonnie Sue and Clint was alone.

"Where have you been?" Jack demanded before his son had a chance to offer an explanation.

"Pa, there is a white woman here, but she isn't Alisha."

"I'm well aware of that!" Jack replied sternly. He was upset with Clint for leaving and disobeying orders.

"I was with this woman, and she's seriously ill." A look of pity clouded Clint's eyes. "My God, Pa! She's been forced to live outdoors. I don't know for sure what's wrong with her, but she's burning up with fever. The little girl who took me to her said that the woman was beaten and also had a miscarriage."

Jack shook his head with sympathy. "The poor woman." He turned to Justin. "We must find a way to help her."

The scout said he'd be right back, and then he reentered the chief's tepee. He emerged a few minutes later and told Jack that he'd received Strong Fox's permission for them to visit his slave.

With Clint leading the way, the three men hurried through the village. Johnny had chosen to remain with the soldiers. He had no interest in seeing some woman who had lived with the Sioux for over a year. In his opinion, any decent woman would choose death over living with Indians; his sister was no exception.

Little Star was sitting beside Bonnie Sue when the men arrived. Clint stood back as his father and Justin went to the woman and knelt next to her. Both men were taken aback somewhat, even though Clint had warned them of her piteous condition.

Bonnie Sue was awake, and looking at them through fever-glazed eyes, she pleaded, "Don't leave me behind! . . . Please have mercy!" She had no control over the hard sobs that suddenly shook her pathetically thin frame. She was so afraid they'd leave her!

"Now, ma'am, you just dry up them tears," the scout murmured, as though speaking to a child. "There ain't no way we're gonna leave this camp without you."

The man's promise made Jack stiffen, for he knew the woman had only one ticket out of this village; a ticket representing five steers and three horses.

Justin was perfectly aware of Jack's reluctance, but he knew this was not the time to discuss it. "We need to check her over," he said to Jack.

Speaking for the first time since the men had appeared, Little Star told them, "Golden Hair keeps bleeding."

Jack and Justin exchanged worried glances, the woman's condition sounded grave.

"Ma'am," the scout said, blushing beneath his thick beard, "we're gonna have to have a look at you. But Mr. Stevens and me, well he's a widower and I'm a married man, so it's . . ."

243

Bonnie Sue's weak voice interrupted, saving him further embarrassment, "I understand, and I won't take offense."

"Thank you, ma'am," the scout mumbled shyly.

Her smile was feeble. "No—I'm the one who should be thanking you." Turning her eyes to Jack, she added humbly, "And I also thank you, sir."

Using extreme care, Justin's large hands went to the covers and drew them downward past her wasted frame. "When did you last eat?" he asked.

"I don't know," Bonnie Sue answered.

"Golden Hair too sick to eat for many days," Little Star explained.

Bonnie Sue was unclothed beneath her waist, and when the covers dropped past this point, the two men were immediately alarmed. Although Little Star had placed a thick pad between Bonnie Sue's legs, blood had soaked through and was shining a bright red.

"Do you know anything about miscarriages?" Justin asked Jack.

"Yes, a little. My wife had two of them. She should be packed and her hips elevated."

"First, we have to get her out of this village," Justin remarked. He drew the blankets back over her, then, standing, motioned for Jack to follow.

Before he could do so, Bonnie Sue reached over and grabbed Jack's arm. Considering her weakened condition, he was shocked by the strength in her grip. She was wild with fear of them leaving her. "Please, don't forsake me! . . . Dear God, I'm begging you!"

Her plea had sapped what little strength she had left, and her hand dropped to her side. Gently, Jack placed her arm beneath the covers. He groped for the right words to console her, but before he could find them, Bonnie Sue drifted into a restless sleep.

Chapter Twenty-Two

Loretta and Joel were sitting on the sofa in Loretta's parlor. She leaned into his embrace and kissed him with a passion that sent his blood racing. "I can hardly believe that this time next week we'll be married!" she exclaimed joyously.

Smiling, he replied, "Believe it, my darling." His lips met hers again, and while pressing her against his chest, he kissed her ardently.

Removing his arms from her, Joel edged a little way down the sofa and groaned, "Sweetheart, if you insist on waiting until our wedding night, I wish you wouldn't kiss me so passionately." He fidgeted uncomfortably, for it had been a long time since he'd made love to a woman.

Loretta felt self-conscious and silently chastised herself for responding so heatedly. Her determination to save herself for marriage and Joel's pressing need to have her before their wedding had been a constant strain between them. Now, feeling contrite, she wondered if perhaps she had been behaving childishly. Just because she was still a virgin didn't mean she had to continue to act like one. After all, she was twenty-eight years old and a full-grown woman. Joel loved her, she was sure that he did. Maybe it was unfair to keep refusing him what he needed the most, a woman who would love him completely. She had never imagined giving herself to a man who wasn't her husband, but soon she and Joel would be man and wife. Would it really make that much difference if she gave in to him a week early? Although she was somewhat naive, she knew that he wanted her desperately. She in turn needed him as much as he needed her, for Joel had awakened a passion in her that she had never known before.

Her mind made up, Loretta stood, reached for Joel's hands, and urged him to his feet. Gazing into his hazel eyes, she murmured lovingly, "Darling, spend the night with me."

Startled, he stammered, "But . . . but Loretta, surely you understand what that would mean."

She smiled sweetly. "Of course I do. Joel, I want you to make love to me."

"Are you sure?" he pressed her. "I can wait until our wedding night." He hesitated. "Although I must admit, it's becoming very difficult for me to do so."

Grasping his hand firmly, she began leading him to her bedroom. "I hope you won't find me disappointing. I've had no experience."

He grinned wryly. "I've had enough experience for both of us."

She smiled knowingly. "I just bet you have, you handsome rogue. But from this moment on, your philandering is over."

Following her into the bedroom, he said lightly, "You'll get no argument from me." She was walking in front of him, and catching her around the waist, he swung her into his arms. "Loretta Ingalls, you're the only woman I'll ever want."

"Promise?" she asked pertly.

"You have my word," he answered, then kissed her with such ardor that it seemed to take her breath away. Lifting her, he carried her to the bedside, placed her on her feet, and kissed her again.

"Let me undress you," he murmured, his voice heavy with passion.

Blushing, she whispered, "Joel, I'm afraid."

"Don't be," he said soothingly. "I love you, and I want to possess you completely, but I know how to be gentle." He turned her around so that he could undo the buttons at the back of her dress. Then he slipped the garment past her shoulders and let it drop at her feet. Moving her so that she was again facing him, he removed her petticoat and swept her into his arms and onto the bed. Quickly he took off her slippers, then reached for the band of her pantalets. Slowly, so her beauty would be revealed seductively, he slipped her final undergarment past her hips, down her legs and onto the floor of the bed.

His eyes filled with desire as he boldly studied her supple curves. Leisurely, he examined her full breasts, then looked downward to the reddish lushness between her slender legs. Bending over, he placed his mouth against one of her breasts and his tongue flickered over her nipple.

Loretta gasped as a fiery longing filled her senses. Lying beside her he continued his sensual caresses as his lips and tongue relished her soft, lovely mounds. Her passion was ignited, and when his mouth suddenly claimed hers in a demanding kiss, she responded fervently.

His need to consummate their love was now overpowering, and leaving the bed, he began to undress quickly. Casting aside her inhibitions, Loretta daringly watched as he disrobed, and when he stood before her unclad, her eyes became glued to his erection. She had never before seen a man fully aroused and was fascinated.

Returning to her arms, he placed his frame over hers. He probed gently, wishing he didn't have to give her a moment of pain. However, knowing it couldn't be avoided, he plunged into her deeply.

Loretta moaned and strained against him.

"Relax, sweetheart," he murmured.

She did as he told her, and as her pain magically vanished it was replaced with a pleasure so exciting that she began to arch beneath him.

Losing himself in the hot folds of her depths, Joel moved against her aggressively. Absorbed in his own bliss and aroused beyond conscious thought, he whispered with unforgotten longing, "Bonnie Sue . . . Bonnie Sue."

Joel was so engulfed in pleasure that he wasn't aware of Loretta's sudden tautness. As she stiffened beneath him, his climax was about to erupt, and while holding her tightly, he shoved his thighs to hers and sought total completion.

Kissing her lightly, he rolled to her side and stretched out. "Sweetheart," he said breathlessly, "you were superb."

Loretta said nothing as tears gushed from her eyes.

"Are you all right?" he asked, raising up to look into her face. He was startled to see her deep distress.

She sniffled and wiped at her tears. Leaving by the far side of the bed, she went to her armoire and removed her robe. Slipping it on, she left the room.

Joel was totally baffled, for he didn't realize that he had called her Bonnie Sue. Dressing hastily, he left the bedroom and found Loretta sitting on the sofa, staring vacantly across the room.

Going to her and sitting beside her, he questioned urgently, "Honey, what's wrong?"

She had never been so emotionally wounded, and as fresh tears came to her eyes, she answered shakily, "While we were making love, you whispered Bonnie Sue."

"Oh, my God!" he gazed, sincerely upset. "Loretta, please forgive me!"

"You're still in love with her, aren't you?" she asked, her voice quaking.

Rising, he stepped to a small table where Loretta kept his bottle of brandy. He poured himself a liberal amount before returning to sit at her side. He quaffed down the liquor, then said softly, "Yes, I still love Bonnie Sue. I'll always love her. She was my first love and my wife." His tone became anxious, "But Loretta, she's dead, and my love is in the past."

"The past?" she asked sharply. "No, your love isn't in the past. If it was, you wouldn't have called her name."

Joel slumped against the sofa, then murmured, "Loretta, if you can't forgive me for what I did, then we shouldn't get married, for you'd always hold it against me. It was only a slip of the tongue, but in your mind you'd let it fester and grow until eventually it destroyed us."

"Not get married!" she cried. The possibility stabbed painfully into her heart. She loved Joel and believed she'd never love another man. He was her life, her world! She couldn't bear the thought of losing him! "No, Joel," she said desperately. "I don't want us to call off our wedding."

"Then you forgive me?" he asked hopefully.

"Yes," she replied without pause. "I think I could forgive you anything."

He placed his empty glass on the coffee table, then taking her into his arms, murmured, "Loretta, I'm sincerely sorry for what I did to you. It won't happen again, I promise."

Loretta wasn't so sure he'd be able to keep his promise, for she felt that his love for Bonnie Sue was still very much alive. However, she accepted what she could not change. Furthermore, surely he'd eventually get over this lost love and truly put it in the past. After all, Bonnie Sue couldn't possibly pose a serious threat to her and Joel.

Camped a short way from the soldiers, the three Stevenses set about their small campfire. Night had fallen over the landscape, but Chief Bear Claw's village was still within their sights. Expecting Justin's return from the Indian camp, they kept glancing in that direction hoping to see the scout coming their way.

Justin had gone to the village to see Strong Fox and to bargain for his slave's freedom. The scout had agreed to do so because Jack had insisted, but he was sure that the effort was a wasted one. Jack had told him to offer Strong Fox blankets, cooking utensils, and several trinkets. Before leaving for the conference, Justin had warned Jack that the warrior would flatly refuse, because Strong Fox wanted the cattle and horses and would trade for nothing less.

"I wonder what's keeping Smith," Clint mumbled, anxious for the man's return.

"I don't know," Jack replied. "I just pray to God that Strong Fox will accept our offer."

"What if he doesn't, Pa?" Johnny asked. "What are you gonna do?"

Jack had no answer, for he didn't know yet what he'd do. His face was etched with worry as he looked at Johnny and merely shrugged.

Seeing his father's indecision, Johnny challenged, "Surely you aren't considering trading the horses and steers for that white squaw!"

"She isn't a white squaw!" Clint snapped angrily. "She's a slave."

"Slave, white squaw, what's the difference?" his brother ranted. "She's been sleeping with a Sioux buck, hasn't she?"

Jack cut in, "She certainly hasn't done so by choice."

Johnny's expression was one of distaste. "Any decent woman would kill herself before submitting to a dirty Indian buck. If you ask me, she probably enjoyed wallowing with him on his stinkin' buffalo rug!"

"Well, no one asked you!" Clint said harshly. "So keep your damned opinions to yourself!" Worried about Jack's reaction to Johnny's comments, he looked at his father hesitantly.

Jack was seething, and he had to call upon all his will power to keep from hitting his own son. A threatening rage glared in his eyes, and seeing this, Johnny instinctively recoiled.

In a desperate effort to cover his blunder, Johnny remarked hastily, "Pa, I know what you're thinking. But I wasn't insinuating that Alisha should kill herself. I mean, if she's been with an Indian, I'm sure that he had to force . . ."

Interrupting, Jack said between gritted teeth, "Shut up, Johnny! If you open your mouth again, I'm going to shut it for you!"

"Here comes Smith," Clint spoke up, grateful for the man's timing, for he knew his father's patience with Johnny had reached its limit.

Joining the Stevenses, Justin sat down and helped himself to a cup of coffee. He took a drink before commenting, "Strong Fox refused your offer. He said that if you want the woman, you'll have to give him the livestock."

Jack groaned. "Isn't there any other way that we can obtain her release?"

Justin shook his head. "Strong Fox gave you permission to see his slave because he hoped if you saw her condition you'd be compelled to help her. He figures you to be a man of compassion."

"I do have compassion," Jack remarked. "But regardless of my feelings for this poor, helpless woman, my daughter must come first. If I give Strong Fox the livestock, I'll have nothing of value to trade for Alisha. Which means I'd have to return to the ranch for more horses and cattle, and by then it'd be too late for me to come back into the Hills. I'd be forced to wait until Spring."

"Everything you said is true," Smith replied quietly. Eyeing Jack levelly, he continued, "So I reckon you're gonna have to leave that woman here to die."

"Even if I were to trade for her, there's no guarantee that she won't die before we can get her to the fort."

"You're right again," the scout mumbled dryly.

Jack felt as though Justin's eyes could see into his very soul. Besieged by guilt, he looked away from the scout.

Johnny, unaware of the tension between the scout and his father, said eagerly, "Hell, why don't the soldiers just ride into the village and take the woman!"

Smith looked at Johnny as though he were daft. "There's thirty troopers here and about two hundred warriors in that village. Now just how in the hell do you suggest they take that woman by force?"

"Actually," Clint began, "in a roundabout way, Johnny made a good point. Why can't the lieutenant send a messenger back to the fort? Then Colonel Johnson can send troops to Bear Claw's village and demand the woman's release."

Justin liked Clint, and he answered with tolerance. "In the first place, by the time all that could be arranged, the woman would most likely be dead. But

252

just for the sake of argument, let's say the colonel sends troops here and the woman ain't dead. I can guarantee you that the moment the soldiers attempt an attack, Strong Fox or his wife will slit the woman's throat. But none of this matters a good damn, 'cause the colonel ain't gonna send no troops."

"Why wouldn't he try to rescue her?" Clint asked, surprised. "Good God, she's a white woman!"

"Our government officials in Washington don't want a war with the Sioux. Not at present, anyhow. They're too busy seeing to it that the Army wipes out the Comanches and Kiowas, or places them on reservations. When they get that over with, then they'll concentrate on terminating the Sioux. Our government is not only shrewd but devious as hell. They got all the Sioux up here in the Hills where they want 'em. When it comes time to get rid of 'em, it'll be easy for the Army to round 'em up. Now these government officials have it all strategically planned, and they ain't gonna take a chance on war erupting with the Sioux over one white woman. They don't want any fightin' goin' on between the Sioux and the Army until they themselves decide it's time. Now, Colonel Johnson is aware of this, and he ain't gonna send troops into these Hills with orders to attack Bear Claw's village, 'cause he knows it'll anger all the Sioux, which might very well end in an all-out war. Don't get me wrong; the colonel is a decent, compassionate man—but he's got his orders and he won't disobey them. Sometimes an officer has got to turn his heart into stone."

"And sometimes a father has to turn his heart into stone," Jack declared firmly. "I'm sorry, Smith, but I must harden my heart toward this woman and leave her behind. Alisha's life is too important to me."

Justin nodded somberly. "I understand."

"Someone's coming," Clint remarked, catching sight

of a small figure approaching through the darkness.

"It's Strong Fox's daughter," Justin said, recognizing her.

Picking up her pace, the child hurried to the white men. Reaching the campfire, she looked directly at Justin, and then to Jack. "Golden Hair, she begs to see you both," Little Star began. "My father tell me I come and get you so you can see Golden Hair."

"I'm surprised the man gave his permission," Jack replied.

Justin wasn't surprised, for he knew it was another attempt on Strong Fox's part to play on Stevens' sympathy. However, he kept his speculation to himself. "Well, let's go," he said to Jack.

"All right," he agreed reluctantly. He dreaded telling the woman that he couldn't help her.

Before leaving to fetch the white men, Little Star had placed a lit lantern beside Bonnie Sue's pallet, and when Justin and Jack walked around to the side of the tepee, they could see her plainly. They knelt beside her.

Bonnie Sue had never been so apprehensive. Why had these men stayed away so long? She had thought they would come after her before it grew dark. When night descended, she had waited anxiously for their arrival; then as the darkness deepened and they still hadn't come, she had begun to panic. Dearest God, surely they weren't planning to leave her in this village! They had promised to help her! Bonnie Sue knew if they abandoned her, she'd not be able to physically stand it; furthermore, she was barely holding on to her sanity.

"Did you send for us, ma'am?" Justin asked.

"Yes," she whispered, her heart pounding anxiously. "When are we leaving? Please, make it soon!"

The scout cast Jack a sidelong glance. "I reckon it's your place to tell the lady what's goin' on."

Bonnie Sue looked over at the other man. Reading the truth on his face, she cried wretchedly, "Oh God, no! . . . no!"

"I'm sorry, ma'am," Jack groaned. "Please forgive me."

"No! . . . no!" Bonnie Sue grieved hysterically.

Little Star had been standing close by, listening. Now, rushing up to Jack, she said excitedly, "But Strong Fox say he trade Golden Hair for horses and cattle. Why you not trade and save Golden Hair?"

Jack had remained kneeling at Bonnie Sue's side, and reaching over, Bonnie Sue grabbed at his ankles as though she were humbling herself before him. "Dear God, give Strong Fox the animals!"

"But you don't understand," Jack attempted to explain.

Using what little strength she could muster, Bonnie Sue raised up enough to lay her face across Jack's boots. "I'm begging you! . . . Don't leave me!"

Jack groaned with defeat, and his wide shoulders shook with deep sobs as he relented, "I won't leave you." God help him, he couldn't forsake this helpless, pitiful woman! If he did, he knew he'd never forgive himself, and her pathetic pleas would forever torture his mind.

"Thank you! . . . Thank you!" Bonnie Sue cried, and Jack was shocked when the woman actually grabbed his hands and kissed them.

Embarrassed, he carefully withdrew his hands; then, giving in to his own grief, Jack cried hoarsely, "Alisha, please forgive me!"

Justin placed a hand on the man's trembling shoulder. "Stevens, I ain't never admired a man more than I admire you at this moment."

255

It took a little while for Jack to manage a semblance of composure. "You can tell Strong Fox that he can have the livestock."

"The soldiers have a buckboard. After I talk to Strong Fox, I'll have the lieutenant see to it that a place is cleared for the woman, then we'll take her to the wagon."

He merely nodded his agreement, and as Justin stood to leave, Jack started to follow, but Bonnie Sue's hand suddenly clutched at his pants leg.

"Don't leave me!" she pleaded.

"Ma'am, I need to talk to my sons; I'll be right back."

But Bonnie Sue was afraid that if he left, he'd never return. Irrationally, she begged, "Don't leave me . . . please!"

Conceding, Jack sat down close to her side. Glancing up at Justin, he asked, "Will you explain everything to Clint and Johnny?"

Smith assured him that he would, then left.

Bonnie Sue reached for Jack's hand and clasped it tightly. She had no intention of letting it go; she would hold on to this man for dear life! Bringing his hand up to her face, she rested it against her fevered cheek, and Jack could feel her tears. Gently, he tried to slip his hand from hers, but her grip tightened and he let her keep her hold on him.

Jack Stevens had become Bonnie Sue's lifeline, and she clung to him like a drowning woman holding desperately to her only means of survival.

Chapter Twenty-Three

The day was crisp and refreshing, with a touch of autumn in the air. It was a good day for working outdoors, and Spotted Fawn had suggested that she and Alisha sit outside while weaving their baskets. They had placed buffalo rugs in front of the tepee, and then had gathered up what they'd need to carry out their tasks.

Now, sitting cross-legged on the rug, Alisha worked diligently, but slowly, on her project. It was her first attempt at basket-weaving, and Spotted Fawn had assured her that she'd soon get the hang of it.

Since Alisha was a beginner, Spotted Fawn had chosen a simple pattern. It was a checkerwork design in which the warp and weft passed over and under another singly, then the rows of warp were placed side by side and the weft splints woven in and out for the width of the warp. The next weft splint, alternating with the first, would go under and over, out and in, in such a manner that the first would be held in place by the rise of the warp.

Although Alisha continued to give her work careful consideration, her thoughts had drifted to Black Wolf. She had now lived with him for over two weeks, yet they had made no headway in resolving their personal differences. Black Wolf had made it very clear that he intended to remain here with his father and his father's people, and even though Alisha was beginning to feel more at ease among the Sioux, she still longed for her own world. However, she now knew that she loved Black Wolf too much to leave him by choice. Surely they could find a way to compromise! Suddenly her eyes lit up with hope as a possible solution occurred to her. Why couldn't she and Black Wolf divide their time between her life and his? They could spend six months with his people and then six months with hers. That way, neither of them would feel as though they were alienating themselves from their families.

But would Black Wolf agree with her solution? Did he love her enough to meet her halfway? She paused. Why was she letting her thoughts flow so rashly? Black Wolf had never told her that he loved her, so why was she acting on the assumption that he did? Well, she decided, feeling somewhat depressed, if he ever professes his love, I'll tell him of these plans. If he truly loves me, then I'm sure he'll go along with them.

As her thoughts lingered on the man she adored, she sighed deeply. Yesterday, Black Wolf and David had left with a hunting party and were not due back until sometime tomorrow. She missed them both, especially Black Wolf.

Suddenly becoming aware of a commotion in the village, Alisha looked up from her work. She saw that quite a few people were pointing toward the edge of the camp. Placing her partially completed basket on the rug, she stood to have a clearer view. The sun's brightness was blinding, causing her to shade her eyes with her hand and squint in order to see what was happening. She gasped with surprise as she made out the shapes of two white men on horseback. The visitors, while leading three pack mules, rode slowly into the village. As they came closer, Alisha could tell by their appearance that they were trappers. Their clothes were a mixture of furs and buckskins, and both men had long hair and full beards.

Rising and standing beside Alisha, Spotted Fawn looked closely at the two trappers.

"Do you know these men?" Alisha asked her.

"Yes, they have been here before. They come to trade."

Continuing her observation, Alisha watched as the mountaineers pulled up their horses and dismounted. They were immediately surrounded by curious women and children who were anxious to see what goods the men had brought.

Alisha wondered if by chance these trappers would know if there was a search party looking for her. They might have run across the searchers in their travels. She was still afraid that Jesse Wyatt might have murdered her father. She was also worried that her brothers had ventured into the Hills in order to find her. Although she knew it was a slim possibility that these trappers knew anything at all, still she intended to ask them.

"Spotted Fawn," she began, "when the men have finished trading, will you please ask them to come to my lodge? I need to talk to them."

The Indian woman was uncertain. "I do not think Black Wolf would want you talking to these men."

Alisha frowned impatiently. "Black Wolf doesn't have the right to tell me who I can or cannot talk to." Pressingly, she added, "Spotted Fawn, it's very important that I talk with those men. It concerns my family."

The girl first hesitated, then relented. "I will tell them you want to see them," she replied. Spotted Fawn hoped that her cousin wouldn't be angry with her, but after all, Alisha was a guest and had a right to see whomever she pleased.

"Thank you," Alisha said warmly. She glanced back toward the trappers, but with so many people gathered around them, she could barely make out the two visitors. She hoped with all her heart that the men would know something about her father and brothers.

Alisha was inside her lodge waiting anxiously when the two men arrived. Spotted Fawn showed them into the tepee, then left so Alisha could talk in privacy.

The trappers were astounded to find such a beautiful white woman living among the Sioux. Alisha was standing by the lodge fire, and the men's eyes roamed appreciatively over her well-endowed curves, which her Indian dress clearly defined.

Welcoming them, Alisha said politely, "Please come in and have a seat."

They hadn't yet overcome their shock at finding her, and their steps were hesitant as they moved over to sit by the fire.

Taking a seat across from them, Alisha smiled. "I imagine you both are quite surprised by my presence."

"Surprised is putting it mildly," the larger of the two answered.

"First, before I explain why I sent for you, I think I should tell you how I came to be in this village."

They didn't say anything, but their interest was piqued, and they listened attentively as Alisha's story unfolded. She spoke vividly about her father and brothers; however, she wasn't about to confide her personal affairs, and although parts of her story were sketchy and lacked details, the men were able to draw a general picture.

Finishing her explanation, Alisha waited for one of

them to say something, but when they remained mute and merely stared at her, she continued, "I wanted to talk to you because I was hoping that you might have run across a search party."

The man who had spoken earlier smiled largely, then answered, "As a matter of fact, Ma'am, we did see some men who said they was lookin' for a woman named Alisha."

"How long ago did you see them?" she asked, astonished.

"It's been a week or so," he answered deceitfully. Nudging his companion with his elbow, he questioned, "Ain't it been that long, Doug?"

"Yeah . . . yeah, I reckon so, Sam," he stammered, wondering why his partner was fibbing to this woman.

Sam feigned a somber expression. "I'm sorry to tell you this, ma'am, but I got bad news for you."

"Bad news?" she repeated.

"Yes'm," he replied, lying through his teeth. Sam Malone was not only dishonest, but also calculating. His deceptive mind had quickly conjured up a ploy in which to trap Alisha. When she had been explaining everything, he had listened alertly; especially when she was talking about Jack, Clint and Johnny. Now, continuing, he told her, "We run across your brothers. They had some men with 'em; I reckon they was cowhands. Anyway, the one named Clint asked us if we had seen you, and we told him that we hadn't seen no white woman. He then told us to keep an eye out for you, and if we could get you home, there would be a reward waitin' for us."

"I regret cheating you out of a reward," she interrupted. "But as soon as Black Wolf returns, I'll ask him to find my brothers and bring them here."

"Ma'am, you didn't let me finish," Sam remarked, sounding urgent. "While your pa was searchin' for you, he was shot by the Sioux."

"Papa shot!" she cried, horrified.

"That's what your brother told us, Ma'am. It seems some of the men took your pa back to the ranch."

"How seriously was he injured?"

Sam pretended to be hesitant about answering. "I'm sorry to be the one to tell you this, but Clint said he was hurt real bad. In fact, he told us that he was goin' to give up lookin' for you and return home to check on your pa." The trapper managed successfully to look quite noble. "Now, Miss Stevens, I ain't gonna lie to you. My partner and me, we could sure use that reward money, but that ain't the main reason I'm offerin' to take you home. I ain't educated, but I still consider myself a gentleman, so I'm offerin' to help you."

"Th . . . thank you," she stammered absently, her thoughts on her father. Oh God, he couldn't be dead! He just couldn't!

"Well?" Sam pressed her. "Do you want us to help you?"

"I appreciate your offer, but when I tell Black Wolf about Papa, I'm sure he'll take me home."

The man's devious mind was on target. "But I thought you said that Black Wolf has refused to escort you home 'cause Running Horse is sick."

"Yes, that's true," she replied.

"So what makes you think he's gonna change his mind just 'cause your own pa is sick? To take you back, he's still gonna have to leave Running Horse. The way I see it, he's gonna have to choose between your pa and his. Now, just who do you think he'll choose?"

"I don't know," she whispered, admitting to herself that Sam had made a good point.

"Can I give you a little advice?" the burly trapper asked.

"Yes, of course," she answered.

"Why don't you just let us take you to your pa? That way, Black Wolf won't have to make a choice."

Alisha's thoughts raced rapidly. Should she do as Sam suggested? But if she were to leave with these men, would she ever see Black Wolf again? Suddenly, her conscience intruded, impaling her with guilt. Why was she worrying about Black Wolf? Her thoughts should be solely with her father!

"Miss Stevens," Sam began. "I don't think it's right for you to be stayin' here. After all, the Sioux shot your pa, and you shouldn't be so friendly with 'em."

Sam's words caused Alisha to feel even more guilt; that had been his intent.

"All right," Alisha decided. "I'll leave with you."

Victorious, the trapper smiled inwardly. "It might be best if these Indians don't know you're plannin' to leave with us. Doug and me will camp 'bout a mile to the east. An hour or so before daylight, can you manage to get a horse and slip off to our camp?"

"Yes, I can," she assured him.

"Good!" he remarked. "We'll be waitin' for you." He got to his feet, and his companion did the same. "If we travel fast and hard, we can reach your ranch in seven, maybe eight days."

Alisha didn't rise to show them out; she felt too emotionally weak to make the effort.

Again, Sam made a point of telling her that he'd see her at the camp, then he and Doug left.

As the two trappers headed toward their horses and mules, Doug asked pressingly, "Why did you tell her all them lies?"

Sam guffawed heartily. "This is one winter we ain't gonna be closed up in our cabin without a woman to pleasure us."

"You mean we're gonna keep her?"

"Why the hell not?" he questioned eagerly.

263

"But what if we get caught?"

"Whose gonna catch us? If her brothers are lookin' for her, they're gonna be searchin' Sioux villages." He grinned complacently. "I bet you they'll ride into one village too many and that'll be the end of 'em. Some of these Sioux shoot white men on sight; Two Moons, for instance."

Doug agreed. "You're right, Sam. If anyone is lookin' for the woman, they're probably dead by now." He grew a little worried. "But what about Black Wolf? Do you reckon he'll come after her?"

Black Wolf was the only flaw in Sam's ploy, and the man feared that the warrior might foul up his scheme. However, it was a risk he was willing to take.

Early the next morning, Alisha was relatively sure that she'd encounter no problems slipping away from the Indian camp, for she was treated as a guest and was not under guard. Her own clothes had been ruined during her long, difficult trip to Running Horse's village, so she had no choice but to wear one of the outfits that Spotted Fawn had loaned her. She chose a simple suede dress with fringed leggings, plus a buffalo robe, for the nights were chilly. She gathered up a few personal belongings and her riding gear, then leaving the tepee, she hurried to the gelding that had belonged to Joe Wyatt. The horse, standing apart from the Indian ponies, was grazing quietly. He was familiar with Alisha's scent and didn't balk or run when she approached. She had him saddled quickly, and after securing her belongings, she mounted, turned him about, and headed east.

Alisha tried to keep Black Wolf from her thoughts as she traveled toward the trappers' camp. She didn't want to think about him or try to imagine what he'd do when he returned home to find her gone. Would he come after her? In a way, she hoped he would, for it would prove his love. But in another way, she hoped that he wouldn't pursue her. He might refuse to take her to her father, and, dear God, how could she go all winter not knowing if her father was alive or dead? It would be more than she could bear!

As Alisha had sat through the long night, waiting for the time to leave, she couldn't be sure if she was doing the right thing. But now, as her horse's long strides took her closer to the trappers, she decided that she had made the correct decision. This way, Black Wolf wouldn't be forced to choose between her father and his. The thought that she might never see Black Wolf again brought a surge of tears to her eyes. Blinking them back, she told herself that if he truly loved her, someday, when the time was right, he'd find her.

Dawn was still an hour away, and a distant flickering light gleamed in the darkness. Looking closely, Alisha saw that the brightness was coming from the trappers' campfire. As she drew nearer, she could detect the aroma of freshly brewed coffee.

Doug and Sam were aware of Alisha's arrival, and as she rode into camp, they were waiting for her.

Stepping to her horse, Sam assisted her from the saddle. "Would you like a cup of coffee before we pull out?"

"Yes, thank you," she answered. Glancing up into his bearded face, she favored him with a warm smile, for she was quite impressed with the man's gentleness and integrity.

Doug poured the coffee and brought it to her. Then, as she sipped the hot beverage, the men set about breaking camp.

They had the task finished in quick order, and the eastern horizon was still pitch black when Alisha and her companions rode out.

Alisha was extremely tired, and giving in to her fatigue, she gave no thought to the direction the trappers had taken. As she kept her horse plodding alongside Sam's, she was totally unaware of the men's treachery until the sun began its ascent.

Shaking off her lethargy, she straightened her posture and sat upright. Looking away from the rising sun, she turned to Sam. "We're heading north!" she exclaimed.

He grinned slyly. "That's right."

"But we should be headed southeast!"

Doug was riding a short way in front of them, and Sam called, "Did you hear that, Doug? The lady says we're goin' the wrong way."

Glancing over his shoulder, he smiled at Alisha. "We're headed for Canada."

"Canada!" she gasped.

"We got us a trappin' cabin up there on the border," Sam explained. "It's so damned far away from civilization that we don't see another soul all winter. Them winter months are long and cold without a woman to cuddle with." He laughed. "But this will be one winter when Doug and me are gonna have a little woman to keep us warm."

Alisha's eyes flared angrily. "You lying, dirty . . ."

His hand shot out and grabbed her arm. Squeezing painfully, he threatened harshly, "Let's get one thing straight right now. If you don't keep a civil tongue, I'm gonna knock you around until you learn to behave! I won't tolerate no woman talkin' back to me!"

He removed his large hand, and her arm actually ached from his brutal grasp. Grimacing, she remarked sharply, "You didn't see my brothers after all. Everything you told me was a lie!"

"I ain't never laid eyes on your brothers. But if they

266

was crazy enough to come into these Hills, they're probably dead by now. So if you're hopin' they might rescue you, then you're hopin' for somethin' that ain't gonna happen."

"Maybe they won't save me, but Black Wolf will!" She had spouted the threat impulsively, and it wasn't until the words had passed her lips that she wondered if her threat was hollow. Would Black Wolf try to find her? Did he know these two men enough to realize that they had tricked her? Or would he be so angry at her for running away that he'd leave her to her fate?

"I ain't scared of Black Wolf," Sam lied. Truthfully, he considered Black Wolf a serious threat and was hoping the warrior wouldn't decide to come after the woman. Abducting Alisha carried a certain amount of risk, and Sam was fully aware of the danger involved. However, he was determined to keep Alisha and would face any consequences should they arise.

Chapter Twenty-Four

Jack placed a hand on Bonnie Sue's brow and checked her fever. She felt considerably cooler, and he began to be more optimistic about her condition. She had been under his care now for two days, and more than once he had feared she was dying.

Justin, along with Clint's help, had used blankets to erect a shelter for the buckboard, affording Bonnie Sue some privacy.

Jack had ridden in the wagon since they had left Chief Bear Claw's village. A couple of times when Bonnie Sue had been sleeping, he had attempted to take a break and let Justin or Clint stay with the woman, but both times she had somehow sensed his departure; awakening, she had deliriously begged him not to leave her. Jack soon realized that for some reason he had become this woman's life line, and she clung to him with all her might.

Now, as the buckboard suddenly rolled over a large rock, the rough jolt shook its foundation, waking Bonnie Sue.

Her eyes open wide, she looked quickly to her side, and seeing Jack, smiled.

She had a pretty smile, and Jack knew that if she

weren't so thin and ill she'd be a beautiful woman. Looking into her eyes, he was pleased to note that they were now lucid. "How do you feel?" he asked.

"I think I'm beginning to feel better." Her smile deepened. "I'm hungry. Is that a good sign?"

A large grin spread across Jack's rugged face. "You bet that's a good sign!" Parting the hanging blanket so that he could see outside, he saw Clint riding at the rear of the wagon. "Tell Justin we're going to stop here for lunch. The lady says she's hungry."

As Clint rode past the buckboard to find Justin, Jack started to reposition the blanket but was deterred by Bonnie Sue's voice: "Please, leave it open. I want to see the sunshine."

"It's a lovely day, ma'am," Jack said, spreading the cover even wider so that more sunlight could enter.

"You don't have to call me ma'am. My name is Bonnie Sue."

The wagon came to a slow stop, and they could hear the lieutenant issuing orders as the men dismounted for a lunch break.

"Bonnie Sue." Jack said the name thoughtfully. "What's your last name?"

"Carson," she replied.

Joel had talked often to Jack about his wife and the way in which she had been abducted and supposedly murdered. "Bonnie Sue," he began, wondering if this woman could be Joel's wife. "Do you have a husband named Joel?"

"Do you know Joel?" she asked. The possibility that this man might know her husband was shocking.

"Yes, I do. He owns a saloon in Backwater. The town's a few miles from my ranch."

"But didn't he go on to San Francisco?"

"He didn't want to go without you. Joel has talked often about you, and he said that after he lost you, he

269

just wandered around from one town to another until his travels finally brought him to Backwater. He won the Golden Horseshoe in a card game, so he decided to stay in town."

"How far are we from your ranch and Backwater?" she asked excitedly.

"We're about a week's ride away."

She could hardly believe that Joel was so close. She felt as though it were a miracle!

"Bonnie Sue," he explained, "the soldiers plan to take you to Fort Laramie. When we reach the foot of the Hills, the fort and Backwater are in two different directions. My sons and I will be leaving you and the others to head for home. But, of course, I'll contact Joel and let him know that you're alive and that you're at Fort Laramie."

"No!" she exclaimed. "I don't want to go to the fort! Let me go with you!"

"But, ma'am, we'll be traveling on horseback, and you're too ill to ride."

"Ask the lieutenant if we can borrow this wagon." She could tell he was hesitant. "Please take me with you! Joel and I will be together so much sooner if I can go with you."

He didn't have the heart to refuse her. "All right, I'll talk to Lieutenant Wilkinson." He patted her hand comfortingly. "I'm sure he'll loan us the wagon." He gave her an encouraging smile, then left.

Jack, his sons, the lieutenant, and Justin stood a distance from the wagon. The elder Stevens had called the meeting, and the others now waited for him to explain why he had wanted a conference.

"The lady's name is Bonnie Sue Carson." Jack looked from Clint to Johnny. "She's Joel's wife."

"Well I'll be damned!" Johnny exclaimed.

Clint smiled broadly. "Joel will be wild."

Justin then remarked, "I take it you all know this woman's husband."

"Yes," Jack answered. "He owns a saloon in Backwater." He gave Lieutenant Wilkinson his attention. "Mrs. Carson wants to see her husband as soon as possible, so I'd like your permission to borrow the wagon. I'll take her to my home, then go into town and get Joel."

The lieutenant nodded. "I'm sure it'll be all right if you take the buckboard."

"I'll return it as soon as possible."

"Don't worry about it," the officer said politely. "The lady being reunited with her husband is much more important than a buckboard."

"Mr. Stevens," Justin began, "I'm gonna head farther north and keep searchin' for your daughter."

"By yourself?" Jack questioned.

"If I take the soldiers and happen to find your daughter, whoever has her is gonna expect the Army to bargain for her. As we know, we done lost the only bargaining power we had. Besides, just the sight of soldiers can cause some of these Sioux to get their dander up. Alone, I'd have a better chance of gettin' your daughter back."

"Without anything to trade?" Jack asked.

"There are other ways to get her back," he drawled.

Understanding, Clint surmised, "If it becomes necessary, you're planning to help her escape, aren't you?"

"Maybe," he said.

"Then let me go with you. You might need my help," Clint declared.

"Thanks for offerin', but I work better alone." Seeing Clint's disappointment, he added considerately,

"You ain't had no experience. You're a cowboy, not an Indian fighter. I can't quite picture you slippin' into a Sioux camp, makin' your way to your sister and sneakin' her out without wakin' up the entire village. Have you ever had to slit a man's throat so you could kill him without making any noise?"

"No, of course not," Clint answered, relenting.

Justin looked at Jack. "I can't stay away from the fort indefinitely, but I'll look around for another week or so. I'll stop by your ranch before returning home and let you know if I learn anything. If I don't find her and you still want to continue the search in the Spring, notify Major Landon and he'll see that you have a military escort."

Shaking the scout's hand, Jack replied, "I appreciate what you are doing, and my prayers will be with you."

"Like I said, I'll stop by your ranch in a week or so." With that, Justin left the other men to get ready to leave.

As the Stevenses were watching Smith's departure, Lieutenant Wilkinson said with obvious respect, "You men have the best scout in the west looking for Miss Stevens. Furthermore, if she has to be stolen back, Justin Smith is the only man I know of who can do the job."

Cooking smoke from the tepees' open flaps swirled upwards to disappear into the billowing clouds, and the savory aromas permeated the air with a mixture of delicious, mouth-watering scents.

As the Sioux hunting party neared Running Horse's village, the appetizing odors reached them before the encampment came within their view.

David, riding beside Black Wolf, uttered hungrily, "I sure hope dinner tastes as good as it smells."

272

Black Wolf smiled. "So do I." He was in an especially good mood, for their hunt had been successful. However, their ample supply of meat was not the primary reason for his high spirits. During his absence from Alisha, Black Wolf had given their relationship considerable thought. He had fallen deeply in love with her and didn't try to foolishly deny it to himself. She was everything he wanted in a woman: compassionate, honest, dependable, and loving. It had taken him thirty years to fall in love, and now that he had found her, he wasn't about to lose her. Their different worlds were a serious problem, but he believed this conflict could be resolved through compromise. Together they would find a way to work it out. He was quite willing to meet her halfway, and perhaps even go further than that if it should become necessary.

Several people ran to greet the men as they rode into the village, and Black Wolf wasn't surprised to see that Spotted Fawn was among them. He had no reason to think anything was amiss until she hurried to the side of his horse and yelled for him to stop.

Pulling up the pinto, and noticing the worry on her face, he asked urgently, "What's wrong?" Was it Running Horse? Had he taken a turn for the worse? Dear God, surely nothing had happened to Alisha!

"Black Wolf," she began excitedly, "Alisha is gone!"

David had reined in beside Black Wolf, and hearing what Spotted Fawn had said, exclaimed, "What do you mean, she's gone?"

Although her reply seemed to be a response to David's question, she looked at Black Wolf as she explained, "The trappers called Doug and Sam came here yesterday. Alisha spoke alone with them, but then this morning, when I went to your lodge, she was gone. I am sure she is with these white men, for she took her horse and some of her things."

A cold rage glinted in Black Wolf's eyes. He had been a fool to think that Alisha loved him! She had deserted him at the first opportunity! Not only had she left him, but she had done so with two unsavory characters.

"You must go after her!" Spotted Fawn pleaded. "I do not trust those men! Alisha might be in danger!"

"Apparently she left with them on her own accord!" Black Wolf snapped, consumed by anger. Although he had spoken harshly, he still intended to pursue her. Spotted Fawn was right—Alisha probably *was* in danger. Doug and Sam had most likely promised to take her home, and she had been foolish enough to believe them. However, his belief that she had been tricked didn't lessen his wrath. He considered her departure a personal betrayal, as well as proof that she didn't love him.

Black Wolf already had provisions packed on his horse, so it wasn't necessary for him to go to his lodge. He looked at David. "I'll be back as soon as I can, and I'll have Alisha with me."

"I want to go with you!" the boy said eagerly.

"No, stay here," Black Wolf answered, adamant. Jerking the reins, he urged the pinto into a steady canter, then as he rode out of the village, he sent the horse into a full gallop. Alisha had left early this morning, which meant she and the trappers had half a day's head start on him. He'd have to travel fast and nonstop to catch up to them by nightfall.

David had watched Black Wolf until he was out of sight, then had tended to his horse and turned him loose to graze with several Indian ponies.

Going to Kicking Buffalo's lodge, David was hesitant to enter. However, it was his home, so he stepped inside. The interior was dark compared to the bright sunshine outside, and it took a moment for David's eyes to grow accustomed to the change. He expected to see Basket-Weaver and Spotted Fawn tending to dinner as Kicking Buffalo sat by the fire, but glancing about, he was surprised to find them gone. There was no one inside the tepee except for Flying Hawk.

David looked toward the Indian boy's bed and was actually pleased to see that he was now sitting up. The deep cuts the bear had delivered across Flying Hawk's chest had become infected, and for days the boy's body had been racked with fever. His serious condition had been life-threatening, and it had taken several days for his fever to break. In spite of Flying Hawk's illness, his family had remembered to thank David for his courageous rescue, and their thankfulness had been demonstrative. David had found this a little embarrassing, for he didn't think he had done anything worth so much praise. But because of their constant concern for Flying Hawk, David was able to make himself as scarce and as inconspicuous as possible.

Since the day the boys had encountered the bear, they hadn't talked to each other, which suited David fine, for he still considered Flying Hawk his adversary.

Now, finding only Flying Hawk in the lodge, David started to turn around and dart back outside.

"Wait!" Flying Hawk called.

David paused, then turned about. "What do you want?" he asked, immediately on his guard.

"Come closer. I want us to talk."

"I doubt if we have anything to talk about," David answered, frowning.

Flying Hawk smiled sincerely. "Bear Fighter, I want us to be friends."

David wasn't sure which surprised him more, his new name or Flying Hawk's offer of friendship. He didn't question the other boy's sincerity, for David already knew that deceitfulness was never practiced among the Sioux.

Taken aback, David mumbled without anger, "Bear Fighter? How did I get that name?"

"Did you not fight off the bear?"

"All I did was throw a rock at a damned little cub."

Flying Hawk laughed warmly. "Yes, but we cannot call you Cub Fighter. It is not a fitting name for one so brave."

David found himself smiling. "Well, I don't know if I'm all that brave or not, but Bear Fighter is definitely an improvement over Squaw Eyes."

Motioning for David to come closer, Flying Hawk said, "Come; sit beside me."

Complying, David moved over and took a seat next to the other boy's bed.

"I asked my family to leave us alone so we could talk privately," Flying Hawk began. "While recovering, I have had much time to think. The white soldiers killed my mother and father, and this put much hate in my heart for all your people. Black Wolf told me this hate was wrong. He was right. It is wrong for me to hate you only because your skin is white. A man should be judged by his worth alone. Also, it shames me to admit that I was jealous of your relationship with Black Wolf." His dark eyes met David's without wavering. "You saved my life, and for this I will always be your friend. If you choose not to return this friendship, then I will understand. But my feelings will not change. I will continue to feel only warmth for you."

David studied Flying Hawk for a moment, and was surprised to realize that his own feelings were the same. He no longer wished them to be enemies. Quite the contrary, he was longing for a friend his own age. And in spite of the animosity that had existed between them,

David had nonetheless respected Flying Hawk. The Indian boy had always been direct and honest.

Smiling affably, David offered Flying Hawk his hand. "Let's shake to our friendship."

Eager to seal their agreement, Flying Hawk placed his hand in David's. Then, as the boys shook hands, Flying Hawk swore, "From this moment forward, we will be as brothers. I will hold this bond between us sacred, and when your people and the Sioux are at war, I will still love you as a brother. If, someday, we find ourselves facing each other on the battlefield, I will lay down my weapon before you and let you take my life."

David increased his grip on Flying Hawk's hand. The other boy's pledge had moved him deeply. "No, my brother, I could never take your life. When our people go to war, we won't let their conflict come between us."

Their eyes met and held for a moment, then as David broke their handshake, he asked, "Were you an only child?"

"No, I had a younger brother, but he died last winter. He was sick many days. He had the sickness called pneumonia."

"I never had any brothers or sisters."

Flying Hawk smiled. "You now have a brother, Bear Fighter. And soon all my friends will be yours, for I will tell them that we are brothers."

At that moment, Kicking Buffalo entered his home, and having overheard Flying Hawk's words, he said strongly, "I am glad you boys are as brothers. When Black Wolf hears this, he will be pleased."

The mention of Black Wolf made David think about Alisha. He hoped desperately that Black Wolf would catch up to her before anything bad happened. Alisha's departure with the two trappers had come as a shock to David. He couldn't understand why she had done something so foolish; furthermore, just like Black

Wolf, he considered her desertion a personal betrayal. How could she have gone off without even telling him goodbye? Also, he'd been aware of Black Wolf's anger and didn't blame the man for feeling that way. In David's opinion, it seemed that she had abandoned not only him but Black Wolf as well. Her actions had David totally mystified. How could she have been so callous to Black Wolf? After all, the warrior had not only saved her life but had treated her well. Furthermore, David had a strong feeling that Black Wolf was in love with Alisha, and it had probably hurt him deeply to find that she had forsaken him.

Chapter Twenty-Five

Sam didn't try to find a place to stop until the sun had made a full descent and darkness cloaked the landscape. As the threesome rode into an area that was well-hidden by bordering shrubbery, Sam gave the surroundings a close inspection and decided it was a good location. Pulling up his horse, he told the others to dismount.

Alisha was slow getting down from her horse, for she was extremely fatigued. The day had been long and tiring, and since she'd had no sleep the night before, she now felt as though she were about to collapse from exhaustion. Taking a rolled blanket from behind her saddle, she tucked it under her arm, stepped to a large spruce, then spread the blanket and sat down. Leaning back against the tree's trunk, she watched the two trappers. Now that they had stopped for the night, Alisha began to feel really frightened. Would Sam and Doug decide to force themselves on her? Alisha was certain that they wouldn't leave her unmolested until they reached their cabin.

Her eyes became glazed with desperation as she looked around. If only she could find a way to escape! But how? How? It's hopeless, she thought frantically.

There's no chance for escape! Oh Black Wolf, please . . . please come after me! You can save me; I know you can! She grieved inwardly, for she believed there was a good possibility that he wouldn't pursue her. He might think that these men were taking her home and would decide to let her go without his interference.

Clearing her mind, Alisha listened as Sam began talking to his companion. "Doug, we'd better leave the horses saddled in case we have to make a quick getaway. Also, I don't think we should make a fire. We can eat jerky for supper. Get your rifle and take the first watch."

"Why do I have to take the first watch?" he whined.

"'Cause I said so," Sam stated firmly.

"You ain't my boss," the other man argued, his expression resentful. "I know why you're wantin' me to take the first watch. You're aimin' to poke the woman."

"So?" Sam challenged.

"How come you get to poke her first?"

The burly trapper grinned confidently. "I get her first 'cause I'm bigger than you are." His beady eyes narrowed into angry slits. "Now get your rifle and get in those bushes and keep a lookout for Black Wolf. That damned half-breed is liable to come after the woman."

For a dangerous moment, Doug considered disobeying, but his common sense intervened. He knew he couldn't beat Sam in a fight, for the man was too big and strong.

"All right," Doug mumbled, "I'll do as you say."

The two trappers had been partners for a long time, and Sam had a certain fondness for Doug. To cheer him up, he said brightly, "While I'm takin' the second watch, you can have the woman."

Agreeing, Doug stepped to his horse and got his rifle,

then cradling it across his arms, he headed for the shrubbery.

Alisha had overheard their discussion, and as Sam turned to eye her lewdly, she bolted to her feet. Frantic, she made a desperate effort to run, but moving incredibly fast, Sam reached her, swung her around, and lifted her into his arms.

She tried to scream, but before she could, his lips were on hers. His mouth was wet and brutally rough, and she fought wildly against his sickening kiss.

Meanwhile, Doug hadn't ventured very far into the shrubbery, for he wanted to watch Sam as he took the woman. He could hardly wait for his partner to strip off her clothes so he could take a secret peek at her body. Just the thought of her nudity made him grow hard. Determined to observe the rape scene, he found a place to conceal himself, and squatting behind a heavy bush, he placed his rifle at his side. Then before parting the foliage, he undid his trousers and freed his erection. When Sam forced himself on their beautiful captive, Doug intended to bring on his own climax.

Doug continued to look on as Sam carried Alisha back to the spruce and dropped her struggling body onto the spread blanket. The exciting action held his undivided attention, and the unsuspecting trapper was totally unaware of the warrior who was slipping up behind him.

Black Wolf moved stealthily, and creeping closer to Doug, he raised his rifle, then brought the butt of the weapon down across the man's head. The solid blow knocked Doug unconscious, and he fell over limply.

A murderous glare shone in Black Wolf's vivid blue eyes as he looked toward the camp area and saw Sam wrestling with Alisha. The huge trapper was in the process of tugging at her leggings when Black Wolf stepped out of the shrubbery.

Sam was so absorbed in his act of violence that he was completely oblivious to Black Wolf's presence. Silently, the warrior approached the trapper from behind.

Alisha had continued to fight relentlessly, making it quite impossible for Sam to remove her leggings. Deciding it was time to show the woman who was boss, Sam raised his arm to strike her a severe blow, but a cold rifle barrel suddenly touched the back of his head. Sam froze, and his erection shriveled.

"Get up and step away from the woman," Black Wolf demanded. He moved the rifle so that it was no longer touching Sam's head, but he kept the weapon cocked and ready to fire.

Carefully, the trapper did as he was told. Backing away with his hands in the air, he pleaded, "You ain't gonna kill me, are you? It ain't as though the woman was harmed; you got here before I could do anything."

Bending over, while keeping his eyes on Sam, Black Wolf grasped Alisha by the arm and pulled her to her feet. Then, handing her the rifle, he said hastily, "If Sam makes a move, shoot him."

As she took the weapon and pointed it at the trapper, she wanted desperately to thank Black Wolf for saving her, but there was a strange hardness in his eyes that held her at bay. She could sense that his anger was not aimed entirely at the trappers, but included her as well.

Moving quickly, Black Wolf went back into the shrubbery and retrieved Doug's rifle. The trapper was still unconscious, and grabbing him by the neck of his jacket, Black Wolf dragged the man's body into camp and over to Sam. Then, keeping Doug's rifle, Black Wolf stepped to the men's horses and pack mules. They had been tethered, and freeing all of them except for Alisha's mount, he cocked the rifle and fired several shots into the air. The animals took off with a bolt and were soon running frantically in different directions.

"Why'd you do that for?" Sam asked urgently.

Walking toward Alisha, Black Wolf answered, "I just wanted to make sure that you won't be following us. It'll take you all day tomorrow to round up your horses and mules." Touching Alisha's arm, he urged, "Let's go."

As she was following him to her horse, Sam called, "But you got to leave us Doug's rifle. We got to have a way to protect ourselves, and my gun is on my horse."

Helping Alisha mount, Black Wolf shouted, "As I'm leaving, I'll throw the rifle into the shrubbery. Then all you have to do is find it. But there's only a couple of shells left, so if I were you, I wouldn't waste any shots."

Alisha handed Black Wolf his own rifle, and he slipped it into the scabbard, then swung up onto the saddle behind her. While still watching Sam, he backed the horse, then when they were in the shrubbery, he sent the gelding into a gallop. When they were safely out of Sam's vision, he pitched Doug's gun into the bushes.

Black Wolf had left his pinto a distance away because he had wanted to approach on foot. Now, as they rode up to his horse, he didn't dismount; instead he grabbed the steed's reins to lead him.

"Why aren't you riding your horse?" Alisha asked.

"In order to catch up to you by nightfall, I had to push the pinto, and now he's exhausted."

Turning so she could see the horse, she was alarmed to find that the animal was indeed worn out. "Will he be all right?" she asked anxiously.

"I hope so," he replied. "There's a good place up ahead to camp. Following a night's rest, maybe he'll be fine. The horse is old, and I shouldn't have pushed him so hard."

Alisha didn't say anything. If the pinto didn't

recover, it would be her fault! As she took another quick look at the tired horse, she was engulfed with a mixture of guilt and depression. If the pinto were to die, would Black Wolf hold her to blame?

As soon as they reached the area where Black Wolf intended for them to spend the night, he swung down from Alisha's horse and went to the pinto. He unsaddled the steed quickly, then used a blanket to rub him down.

Alisha took it upon herself to unsaddle her own horse, and when she was finished, she looked for a place to sit. She had left her blanket back at the other camp, and Black Wolf was using his on the pinto, so she chose to sit down on a soft bed of grass. Drawing up her knees, and crossing her arms over them, she watched Black Wolf as he tended to his horse. He had said very littlie since they'd left the trappers, and Alisha was now certain that he was angry with her. But surely when she had a chance to explain why she had gone with Sam and Doug, Black Wolf would understand.

Completing the rubdown, Black Wolf spread the blanket over the pinto's back, then giving the horse an affectionate pat on the neck, he turned around and faced Alisha.

The coldness in Black Wolf's eyes caused her to tense up, and as he began walking toward her, she waited apprehensively.

Pausing in front of her and glaring down into her watching eyes, he said sharply, "I thought you were different from other white women, but now I realize I was badly mistaken! You apparently find living with Indians so repulsive and degrading that you'll grasp at any opportunity to leave."

She stood up quickly. "But, Black Wolf, you don't understand. . . ."

"The hell I don't!" he raged. How could he have been so blind to her character? He had actually started to believe that she cared about him and his people!

His unjust anger aroused Alisha's own wrath. "If you'll let me explain . . ."

Again, he rudely interrupted, "No explanation is necessary! As far as I'm concerned, hereafter you can do as you please! If you attempt to leave my village again, don't expect me to come after you!"

Her temper flared, and reacting to the heat of the moment, she said irrationally, "In that case I'll leave now! If I keep to a southeasterly course, I can find my way out of these Hills and back home!"

She attempted to brush past him, but his arm lunged and grabbed her waist. Jerking her roughly against his powerful frame, he spoke gruffly. "You little fool! What chance do you think you'd have by yourself?"

Reacting angrily, she spouted, "I'd rather take my chances alone than be dependent on you!"

"I should let you leave," he grumbled through gritted teeth.

"Then why don't you?" she lashed out.

"I don't want your safety preying on my conscience. If you try to leave these Hills without proper protection, you'll end up dead or raped!"

"Raped?" she snapped petulantly. "If I remember correctly, I was under your protection when I lost my virginity!"

"I don't remember you putting up much resistance!" he retorted.

Her anger now steaming, she pushed against him as she tried vainly to free herself from his firm hold. "Turn me loose!" she demanded furiously.

"I'll turn you loose when I'm damned good and ready!" he remarked bluntly. He drew her closer, pinning her against him. "But before I do so, I intend to make love to you." Black Wolf's better judgment warned him to free her, but Alisha's struggles had aroused his passion, and he no longer had the will power to turn her away.

His cold, callous attitude put her in a rage. "If you take me, it'll be by force! I'll fight you!"

"Good!" he declared flippantly. "I've always enjoyed a woman with spirit."

"You unfeeling, pompous brute!" she ranted.

Letting her remarks pass, he lifted her into his arms, then kneeling, laid her on the grass.

As his body came down on hers, trapping her beneath him, she said angrily, "If you force yourself on me, then you're no better than Sam!"

"Apparently you liked Sam, or else you wouldn't have been so willing to leave with him."

"I didn't know he was a vile, lying weasel!"

Black Wolf looked at her seriously. "Do you really want to go home so badly that you're willing to take your chances with any man who comes along?"

Still perturbed, she muttered tartly, "What do you think?"

"I don't think it's your father you're longing to see, but your fiancé."

"Fiancé?" she questioned. She was confused until she recalled telling Black Wolf that she and Todd were engaged.

Alisha was about to admit that she had fibbed, when Black Wolf uttered hoarsely, "I'm tired of talking!"

"Then let me up!" she demanded.

"I'll let you up when I'm finished with you!" he promised. She started to protest, but before she could, his mouth was on hers, branding her lips in a fiery kiss.

Alisha forced herself not to surrender, for she believed he only wanted her to satisfy his lust. He hadn't rescued her from those trappers because he loved her; he had saved her so he'd have a woman to share his bed. He was no better than Sam and Doug!

Interrupting his forceful kiss, he rolled to lie at her side. Immediately, she attempted to sit up, but his strength easily held her down. Imprisoning her with one arm, he moved the other one down her slender form. Lifting the hem of her dress, he shoved it up to her waist, then with astonishing quickness, he pulled off her leggings. Dressed Indian-style, she wasn't wearing an undergarment, and her soft thighs were bare.

Moving back over her, he knelt between her legs and undid his buckskin trousers. Now submissive, Alisha looked deeply into his eyes and tried to find a trace of warmth in them. Feeling her scrutiny, he met her gaze, and his stare was ice-cold. As he continued to look at her, her vulnerability began to soften his heart and cool his rage.

However, Alisha was not aware of this change taking place within Black Wolf, and she spouted indignantly, "I despise you!"

"Do you?" he said calmly. "We'll see just how much you despise me, you little vixen." He was still kneeling between her legs, and her womanly core was open to his touch. Moving his hand to the center of her pleasure, he probed gently with his finger. He gazed downward and watched with desire as his finger moved in and out.

Alisha didn't want to respond, but her resolutions soon deserted her, and Black Wolf had her under his power. His stimulating rhythm set her passion ablaze, and her hips arched as she welcomed his fondling.

His own need was burning, and moving his hands to his trousers, he slipped them down past his muscular thighs.

Her anger now totally supplanted with passion, Alisha's gaze went to his jutting hardness. Anxious to feel him deep inside her, she moaned wantonly, "Take me now, Black Wolf."

Slipping his hands under her knees, he raised her legs and placed them over his shoulders. This position was new to Alisha, and a little frightened, she gasped softly.

Positioning himself so that he could plunge into her hot depths, he uttered thickly, "I've never wanted you as badly as I do right now."

"Then take me, darling," she pleaded, her whole being on fire for this man who could arouse her to such wonderful heights.

Leaning forward, he shoved his erection far into her enfolding heat, and his entrance was so exciting that Alisha cried out with unbearable pleasure.

As his hips began moving rapidly, she locked her ankles about his neck, then bent her legs so that he could lower his chest against hers.

He pressed his lips to hers in a passionate, breathtaking kiss, and as Alisha surrendered ecstatically, her mouth blended with his as their tongues met in sensual love play.

Carefully, he moved her legs down until they were wrapped about his waist, then easing his hands under her hips, he elevated her thighs. Pulling her up against him, he pounded into her aggressively. On fire with passion, she equaled each demanding thrust until, explosively, they climbed to love's fiery climax. Clinging tightly, they found wondrous release as their bodies trembled with complete fulfillment.

Black Wolf remained on top of her for a moment, then withdrawing, he moved to lie at her side.

Alisha hoped he'd tell her that he loved her, and she waited anxiously for him to do so.

Lying on his back, Black Wolf gazed up at the thousands of stars glimmering in the dark sky. He was no longer angry at Alisha; his anger was now aimed exclusively at himself. He'd been a fool to let down his guard and fall in love with a white woman. A bitter frown hardened his handsome features as he remembered how only this morning he had hoped he and Alisha would find a way to resolve their personal differences. He had wanted it so badly that he'd been willing to meet her halfway and more if necessary. Well, he thought sourly, I was a fool! Apparently, Alisha wants her home more than she wants me. His frown deepened. Also, she's probably anxious to return to her rich fiancé, who can offer her a life of luxury. Cutting off his thoughts brusquely, Black Wolf got to his feet and pulled up his trousers.

Watching him, Alisha sighed sadly. He doesn't love me, she thought. Her movements were slow as she sat up and put on her leggings.

When Black Wolf suddenly spoke, it was so unexpected that Alisha was a little startled. "We'll have to use the horses' blankets for a bed. The buffalo robe you brought will suffice for cover."

She nodded agreeably, her placid mood belying her inner turbulence. As Black Wolf left her side to walk over to the horses, she watched him through a tearful blur. She had to fight the urge to run after him, throw herself into his arms, and beg him to love her! But she valued her pride, and her self-respect kept her riveted to the spot.

Carrying the blankets and the robe, Black Wolf returned and placed them beside Alisha. "I brought some provisions, so as soon as I start a fire, we can have something to eat."

Again, she simply nodded. It seemed ironic that they could be lovers one minute, casual friends the next.

Mistaking her silence for homesickness, Black Wolf said kindly, "Just because things didn't work out with Doug and Sam doesn't mean you won't get home before winter sets in. If Running Horses health keeps improving, we'll leave in another week or so."

She hadn't expected him to take her home before winter, and his offer to do so came as a surprise. Was he anxious to get rid of her? Was he still upset because she had left with the two trappers? She hadn't yet explained to Black Wolf how Sam had told her that her father was seriously wounded. Deciding now was the time to explain, she said hesitantly, "Black Wolf, I want to tell you why I left with Doug and Sam."

He cut her off abruptly, "You don't owe me any explanations. You're free to do as you please." With that he turned to start the campfire.

"Have it your way, Black Wolf!" she uttered beneath her breath. "I'm not going to throw myself at your feet!" As she spread out the horse blankets and the robe, Alisha decided that the sooner she got away from Black Wolf, the better! Surely once she was back home with her father and brothers, she'd find a way to get over this man who could wreak such havoc with her emotions!

Chapter Twenty-Six

A bright shaft of sunlight fell across Alisha's face, awakening her from a deep slumber. She stretched beneath the heavy buffalo robe and slowly opened her eyes. For a moment her drowsiness left her disoriented, and she was puzzled to find herself sleeping outdoors. Then, quickly, it all came back to her; her abduction, Black Wolf's rescue, and the evening they had spent together. A shadow of sadness darkened her pretty features as she recalled the night before. Following their passionate union, they had become as cold as strangers. Although Black Wolf had slept beside her and shared her cover, their proximity hadn't warmed the coldness that had developed between them.

Black Wolf was no longer at her side, and wondering where he was, she sat upright. She looked about quickly but couldn't find him. Leaving the pallet, she got to her feet and called, "Black Wolf?"

From the near distance, she heard his response. "I'm over here."

His voice had come from the other side of the brush, and she hurried through the foliage. As she stepped free of the thick bushes onto a patch of open ground, the sight before her caused her to halt abruptly. She gasped with alarm as she saw Black Wolf sitting beside the fallen pinto. The horse was lying on its side; its breathing was labored.

Moving hesitantly, she went to Black Wolf and knelt. Tears came to her eyes as she gazed at the pinto. "Is he going to . . . ?"

"Die?" Black Wolf finished for her. His voice was filled with sadness as he continued, "Yes, he's dying."

"I'm sorry!" Alisha cried. Guilt hit her sharply, for she felt the horse's impending death was all her fault. If she hadn't left with Sam and Doug, Black Wolf wouldn't have been forced to push the pinto beyond its limit to catch up to her.

Quietly, Black Wolf murmured, "When I woke up this morning and went to check on him, he was barely able to stand. I tried leading him, hoping if I could force him to walk, he wouldn't lie down and give up." He paused, then added somberly, "He tried to appease me, but I was asking too much of him. It's time for him to die, and he was able to accept that, but I kept trying to make him live. Finally, the last of his strength gave way and he lay down." Black Wolf placed a gentle hand on the pinto's neck and patted him. He smiled wistfully. "He's been a damned good horse. More than once his obedience and intelligence have saved my life."

"How long have you had him?"

"My father gave me the horse when I was eighteen. Running Horse had captured a herd of wild horses and the pinto was among them."

"Did you give him a name?"

"Yes, I called him Kola."

"What does Kola mean?"

"Friend," he answered softly.

Brushing at the tears that were now streaming from her eyes, Alisha murmured, "I had a white stallion, and I was very fond of him. Although I didn't have him nearly as long as you've had the pinto, I think I understand how you feel. When the Wyatt brothers abducted me, I tried to make a run for it, and my horse was wounded as I was trying to escape. The fall broke his leg, and as I was leaving with Joe and Walter, Jesse shot the stallion." Relating the way in which her horse had died filled her with more guilt, for she had never stopped blaming herself. Now, once again, she was feeling responsible for a horse's death. Sobs emerging, she moaned brokenly, "Oh Black Wolf, I'm so sorry! It's all my fault that your horse is dying!"

"Don't blame yourself, Alisha. When I decided to go after you, I should've left the pinto at the village and taken another horse. In fact, I should've stopped riding him a long time ago."

"The young stallion you traded to Two Moons for David, had you planned for the horse to be the pinto's replacement?"

"Yes," he replied, his voice so low that his answer was almost inaudible. "Alisha, would you mind leaving me alone?"

She understood. "I'll make some coffee." Standing, she took one last look at the pinto, then hurried back to camp.

Alisha had the coffee prepared and was sitting beside the campfire when Black Wolf came through the thicket. He walked over slowly and sat beside her.

As she poured him a cup of coffee, she asked, "Is he dead?"

Accepting the proffered cup, he replied, "Yes." He took a couple of drinks, then continued, "I'll take you back to the village, then return for my riding gear."

She longed desperately to take him in her arms and console him, but she had a feeling that he'd rather

293

she didn't.

He finished his coffee in three quick swallows, got to his feet, and said curtly, "Let's go. The sooner I get you back, the sooner I can return for my things."

"Don't you want some breakfast?" she asked.

"No, thanks, but if you're hungry . . ."

She interrupted. "No, I don't want anything to eat."

He moved away and began to saddle the other horse. Watching, Alisha longed again to go to Black Wolf and hold him close. She wanted him to share his grief with her, but he seemed determined to remain withdrawn. Why should he turn to me for consolation? she asked herself. Regardless of what he said, he probably blames me for the pinto's death. And he's right! It is my fault! How could I have been so foolish as to believe everything Sam told me?

Looking away from Black Wolf, she quickly set about breaking camp. She was just finishing when Black Wolf walked up to her side.

Evenly he remarked, "As soon as we get back to the village, I'll check on my father's condition. If he still seems to be improving, I'll take you home before winter sets in."

Although a large part of her wanted to stay with Black Wolf forever, she knew she had to get back home. Her family were probably half out of their minds with worry. At this time, she couldn't be selfish and think only of what she wanted. If only Black Wolf would ask her to marry him, then she could return home, let her father and brothers know she was well, and marry Black Wolf; then they could live wherever he pleased. She wouldn't care where they made their home, so long as they were together! But she didn't think Black Wolf wanted to share his life with her; he'd made no commitments, nor had he pledged his love.

Conceding, and granting him what she thought he

wanted, she answered softly, "I hope Running Horse is doing well, for I'm anxious to go home."

Against his will, jealousy surfaced. "I imagine your fiancé will be happy to see you. When do you plan to marry him?"

"I . . . I haven't set a date," she stammered. Should she tell Black Wolf the truth? After short deliberation, she decided against it. Her deceit would probably only give him more cause to distrust her. Since he'd rescued her from Sam and Doug, she'd sensed that he now considered her untrustworthy.

As Black Wolf kicked loose dirt over the fire to smother the flames, Alisha went to her horse and mounted.

Later, Black Wolf had left Alisha at their lodge and then had gone to see Running Horse. The trip back to the village had seemed interminable to Alisha, for Black Wolf had remained withdrawn and quiet throughout the journey. If only she had the power to see into his mind, but his thoughts were a total mystery to her. Did he love her, or did he just consider her his responsibility? Did his reason for rescuing her have nothing whatsoever to do with love? Maybe his motive had been governed by lust alone. But if that was true, he wouldn't be planning to take her home, unless he was growing tired of her.

Pacing the restricted enclosure of the lodge, Alisha could find no answers to these pressing questions. Deciding to set her mind on a different course, she started thinking about preparing dinner. She had taken a step toward the lodge fire when she suddenly heard David asking permission to enter her home.

"Come in, David," she said clearly.

He entered, and giving the interior a quick glance, he

asked, "Where's Black Wolf?"

"He's visiting his father."

Moving to her side, David demanded a little harshly, "Why did you run away?"

"I wouldn't call it running away," she answered.

His brow furrowed. "Oh?"

"Those trappers tricked me. They said they'd take me home, when actually they planned to take me to their cabin, which is on the Canadian border."

"Alisha, if you wanted to go home so badly, why didn't you tell Black Wolf how much it meant to you? If you'd made your feelings clear, I think he'd have found a way to send you back."

"I didn't want to go home as badly as you think. I was willing to stay here for the winter. But the trappers told me that they had run across my brothers. They said that my oldest brother had told them that my father had been shot and was seriously wounded. I was desperate to get home because I was worried about my father."

David smiled. "I understand, and now I can see why you acted so rashly. Did you tell Black Wolf why you left?"

"No," she answered.

"You intend to tell him, don't you?"

She shook her head. "I don't think so. Black Wolf hopes to take me home before winter. So why I left with the trappers doesn't really matter. Besides, I don't think he cares to know what prompted me to leave."

Alisha's dilemma slipped from David's thoughts. "Does Black Wolf plan for me to leave at the same time you do?"

"I don't know," she replied. "I suppose he does."

David looked disappointed. "But I was just beginning to like it here. Flying Hawk and I are now good friends."

"I'm pleased to hear that you boys finally settled your differences." She smiled warmly and placed a hand on David's shoulder. "If you're worried about what will happen to you when you leave here, I'm sure my father will offer you a home at the Bar-S. You'll like living at the ranch."

David nodded and mumbled his thanks. He was sincerely grateful to Alisha for offering him a home, but nevertheless he had been looking forward to spending the winter with Flying Hawk.

His sadness was apparent. "Why do you look so unhappy?" Alisha asked with concern.

"I'm gonna miss Flying Hawk. But most of all, I'm going to miss Black Wolf."

"So will I," she murmured, her mood somber.

Alisha was tending to dinner when Black Wolf returned from visiting Running Horse.

As he entered the lodge, she asked, "How's your father?"

Going to his bed and sitting, he answered, "He's doing as well as can be expected." He motioned for her to join him.

She went to his side and sat down.

"I still have a couple of weeks hunting to do before we can leave. I not only need to hunt meat for my own lodge, but also for Running Horse's. When I manage to get enough food stored, I'll take you home."

She nodded agreeably, although she was longing to fling herself into his arms and tell him how much she loved him. Remaining calm, she asked, "What about David?"

Black Wolf was not aware that David and Flying Hawk had become friends, and believing David would be more than happy to leave, he replied, "You once said that your father would give him a home, so the boy will leave with us."

She mistakingly thought he was being callous and unfeeling. "You're very good at ruling David's life, as well as my own. First, you tell us we are to live here, and now you tell us we're to live at the Bar-S. You have never bothered to ask us where we want to live."

He stood up abruptly. "I never thought there was any doubt where you wanted to be."

"That's beside the point. You've never bothered to ask!"

"Nor do I intend to ask now!" he said short-temperedly. "I already know you want to be with your fiancé!" He turned to walk away.

"Where are you going?" she demanded.

"I need to go back and get my saddle and gear."

"But it's a long way to travel. Why don't you wait and leave in the morning?"

"I'd rather leave now," he mumbled.

She came close to arguing with him but refrained from doing so. Vexed, she spouted, "Go; and I don't care if you never come back!"

He grinned coldly. "I'll be back, Madam, for I intend to personally escort you onto the Bar-S and place you in your father's care and out of mine." With that, he spun about and stalked out of the lodge.

Black Wolf had been gone only a few minutes when Spotted Fawn arrived, and the moment she entered the tepee, she floored Alisha with the news that Black Wolf had told her to show Alisha the proper method for making up another bed.

"So Black Wolf wants separate beds, does he?" Alisha fumed. "How dare he make such a decision without consulting me!"

The white woman's petulance was upsetting to Spotted Fawn, and she was hesitant to begin carrying

298

out Black Wolf's request.

"Very well!" Alisha remarked. "Black Wolf's wish is my command, so let's get the other bed prepared."

Alisha's inner pain was well concealed as she helped Spotted Fawn with the chore, and the young Indian woman hadn't the slighest notion that her friend's heart was breaking. For Alisha was now certain that Black Wolf didn't love her.

Dawn was only a few minutes away when Black Wolf returned to the village. He slipped quietly into his lodge and stored his gear in the corner. Alisha's bed was placed on the opposite side of Black Wolf's, and stepping silently to her side, he knelt close. She was sound asleep, and his gaze lingered as he studied her. As he admired her beauty, he was almost tempted to wake her and demand that they talk about their personal differences. But he believed it would prove to be a total waste of time, for he was sure there was no way for them to resolve their problems. Alisha's loyalty belonged to her family and fiancé. For a short time he had hoped he was first in her life, but if she loved him above all else, she'd never have left with Doug and Sam.

He sighed deeply and resigned himself to life without her. He'd been a fool to break his vow never to fall in love with a white woman. He'd always known it would eventually lead to heartache. A tiny, rueful smile curled at his lips as he placed a kiss on his fingertips, then touched Alisha's brow. Barely above a whisper, he pledged, "I love you, Alisha Stevens. But sometimes love is knowing when to let go."

Standing, he went quietly to his own bed and lay down. Folding his arms beneath his head, he gazed up through the open smoke flap. It was going to be a clear day, and as the sky lightened with the breaking dawn, only the Morning Star could be seen.

Black Wolf missed Alisha's presence at his side, and his whole being ached to feel her snuggled against him. Deciding on two separate beds had been a hard decision for him to make. But believing his and Alisha's parting inevitable, he knew the sooner he grew accustomed to sleeping without her, the better.

Chapter Twenty-Seven

Loretta and Joel were sitting on the sofa wrapped in each other's arms. Loretta had never been so happy, and as she snuggled against the man she loved, a small but radiant smile spread across her face. Tomorrow morning at ten o'clock, she and Joel were to meet at the church, get married, then leave the next day for Fort Laramie. Loretta was still finding it hard to believe that a man as handsome and as debonair as Joel Carson could be in love with her. She intended to dedicate the rest of her life to making him happy.

"I'd better get back to the hotel and get a good night's rest so I'll be an alert bridegroom." Joel had sold his saloon and was now staying at the hotel.

Cuddling closer, she murmured, "Must you go?"

He placed a kiss on her forehead, then standing, drew her to her feet and back into his embrace. She gazed up at him, and for a moment, he admired her glowing beauty. Smiling tenderly, he told her, "You barely resemble the woman who came to my quarters with Alisha Stevens. Although you did a good job of hiding your beauty with matronly dresses and a severe hairdo, I nonetheless knew you were beautiful." Placing his hands on her shoulders, he held her at arms' length, and as his gaze roamed over her, he continued, "Your transformation is astounding."

Dressed in a colorful, stylish gown with her auburn hair cascading freely, Loretta Ingalls was indeed a fetching sight.

"I want to look pretty for you," she replied. "I'd never want you to be ashamed of me."

"You'll always make me proud," he assured her.

Her eyes gleaming with joy, she cried ecstatically, "I can't wait to be your wife!"

He withdrew his pocket watch and checked the time. "Well, it's now eight o'clock, so you have only fourteen more hours to wait."

"They'll be the longest fourteen hours of my life," she remarked.

"And mine," he whispered.

A couple of firm knocks suddenly sounded at the front door.

"I wonder who's calling?" Loretta pondered.

She started to answer the knocks, but Joel said quickly, "I'll see who it is."

Leaving the parlor, Joel stepped into the foyer and opened the door. He was surprised to see Jack and Clint. "Please come in," he invited.

As the two men entered, they removed their hats, and taking them, Joel hung them on the wall rack located beside the door, then showed the visitors into the parlor.

"Have you news of Alisha?" Loretta asked, moving over to stand at Joel's side.

"No, ma'am," Jack replied, trying not to stare at her too conspicuously, but he was finding it difficult to keep his eyes turned away. He'd only seen Loretta once, and although at the time she hadn't made much of an impression on him, he remembered that she had seemed a little plain. But the woman who now stood before him was striking. Tearing his gaze from Loretta, Jack looked at Joel and said, "Clint and I went to the Golden Horseshoe and were told that you had sold out and that you were now staying at the hotel. When we went there to see you, the desk clerk told us we'd probably find you here."

Placing his arm around Loretta's shoulders, Joel said happily, "Tomorrow morning, Miss Ingalls and I are getting married."

Although Joel's news disturbed Clint and Jack, they managed to maintain their composure.

Joel waited for their congratulations, but when it became apparent that they weren't about to express their good wishes, he began to wonder if something was wrong. Why had Clint and Jack come into town to see him? What was so important that they had ridden in tonight instead of waiting until tomorrow?

"Joel," Jack began hesitantly, "we need to talk to you." He cast Loretta a worried look and wondered if he and Clint should speak alone with Joel. However, what he had to tell Joel also concerned Miss Ingalls, so Jack decided to deliver his shocking news to both of them.

"Is something wrong?" Joel asked, his curiosity building.

"Not exactly," Jack mumbled.

"Would you two care to sit down?" Loretta asked, gesturing toward the sofa.

"No thank you, ma'am," Jack replied. He centered his attention on Joel. "While the others and I were searching for Alisha, we heard there was a white woman at Chief Bear Claw's village. When we arrived at this village, we learned that she wasn't Alisha. This woman had been a slave for over a year, and when we found her, she was in poor health. Although I'm happy to announce that she's now doing much better."

"Did you bring her back with you?" Loretta queried.

It was Clint who answered. "Yes, she's at the ranch. Before looking for Joel, we visited Doctor Blackburn and asked him to ride to the Bar-S and see her."

"Who is this woman?" Joel questioned. That she could be Bonnie Sue hadn't entered his mind, for he was certain that his wife was dead.

Carefully, Jack replied, "Joel, I have something very shocking to tell you, so try to prepare yourself."

As a strange feeling suddenly came over him, Joel removed his arm from about Loretta and stepped closer to Jack. "What is it?"

"The woman at our ranch is Bonnie Sue."

"What!" he gasped, his face paling. "Are you sure?"

"Believe me, Joel, she's your wife," Jack replied, watching the man closely.

Joel tottered, and reacting alertly, Jack moved forward and grabbed the man's arm in a supportive hold.

"My God!" Joel moaned. "I can't believe what you're telling me! Bonnie Sue was murdered! I saw her body!"

Clint explained, "The burned body was that of a Kiowa squaw. The Indians who abducted your wife wanted you to think it was Bonnie Sue. That's why her wedding ring was placed on the squaw's finger."

Shakily, Joel went to the sofa and sat down. Leaning over, he rested his head in his hands. As the shock hit him full force, his wide shoulders shook, and deep, ripping sobs tore from his throat.

It was Clint who went to Joel to comfort him, for Jack's attention was now solely on Loretta. The woman looked dangerously pale, and he was afraid she was about to pass out.

Going to Loretta's side, Jack asked gently, "Are you all right, ma'am?"

She answered raspingly, "I . . . I think so." Her eyes,

glazed wildly, turned to Joel. She wanted to fling herself into his arms and beg him not to leave her, but she was so numb that she couldn't move.

Suddenly, Joel bolted from the sofa. Now, as it fully dawned on him that Bonnie Sue was alive, his mood became ecstatic. "Dear God!" he cried joyously. "She's alive! Bonnie Sue is alive!" Taking the others unexpectedly, he darted across the parlor and toward the foyer.

"Where are you going?" Jack called.

"To see my wife!" he replied, his tone ringing with elation.

Nodding at Clint, Jack said, "You'd better go with him."

As Joel rushed outside with Clint following, Loretta stood transfixed, her eyes staring with disbelief. Joel didn't even bother to tell me goodbye! she lamented. My God, he didn't even say goodbye!

Jack watched Loretta with understanding, for he'd also been aware that Joel hadn't said anything to her. Wrapped up in his own joy, Joel had forgotten Loretta Ingalls' existence.

Distraught, the young woman bowed her head, and as tears gushed from her eyes, her small shoulders shook violently. She hadn't wanted to break down in front of Mr. Stevens, but she could no longer hold back her grief. She had lost Joel forever! Bonnie Sue was alive and had returned to reclaim her husband!

Jack felt ill at ease. He wasn't sure if he should offer his comfort. He and the school teacher were barely acquainted, and if he were to take her in his arms to try and console her, she might find his gesture offensive. As Loretta's tears continued to flow, Stevens sighed deeply. First Bonnie Sue had needed his succor, and now this woman needed his help. Tentatively, he reached for her and was somewhat surprised when she

305

went into his embrace. He held her close, and as he murmured words of comfort, he wondered if Alisha had someone to give her consolation, or was she facing her tribulations alone?

It was a long time before Loretta's tears began to dwindle; nonetheless, Jack kept her tenderly in his strong arms.

Stepping back and wiping at her wet cheeks, Loretta said apologetically, "Mr. Stevens, please forgive me."

"You don't need to apologize, ma'am," he replied. Taking her arm, he led her to the sofa and urged her to sit down. "Miss Ingalls, with your permission, I'll go to the kitchen and fix a pot of coffee."

"Yes . . . yes, of course," she stammered, his offer registering vaguely.

The moment Jack left the room, Loretta was once again hit with hard sobs. Leaning her head against the arm of the sofa, she surrendered to her heartache. She felt as though she didn't want to live without Joel. Now that she had lost him, she had lost her reason for existing! He was her world, her heart, and the very core of her life!

By the time Jack returned with the coffee, Loretta had managed to regain a semblance of composure, but her reserve hung by a mere thread.

Sitting beside her, Jack placed the warm cup in her hands. She tried to guide the cup to her mouth, but her hands were shaking so badly that the simple act was impossible. Jack placed his hand over her trembling ones, and with his assistance she was able to take a sip of the hot brew. Then, taking the cup, he placed it on the table.

"Why did Joel sell the Golden Horseshoe?" Stevens asked. "Were you against his owning a saloon?"

"We weren't planning to stay here in Backwater. The day after tomorrow, we intended to travel to Fort

Laramie, winter at the fort, then come spring, join a wagon train and journey to San Francisco. Todd Miller's aunt has moved to town, and she has been hired to replace me and will begin teaching on Monday. Which means this home is now hers. The townspeople built this house so whoever is teaching school will have a place to live."

"When does Todd's aunt plan to move in?"

"Sunday," she answered.

"This is Thursday, so that only gives you two days to find new accommodations."

Loretta shrugged as though the prospect of being homeless was of little importance. "I suppose I should go back to Fort Sill, but at present I don't have enough money to pay my fare."

Jack settled himself comfortably, and as he sipped his coffee, he gave Loretta's predicament deep thought. He knew he should find a way to help her, for she was too distressed to help herself. It didn't take long for him to come up with a solution. Finishing his drink, and putting down the empty cup, he began, "Miss Ingalls, my housekeeper, Mary Cummings, is getting on in years, and running my household takes a lot of work. She not only has the cleaning to take care of, but she also cooks, washes clothes, and does all the shopping. Alisha always helped her, but now all the work has fallen on Mary."

Loretta looked at him with a puzzled expression. She hadn't grasped that he was about to offer her a job.

Seeing her bewilderment, Jack explained, "Ma'am, would you like to come to work as Mary's assistant? I have a large home, and you'll have a room to yourself."

"Mr. Stevens," she began kindly. "Are you offering me employment or charity?"

He smiled. "Miss Ingalls, believe me, you will earn your wages. Mary runs a meticulous household, and

307

since my sons and I aren't as neat as we should be, it takes a lot of work to keep everything in order."

"Won't Mary resent my presence?"

"She'll welcome the extra help," he assured her.

Loretta started to accept his generous offer, then hesitated. "But Mr. Stevens, Joel's wife is staying at your home. I couldn't possibly. . . ."

"I understand," he replied. "But her stay is only temporary, and as soon as Joel finds them a place to live, I'll come into town and move you to my home. Until then, you can stay at the hotel. I'll take care of the bill." She made a move to protest, but he proceeded quickly, "You needn't consider it charity, I'll deduct the cost from your wages."

"Mr. Stevens, I think your generosity stems from kindness and not necessity."

His eyes twinkled. "Miss Ingalls, haven't you ever heard the old saying, never look a gift horse in the mouth?"

Loretta laughed, and the unexpected sound of her own laughter shocked her. Her heart was breaking, and her world was crumbling at her feet, yet this man had made her laugh!

Loretta's hands, clasped together tightly, were resting in her lap. Reaching over, Jack patted them lightly. "Ma'am, your laughter is like music to my ears. I know that right now you probably feel as though you'll never be happy again. But take it from someone who is a lot older and wiser than yourself, this isn't the end of the world. In time, you'll get over Joel and love again."

She wasn't so sure, but not wanting to openly disagree with this man who was being so kind, she smiled as though she believed his words.

Standing, Jack said briskly, "Well, I need to get back to the ranch. I'll return Sunday morning and help you check into the hotel. It should only be a few more days before you can move out to the Bar-S."

She started to get up, but he remarked hastily, "Don't bother to show me out. You just sit there and drink your coffee." He turned about to leave, but pausing, he asked, "Miss Ingalls, are you going to be all right?"

"Yes," she whispered. "I'll be fine, thanks to you." A trace of tears returned to her eyes, but this time they were a sign of gratitude.

"Promise me you'll take care," he insisted. Jack watched her closely as he waited for her assurance. Her long auburn hair was falling about her face in a seductive disarray, and her cheeks were becomingly flushed. Her beauty struck Jack with a force, and for a moment he was taken aback.

"I promise," she replied with a smile.

"Good," he declared, favoring her with an encouraging wink. Then leaving the parlor, he grabbed his hat from the rack and let himself out of the house.

Jack Stevens' two-story framed house sat atop a small incline overlooking his land, which stretched farther than the eye could see. The corrals and the barn stood a good distance from the house so the strong odors which always permeated these areas wouldn't drift through the open windows and into the house.

Now, as Clint and Joel rode up to the hitching rail, they recognized Doctor Blackburn's buggy.

Dismounting swiftly, Joel remarked, "I pray the doctor will say Bonnie Sue's going to be all right."

Getting down from his own horse, Clint replied, "I'm sure she'll be fine."

They hurried up the front steps and across the porch. Opening the door, Clint moved back and gestured for

Joel to precede him.

As they entered, Doctor Blackburn was descending the staircase, his black bag in hand. "Joel," he said heartily, "I'm glad to see you're here."

"How's my wife?" he asked pressingly.

Finishing his descent, the doctor went to Joel and stood in front of him. Absently, he brushed a hand over his gray goatee, and his aged face was etched with a trace of worry. "Bonnie Sue seems to be making a complete recovery, but she's still very frail. She may never regain her full strength."

"My wife has always been fragile. As a child, she was sickly."

Doctor Blackburn spoke firmly. "Bonnie Sue needs good care. You must make sure she takes it easy and doesn't exert herself."

"Is she too weak to travel to Fort Laramie?"

The doctor thought a moment. "No, not if you travel leisurely. But wait another week before making the trip."

He answered hastily, "I will." Joel's eyes darted to the stairway.

Understanding how anxious he must be to see Bonnie Sue, Doctor Blackburn said with a smile, "Why are you standing here, why don't you go to your wife?"

As Joel raced up the stairs, the doctor called, "She's in the second room to your right."

Finding his way, Joel knocked softly, then swinging open the door, he darted inside. The room was lit by a solitary lamp placed on the bedside table. Its soft glow fell across Bonnie Sue, who was sitting up and leaning back against two large feather pillows.

"Joel!" she cried, holding out her arms.

Her husband practically flew to her side and into her embrace. Sitting on the edge of the bed, he drew her close and rocked her back and forth as he moaned

310

huskily, "Bonnie Sue! . . . Bonnie Sue! . . . I love you, sweetheart!"

Her tears, mingling with Joel's, rolled steadily down her pale cheeks. "Oh my darling! . . . My darling! . . . I thought I'd never see you again!"

"Thank God you're alive!" he exclaimed.

Pressing her hand to the back of his neck, she urged his lips to hers. Their lips blended together in a passionate exchange, tasting and relishing the sweetness they had believed was lost forever.

Joel's pulse beat wildly as he continued to savor his wife's kiss; and totally enthralled with Bonnie Sue, his thoughts and heart were now completely devoid of Loretta Ingalls.

Joel stayed with Bonnie Sue until she fell asleep, then as he left her room, he found Johnny waiting for him in the hall.

"Pa's in the study, and he wants to talk to you."

Joel nodded. "All right." This was not his first visit to the Bar-S, and he headed toward the study. But he was detained by Johnny's hand on his arm.

"Joel," he began uneasily, "about that debt I owe you . . ."

"Don't worry about it. I tore up your note a long time ago." Without bothering to offer an explanation, the man left Johnny, hastened down the stairway, and went to the study, where he found Jack seated behind his oak desk with a decanter of brandy and two glasses.

Stevens motioned for Joel to take the chair in front of the desk, then as he poured the drinks, he asked, "Is Bonnie Sue asleep?"

"Yes," he answered, accepting the proffered glass. He took a large swallow of the potent liquor. Then leaning back in the chair, he stretched out his long legs and relaxed. The brandy was soothing, and for the first time since he'd learned that his wife was alive, he began to unwind. "Bonnie Sue told me everything you did for her. Jack, there are no words to express how grateful I am."

"I understand, but your thanks aren't necessary."

"Perhaps, but, God, I do thank you!" Joel took another liberal swig. "I think I'm still in shock. I guess it'll take awhile for the shock to wear off. Bonnie Sue alive! What a wonderful miracle! I've always loved her from the depth of my soul."

Jack regarded him a little critically. "Aren't you forgetting somebody else?"

For a fleeting moment, Joel seemed confused, but his expression quickly became remorseful. "Loretta!" he whispered.

"Joel," the other man began sternly, "you didn't even have the common courtesy to tell the lady goodbye."

Joel finished off his drink, and Jack gestured for him to pour himself another one. Doing so, Joel admonished himself. "I treated Loretta terribly, but I was so beside myself that I was incapable of rational behavior."

Jack decided not to judge the other man so harshly. "Under identical circumstances, I might have done the same thing."

"What am I going to do about Loretta?" he lamented.

"There's nothing you can do except go to town and tell her goodbye, then as soon as Bonnie Sue is well, leave Backwater and stay out of Miss Ingalls' life. Once you're gone, she'll pick up the pieces and start over."

"But you don't understand. Loretta lost her job, and now she has no means of support." His face lightened. "I'll give her enough money to return to Fort Sill.

Maybe she'll be able to resume teaching at the reservation."

"If I were you, I wouldn't make her that offer. Although I know your heart is in the right place, it sounds more like you're trying to buy her off and ease your own conscience. Miss Ingalls will most likely find your proposition degrading. Besides, you don't have to worry about her welfare. I told her she could work here as a housekeeper, and she has accepted the job."

Though Joel was relieved, his actions had flooded him with guilt. He had sincerely loved Loretta, he still loved her, so why was he feeling as though she were a burden that Jack had lifted from his shoulders?

Reading his thoughts, Jack said considerately, "Don't feel so guilty. When you became involved with Miss Ingalls, how could you know it would come to this? Bonnie Sue is your wife and you loved her first."

"And I love her more," Joel added. "I've always known I'd never love another woman as much as I love Bonnie Sue. The way I feel about my wife is a feeling that only happens once in a lifetime."

Jack smiled introspectively. "I envy you. Some of us never experience that kind of love."

The other man looked at him with surprise. "But you were married."

"Yes, but that doesn't mean I loved my wife in the same way you love Bonnie Sue. I guess you could say I was manipulated into marriage. She told me she was pregnant, then after I married her, she admitted that she had lied."

"Why did she want to trap you?"

"Sally always got what she wanted, even if she had to cheat and lie to get it. And she wanted to become Mrs. Jack Stevens, so she set her snare and I fell into it." Jack paused and took a drink of his brandy. "I tried to

313

make the most of our marriage. Sally was a beautiful woman, and although I wasn't in love with her, I can't deny that I didn't desire her. She died in childbirth. The baby was stillborn. Sally never wanted our fourth child; in fact, she never especially wanted any of our children. She was always worried that the pregnancies would ruin her hourglass figure. In a way, I guess her death was my fault. One night she demanded separate bedrooms and a platonic marriage. I never really forgave her for tricking me into marrying her. I lost my temper and forced myself on her, and even though I agreed afterwards to her terms, it was too late, for that was the night when our fourth child was conceived."

"Why haven't you remarried?"

"For years I was too embittered. By the time I could forget all the past pain and rage, I was too old and set in my ways to fall in love."

"I don't buy that excuse," Joel rebuked. "You aren't too old for love."

"Snow on the chimney, but a fire in the hearth?"

Joel chuckled. "Yeah, I guess that's what I was trying to say."

His expression serious, Jack said, "My kids don't know the truth about my marriage."

"You needn't worry. I won't say anything."

Jack changed the subject. "You and Bonnie Sue are welcome to stay here until she's able to travel. I'll have one of my men hitch up the buckboard so you can go into Backwater and pick up your belongings. And while you're in town, don't you think you should pay a call on Miss Ingalls?"

Joel heaved a sigh. "God, I dread facing her! What can I possibly say to ease her pain?"

Jack didn't answer, but then Joel hadn't expected him to offer a solution. He knew that in the end there was no way to avoid breaking Loretta's heart.

Chapter Twenty-Eight

Loretta stood at the window, looking down at the Golden Horseshoe across the street. Her hotel room was on the second floor, and since the day Jack had helped her check in, she had spent a lot of time gazing out the window, for the sight of the saloon made her feel closer to Joel.

Now, with a heavy sigh, she turned away and sat on the edge of the bed. She wondered if Joel and his wife had left for Fort Laramie. A week had passed since Bonnie Sue had miraculously shown up alive, during which time Loretta had become a recluse, never venturing from her hotel room unless it was absolutely necessary.

The day before, Jack had come to inform her that he was quite sure Joel and Bonnie Sue would be leaving within the next twenty-four hours. Loretta supposed today, or by tomorrow at the latest, Mr. Stevens would be arriving to take her to the Bar-S. She wasn't sure if she'd make a competent housekeeper, for she had spent her entire adult life teaching school. She shrugged her small shoulders as though failing or succeeding at her new occupation was irrelevant. She'd do the best job she could, and if it wasn't up to Mary Cummings' standards, then she'd simply find a way to return to Fort Sill.

Loretta knew she should take more interest in her new work, for she owed it to Mr. Stevens to try and please him. But she couldn't muster any form of enthusiasm. Joel had been her life, and now without him, she felt only half-alive.

Moving listlessly, she stretched out on the bed, and drawing back the spread, she fluffed one of the pillows and tucked it beneath her head. Staring up at the plastered ceiling, she allowed her thoughts to drift back to the night Joel had told her goodbye. He had come to town to pick up his belongings, then before returning to the Bar-S to be with his wife, he had stopped at Loretta's home.

Remembering their parting in vivid detail caused a surge of tears to fill her eyes. Joel's visit had been short and straight to the point. He still loved Bonnie Sue and his place was now with her. He'd made a clumsy attempt to tell Loretta that he was sorry, but she had told him that she understood and that an apology wasn't necessary.

I made it so easy for him to step out of my life and back into his wife's, she thought bitterly. Maybe I should have found a way to make him hurt the way I was hurting. But if I had, what difference would it have made? He'd still be with Bonnie Sue and I'd still be lying here alone with my heart breaking. Besides, Joel's not to blame for what happened, so why do I keep feeling so resentful toward him? Is it because he found it so easy to leave me?

Loretta's thoughts were suddenly interrupted by a knock at the door.

"Who's there?" she called.

"Jack Stevens," came the reply.

Leaving the bed, Loretta opened the door. "Please come in, Mr. Stevens."

Concern registered in Jack's eyes as, entering the room, he took a close look at Loretta. Her mussed hair was tangled, giving the impression that it hadn't been thoroughly brushed in days, and she was wearing one of her old, unflattering gowns.

"Are they gone?" she asked dryly.

"Yes, they left this morning."

Moving away, she went back to the window and gazed outside. "I'm glad he's gone," she said unemotionally. "Now I don't have to worry about running into him. I was afraid to even leave this room and step outside for fear of coming in contact with him." Almost inaudibly, she added, "I'm glad they're both gone."

"They have names, you might try using them."

She didn't offer a response.

Jack decided to let the matter rest. "Miss Ingalls, I have a few things to take care of in town, but I'll be back shortly. How long will it take you to pack?"

"Not long," she murmured, still looking outside, her back turned toward Jack.

The door had been left standing open, and when Jack suddenly shoved it closed with a loud bang, the sound caused Loretta to whirl around.

Impatient with her listless attitude, Jack remarked sternly, "Ma'am, I'm usually very sympathetic, but I cannot tolerate self-pity."

"I'm sorry," she replied quickly before he could say more. "I'll try to improve my disposition."

His heart softening, Jack said gently, "It's never easy to lose someone you love. But there is a cure for a broken heart, and it works every time."

"What is that?" she asked, vaguely interested.

"Fall in love again. It's like falling off a horse—

317

you've got to get right back on."

Loretta laughed lightly. "But I've never ridden a horse."

He was surprised. "Never?"

Her eyes twinkled. "I'm a greenhorn."

"Well, the first thing I'm gonna do is teach you. You can't live on a ranch and not know how to ride a horse."

"You can't?"

"No, it's against house rules," he teased.

Stepping away from the window and moving closer to her visitor, she said sincerely, "Mr. Stevens, you're very good for me. You always lift my spirits."

He smiled wryly. "When I come back, I hope I'll find you in a pretty dress with your hair all groomed. You're a beautiful woman, Miss Ingalls, and you shouldn't try to hide your beauty."

"Very well, Mr. Stevens. You're now my employer and if you want me to dress stylishly, I will."

"Don't do it for me! Do it for yourself. There's a lot of eligible bachelors around, and it's only a matter of time before they'll be coming to the Bar-S to court one of the prettiest ladies in these parts."

She started to tell him that she wasn't interested in courting, but decided to let the subject drop. Loretta was sure she'd never fall in love again. Her heart was broken, and there wasn't a man alive who could mend it. She sometimes felt as though she'd never even smile or laugh again. Except when I'm with Jack Stevens, she suddenly realized. For some reason, when he's with me, I'm no longer depressed.

When Black Wolf entered his lodge, he saw Alisha sitting on her bed with his mother's Bible open in her lap.

318

His presence startled Alisha and her gaze flew to his. Black Wolf had left three days ago to go hunting, and she hadn't been expecting his return for another day or so.

"Aren't you back early?" she asked.

Storing his gear in the corner, he answered, "The hunt was more successful than I thought it'd be, so I shortened the trip."

Alisha watched him thoughtfully as he went to the lodge fire and poured himself a cup of coffee. Since the day Black Wolf had decided that they should sleep in separate beds, their relationship had been cordial but distant. She knew their present living arrangements would be almost unbearable if Black Wolf weren't away so often. His hunting excursions always lasted for days. When he returned it was only for a night, and then the next morning he'd be gone again.

Deciding to fix dinner, Alisha started to close the Bible and put it away. However, as the name Charles Lansing crossed her mind, she said to Black Wolf, "Why did your mother decide to name you Charles Lansing?"

"It was her father's name," he answered.

Putting the Bible aside, she stood and walked over to Black Wolf. Sitting beside him, she said, "I know a man whose name is Charles Lansing. He owns a large ranch which borders the north side of the Bar-S. He and Papa are good friends. He's in his late sixties or early seventies, so he's the right age to be your grandfather."

"I seriously doubt that he is. My mother and her folks were living in Northern Texas when Running Horse found her. Is this man from Texas?"

"I don't know," she answered. "I've known him all my life, but he's never said anything about coming from Texas." She thought for a moment, then said eagerly, "But he became a successful rancher through breeding Texas longhorns, so maybe he used to live in Texas."

"Does he have a family?"

"He's a widower. His wife died a long time ago. As far as I know, they never had any children."

"The name Charles Lansing isn't uncommon, so I'm sure it's only a coincidence. There are probably a lot of men with that name."

Black Wolf stood abruptly, and she asked, "Where are you going?"

"To see Running Horse," he answered. "I won't be gone long."

When he left, she moved back to the Bible, picked it up, and returned it to its rightful place. As she laid it on top of the stacked books, she couldn't help but wonder if the Charles Lansing she knew could be Black Wolf's grandfather. No, she suddenly decided. Black Wolf is right, the names are only coincidental. That Charles could be Abigal's father may not be impossible, but it is certainly improbable.

"You didn't learn anything at all?" Jack asked Justin. He was beginning to fear that Alisha might never be found.

The two men were in Jack's study, seated at his desk. Justin had a glass of bourbon in his hand, and he helped himself to a big swig before answering, "Like I done told you, my search didn't turn up a thing. I visited several villages, but no one knew anything about a white woman."

"They could be lying!" Jack argued.

"Yep, they could be." The scout didn't deny it.

Justin had arrived at the Bar-S a short time ago, and

immediately upon his arrival, Jack had ushered him into the study. Stevens had hoped desperately for some encouraging news and had been sorely disappointed to learn that Justin's search had been unsuccessful.

Sighing deeply, Jack said honestly, "Smith, I want to thank you again for trying to find my daughter."

"I'm sorry it didn't work out."

"It's a long way to Fort Laramie. Please accept my hospitality and spend the night here."

Justin finished his drink, then put the glass on the desk. "Thank you, Mr. Stevens. I appreciate your offer."

Standing, Jack said, "I'll have Mary prepare you a room. We always eat at eight, so that gives you plenty of time to rest before dinner."

Before Jack could leave to search for Mary, the study door opened and the woman appeared as though by magic. "Excuse me, but Mr. Lansing is here."

"Charles!" Jack exclaimed. "Show him in."

Lansing had been poised behind the servant, and sweeping past her, he entered the room on long strides.

Jack greeted his friend with a firm handshake. "Charles, this is a pleasant surprise. When did you get back from St. Louis?"

"Yesterday," he answered. "I heard about Alisha, and I came to express my concern."

"Thank you, Charles."

"Have you heard anything about her?"

"No, I'm sorry to say."

Lansing's face turned bitter, and a cold rage flickered in his blue eyes. "These damned Indians! Any warrior caught capturing a white woman should be castrated, then hung by his . . ." It was at that moment that he noticed Justin. When Jack's visitor had entered the room, Justin had gotten to his feet, and he was now

321

standing beside his chair. Continuing, Charles mumbled an apology. "I'm sorry, I didn't realize you had company." To Justin, he remarked, "I hope I didn't offend you, sir."

"No offense taken," the scout assured him.

"Charles," Jack began, "I'd like you to meet Justin Smith. He's Fort Laramie's head scout."

Crossing over to shake Justin's hand, Charles said amicably, "I'm glad to meet you."

Explaining, Jack proceeded, "Mr. Smith has been searching for Alisha." He drew up another chair, and when his guests were seated, he handed them each a glass of bourbon.

Then, as Jack was taking his place behind the desk, Justin remarked offhandedly, "I have a friend named Charles Lansing."

"Oh?" Charles questioned politely. "Does he live in these parts?"

Justin grinned. "Well, in a way he does. He lives in the Black Hills. You see, his name ain't really Charles Lansing. He's a half-breed. His father named him Black Wolf, but his white mother wanted him to have a Christian name, so she named him Charles Lansing after her father."

The elderly man's face paled imperceptibly. "This Black Wolf, do you know how old he is?"

"Somewhere around thirty, I reckon."

"What is his mother's name?"

"Abigal," Justin answered.

Lansing's face now turned ashen. "My God!" he choked.

"Charles, what's wrong?" Jack asked urgently.

It was a moment before the man could find his voice, and when he did, he completely ignored Jack. The scout had his undivided attention. "Tell me everything you know about Black Wolf and his mother."

322

Justin eyed him suspiciously. "I ain't gonna go no further till you tell me why you're so damned interested."

Sitting rigidly, Charles spoke in a strained voice. "Over thirty years ago, my wife and I had a small homestead in Northern Texas. We had one child, a daughter named Abigal, who grew to be eighteen. There had been a lot of unrest between the settlers and the Comanches and I told my wife and daughter to stay close to the house. Abigal disobeyed and went down to the river." A sob caught in his throat and he paused. "We never saw our daughter again. When I went to look for her, I could see by the tracks left in the wet bank that she had been taken by Indians. I notified the Texas Rangers, and although we searched thoroughly, we never found her. The search dragged on for two years. My wife never recovered from her grief, and she finally pined away. She was never a healthy woman, and her heart just wasn't strong enough to endure.

"After my wife died, I decided to move away. I had no definite route in mind, but my travels finally brought me here to Wyoming. When I saw that the cattle in this region were poor specimens, I returned to Texas, bought a herd of longhorns, and drove them back here. Through these Texas longhorns, I eventually made my fortune. But I never really stopped searching for Abigal. In fact, I'm still searching and hoping. You see, I have contacts in different places and was notified recently that a white woman who had been captured years ago by the Comanches had been taken to St. Louis." He sighed regretfully. "That's why I was in St. Louis, but, of course, the woman wasn't my Abigal."

"Black Wolf isn't Comanche, he's Sioux," Justin stated.

"Maybe that's why the rangers and I were unable to

find Abigal. We took for granted that she was kidnapped by Comanches."

"Well, you were in Comanche territory, but the Sioux are nomadic, and their warriors like to wander. It wouldn't be that unlikely for a band of Sioux to wander into Texas."

"Charles," Jack spoke up, his expression depicting his shock. "Why haven't you ever told me about all this?"

"When I decided to make Wyoming my home, I vowed to keep my grief to myself."

"You should've told me. Grief is harder to carry when you have no one to share it with."

"Maybe," he relented. "But I chose to grieve in private and saw no reason to change my mind." He turned to Justin. "Now that I've explained everything, will you please tell me what you know about Black Wolf's mother?"

"Not that much," the scout answered. "Black Wolf seldom talks about her. At least, he never has to me." Justin took a large drink of his bourbon. He wished he could spare the man his next statement, but he knew it had to be said. "Black Wolf's mother died five years ago."

"Died?" he repeated, as though the word was foreign.

"She contracted smallpox."

Charles' body slumped, and his glass fell from his hand and onto the floor.

Rising, Jack hurried to his friend's side. Placing a hand on the man's shoulder, he said firmly, "Charles, you don't know that this woman was your daughter."

"How many Abigals with fathers named Charles Lansing do you think have been stolen by Indians? Are you going to tell me that this is all coincidental?"

"It could be," Jack uttered, but not convincingly.

Suddenly, sitting upright, Charles said briskly, "Mr. Smith, will you take me to Black Wolf? I'll pay you handsomely."

"First of all, I wouldn't take your money, but secondly, and most importantly, it's gettin' too late in the season to be traveling into the Black Hills."

"If we were to leave right away, we could get back before winter breaks."

"Yep, I reckon we could," Justin drawled. He was considering offering the man his services.

"Charles," Jack began, "can't this wait until spring?"

"If you thought you had a grandson in the Hills whom you had never seen, could you wait until spring?"

"I have a daughter up there, and God help me, I'm forced to wait until spring to look for her."

"But this situation is different," Justin explained. "I know where Black Wolf is and we can travel straight to his village. Lookin' for your daughter ain't the same. To find her, we have to stop at every village we can locate. That takes a helluva lot of time."

"Does this mean you're considering taking me to Black Wolf?" Charles asked excitedly.

Justin thought for a moment. He didn't want to trek back into the Hills. He was anxious to return home and see his wife and infant daughter. However, Charles Lansing had his sympathy, and he didn't have the heart to turn him down. "We'll leave in the morning." Looking at Jack, he asked, "Would you mind sending one of your men into town and have him wire Major Landon? The major needs to know what I'm up to so he won't be wondering about me."

Jack nodded agreeably, then remarked, "With your permission, my sons and I will accompany you two."

"I don't object to y'all comin' along, but we can't be stoppin' at villages to ask about your daughter. We ain't got much time, so we got to use it sparingly."

"I understand," Jack replied. "However, you're going to a Sioux camp, and there's always a chance that Alisha might be there."

"You won't find your daughter at Running Horse's village," Justin declared without hesitation. "He refuses to keep any white captives."

Chapter Twenty-Nine

As Alisha was preparing for bed, Black Wolf returned from his most recent hunting excursion. The lodge was lit by one kerosene lamp, and as the powerful warrior entered, the flickering light illuminated his bronze complexion and his blue eyes shined with the radiance of sapphires.

Although Black Wolf gave Alisha a passing glance, his quick appraisal noted her stunning beauty. Enclosed inside the warm lodge, she wasn't wearing leggings, and her Indian dress barely touched her knees, leaving her long, slender legs revealed. She was kneeling beside her bed, which had caused her garment to move up, exposing her soft, creamy thighs. Alisha's long, flaxen hair was falling freely about her pretty face, and even though Black Wolf's perusal had been superficial, he'd noticed a trace of sadness in her large brown eyes.

As he was putting away his hunting equipment, Alisha stood and asked, "Would you like something to eat?"

"No, thanks," he answered. "I'm not hungry, but I am tired, so I think I'll go to the river, take a quick bath, then go to bed."

"Isn't it a little chilly to wash outside?"

"A quick dip in the river will be rejuvenating. I'll stop by Kicking Buffalo's lodge and ask David if he wants to join me. I've been away so much lately that I haven't had a chance to spend any time with the boy."

Alisha's tone was laced with a note of bitterness. "You never have time for anyone. Even Running Horse very seldom sees you." She wanted to add how much she herself resented his continual absence, but her pride buried the complaint.

Black Wolf shrugged as though her remonstrance was of no importance.

His cold aloofness was not only painful to Alisha, but it also provoked her anger. Reacting to the moment, she snapped, "Well, I certainly hope these hunting trips will soon be over. I'm getting tired of sitting in this tepee, waiting for you to finally decide to take me home." Part of what she said was true. She was tired of staying in this lodge, but only because Black Wolf didn't truly share it with her. He was gone so much, and then when he did return, his disposition was so cold that she was sure he resented her presence in his home.

Her vexation was contagious, but Black Wolf managed to keep his ire concealed and remarked with a false air of nonchalance, "It pleases me to announce that I have only one more trip to make, then I can deliver you to the Bar-S and have you out of my life for good."

To Alisha his words were sharp and painful, and they cut deeply into her heart. Returning to kneel beside her bed, she drew back the top cover, and hiding her hurt beneath a calm facade, she asked, "How much longer before we can leave?"

"A week, two at the most," he answered. She lay down on her pallet, and his vivid blue eyes were searing as they watched her every move.

Reclining gracefully, Alisha rolled to lie on her side, turning her back toward Black Wolf. She didn't bother to draw up the top blanket, and her slender frame was clearly in view. Alisha's suede dress clung provocatively to her supple curves, and as Black Wolf's eyes continued to brand her beauty, he had to call upon all his will power to keep from taking this woman who could so easily set his passion ablaze. He was burning with need, and it was infuriating to Black Wolf that Alisha could kindle this flame within him without even trying. She hadn't tempted him on purpose and was probably totally unaware that she was a picture of seduction.

Black Wolf's defenses were weakening, and knowing he'd succumb to Alisha's alluring charms if he didn't leave right away, he hurriedly gathered up what he needed for his bath and left.

Stepping outside, he welcomed the brisk night air, for it seemed to cool his passion. As he headed in the direction of Kicking Buffalo's lodge, he began to question his sanity. Why was he sharing his lodge with a woman as beautiful as Alisha and keeping their relationship platonic? What was wrong with him? Had he lost his virility?

A bitter frown came to his face, for he knew his sanity was intact and his sexual drive was not in danger. In all honesty, he avoided Alisha because he was afraid of having his heart broken, and his only defense was to keep an impersonal breach between them.

As Black Wolf's thoughts flowed, his frown deepened. He had never been so angry with himself as he was at this moment. Since manhood, he'd managed successfully to abide by his vow to never fall in love with a white woman. Once before, he had almost strayed from his promise. When he had first met the woman Major Landon was to marry, Black Wolf had been quite taken with her charms, but it had only been a passing attraction. However, this time it was different. Alisha was not a passing desire; she was in his heart and soul. He loved her with every fiber of his being. Black Wolf was certain that Alisha didn't return his love and was pining for home and her fiancé. If she cared about him the way he cared about her, she'd never have left with Doug and Sam. By God, it still galled him that she had run away without bothering even to tell him goodbye! If it had been the other way around, he could never have hurt her in such a callous fashion!

Reaching his uncle's lodge, Black Wolf cleared his mind of Alisha and asked for permission to enter the tepee. Receiving consent, he stepped inside and invited David to join him for a quick dip in the river.

David had missed being with Black Wolf, and he agreed hastily. He had his things gathered quickly, then left with his friend and kept his strides even with the warrior's as they walked down to the water.

They stopped at a secluded spot a short way from the village. As he began to undress, David remarked, "That water's going to be cold."

Black Wolf shook his head. "Actually it will be a lot warmer in the water than out. The river is fairly deep and hasn't turned cold yet."

David, now stripped, rushed to the river's edge. The evening breeze brushed coolly over his naked flesh, and he shivered as he waded into the water. When it was up to his knees, he dived into the deeper part of the river. The water wrapped around him like a thermal cocoon, warming his cold body almost instantly.

As Black Wolf swam toward him, he called exultantly, "I told you it'd be warm, didn't I?"

"Feels great!" David returned, and as the man drew closer, he playfully splashed water in his direction before swimming farther out.

Later, dressed warmly, the man and boy sat on the bank. The rays from the full moon glistened on the rippling waves, casting a golden hue over the river. The soft noises of nocturnal creatures and sounds from the village mingled, then drifted in harmony over the night-enshrouded land.

Presently content with their own thoughts, Black Wolf and David sat silently. The evening breeze, which was blowing lightly, dried their wet hair with a billowing caress.

It was David who spoke first. "I'm going to miss these Hills, this village, and Flying Hawk," he murmured wistfully. He turned his gaze to Black Wolf. "I'll miss you too."

"You'll be missed in return," he replied. Then, with an encouraging smile, he added, "But I'm sure you'll like living on a ranch. It takes a lot of work to keep a place like the Bar-S operating, so you'll probably be too busy to spend much time missing anyone."

David's expression lightened somewhat as he answered honestly, "In a way, I'm looking forward to living on a ranch. I've always wondered what ranching is like." He grinned as he continued, "And if Alisha's family are as nice as she is, then I know I'll be welcomed."

His reference to Alisha caused a look of bitterness to shadow Black Wolf's face. Seeing this, David asked, "What's wrong?"

"Nothing," he mumbled, and was about to abruptly change the subject, but David didn't give him a chance.

"I know something is wrong between you and

Alisha. Since that time when she left with those trappers, she's been acting differently and so have you. Whenever I try to talk to her about what's wrong, she refuses to discuss it."

"You needn't worry, David. Alisha is merely homesick and is impatient to leave. Unlike you, she wasn't able to adjust to her surroundings, nor was she fortunate enough to develop a close friendship similar to yours and Flying Hawk's." Black Wolf was now aware that the boys had settled their dispute and a strong friendship had ensued.

"You've been away so much lately that you don't know what's going on. Alisha has adjusted, and she and Spotted Fawn are close friends. In fact, a lot of the women in the village like Alisha."

Black Wolf was surprised. "I didn't know she was even visiting with other women."

"How could you know?" David countered. "You're never home long enough to know what's happening."

"Maybe she has adapted somewhat, but she's still anxious to leave; otherwise she wouldn't have left with Doug and Sam."

"Hasn't she told you why she ran off with them?" David exclaimed.

"What are you talking about?"

"The day you brought her back, she told me she wasn't going to tell you why she left, but I thought by now she'd have changed her mind."

His interest aroused, Black Wolf demanded, "What hasn't she told me?"

"The trappers lied to Alisha. They said that they'd run across a search party led by her brothers. Sam told Alisha that her oldest brother, Clint, had told him that her father had been shot by the Sioux and was seriously wounded. She didn't leave this village to get away

332

from you. She left because she was worried about her father."

Black Wolf didn't say anything. He wanted to thoroughly digest everything David had revealed. Why hadn't Alisha told him about this? He tried to think of a logical explanation but came up blank. Well, there was only one way to find out and that was to come right out and ask her.

Getting to his feet, Black Wolf said, "I'm going hunting in the morning, and this time I'll be gone about a week. When I return, I plan to take you and Alisha to the Bar-S. So I'll see you when I get back." Anxious to see Alisha, he continued hastily, "It's late; I'm going to turn in."

Standing, David relied, "I know you're planning to talk to Alisha. I hope you two make up."

Black Wolf's smile was bittersweet. "I wish our problems were that simple, but they're too complicated to be resolved merely by 'making up.'"

Alisha was asleep when Black Wolf returned, and he stepped quietly to her side and knelt. She had the cover drawn up past her shoulders and he wondered if she was wearing any clothes. It'd been a long time since he had seen her undressed, and just the thought of her nakedness made his passion spring to life. Moving noiselessly, he stood and stripped off his own clothing, then using care he lay beside her. She didn't stir and was still sleeping soundly.

She was lying on her side, and cuddling behind her, he placed an arm across her waist. "Alisha," he whispered, his lips next to her ear.

Alisha awoke slowly, and at first she thought she must be dreaming, for she could've sworn that she'd heard Black Wolf call her name. Suddenly becoming aware of his closeness, she rolled onto her back.

"Black Wolf!" she gasped. "What are you doing here?"

Leaning up, he gazed down into her bewildered face. "What do you think I'm doing?"

Perturbed, she spat, "If you think for one minute that you can come to my bed and help yourself, then you are badly mistaken!"

His grin askew, he promised, "I not only intend to help myself, but I also aim to have seconds."

"You arrogant cad!" Her temper was boiling. "How dare you treat me as though I'm a kept woman!"

Paying no heed to her anger, he replied calmly, "At present you are my woman, and you're under my keep, so let's stop this silly bickering and make love."

She made a futile attempt to rise, but his large frame was suddenly over hers, trapping her beneath him.

"Let me up!" she said furiously.

Resting on one elbow, he looked deeply into her flashing eyes. The lamp was still lit, making it easy for him to see her. He decided to completely disregard her demands. "We have something very important to discuss, but it can wait until afterwards."

"After what?" she snapped.

"After I get my fill of you," he murmured thickly, although he knew he could love her for an eternity and still hunger for more.

Knowing it would be useless to fight, she remarked coldly, "Then get on with it and get it over with!"

Black Wolf chuckled. "So you plan to pretend indifference, do you?" He moved over and stretched out at her side. "We'll just see how long you can remain unresponsive."

Alisha swallowed nervously. Could she possibly lie here submissively and let him have his way with her?

Would her body betray her? She sighed defeatedly, for she already knew that she'd surrender. How could she do otherwise? She loved this man with all her heart.

With one downward sweep, he had the cover tossed to the foot of the bed. She was unclothed, and his blue eyes filled with desire as they traveled leisurely over her bare loveliness.

His breathing deepened with passion as he leaned over and claimed her lips with his. Black Wolf's kiss was demanding, all-consuming; and casting aside her doubts, Alisha looped her arms about his neck. Her tongue darted forward to meet his; the contact was sensual and inviting.

As his mouth continued to relish hers, Black Wolf's hand moved to her breasts, feeling one and then the other. A soft gasp escaped Alisha's throat as his hand dipped farther down, and finding the core of her pleasure, he caressed her until he had her writhing in ecstasy.

As his lips conquered hers over and over again, he continued his fondling until he brought her to such heights of rapture that she thrust upwards against his probing finger. Just when she thought she could take no more of this wonderful torture, Black Wolf slid down the bed, and spreading apart her legs, moved between them. Placing his hands beneath her hips, he brought her love mound up to his mouth.

Alisha cried out loud with intense longing as his lips and tongue sent her soaring upwards to passion's breathtaking apex.

Black Wolf's need was now flying as high as Alisha's, and rising to his knees, he started to place her legs over his shoulders and plunge deeply within her, but she stopped him by whispering, "No, Black Wolf, not yet." His manhood was hard and throbbing for relief, and as she studied his superb maleness, she eased herself down the bed. When she reached him, she sat upright, and before taking him into her mouth, she murmured sensually, "I want to love you as intimately as you love me."

The touch of her warm lips was thrilling to Black Wolf, and when her tongue brushed against him, his powerful frame trembled. Lacing his fingers through her flowing hair, he encouraged her to continue.

He was soon drawing dangerously close to climaxing, and breaking away, he grasped her at the waist. Easily, his strong arms turned her over. Telling her to rest on her hands and knees, he took his place behind her rounded buttocks. Holding tightly to her slim hips, he brought her against him and guided his shaft far into her womanly depths.

Although this position was new to Alisha, she instinctively knew how to respond. Leaning her weight on her bent arms, she allowed his hardness to dip even farther inside. His maleness filled her with joy, and she pushed back and forth, loving the feel of him moving in and out.

No woman had ever aroused Black Wolf so passionately, and losing himself in their fiery joining, he pounded into her vigorously. His fulfillment culminated powerfully, and achieving her own completion, Alisha found wonderful appeasement simultaneously with the man she loved.

Drained, Black Wolf dropped limply onto the bed. He held out his arms, and she went into them and cuddled close.

Alisha remained quiet, waiting for Black Wolf to say something. This time, would he profess his love? Or had he used her only to satisfy his lust? Earlier, he had said that they had something important to discuss. What had he meant? Did he want to talk about their future? Alisha tried to curb her expectations, but she

336

failed and her hopes began to rise. Was Black Wolf planning to ask her to marry him?

"Alisha," Black Wolf finally began, "why didn't you tell me the truth about Sam and Doug?"

"Wh . . . what do you mean?" she stammered. Her spirits tumbled. Black Wolf didn't want to discuss marriage, he wanted to discuss those trappers!

"David said that Sam told you that your father had been shot while searching for you."

"So?" Alisha mumbled, her tone somewhat irritable. She moved out of his arms, and although she remained at his side, she made sure no part of her was touching him. Why had she allowed her hopes to soar just so this man could send them plunging? Would she never learn? Black Wolf wasn't going to proclaim his love, because he didn't love her.

Sounding short-tempered, he remarked, "You should've told me why you left with Sam and Doug."

"Why?" she questioned sharply. "What difference would it have made?"

A trace of a frown crossed his face. Damn, why must she be so difficult? Didn't she understand that if he had known the truth, he wouldn't have been so angry? Maybe she does understand, he thought dejectedly, and doesn't care.

Black Wolf decided to drop the subject, for it wasn't bringing the results he had hoped for. Discussing why she had left with the trappers wasn't going to be a step toward resolving their problems. Furthermore, she'd probably have taken off with them even if Sam hadn't told her that her father was wounded. Alisha wanted to go home and would grasp any opportunity to do so. Is she that desperate to be reunited with her fiancé? he wondered bitterly. But, damn it, if she loves Miller, then why is she being unfaithful to him? Not only is she cheating, but she's apparently doing so without feeling

337

any guilt.

The more Black Wolf thought about the deceit he believed Alisha was practicing, the angrier he became. Decisively, he swore to cast her out of his life and out of his heart! He wanted a wife he could trust. Obviously Alisha was the kind of a woman a man couldn't trust any farther than he could see her!

Alisha was finding Black Wolf's attitude irritating. He was so arrogant, so demanding! The man had come to her bed, taken advantage of her love, and now had the gall to treat her impersonally! He was stripping away her self-respect and she was submissively letting him get away with it. Deciding it was time for her to protect her pride as well as her heart, she muttered with feigned indifference, "Now that we have both satisfied our passions, don't you think you should sleep in your own bed?"

Her words set fire to Black Wolf's smoldering anger. His wrath burning out of control, he raised himself up and gazed darkly into her face. "I'll leave this bed when I'm ready."

"And just when might that be?" she asked tartly.

"When I joined you in this bed, I told you I intended to have seconds, and I'm about to do just that."

Before she could protest, his lips were suddenly on hers, claiming her mouth with a kiss so forcefully passionate that Alisha's defenses were destroyed; and surrendering, her arms went around his neck.

Moving his large frame over hers, Black Wolf wrapped an arm around her waist, lifting her thighs to his. He entered her suddenly, his maleness filling her with breathtaking ecstasy.

Black Wolf kissed her again as he began to move inside her, and as wondrous chills coursed throughout her, she met him thrust for thrust.

His passion unbridled, Black Wolf took her aggressively, and she responded wantonly to his demanding love. Their hostilities became nonexistent as they became totally engulfed in their erotic joining.

Black Wolf's release came to him with a demanding force, and experiencing her own peak of pleasure, Alisha arched her hips to his as, together, they sought total completion.

He remained inside her until his breathing calmed and returned to normal, then withdrawing, he raised up and sprang to his feet. Looking down at her with an expression she couldn't discern, he uttered with frigid detachment, "Thank you for satisfying my needs."

Holding back the tears that were threatening to overflow, she equaled his coldness, "And I thank you for doing likewise."

He grinned cynically. "In a way, I envy your future husband, for he'll never have need of a prostitute to appease his passion. His own wife's ardor is equal to that of any whore's."

Bolting from the bed, Alisha drew back her arm to slap him, but he caught her wrist in midflight. Grasping her firmly, he forced her back down to her pallet.

He began to dress hastily, and she watched him through tear-glazed eyes. Whore! Was that his opinion of her? Oh, I hate him! she cried to herself. I hate him! . . . I hate him! But even as she silently spouted the words, she knew they were untrue.

Dressed, Black Wolf whirled away, and stepping to the corner of the lodge, he gathered his hunting gear, then grabbed his packed provisions, went to the closed flap and swung it aside. Pausing, he turned to look at Alisha. "As you can see, I decided to leave tonight instead of in the morning. I'll be back in about a week, then I promise you faithfully that I'll take you home."

She held tenaciously to her pride. "I'll be counting the days, so try not to be late."

His eyes pierced hers, and his expression was so violent that she instinctively recoiled. "I won't be late," he grumbled, then without further words, he darted outside.

The moment he was gone, Alisha fell back on her bed and gave in to her tears.

Chapter Thirty

As dawn cast a reddish glow across the eastern horizon, Black Wolf pulled up his sorrel stallion and dismounted. Remaining beside the horse, he patted the animal's neck and spoke gently to him. When Running Horse had learned of the pinto's death, he had given his son this young horse. The chief owned a large herd, and he had told Kicking Buffalo to choose the best stallion from among them as a gift for Black Wolf.

The sun continued to rise, and as its brightness consumed the fading shadows of night, Black Wolf remained standing beside his horse. He stood as though transfixed, and his vivid blue eyes, now sad, were fixed on the grave that lay in the near distance. At one end of the mount a small headstone had been erected.

Daylight was in full bloom before Black Wolf finally moved, and turning to his horse, he reached inside the saddle bags and removed a pemmican cake. Taking his canteen, he strolled to a tall spruce and sat down within its shade. His back was now turned toward the solitary grave, an as he ate his cold breakfast, his gaze swept over the rolling hills outlining the earth's edge. Their eminence towered over the land, and the lofty peaks, reflecting a deep purple, cast a magenta shadow across the forest-covered slopes. The azure sky was dotted with clusters of white billowing clouds, their downiness touching the high summits like soft balls of cotton.

Nature's painting was breathtaking in its glory, and although Black Wolf seldom failed to admire its beauty, this morning he was too troubled to do so, for his thoughts were filled with Alisha. Last night he had gone against his better judgment and had succumbed to his need for her. Now he was regretting his actions. He should've stuck by his resolutions to try to keep their relationship impersonal. However, when David told him the truth about why she had left with the trappers, the revelation had given Black Wolf a reason to hope. But apparently his expectations had been for naught. Alisha had made it very plain that although she desired him physically, that was as far as her feelings went.

Deciding it was time to move on, Black Wolf finished eating, then took a large swallow of water. Getting to his feet, he went back to the horse and replaced the canteen. Although he was ready to leave, Black Wolf didn't mount; instead, he left the stallion's side and walked slowly over to the lonely grave.

Kneeling, he gazed somberly at the small headstone. Black Wolf had ordered it himself, and wanting to keep the inscription simple, had told the carver what to inscribe. Now, speaking quietly, he read the words out loud. "Abigal Ruth Lansing: Born 1820; Died 1863." Black Wolf paused as he recalled the day when he'd told the stone-carver what to write. Although he'd ordered a short epitaph, he hadn't wanted it to sound cold and stoical, so beneath the two dates lay another inscription. Continuing, Black Wolf read softly, "She was deeply loved."

*   *   *

"My wife and I loved Abigal," Charles Lansing was saying to Justin. "Since she was an only child, maybe we loved her too much."

The five travelers were on horseback, the scout and Lansing taking the lead. Jack and Clint were riding in the middle, and Johnny was lagging behind.

Glancing at Justin, Charles proceeded, "Do you think parents' can give a child too much love?"

Thinking about his own daughter, who was her father's pride and joy, the scout answered, "Nope, I sure don't."

Charles was silent for a time as his thoughts centered on Abigal's son. He was curious about this man he believed was his grandson. He was called Black Wolf, yet Abigal had wanted him to carry her father's name. Lansing wondered if his namesake had inherited any of his own characteristics. Would he favor the Lansings, or was he all Sioux? When he met Black Wolf, would he be able to see him as his grandson? Was he capable of seeing the Lansing bearing beneath Black Wolf's savage exterior? Charles was deeply worried, for he feared it might be impossible for him and his grandson to accept each other. After all, Abigal's son had been raised as a Sioux, and by the white man's standards, was uncivilized. Furthermore, he might even harbor hostilities toward his mother's people.

Deciding to probe Justin about his grandson, Charles asked, "How long have you known Black Wolf?"

"Ten, twelve years, I reckon," he drawled.

"Will I have much trouble communicating with him?"

Justin looked at Charles a little dubiously.

"How well does he speak English?"

The scout smiled expansively. "He speaks English a helluva lot better than I do."

"Then he has mastered the language?"

"As well as a college graduate."

Charles was astonished. "Are you telling me that Black Wolf can speak English as though it were his own language?"

"His mother taught him, and from what Black Wolf has told me, she was downright strict."

The other man smiled with fond remembrance. "Abigal wanted to be a school teacher. My wife, Ruth, taught school before she and I were married."

"Abigal didn't teach Black Wolf only English, but all the basic subjects. Running Horse always found a way to get her the books she needed. Not only textbooks, but works of literature. Black Wolf has quite a collection of reading material, and I reckon he's read all them books. He's not only smart, but has what you could call polished manners."

Charles' disbelief deepened. "Black Wolf is well-read? I can hardly believe that a Sioux warrior can be not only educated, but also cultured."

The scout chuckled. "Black Wolf has shocked a lot of people with his . . . his . . ." Justin couldn't find the right words to get his point across.

"'Savoir-faire'?" Charles prompted.

"What in the hell does that mean?" the scout asked, his face blank.

"It's French, meaning knowledge of just what to do in any situation."

Nodding somewhat hesitantly, Justin agreed, "Yeah, I reckon that's what I was tryin' to say. Anyhow, Black Wolf has a shockin' affect on people when they meet him for the first time. When him and Major Landon traveled to Washington D.C. a few years back, he shocked a bunch of them government officials. You see they was all prepared to meet a wild half-breed."

Charles was struck with pride for this grandson

whom he had never met. "I can well imagine their surprise. Why did Black Wolf go to Washington?"

"The Army uses Black Wolf a lot when it comes time to talk treaties."

Eagerly, Charles remarked, "I'm anxious to meet Black Wolf. A few minutes ago I was worried that our different cultures might make it impossible for us to communicate. But you have certainly put my mind at ease." A large reverent smile crossed his face as he added, "Apparently, my grandson is stupendous."

Meanwhile, as Justin and Charles continued to discuss Black Wolf, Clint began a conversation with his father. "Pa," he said softly so he wouldn't be overheard. "You're being unusually quiet. I know you're worried about Alisha, but I have a feeling something else is upsetting you. Would you like to tell me about it?"

"You know me very well," Jack replied, smiling a little ruefully.

"We're a lot alike, Pa. I guess that's why I can sense your feelings."

"You're right, son. I am troubled, and it's more than Alisha's abduction."

"Is it Johnny?" he asked in a hushed tone.

Jack frowned slightly. "I'm always worried about Johnny. But, this time, he's not the one on my mind. It's Miss Ingalls."

Clint was surprised. "Why are you worried about her?"

"I'm thinking that maybe I shouldn't have left her. She hasn't had time to recover from losing Joel, and she probably needs a friend. She told me that I was good for her and lifted her spirits. This trip to Running Horse's village will most likely prove to be a wasted effort as far as finding Alisha. Choosing to accompany Charles and Smith was probably foolish. We should've

345

stayed home. Johnny didn't even want to come, and I'm beginning to feel bad about insisting that he make this trip."

"But your concern lies mostly with Miss Ingalls, doesn't it?"

Jack expelled a heavy sigh. "For some reason, I can't get her out of my mind."

Watching his father closely, Clint implied, "Maybe your feelings for Miss Ingalls run deeper than you realize."

"Exactly what are you insinuating?"

"You could be falling in love," he replied, grinning.

"That's absurd," his father denied quickly. "She's much too young for me."

"What's age got to do with it? Besides, Pa, you're only forty-nine. It'll be a long time yet before you're over the hill."

Jack laughed heartily. "I already went over the hill, and it's a whole lot better than the other side was."

"But it's lonely, isn't it?"

His countenace was now sober. "Sometimes it gets lonely, but I have the Bar-S and my kids to compensate."

"If you ask me, you made a poor trade."

"Well, I didn't ask you, so let's drop the subject."

But Clint wasn't ready to relent. "You know, I've always wondered why you never remarried. Did you love Ma so much that you couldn't find it in your heart to love again?"

"I never knew you were a romantic," Jack mumbled, evading the question. Then, before Clint could continue, he urged his horse forward, and catching up to Justin and Charles, rode alongside them.

Clint wasn't surprised that his father had dodged his questions. He had tried often to get Jack to talk to him about his mother, and he'd always avoided discussing her at length. However, at the moment Clint's thoughts weren't on his parents' marriage, but were centered on his father's relationship with Loretta Ingalls. He wondered if Jack was indeed falling in love. A shadow of a smile teased his lips as the possibility became quite feasible. However, it was a little hard for him to imagine having a stepmother only a couple of years older than himself. As his musings proceeded, the smile faded. His father had been right, he was a romantic. He already had Jack and Loretta married, although he was perfectly aware that she was still very much in love with Joel Carson.

Clint's thoughts now wandered to Joel and Bonnie Sue. He hoped they had made it safely to Fort Laramie. Jack had advised them to take the stagecoach, but Bonnie Sue had wanted to return the buckboard that had been loaned by Lieutenant Wilkinson. A look of concern came to Clint's eyes as a vision of Joel's wife flashed before him. He knew the young woman had supposedly recovered from her miscarriage, but she still seemed very frail. But with proper nourishment and tender care, surely her health would improve. In the meantime, Clint hoped Bonnie Sue wouldn't come down with a serious illness, for in her weakened condition, he doubted if she would have the strength to survive.

"Thank you for inviting us to dinner, Mrs. Landon," Bonnie Sue said cordially as the major's wife showed her and Joel into the small, tastefully furnished parlor.

"You're more than welcome," their hostess replied. "But I do wish you'd call me Suzanne."

Bonnie Sue told the woman that she too must use their first names.

After her guests had been seated on the sofa and

served aperitifs, Suzanne sat on the chair facing them and said apologetically, "I'm afraid my husband is going to be a few minutes late. He's in a meeting with Colonel Johnson."

"We understand," Joel answered. Taking a sip of his brandy, he studied the major's wife over the rim of his glass. She was a strikingly beautiful woman, her blond hair worn in a flattering upsweep and her pale blue gown the latest fashion. Swallowing a liberal amount of the liquor, he then turned his eyes to his wife. Deep concern came over him as he took note of Bonnie Sue's frailty and pallor. He experienced a pang of anxiety. Bonnie Sue wasn't recovering as well as he had hoped. As he continued to watch her, she was suddenly struck with a coughing bout. Putting down his glass, he reached into his shirt pocket and withdrew a handkerchief. Handing it to her, he asked urgently, "Darling, are you all right?"

She coughed into the handkerchief, then having cleared her lungs somewhat, she answered weakly, "Yes, I'll be fine."

"We have two doctors here at the fort," Suzanne told Bonnie Sue. "Tomorrow you should see about having one of them take a look at you. That cough could get worse."

"She's been coughing a lot for the last couple of days," Joel explained.

"Then by all means, she must see a doctor," the major's wife replied.

Before they could further discuss Bonnie Sue's condition, the Landons' young daughter walked into the room. She was wearing her nightgown and a robe, and going to her mother, she kissed her on the cheek. "Good night, Mama," she murmured.

"Kara, I'd like you to meet Bonnie Sue and Joel Carson. They plan to winter here at the fort, then come

348

spring, journey to San Francisco."

The five-year-old smiled and said good night to the couple before leaving the parlor to go to bed.

Suzanne's eyes had followed her daughter out of the room, and when she turned back to acknowledge her guests, she noticed that Bonnie Sue appeared melancholic. "Is anything wrong?" she asked her.

"Is Kara part Indian?" she queried, then realizing her prodding was rude, continued, "Forgive me. I had no right to ask such a personal question."

Smiling, Suzanne answered, "No, that's all right. Kara is our adopted daughter. Her father is white but her mother was Sioux."

Wistfully, Bonnie Sue murmured, "Kara reminds me of Little Star."

The major's wife was aware of Bonnie Sue's past captivity and figured Little Star had lived in Bear Claw's village. "Is Little Star Kara's age?"

"She's a little older. Little Star is a very sweet child, and when I was ill, she took care of me."

At that moment, Major Landon entered his home, and as his wife rose to greet him, Joel grasped the opportunity to ask Bonnie Sue secretively, "Darling, are you sure you feel well enough to stay for dinner?"

She smiled reassuringly. "Yes, Joel, I feel fine. I want to stay for dinner. It's been so long since I socialized, and the major and his wife are so nice."

Squeezing her hand, he replied gently, "I understand. We'll stay, but if you start feeling ill . . ."

She interrupted, "Darling, please stop worrying about me."

Joel agreed to do so, but it was with misgivings, for he was gravely worried about his wife's health. She was recovering so slowly, and now this cough . . . dear God, what if he were to lose her a second time? He quickly dispelled the heart-wrenching thought. Bonnie

Sue would be fine, and in the spring they'd go to San Francisco and fulfill their dream.

Bonnie Sue, lying in bed, watched her husband as he extinguished the lamp, then as he lay beside her, she cuddled close. "Joel," she began, "I had such an enjoyable evening with the Landons."

"So did I," he answered honestly, wrapping his arms about her and drawing her even closer.

"Unlike the major and his wife, some people here at the fort look at me as though I were a freak. Some of them probably think I should have chosen death over living with the Sioux."

Joel wished he could dispute what she had said, but he knew it was the truth. "Don't let it bother you, honey. When we get to San Franciso, no one will know about your captivity."

"You will," she said, then wished she could withdraw the words.

"What are you trying to say?" he asked, raising up. The window curtains were open, allowing the moonlight to filter into the room. Joel could see her face plainly, and when she didn't answer, he gazed deeply into her eyes and asked again, "What are you trying to say?"

"Nothing," she sighed, attempting to evade the issue.

"Answer me!" he insisted.

"All right," she relented, deciding it might be better to express herself. "Since we've been reunited, you haven't made love to me, and I think it's because . . . because . . ." Her voice faltered and her conviction weakened.

"Go on," he encouraged.

Tears emerging, she moaned, "I'm afraid that you don't want to make love to me because of Strong Fox.

You don't want a woman who has been taken by a Sioux warrior."

"No, Bonnie Sue," he denied almost too quickly. "I've been concerned about your health. I think you should be completely recovered before we . . ."

"I am sufficiently recovered," she cut in.

Moving to the edge of the bed, Joel swung his legs over the side, and leaning his head in his hands, he said weakly, "I still think we should wait a little longer."

Sitting up, she remarked, "You mean a little longer for you to accept the fact that your wife was raped time and time again by an Indian."

"No, of course that's not what I meant. I'm only concerned about your health."

"Joel, if you truly believe that, then you are lying not only to me but also to yourself."

Turning, he reached for her hand, "Bonnie Sue," he pleaded.

Avoiding his touch, she lay back down and rolled to her side, presenting him her back. "Leave me alone," she cried.

"Darling, please . . ."

"For God's sake, Joel! Haven't I suffered enough?"

He looked on as, all at once, she was struck with a coughing fit so violent that her body shook with its force.

Grasping her shaking shoulders, Joel drew her into his arms and held her close until the spasm passed. Keeping her in his embrace, he murmured, "I love you, Bonnie Sue. I swear to God that I do!"

Tears falling copiously, she wrapped her arms about him and leaned willingly against his chest. "I know you do, Joel. And I love you too."

"We'll make love again, darling. Believe me, we will. As soon as you're a little better." Even as Joel said the words, he knew he was merely using her frailty to avoid facing the truth. Bonnie Sue had been right; her relationship with Strong Fox did keep gnawing at him. Everytime he thought about making love to his wife, he could envision that warrior taking her whenever and however he pleased. Joel knew he had to find a way to block it from his mind, or else he might never be a husband to Bonnie Sue in every sense of the word.

Holding his wife tightly and rocking her back and forth, he crooned in a soothing tone, "In time, darling. Just a little more time and we'll be as close as we ever were." As self-bitterness coupled with guilt welled up inside him, he wondered if he was trying to convince Bonnie Sue, or was he trying to convince himself?

Chapter Thirty-One

Alisha was just beginning to prepare lunch when Spotted Fawn rushed into her lodge and exclaimed, "There are white men in the village!"

Excited, Alisha asked, "Do you know them?"

"I know the one called Justin Smith. He is a scout from Fort Laramie. But I have never seen the men who are with him."

"Do they look like trappers?"

Spotted Fawn shook her head. "No, they are not trappers."

Alisha's heart began to beat rapidly. Could these men possibly be her father and brothers? "Where are they?" she asked.

"Justin Smith went inside Running Horse's lodge, but the other men are still mounted at the edge of the village."

"How many men are there?"

"Four men are with Justin Smith."

"Did you see them very well? Can you describe them?"

"I did not look at them all that closely, for I came here to tell you."

Suddenly, wondering why she was standing here

asking questions when she could find the answers herself, Alisha darted outside.

Peering into the distance, Alisha could barely make out four mounted men. She began hurrying toward them with Spotted Fawn close at her side. As she drew nearer the visitors, they became distinguishable, and recognizing them, she cried joyously, "Papa!"

Jack was sitting on horseback, and his mount was next to Lansing's; Clint and Johnny, still mounted, were close behind. Now, hearing Alisha's voice, Jack stiffened as his eyes darted in her direction. Catching sight of his daughter rushing toward him, he dismounted with haste and stepped forward to greet her.

Flinging herself into her father's outstretched arms, Alisha hugged him enthusiastically. "Oh Papa! . . . Papa!" she cried, thankful that he was alive and well.

Before Jack had a chance to recover from his shock of finding her, Clint and Johnny were there, waiting to embrace their sister.

Charles got down from his horse, and after Alisha had been greeted by her family, he also hugged her and placed an affectionate kiss on her cheek.

As a semblance of calmness finally came over the happy gathering, Jack took time to study his daughter. He wasn't surprised to see her dressed in Indian clothing, but he was indeed amazed to find that she appeared to be perfectly well and in good spirits.

Knowing this was not the time to flood her with questions, Jack drew her back into his arms and uttered, "I thank God that you're alive and apparently all right."

"Papa, I have so much to tell you," Alisha breathed.

It was then that Jack noticed the pretty Indian woman who was standing close by, watching the proceedings.

Although it had taken Jack awhile to notice Spotted

Fawn, Johnny had been aware of her for quite some time. She, in turn, was acutely conscious of Johnny's good looks and sensual presence.

As Alisha was introducing them to Spotted Fawn, Justin, having concluded his business with Running Horse, joined the group. More introductions and explanations ensued, then Alisha suggested that they all go to her lodge, where they could talk and have lunch. Spotted Fawn offered to help prepare the food, and Alisha gladly accepted her assistance.

Johnny fell into stride beside Spotted Fawn as they all left for Alisha's lodge. The white man's closeness sent the young Indian woman's pulse racing. Giving him a sidelong glance, and admiring his handsome features, Spotted Fawn was immediately mesmerized. Meanwhile Johnny, eyeing her boldly, was wondering if he'd find an opportunity to seduce her. He'd never had an Indian woman, but he'd always heard that they responded more wantonly than whores. Just the thought of this lovely Sioux maiden squirming and writhing beneath him caused Johnny's manhood to harden.

Charles, out of consideration, waited for Alisha and her family to complete their discussion before joining in the conversation. When Alisha had explained how she'd been rescued by Black Wolf and the way in which he had taken care of both herself and David, Charles had had to force himself to keep quiet. He had wanted desperately to begin questioning her about Black Wolf but knew he should wait until she was finished.

By the time the Stevens' family had concluded their business, lunch was over. Everyone was sitting around the lodge fire, and putting down his empty plate, Charles decided it was now time for him to ask about

Black Wolf. Alisha was seated across from him, and catching her eye, he began urgently, "You said that Black Wolf has gone hunting. When do you expect him to return?"

"Today, or tomorrow at the latest." Alisha looked at him a little curiously. She had been surprised to find Charles Lansing with her family and wondered why he was accompanying them.

Charles' next words satisfied her curiosity. "I have reason to suspect that Black Wolf is my grandson." He glanced at Justin who was sitting beside Clint. "Mr. Smith has known Black Wolf for a long time, and he told me that Black Wolf's mother named him Charles Lansing."

"Yes, that's true," Alisha replied. "Did you have a daughter abducted by Indians?"

"Yes," he answered with a sigh. "It happened over thirty years ago."

Standing, Alisha went to the Bible and picked it up. Returning, she sat beside Charles, and opening the Bible to the pages she wanted him to read, she said, "This belonged to Black Wolf's mother. Do you recognize the handwriting as your daughter's?"

He studied the writing carefully. "Yes, I think it's Abigal's." He continued to read further, then as his breathing deepened, he exclaimed, "She named her daughters Hannah and Rebecca!" Explaining, he told the others, "My sisters were named Hannah and Rebecca!"

Speaking up, Justin drawled, "It's beginnin' to look more and more like Black Wolf's your grandson."

Turning to Alisha, Charles asked, "Where are Abigal's daughters?"

Reaching over, she turned the page, and as Lansing continued to read, he inhaled sharply.

Explaining to the others, Alisha said, "The girls died

356

of pneumonia in their infancy."

"Lansing," Justin began, "Running Horse said he'd meet with you after lunch. If you're ready, I'll take you to his lodge."

Charles rose eagerly. "Let's go."

As soon as the two men left, Jack suggested that Alisha take a walk with him. He needed to talk to her and didn't feel free to do so in Spotted Fawn's presence. As an afterthought, he asked Clint to accompany them. What he had to discuss with Alisha was personal, but Clint was Alisha's oldest brother and had a right to state his opinions. It never crossed his mind to take Johnny along, for he wasn't interested in his youngest son's views.

The moment his family departed, Johnny grasped the opportunity to charm Spotted Fawn. She was sitting next to him, but now that they were alone, she decided to make her excuses and leave. It wasn't proper for her to be alone with this man.

She started to rise, but Johnny's hand was quickly on her arm, detaining her. "Don't rush off," he said smoothly.

"I must go," she murmured, her eyes downcast.

"Why?" he asked. "I won't hurt you."

"It isn't right for me to be alone with a man," she explained. "I am a maiden."

"So?" he questioned.

"We are not chaperoned," she replied hastily, getting to her feet.

Before she could flee, he was at her side and had her swept into his arms. Pushing against him, she pleaded, "Please let me go!"

Favoring her with his most charming smile, he uttered, "You don't really want me to let you go, do you?"

Johnny's closeness was causing her heart to race, and

responding to his sensual presence, she whispered uncertainly, "I am confused."

"Don't be afraid, my beauty, for I won't harm you." He tightened his hold on her, pinning her flush to his hard frame. "Spotted Fawn, do you believe in love at first sight?"

"I . . . I don't know," she stammered, very conscious of his firm desire pressed against her so intimately. A strange, warm feeling came over her, its intensity pinpointed between her thighs, compelling her to press closer to his hardness.

Aware of her response, Johnny grinned to himself. Seducing her was going to be a lot easier than he had thought. "I love you, Spotted Fawn," he lied with calculated deceit. "I fell hopelessly in love with you at first sight."

Coming to her senses, she attempted to push free; but his lips were suddenly on hers, and losing the will to refuse, Spotted Fawn melted into his arms and returned his kiss with awakening passion.

"Meet me tonight," he implored, his lips brushing feather-light caresses over her neck.

"I cannot," she answered feebly. She experienced stimulating shivers as his lips continued their sensual assault.

"Yes you can," he insisted gently.

Surrendering, she murmured, "Tonight when the village is sleeping, follow the river downstream. When you reach the hillside, you'll see a small waterfall. We will meet there."

"All right," he agreed, inwardly gloating over his victory.

This time when she tried to break free, he didn't restrain her.

Hurrying, Spotted Fawn dashed outside, and as she headed for her own lodge, she tried to calm herself. She had never before felt this way. She couldn't completely understand why Alisha's brother had made her feel so wonderfully strange. She wondered if she was falling in love. Yes, that must be it! she decided; I am falling in love. Spotted Fawn had never dreamed that love could happen so quickly, and blindly enchanted with Johnny, she didn't question his honesty. He had claimed to love her, and her young, innocent heart believed him.

When Alisha, Clint, and Jack reached the riverbank, they paused and stood in silence. Alisha knew why her father had wanted this talk, and she was feeling uncomfortable about it. She and Black Wolf were living together, and Jack naturally intended to discuss the situation.

Clearing his voice, Jack began uneasily, "Alisha, what I want to discuss with you is awkward. . . ."

Interrupting, she made it easier for him, "You want to know if Black Wolf and I have been sleeping together, don't you?"

Feeling a trifle embarrassed, he answered, "Yes, I guess that's what I need to know."

She turned her back to him and gazed unseeingly across the river. "I'm no longer innocent, Papa," she whispered.

His intake of breath was strong. "He'll marry you!"

She whirled about. "No!" she exclaimed. "I won't have you insisting that he marry me!"

"Why not?" he asked.

"I don't want to be his wife because you made him marry me! I have my pride!"

"Pride be damned!" Jack raged. "That man stole your innocence, and now, by God, he'll do right by you!"

Clint intervened. "Pa, you aren't thinking rationally. If you force this marriage, Alisha will have to live here. Do you really want her to spend the rest of her life living with Indians?"

Jack groaned. Clint was right, he had spoken impulsively. He couldn't bear the thought of his daughter residing permanently in the Black Hills and living with the Sioux. He considered the matter for a long time, then decided, "Black Wolf will return home with us and marry Alisha, and they can live at the ranch."

Clutching at her father's arm, she begged, "Papa, no! Please don't try and force Black Wolf into doing this!"

"My mind is made up!" he said, his tone adamant.

"But, Papa, you don't understand. Black Wolf will never agree to leave his people!"

His expression softened, he placed his hands on her shoulders and uttered tenderly, "Honey, what if you're pregnant?"

She paled. The possibility hadn't occurred to her.

Noting her pallor, he asked anxiously, "Are you?"

"I don't know," she murmured. "I could be."

"That settles it!" he replied firmly. "Black Wolf will marry you!" She started to continue her protests, but Jack stated inflexibly, "The subject is closed. From here on out, Clint and I will handle things." He looked at his son. "As soon as Black Wolf returns, we'll have a talk with him."

"All right, Pa, if you insist. But I still don't think you should make them get married." Impatiently, he added, "You haven't even bothered to ask Alisha if she loves the man."

Becoming aware of Justin heading in their direction, Jack mumbled grimly, "We'll continue this discussion later."

As the scout joined them, Jack asked, "Did you take

Charles to Running Horse?"

He nodded. "After thirty long years, Lansing is finally meeting the man who stole his daughter. I wonder just what in hell they're gonna say to each other."

"I don't know," Jack replied. "But I hope their meeting is peaceful."

"So do I," Justin agreed. "'Cause if it ain't, and Lansing does somethin' stupid, we might all be minus our scalps."

When Charles entered Running Horse's tepee, the chief was seated beside the lodge fire. He motioned for his visitor to sit across from him, and as he did, Charles was quite taken with his host's impressive appearance. Running Horse's fringed buckskins were embellished with beads of several colors, and about his head, he wore a leather band adorned with three eagle feathers. Charles had heard that the chief was ill, but except for a slight drawnness around the man's mouth, he couldn't distinguish any signs of sickness.

An Indian woman was inside the lodge working on a pair of moccasins, but as soon as Charles was settled at the fire, Running Horse dismissed her.

"Your wife?" Charles asked, his even tone belying his anxious mood.

The chief merely nodded.

"Were you married to that woman and my daughter at the same time?"

An amused smile faintly teased Running Horse's lips. He knew that whites were morally against a man having more than one wife. "When I was married to Little Sparrow, she was my only wife. But a man marries for many different reasons. When Little Sparrow died, I needed a woman to tend my lodge, so I married again."

"Little Sparrow?" Charles repeated.

"Abigal's Sioux name."

"Did you give her that name?"

"Yes, she was small like a sparrow."

Charles strove to remain composed, but his anxieties were building. He must know without a doubt if this man's white wife had been his daughter.

As though he could read Lansing's thoughts, Running Horse picked up a leather pouch, and opening it, removed a piece of jewelry. He carefully pitched it over the lodge fire and it landed beside Charles. "It belonged to Little Sparrow. She was wearing it the day I found her."

His hand trembling slightly, Charles lifted the dainty necklace. Tears smarted his eyes as he opened the heart-shaped locket and saw a miniature likeness of himself and one of his wife. He had given this necklace and the pictures to his daughter on her sixteenth birthday.

Clutching the locket, Charles's shoulders drooped and hard sobs tore at him. "Why?" he groaned. "Dear God, why did you take her away? She was our only child and we loved her so much!"

"I took her because I wanted her," Running Horse answered candidly and with little emotion.

Controlling his grief, Charles looked at the chief with a hard expression. "You simply took what you wanted and to hell with anyone else! Well, your selfishness cost my wife her life! She grieved to death!"

"I am sorry about Little Sparrow's mother," the chief replied, still displaying no emotion.

Finding the man unfeeling, Charles asked gruffly, "My God, have you no conscience?"

It was a long time before Running Horse spoke, and when he did, he said nothing in reference to Charles's last question. "I loved Little Sparrow, and she loved me. We were happy together. She talked often about her parents, but never asked to go back home. My people became her people and my life hers. The only cloud in her life was our son's future. She knew the days of the Sioux as free people are numbered. She longed for Black Wolf to find a place in the white man's world, and that is why she taught him the white man's education. Before she died, I promised her that I would encourage Black Wolf to seek his place with the whites. He is part of them, the same as he is part of the Sioux. My last promise to my wife is my only reason for talking to you. Black Wolf is your grandson, your flesh and blood. I ask you to take him home with you. He cannot choose between his mother's people or his father's until he has truly lived the white man's life."

"Will Black Wolf agree to leaving with me?"

"He will not want to leave, but I can persuade him to do so."

"I came to this village with hopes of establishing a relationship with my grandson. I'm a wealthy man, however, except for Black Wolf, I have no living relatives. If Black Wolf chooses the white man's life, then someday he'll inherit everything I own."

"It would be a mistake to tempt my son with your wealth."

Quickly, Charles assured him, "I didn't intend to."

"Then it is settled. When you leave, Black Wolf will leave with you."

Charles could read in the man's eyes that he now wanted him to depart from his lodge. But refusing to be dismissed so easily, he said firmly, "I think we should discuss Abigal."

His expression stony, Running Horse grumbled, "I did not know the woman called Abigal. I only knew Little Sparrow."

363

"They were one and the same!" Charles argued.

"No, they were not. Your daughter became Sioux. She put her other life behind her."

Lansing eyed him shrewdly. "If that's true, then why did she give her children white names?"

"I did not say she forgot her other life, I said she put it behind her."

"My God!" Charles moaned, facing the truth. "She must have loved you with all her heart!"

Lansing was startled to see a trace of tears come to Running Horse's eyes as he answered, "Soon I will join Little Sparrow in the spirit world, which is good, for when she died, a part of my soul went with her."

Slowly, Charles got to his feet. He started to leave, but then remembering he still had Abigal's necklace, he turned to give it to Running Horse.

"Keep it," the chief told him.

"Thank you," Charles mumbled, thinking how ironic it was that he should say "thank you" to this man. He had spent the last thirty-odd years hating the unknown warrior who had stolen his daughter, and now that he had finally found him, there seemed to be no hostility left. Thirty years can drain a man's bitterness and rage, Charles thought as he headed toward the entrance. For a moment he hesitated, feeling as though there should be more said between them . . . but what? What more could be said?

Once again, Running Horse had the ability to see into Charles's thoughts. This time, he spoke with feeling. "I stole your daughter, but I now give you your grandson. I will not live to see our great-grandchildren; but they will bring joy to your twilight years. I hope you will help Black Wolf to teach them to be proud of their Sioux heritage."

"I will," Charles promised truthfully. "It's the least I can do, for you helped Abigal teach Black Wolf to know his white heritage. Justin Smith told me how you always managed to get Abigal the books she needed."

"You are a good and fair man, Charles Lansing. Little Sparrow never stopped loving you."

His tone tinged with desperation, Charles pleaded, "Why didn't you at least let her come home for a visit?"

"When it came time for me to reclaim her, would you have let her leave with me?"

It was a little while before Charles answered, and when he did, he spoke honestly, "No, I'd have killed you." Without further words, he left the tepee, for now there was truly nothing more to be said.

Chapter Thirty-Two

Looking for Charles, Jack found him down at the river. The man was sitting on the bank, smoking a cheroot. Walking up to him, Stevens asked, "Mind if I join you?"

"Of course not," Charles answered.

Jack sat down beside him. The day was growing late and gray shadows were falling across the landscape. The air was exceptionally warm for the autumn season, and the two men sat comfortably as they admired the golden sunset.

"I dread winter," Charles murmured. "Cold weather's bad for my rheumatism."

"I didn't know you suffered from rheumatism."

"Didn't used to, but for the past couple of winters I've had my problems with it." He looked at his friend, his expression inscrutable. "But you didn't come looking for me to discuss my health, did you?"

"No," Jack answered. "I want to talk to you about Black Wolf."

"I figured you did. He's been living with your daughter, and I can understand your concern. However, I don't know what I can do to help. I don't even know Black Wolf; when we finally meet, he may not

366

even like me. He could very well resent my showing up like this. He's a full-grown man, and having a grandfather so late in his life is not going to mean much to him."

"I'm not looking for your help in this matter," Jack explained. "I just thought I should let you know that I intend to insist that Black Wolf marry Alisha. I plan for them to live at the Bar-S."

"What does Alisha have to say about all this?"

"She's against a forced marriage."

"Black Wolf may also be opposed."

Angrily, Jack muttered, "Then he should have thought of that before taking her innocence. He must take responsibility for his actions."

Charles smiled tolerantly. "Jack, your behavior is strictly that of a father's. In your eyes, your daughter has been wronged, and now you demand justice. Don't you realize that shotgun marriages are seldom happy ones?"

Reflecting back on his own unhappy marriage, Jack had to reluctantly agree with his friend. Sighing, he questioned, "But what if Alisha is pregnant?"

"Is she?" he asked.

"She doesn't know yet."

"Then why don't you simply cross that bridge when you come to it?"

"Maybe I will, but regardless, I still intend to have my talk with Black Wolf." A trace of anger had returned.

They sat silently for awhile, both engulfed in their own musings.

Putting out his cheroot, Charles remarked, "Running Horse wants me to invite Black Wolf to my ranch."

"Are you going to?"

"Yes, of course. I'd like to get to know my grandson,

and if he agrees to live in my home, then we'll have time to really become acquainted."

By now the sun had fully descended, and the men got to their feet. As they began their walk back to the lodge, Jack said, "It's beginning to look as though Black Wolf won't be returning until tomorrow. The man is indeed going to be in for more than one surprise."

"A long lost grandfather and an irate father," Charles added, and although he had spoken lightly, deep inside he was worried.

Alisha had put together makeshift beds for her company, and everyone was sleeping when Johnny slipped soundlessly from the lodge. The village was quiet, and no one was moving about as he headed quickly for the river. Reaching the bank, he started downstream. The sky was overcast, making the night extremely dark, and Johnny had to watch his steps closely as he hurried over the unfamiliar terrain.

It was quite a distance to the waterfall, and Johnny had begun to worry that he had somehow missed it when suddenly, he faintly detected the distant sound of rushing water. Hastening his strides, he made his way through the heavy thicket bordering the river, and as he emerged onto an open patch of land, he saw the small waterfall that cascaded down the hillside.

Spotted Fawn was already there, and stepping out of the dark shadows, she said hesitantly, "I should not be here."

Stepping swiftly to her side, he placed his hands on her shoulders. Gently he told her, "No, don't start having second thoughts. You belong here with me. I am your destiny."

"Do you truly love me, Johnny?" she pleaded.

"Yes . . . yes, of course I do," he lied, drawing her

closer. His mouth descended to hers, and as her lips parted, he intensified their kiss. His hands, moving to her soft buttocks, pressed her against his mounting erection.

As Johnny's lips continued to expertly ravish hers, Spotted Fawn gave in to the feverish feelings coursing wildly through her body. Instinctively she rubbed up against him, and the feel of his hardness set her passion on fire.

Carefully, he eased her down on the high grass, and kneeling over her, removed her leggings. She wore nothing underneath, and as he lifted her dress, he placed his hand on her feminine mound.

His touch was magic, and Spotted Fawn gasped with longing as she spread her legs wider, for she wanted more intimate caressing.

Slowly the moon peeped out from behind the clouds, and its romantic glow shone down upon the lovers.

Johnny could now see Spotted Fawn, and as he moved between her thighs, his vision centered on her dark triangle. With feather-light softness, he brushed his fingers through her downy hair, and the sight of her moist crevice sent his desire soaring. Undoing his trousers, he slipped them past his hips. His protruding manhood was hard and ready.

He positioned himself for penetration, and his haste upset Spotted Fawn. Shouldn't there be more to making love? Wasn't he going to whisper words of endearment? She needed more fondling, and she needed his loving assurance. She was a maiden and was frightened.

"Johnny, no!" she pleaded.

Paying no heed to her plea, he shoved his erection into her, and as he robbed her of her virginity, Spotted Fawn cried out loud.

Thinking only of himself, Johnny penetrated her

roughly, his harsh treatment bringing no pleasure to Spotted Fawn. Tears flooded her eyes and rolled down her cheeks. She had always believed that this moment in her life would be beautiful, but it was ugly and brought only pain.

Johnny's climax erupted profusively, and clutching her hips brutally, he let his seed spurt inside her.

Stretching out at her side, he breathed rapidly. Damn, he had needed a woman! However, he was still not totally satisfied, and he planned to take her again. But first he needed to recuperate.

Spotted Fawn started to get up, but Johnny quickly stopped her. "You aren't leaving, are you?"

"Yes. I do not like this making love. It is painful and . . ."

He interrupted, "That's because you were a virgin. The second time will be good."

"Second time?" she exclaimed. "No!"

Putting his charms to work, Johnny feigned tenderness. "Sweetheart, trust me." He had to find a way to keep her from leaving. He wanted her again, and he planned to find out if Indian women were as passionate as he had heard.

Tentatively she remained at his side. Remembering how wonderful he had initially made her feel, she wanted to give him another chance.

"You won't hurt me again?" she asked innocently.

Raising up, he gazed into her watchful eyes. "Relax, my Indian beauty, and I will soon have you begging me to take you."

She smiled with anticipation.

His hand traveling down to cup her mound, he murmured soothingly, "Open your legs."

She did as he requested, and when his finger entered her warmth, she sighed with longing. As he continued his arousing caress, his lips came down on hers; his tongue darted between her teeth.

All at once, Spotted Fawn tensed, and thinking she was about to demand that he let her up, Johnny asked urgently, "What's the matter? Don't you like what I'm doing to you?"

"Yes, I love it, but I think I heard someone coming."

"Damn!" he cursed, frightened.

They scrambled to their feet, and Johnny was in the process of pulling up his trousers when Kicking Buffalo appeared. His savage, powerful frame, outlined in moonlight, was an awesome sight as he stalked to the couple.

Her hands shaking, Spotted Fawn grasped her leggings and slipped them on.

Now poised before them, Kicking Buffalo glowered at his daughter before turning his heated gaze on Johnny. "White man, you will die!"

"No, Father!" Spotted Fawn cried.

Callously, he shoved her so violently that she went sprawling backwards. Then, pulling his knife, he jabbed the very point of the blade into Johnny's ribs. "We will return to the village; you will die there."

Johnny flinched, and his heart was beating so hard that he could feel it thumping against his chest. He thought about pleading for his life, but in spite of his fear, his common sense told him begging would be useless. A chill crept up his spine, and the hairs on the back of his neck prickled.

Johnny's body weakened, and for a moment he came close to passing out. Then, suddenly, hope surged. Surely Justin Smith could find a way to save him, for these Sioux held the scout in high regard. Smith will find a way to keep Kicking Buffalo from killing me, Johnny thought with desperation. I can't die! I just can't, especially over a damned squaw!

Justin awoke abruptly, and sitting up, looked about

the dark lodge. Seeing that Johnny's pallet was empty, he cursed beneath his breath. Damn it, where in hell was he?

There was a faint disturbance in the village, and wondering if that was what had awakened him, Justin stood and was heading outside when he heard someone walking up behind him. Turning, he saw Alisha.

"What's going on?" she whispered, for she too had been aroused by the disturbing noises.

"I don't know," he answered quietly. "But Johnny's gone, and I got a feelin' he's behind whatever it is."

Her eyes darted to her brother's empty bed. "Oh no!" she groaned.

Alisha was fully dressed, and as Justin darted outside, she followed. Glancing about, she could see a group of warriors gathered, but the blackness of night shadowed them, and she was unable to make out what was happening. As a feeling of apprehension came over her, she clutched at Justin's shirt sleeve. "Can you tell what they're doing?"

The scout's ability to see in the dark was uncanny. "Yep, I know exactly what they're doin'. They're tyin' your brother to a stake."

"What!" she cried.

"Damn it! I was afraid that horny bastard was goin' to stir up trouble!"

"Mr. Smith!" Alisha said sharply.

"Pardon my choice of words, ma'am." He glanced back at the lodge. "I'm glad the others are still sleeping. This way I can find out what happened before any of them wake up. Stay here, Miss Stevens, while I go talk to Kicking Buffalo."

"No, I'm going with you," she remarked, her tone brooking no argument. They headed toward the gathered warriors, and Alisha kept close to his side.

Kicking Buffalo saw their approach, and stepping

away from his comrades, went over to meet them.

"Let me do the talkin'," Justin whispered to Alisha. Then giving Kicking Buffalo his full attention, the scout asked, "What did this man do to offend the Sioux?"

Anger radiating from his dark eyes, the warrior said with a sneer, "He took my daughter. I found them together."

"You actually caught them in the act?" Justin specified.

Kicking Buffalo responded by nodding his head, and as he folded his arms across his chest, his expression dared the scout to try and interfere.

"Your brother's committed a serious offense," Justin said to Alisha.

"Please help him," she pleaded, once again grasping at the man's shirt sleeve.

"I don't know what I can do, but I'll give it a try." Returning his attention to Kicking Buffalo, he asked, "Can we talk alone?"

"We will go down to the river," the warrior decided.

Alisha watched the two men as they walked away, and when they were a good distance from her, she moved uncertainly in Johnny's direction. However, before she could reach him, another warrior seemed to appear out of nowhere. His presence exuded authority, and upon his arrival, complete silence fell over the gathering.

Although Alisha had never seen Black Wolf's father, she didn't have to be told that this man was Running Horse. Her eyes met his, and his gaze was penetrating.

Brusquely, he looked away and walked over to his men. They conversed in their own language, and she had no idea of what was being said.

Leaving the others, Running Horse came to stand at Alisha's side. His black eyes, staring into hers, were intimidating. She wondered if she should retreat back to the safety of her lodge.

Seeing her fear, he said softly, "Do not be afraid." Slowly, he reached over and lifted a strand of her hair. Caressing a silken lock between his fingers, he murmured, "Your hair is the color of freshly fallen snow. I will call you Fallen Snow."

Now, detecting kindness in his gaze, she gathered the courage to plead with him. "Running Horse, please don't let Kicking Buffalo kill my brother!"

Releasing the strand of hair, he said emphatically, "It is not right that I interfere. The white man must pay for what he did."

A little timidly, she asked, "Did . . . did Johnny force himself on Spotted Fawn?"

"No," the chief replied.

"Then no crime was committed." Courage building, she continued, "My brother's actions are no worse than those of your own son. Johnny took Spotted Fawn's innocence, but Black Wolf took mine. Yet my father is not planning to kill Black Wolf for what he did."

She was indeed surprised when Running Horse smiled. "Your words are wise, Fallen Snow. You are not a foolish woman and will be a good wife to my son."

Flushed, Alisha stammered, "Black Wolf and I are not getting married."

He merely looked at her as though he knew more about her future than she did.

Tentatively, she asked, "May I talk to my brother?"

Catching sight of Justin and Kicking Buffalo returning, he answered, "Let us see what they have decided."

Alisha watched the scout closely, hoping to read encouragement in his eyes, but his set expression revealed nothing.

Kicking Buffalo looked directly at Alisha. "I will not kill your brother."

She was so relieved that she sighed aloud, "Thank you!"

"Don't be so fast with your 'thank yous,'" Justin warned her.

"Why not?" she asked.

"In the morning, Johnny will run the gauntlet. His horse will be saddled and waiting at the end of the line. If he successfully runs the gauntlet, he's to mount his horse and leave this village. If he's seen in the Black Hills again by Kicking Buffalo or any of these other warriors, he'll be killed on sight."

"Wh . . . what is the gauntlet?" Alisha asked warily.

"I'll explain it to you later," Justin answered.

Speaking in Alisha's behalf, Running Horse said to Kicking Buffalo, "The woman wishes to talk to her brother."

Black Wolf's uncle didn't express a verbal consent. Instead, he reached for Alisha's arm and led her over to Johnny.

The sight of her brother tied at the stake cut sharply into Alisha's heart. Tears threatening, she cried, "Oh, Johnny, why did you do something so foolish?"

Straining against the ropes binding him, Johnny pleaded hoarsely, "Alisha, ask Smith to help me."

"He has helped you."

"Then why am I still tied to this damned pole?"

Alisha hadn't heard Justin walking up behind her, and when he spoke, his voice startled her. "You're gonna have to remain tied until mornin'."

Fear overwhelming him, Johnny questioned shakily, "What will happen to me in the morning?"

"Well, for one thing, you're gonna be banished from this village."

"That's the good news; now tell me the bad."

"You're gonna run the gauntlet." Justin believed young Stevens deserved his punishment, and didn't try to repress his grin.

Johnny, somewhat familiar with the gauntlet, was furious with the scout. Viciously, he grumbled, "Smith, if I wasn't tied to this pole, I'd knock that obnoxious grin off your ugly face!"

"Johnny!" Alisha exclaimed reproachfully.

His grin widening, Smith answered calmly, "Stevens, I'm gonna enjoy watchin' you run the gauntlet."

"Stop it! Both of you!" Alisha demanded.

Touching her arm, Justin prodded, "Come on, ma'am. We need to go back to the lodge and wake the others."

Alisha cast Johnny a loving glance before accompanying Justin. As they headed for the lodge, she groaned, "I dread telling Papa what has happened."

"Your brother's punishment ain't no more than he deserves. I warned him to stay away from these Indian women. He's lucky Kicking Buffalo didn't castr . . ." Catching himself, he substituted, "Didn't slit his throat."

"Maybe he's falling in love with Spotted Fawn," she said, sticking up for Johnny. "After all, Spotted Fawn is very pretty and sweet."

"Miss Stevens," he began tolerantly, "when we were all searchin' for you, more than once I heard Johnny's opinion of Indians, and believe me, there ain't no way that he's goin' to fall in love with a Sioux woman."

"Then why . . . ?" Her question faded into thin air.

"'Cause he's a horny skunk, that's why," Justin mumbled, and this time he didn't offer an aplogy.

She didn't reproach him. "How did you convince Kicking Buffalo to spare Johnny's life?"

"Asked him to," he replied simply.

"And he agreed only because you asked?"

"Once, a long time ago, I saved Kicking Buffalo's life. I reckon he figured he owed me a favor."

They had reached the lodge. Pausing, Alisha expressed her thoughts audibly, "I wish Black Wolf was here."

"It wouldn't make any difference. Johnny would still have to run the gauntlet."

Opening the leather flap, he stood back and motioned for Alisha to precede. Taking a deep breath, and bracing herself for the awaiting ordeal, she entered.

Following, Justin whispered, "Your papa's goin' to be madder than an old wet hen."

"That's putting it mildly," she moaned.

Chapter Thirty-Three

Alisha and the others had gone through two pots of coffee before sunrise, and now as the morning brightness seeped inside the lodge, Alisha unconsciously edged closer to her father. They were sitting at the fire, and aware of her apprehension, Jack placed an arm around her shoulders. Justin had explained the gauntlet in explicit detail, and Alisha was terribly worried about Johnny.

Clint, pacing the lodge, asked the scout, "How much longer does Johnny have?"

"Kicking Buffalo will wait until after breakfast. He might want to punish Johnny, but he won't see any reason to do so on an empty stomach."

Jack, uncomfortable about the favor he needed to ask, broached Justin hesitantly, "Mr. Smith, I hate to impose on you, but I'm concerned over what will happen to Johnny after he leaves this village."

"You want me to stay with your boy, don't you?" the scout guessed.

"If you don't mind," Jack replied quickly.

"I'll tell you what I'll do. I'll take care of Johnny and we'll hole up about five miles from here. How much longer do you think it'll be before you're ready to leave?"

"If Black Wolf returns today, then we should be ready to leave tomorrow." Jack looked questioningly at Charles, who was seated beside Justin.

"Tomorrow will be fine," Lansing answered. "My business with Black Wolf shouldn't take long."

"It's settled then," Justin remarked. "Johnny and I will set up camp and wait for you all to catch up."

"Mr. Smith," Jack began, "I appreciate your help."

"Somebody's got to stay with the boy, and I reckon I'm the best man for the job. Left alone in these Hills, he'd probably get himself scalped."

Johnny's family didn't disagree, for they reluctantly admitted to themselves that the scout's conjecture was probably true.

"Does anybody want more coffee?" Alisha asked. They declined, so she remained cuddled close to her father.

"I'm going to check on Johnny," Clint declared, heading toward the entrance.

"Wait," Justin called, getting to his feet. "He's got guards watchin' him who ain't gonna understand what you're wantin'. So I'd better go with you so I can explain that you're only wantin' to talk to him for a moment."

As the two men were leaving, Jack said to Alisha, "Honey, when it's time for Johnny to run the gauntlet, you are to stay here. I don't want you seeing something so . . . so barbaric. Nor do I want you to be a witness to your brother's shame."

"I understand, Papa," she murmured agreeably. She hadn't planned to view the proceedings, for she certainly didn't want to see Johnny's punishment. When Justin had been explaining the gauntlet, she had known immediately that she wasn't going to watch her brother through that ordeal.

The procedure was simple in its severity. In Johnny's

379

case the gauntlet was to be a punishment. However, it was sometimes used to test nerve and courage. It was formed by placing two lines of men about four paces apart, facing inward. Each person in line had a switch, spear, club, or knife.

On this occasion, Johnny's horse would be saddled and waiting at the far end of the line. Johnny would be forced to dash into the opening between the line and endure the stinging switches while dodging thrusting spears, ducking away from swinging clubs and avoiding jabbing knives. The safety goal would be his horse, and when he reached the animal, his punishment would be over.

Now, thinking about the whole thing, Alisha shivered. "Papa, do you think Johnny will survive?"

"Of course he will," Jack assured her. "Speed is important, and Johnny is quick. He'll run that gauntlet, be on his horse and gone in a flash." For Alisha's sake, he had spoken lightly, but Jack was deeply worried. He was sure that a man could be killed running the gauntlet. If Johnny was to trip and fall, he might be beaten to death before he could manage to get back on his feet. Earlier, while talking privately to Justin, he had relayed this fear to the scout. Although Smith had assured him that Kicking Buffalo wouldn't allow such a thing to happen, Jack hadn't been convinced. The scout might hold the warrior's word sacred, but Jack didn't trust Kicking Buffalo.

"I wonder how Spotted Fawn is holding up through all this," Alisha said softly.

"I don't know," Jack muttered. "But my concern is for Johnny, and at the moment, I can think of nothing else." Worry overtaking him, he drew his daughter into his embrace, and holding her tightly, groaned, "Dear God, I'd run the gauntlet for him if I could. Johnny has a lot of faults, but he's my son and I love him!"

"I know you do, Papa!" Alisha cried, tears flowing. "I love him too!"

Black Wolf knew something was amiss the moment he rode his horse to the top of the hill and looked down upon the village. At this time of morning an encampment should be busy with mundane activities, and one quick glance revealed that no one was carrying out their routine duties.

Black Wolf was leading a second horse, and a dead elk was slung over the animal's back. He jerked on the lead rein, and the pack horse broke into a loping gallop as it followed Black Wolf's stallion down the hillside.

Riding past the outer tepees, Black Wolf noticed that people were gathering at the hub of the village. Fear for his father and Alisha gripped him like a vise.

Justin, leading Johnny's saddled horse, caught sight of Black Wolf's arrival and called out to him.

Black Wolf was surprised to see the scout, and as he guided his stallion in Justin's direction, he glanced about and saw that a gauntlet was about to be run. Reaching his friend, he dismounted and said with a smile, "Justin, it's good to see you."

Smith shook hands with him. "You're here just in time for the show."

The scout continued his strides, and Black Wolf walked beside him. When they reached the far end of the gauntlet line, they held up. Black Wolf looked down the narrow line and was shocked to see a white man waiting to run past the warriors who were standing in formation.

"Who is he?" Black Wolf asked Justin, gesturing toward Johnny.

"His name is Johnny Stevens and he's Alisha's youngest brother."

Black Wolf exhaled a heavy sigh, and when the scout didn't offer any more information, he remarked, "I hope you aren't waiting for me to thank you for bringing Alisha's brother here."

"Nope, I'm waitin' for you to ask me what he did to offend Kicking Buffalo."

Black Wolf answered with impatience, "Justin, just tell me what the hell is going on."

"Last night Kicking Buffalo caught Johnny and Spotted Fawn in a compromising position. They was down at the waterfall."

Anger shone in the other man's eyes, and his large hands doubled into fists, for he was itching to use them on Johnny.

Seeing Black Wolf's wrath, Justin continued quickly, "There ain't no reason for you to beat him up; the gauntlet will be punishment enough." As an afterthought, he added casually, "Besides, if you was to get in a fight with your future brother-in-law, it could cause a lot of family tension."

"What!" Black Wolf exclaimed.

Keeping an insouciant air, the scout pointed toward Clint and Jack, who were standing a distance behind Johnny. "Those are the rest of your future in-laws . . . Alisha's other brother and her father."

"Why did you lead them here?" Black Wolf asked irritably.

"How in the hell was I supposed to know that you had Alisha?"

"What makes you think they're going to be my in-laws?"

"Well, Jack has his daughter, yet he still hasn't left. So I have to surmise that he's waitin' for you with a loaded shotgun." Frowning, he added, "By the way, you made me looked like a damned fool. I guaranteed Jack Stevens that he wouldn't find his daughter at

Running Horse's village."

At that moment, Kicking Buffalo decided to begin the proceedings.

"Where's Alisha?" Black Wolf asked.

"In your lodge."

Having no wish to watch Johnny run the gauntlet, Black Wolf walked away and went to his lodge. Entering, he saw Alisha sitting on her bed.

Startled by Black Wolf's sudden appearance, she rose quickly.

"Justin told me what happened between your brother and Spotted Fawn," he said, his tone even.

She asked pleadingly, "Can't you stop Kicking Buffalo from punishing Johnny in this cruel way?"

All at once, a loud hubbub erupted outside the lodge, ensued by several excited shouts.

Alisha tensed. It was too late; the gauntlet had started.

Watching her, Black Wolf longed to take her in his arms and offer her comfort, but he was sure she would spurn his affections, for it was his people who were inflincting Johnny's punishment.

As the roisterous yells continued, Alisha held back her tears. She tried not to envision Johnny's ordeal, but against her will, the scene kept flashing before her eyes. If only Black Wolf would hold her! She had never needed his comfort as badly as she did now!

Turning away in an effort to keep from embracing her, Black Wolf stepped outside. To Alisha, his departure was proof that he didn't love her.

Black Wolf returned momentarily, and as he did, the vociferous uproar died down. "It's over," he said to Alisha. "Your brother is all right and is leaving."

She sighed gratefully. "Thank goodness he survived."

"Did you think he wouldn't?"

383

"I was afraid . . ." her voice faded.

"Considering his crime, he deserved worse than he got!" Black Wolf grumbled.

"It's not as though he forced himself on Spotted Fawn," she declared, resenting his attitude.

Changing the subject, he asked shortly, "Why did Justin bring your family here?"

"Didn't he tell you why?"

"Alisha, if he had told me, I wouldn't be asking you." He was impatient.

Alisha was uneasy. How was she to tell Black Wolf about Charles Lansing? Finding out that his grandfather was here, was going to be a severe shock. "Black Wolf," she began carefully, "do you remember when I told you that I know a man named Charles Lansing?"

"I remember," he answered, eyeing her intently.

She decided to come straight to the point and omit the details. "Charles Lansing has learned that he's your grandfather. Mr. Smith brought him here to meet you, and my father and brothers accompanied them."

It was a long moment before Black Wolf responded. "What makes the man think he's my grandfather?"

"The proof is indisputable. Black Wolf, believe me, he's Abigal's father."

Hearing the men's arrival, Black Wolf spun on his heel and watched them as they entered the tepee.

The tall, impressive warrior gave the three men reason to pause. "Are you Black Wolf?" Jack asked.

"Yes, I am," he answered, his gaze unwavering.

Charles had been the last to enter, and now as he regarded the impressive Black Wolf, he inhaled sharply. It was obvious that the warrior was a Lansing.

Detecting the man's sharp intake of breath, Black Wolf looked away from Jack to acknowledge Charles. For a tense moment the two men scrutinized each other, each well aware of their mutual similarities.

They were both tall, their strong builds identical, and their eyes were the same shade of blue.

It was Charles who broke the silence. "I can see that you are Abigal's son."

Black Wolf made no reply. Instead, he brushed his way past the men and darted outside. As he was assailed with fresh air, he breathed in deeply. The heavy tension inside his lodge had become suffocating to Black Wolf, and he had needed to get away. Pausing, he brushed a hand across his brow and wasn't surprised to find that he was perspiring. A picture of Jack and Clint crossed his mind as he recalled their stares. He wasn't sure what they wanted from him, and although he intended to find out, he planned to visit first with his father. As he started for Running Horse's tepee, his thoughts turned to Charles. He was also unsure of this man's intent. He couldn't deny that Charles' presence had stirred a warm emotion within him, for after all, the man was Abigal's father, his own flesh and blood.

Arriving at the chief's tepee, Black Wolf announced his presence, then entered. His father was sitting on his bed, and he moved over and took a seat in front of him.

Running Horse quickly dismissed his wife. He waited for her to leave before speaking in Siouan, "My son, was your hunt successful?"

"Yes, Father," he answered. His face was shadowed by a small frown. "It seems a lot has happened in my absence."

"Did you meet your grandfather?"

"I saw him for a moment."

Running Horse raised an eyebrow. "I should think you would have more time for your grandfather."

"I'll talk to him later."

"And Fallen Snow's family? Will you also find time for them?"

"Fallen Snow?" Black Wolf questioned.

"The white women has hair the color of fallen snow."

"When did you meet Alisha?"

"Last night after her brother was found with Spotted Fawn."

Black Wolf expelled a deep sigh. "Yes, Father, I'll find time to talk to her family."

"Fallen Snow's father might want you to marry her."

The younger man shrugged as though it were insignificant. "I'll marry when I'm good and ready and not before."

Running Horse watched his son expectantly as he said, "Charles Lansing wants you to return to his ranch with him for a long visit. I think you should agree to go."

"It's out of the question. Winter will soon be here, and you'll need me."

"I can manage without you. If I should become ill, Kicking Buffalo can take care of everything."

Realizing his father intended to persuade him to leave with Lansing, Black Wolf got abruptly to his feet. He felt that he wasn't up to a disagreement with Running Horse. He had too many pressing matters on his mind. "We'll discuss this later, after I've given it some thought."

Before the chief could protest, Black Wolf left the lodge only to be confronted with Jack and Clint. The two men were poised close to Running Horse's tepee, waiting for him.

"We want to talk to you," Jack said firmly.

Deciding he might as well get it over with, Black Wolf invited them to walk down to the river with him. When they reached the bank, he stood facing them both, his gaze unwavering.

As Jack studied the warrior, he could see a strong resemblance to Charles. Studying him further, Jack realized that Black Wolf looked more white than

Indian. It was his clothes and long hair that made one see him as a Sioux. Dressed in white man's clothing, and with his hair cut shorter, his likeness to his father's people would barely be distinguishable.

"You wanted to talk," Black Wolf reminded him, impatient with the man's scrutiny.

"Black Wolf," Jack began uncertainly, "I want to discuss Alisha. You saved my daughter's life, and for that I'm very grateful. However, you've been living with her, and she has told me that . . . that she is no longer innocent."

He fell silent, for Black Wolf's unyielding gaze was unnerving.

"Go on," Black Wolf remarked.

"Do you plan to marry her?" he asked bluntly.

"If I don't, are you going to stick a shotgun in my back?"

It was Clint who answered. "We haven't thought that far ahead." He was amazed by Black Wolf's decorum, even though Justin had told him that the man was well-polished and educated.

"I don't intend to discuss marrying Alisha until I've had more time to think about it."

"Very well," Jack agreed. "But we're planning to leave in the morning. I hope you'll have an answer for me by then."

The Stevenses turned and began their walk back to the lodge, but were suddenly detained by Black Wolf asking, "Mr. Stevens, don't you object to your daughter living the rest of her life married to a Sioux warrior and living in a Sioux village?"

"Of course I object," Jack replied strongly. "If you marry Alisha, I'll expect you to live at the Bar-S." He waited expectantly for Black Wolf's answer.

However, he didn't receive one, and when Black Wolf sat down on the bank and turned his back, Jack

387

and Clint resumed their stroll to the lodge.

Justin had a small campfire built, and placing a coffee pot over the open flames, he looked over at Johnny.

The young Stevens was sitting on the ground, leaning back against a tree. He was huddled inside his jacket, with a blanket draped over him. Feeling the scout's eyes on him, he turned and met the man's gaze.

Johnny's face hardened with rage as he said threateningly, "Someday, I'll get even with Kicking Buffalo! So help me God, I'll make that man rue the day he made me run that damned gauntlet!" Resentment filled his heart as he remembered the way in which Spotted Fawn's father had not only stripped him of his pride, but also his clothes. Johnny had been forced to run the gauntlet naked. He'd never been so humiliated!

Growing uncomfortable, Johnny changed his position, but the movement brought him pain. There didn't seem to be a part of his body that didn't ache, for he'd been jabbed with weapons and whipped with switches.

"I reckon the gauntlet is a little barbaric," Justin admitted.

"A little!" Johnny exclaimed angrily.

"It serves its purpose though," the scout argued, grinning wryly. "I bet you won't be tryin' to seduce any more Indian maidens."

Johnny scowled, and dismissing Justin's words, he grumbled, "Furthermore, if Pa makes Alisha marry Black Wolf, I'll kill that red-skinned savage before he can say 'I do'!"

Justin chuckled. "You've got just about as much a chance of killin' Black Wolf as a snowball in hell."

"We'll see about that!" the younger man thundered.

"Although I know I'm wastin' my breath, I'm gonna give you a little advice. Forget killin' Black Wolf and forget gettin' even with Kicking Buffalo. If you try either one, you're gonna end up six feet under. Believe me, son, you'll be pushin' up daisies."

"Your philosophy is as ignorant as you are," Johnny said testily.

"Well, I got a little more philosophy for you," Justin drawled. "If you insult me again, I'm gonna kick your rear so hard that the jolt will pop your teeth right out of your mouth."

Deciding not to further incite the large man, Johnny withdrew into a sulk. For the time being, he dismissed Black Wolf from his thoughts. Determination flashed in Johnny's eyes though as he considered getting even with Kicking Buffalo. Someday he'd find a way to even the score; regardless of who he had to hurt, or how he had to go about it, he would somehow achieve his revenge!

Chapter Thirty-Four

Standing in front of Kicking Buffalo's lodge, David had waited for Jack and Clint to leave Black Wolf before walking down to the riverbank.

Now, as he approached the warrior, he asked, "Do you mind if I join you?"

Looking at David, Black Wolf smiled warmly. The boy was dressed in Indian clothing; his tan leggings and suede shirt clung smoothly to his tall, well-developed frame. Admiring his young companion, Black Wolf was again reminded that David would soon become a man worthy of praise.

Sitting down, David brushed at the lock of hair that consistently fell over his forehead. His gesture was futile, for the curly strand refused to stay in place.

Noticing that the boy seemed a little troubled, Black Wolf asked gently, "Son, is something wrong?"

"I'm not sure," he mumbled. "Last night Mr. Lansing and I had a long talk, and he invited me to live at the Longhorn."

"Longhorn?" Black Wolf questioned.

"That's the name of your grandfather's ranch." Almost apologetically, he added, "I hope you don't mind that Mr. Lansing told me that he's your grandfather."

"Of course I don't mind."

"I'm kinda anxious to live at the Longhorn, but I don't want to hurt Alisha's feelings."

Understanding, he asked, "Did you tell Alisha that you'd stay at the Bar-S?"

"Yeah, in a way I did."

"I wouldn't worry about it, David. I'm sure she'll understand."

"I hope you're right," he uttered anxiously.

"Why did you choose the Longhorn?"

David shrugged. "I guess I kinda feel sorry for Mr. Lansing. He doesn't have a family. Alisha's father would offer me a home out of courtesy, but Mr. Lansing is looking for companionship." He smiled a little timidly. "Besides, Mr. Lansing said that you might be staying at the Longhorn."

"Was that an important factor in making your decision?"

"Yeah, I guess," he admitted.

"I doubt if I'll be living at the Longhorn. I prefer to stay here. However, I think your decision is a wise one."

David was disappointed. "I was sure hopin' that you'd be leaving with us."

Black Wolf smiled encouragingly. "I'll visit you in the spring." He started to say more, but he suddenly caught sight of Charles heading in their direction.

Following Black Wolf's gaze, David said hastily, "I'll leave you two alone. I'm sure you have a lot to discuss."

As Lansing arrived, David stood, made his excuses and left. Charles sat beside Black Wolf, but he found the grassy bank a little uncomfortable, for his rheumatism was beginning to pain him.

His discomfort didn't escape Black Wolf's notice. "Are you feeling all right?"

"I'm fine," the older man assured him. He changed his position, which eased his aching joints. "I was hoping that you were as anxious to talk to me as I was to talk to you. It finally dawned on me that you weren't. So I asked Jack if he had seen you, and he told me where you were."

Smiling, Black Wolf added, "So you decided if I wouldn't come to you, you'd come to me."

His blue eyes shining with admiration, Charles remarked, "Black Wolf, you amaze me. Speaking with you is no different than conversing with a white man."

"Why do people set such a store by the color of a man's skin? Do you think Indians are incapable of intelligence?"

"No," he replied. "But I've never met one with your education."

"I'm sure Justin told you that I owe my education to my mother."

"Yes, he did." Sadness shadowed the older man's face. "Tell me about Abigal."

"What exactly do you want to know?"

"Was she truly happy living with Running Horse?"

"She and my father were deeply in love. They suffered through tragedies, but their love endured and grew stronger with the passing of time. Running Horse was her happiness, and she was his."

Tentatively, Charles queried, "Did Running Horse tell you that . . . ?" The question faded on his lips. He felt as though he were overstepping his boundary. He didn't have the right to ask this man to return to the Longhorn with him.

Aware of Lansing's uncertainty, Black Wolf said considerately, "Yes, I know that you want me to visit your ranch. In the spring, I'll try to make it and stay for a week or so."

"A week or so!" Charles exclaimed. "But I want you to stay indefinitely!"

"Don't you think I'm a little old to need a grand-father?" Black Wolf asked archly.

"Your age is irrelevant; it's my age that's important. Next month I'll be seventy years old. My ranch is large, twice the size of the Bar-S and other bordering ranches. I'm getting too old to run the place. Even though I have a reliable foreman, most of the work still falls on me." Anxious, he proceeded rapidly, "I want to teach you how to operate the Longhorn so that I can relax and enjoy the rest of my life. My daughter was stolen from me; I never knew my grandson; but thank God, there's a chance that I can know and love my great-grandchildren. If you and Alisha marry, you can live at the Longhorn, and someday the ranch will be yours, and you'll inherit everything I own."

Black Wolf resented this added burden his grandfather was placing on his shoulders. He had no desire to disappoint the man; in fact, Charles had his understanding and sympathy. But Black Wolf was not ready to commit himself. "I'll think over your proposition."

"Please believe me, I'm not trying to buy your loyalty. I'm merely stating my feelings as honestly as I can."

"I know," Black Wolf murmured.

Getting slowly to his feet, Charles replied, "I'll be waiting anxiously for your decision." He made a move to leave, but hesitating, he asked, "Did Abigal call you Charles?"

"She called me Black Wolf, but in the privacy of our lodge, she often referred to me as Chuck."

Lansing smiled broadly. "When I lived in Texas, everyone knew me as Chuck, but when I moved to Wyoming, I lost the nickname." Cautiously, he asked, "Would you mind if I called you Chuck?"

"Does my Indian name offend you?" Black Wolf asked, his love for the Sioux making him offensive.

"No, it doesn't offend me. But I am honored that Abigal named you after me, and it pleases me to call you Chuck. Somehow, it makes it seem more real that you're actually my grandson."

"I understand," Black Wolf answered truthfully. "I have no objections. If you want to call me Chuck, then by all means, do so."

Knowing that at the moment there was nothing more to be said, Charles left his grandson and returned to the lodge.

Black Wolf remained sitting at the river, his thoughts deep and turbulent. He dreaded hurting Charles Lansing, but after considerable deliberation he had decided to stay with the Sioux. However, he didn't want to lose touch with his grandfather and intended to visit him often.

Standing, he planned to go to Lansing and let him know of his decision, but all at once he noticed Spotted Fawn slipping away from the village. She was on foot and heading toward the woods.

Worried, Black Wolf set out to follow her. When she disappeared into the thick shrubbery and out of sight, he picked up his pace.

Meanwhile, unaware of her cousin's closeness, Spotted Fawn paused beside a towering spruce, and kneeling, she drew the knife that she had concealed beneath her robe. Then slinging the fur wrap from her shoulders, she took a firm hold on the handle of the knife. As she studied the sharp blade, the expression in her eyes was dangerously deranged. Her hands were shaking so badly that she could barely place the cold blade against the inside of her left wrist. She knew that she had to move quickly. First she'd slit one wrist, then the other.

She was determined to kill herself and was so engrossed in doing so that she didn't detect Black Wolf's presence. When he suddenly lurched for the knife and jerked it from her hand, she was shocked.

Throwing the knife to the ground, Black Wolf grasped her arms and pulled her to her feet. Shaking her roughly, he demanded, "What is wrong with you? Have you lost your senses?"

Squirming out of his grasp, she shouted desperately, "I cannot live with the shame I have brought upon myself and upon my family!"

"Do you think killing yourself is the answer?" he shouted back.

"Yes!" she cried. Her determination was obvious. "I will kill myself! If not today, then tomorrow!"

"I won't let you!" he raged.

"You cannot stop me, unless you intend never to let me out of your sight!"

Black Wolf, his voice breaking with emotion, pleaded, "Spotted Fawn, I'm begging you not to do this. Believe me, in time, you'll rise above your feelings of shame, and Kicking Buffalo will find it in his heart to forgive you."

Her eyes downcast, she murmured demurely, "I am no longer a maiden. No young warrior will want me for his wife. If I marry, I will be forced to be a second or third wife to a man who is old."

"You don't know that," he argued.

She lifted her gaze to his. "It does not truly matter, for I cannot continue to live with what I have done. My father will not even speak to me, my mother's eyes are filled with tears, and the people in the village shun me. If I tried to move to another village, my shame would follow me and I would soon be an outcast. I have no other choice but to take my life."

"No, you have another choice," Black Wolf remarked. He sighed with resignation, for it seemed regardless of his reservations, he'd be moving to the Longhorn. There was no doubt in his mind that, given the opportunity, Spotted Fawn would commit suicide. This time he had stopped her, but next time he might fail.

She looked at him with bafflement. "What other choice do I have?"

"Do you know that Charles Lansing is my grandfather?"

"Yes, I heard my parents talking about him."

"He wants me to live at his ranch, and I've decided to take him up on his invitation." Placing his hands on her shoulders, he gazed tenderly down into her face. "I'm taking you with me. In time, if you decide to return to the Sioux, then I'll bring you back. But, for now, you can leave and someday soon you'll lose this self-condemnation and regain your self-respect."

"Black Wolf, are you doing this for my sake? Had you decided to live with your grandfather before finding me?"

"Yes, I had already made the decision." Deceit went against his grain, but in this case he believed it necessary.

A glint of hope shone in Spotted Fawn's eyes. "Do you think your grandfather will object? He might not want me to live in his home."

Smiling reassuringly, he replied, "Don't worry, he won't mind." Black Wolf wasn't as certain as he sounded, but he had a feeling that Charles Lansing would give his permission.

"When will we leave?"

"In the morning."

"Then I need to pack." Her voice saddened. "Also, I must say goodbye to my parents and to Flying Hawk."

"I'll stop by later and talk to your father. Everything considered, I'm sure he'll agree that this move is for the best. At least, for the time being."

She told him that she'd see him later, grabbed her robe, then darted off to start her packing. Left alone, Black Wolf stepped over to the knife and picked it up. Returning to the spruce, he sat down, and while absently toying with the knife, he let his somber thoughts occupy him. He wasn't looking forward to living at the Longhorn, for he preferred to stay with his father. He was worried about Running Horse's health and was afraid that he wouldn't survive the upcoming winter. As his musings drifted to Spotted Fawn, he was certain that he'd made the right decision. It was imperative that he get her away from this village, for he firmly believed that in time she'd get over this shame she was feeling. Furthermore, he was sure that Kicking Buffalo would eventually forgive her. He could only hope and pray that Running Horse would remain in relatively good health until he and Spotted Fawn could return.

Against his will, Alisha crossed his mind. Living at the Longhorn would mean that she wouldn't be out of his life. Their paths were destined to cross again, and loving her the way he did, how could he continue to resist his feelings for her?

Black Wolf could understand Jack's concern over his relationship with Alisha. He had taken Alisha's innocence and owed her a marriage proposal, and Jack apparently wasn't set on his daughter marrying Todd Miller.

Black Wolf pondered whether or not Alisha would agree to marry him if he were to propose. He felt that she didn't love him, but that didn't mean that he might never win her love. He sighed disconsolately, for he knew at present he'd find no answers to these questions.

Meanwhile, as Black Wolf pondered a possible future with Alisha, she and David were taking a walk. David had come to the lodge and asked Alisha if he could talk alone with her.

Now, as they strolled leisurely toward the area where

Black Wolf had encountered Spotted Fawn, David remarked with hesitation, "Alisha, I needed to talk to you because I have something important to tell you."

She turned her head and looked at him. He was taller than Alisha and she had to raise her gaze to see into his face. For a moment she became mesmerized by his dark emerald-colored eyes and long black lashes. She found their beauty enchanting.

David continued, "Mr. Lansing invited me to live at his ranch, and I told him that I would." He sounded apologetic. "Alisha, I appreciate you asking me to stay at the Bar-S, but . . ."

She interrupted. "David, I think that's a marvelous idea. Charles lives alone, and you'll be such wonderful company for him. And if you're interested in ranching, he can teach you everything you need to know." Affectionately, she reached over and squeezed his hand. "The Longhorn isn't all that far from the Bar-S, so we'll see each other often."

He grinned happily. "I'm sure relieved that you understand. I was afraid that you'd be mad at me."

"Nonsense!" she insisted fondly.

They were now drawing nearer to where Black Wolf was sitting; however, they were completely unaware of his close presence. But Alisha and David hadn't yet come within Black Wolf's hearing.

"Alisha," David began, "do you think Black Wolf will decide to visit his grandfather?"

"I don't know, but I seriously doubt it. He won't want to leave Running Horse."

"I know this is none of my business, but aren't you and Black Wolf getting married?"

"Whatever gave you that idea?" she exclaimed, her cheeks flushed, hoping desperately that Black Wolf had mentioned it to David.

The lad shrugged. "I was just hoping you two had fallen in love."

Alisha tried to hide her disappointment, but she failed, and David could see her sadness.

"If Black Wolf were to ask you to marry him, would you?"

"Yes, if he asked because he loves me. But if he asked out of obligation, or because Papa insisted, then I'd flatly refuse."

Unknowingly, they had now walked so close to Black Wolf that he was able to hear their next words; and seated beneath the tall spruce, he was concealed from their vision.

"Why would you be dead set against marrying Black Wolf?" David asked.

"I would find it too humiliating and degrading!" Alisha declared, resentment heavy in her voice.

Humiliating and degrading! The words cut sharply into Black Wolf, bringing a moment of pain before it was supplanted by rage. So that was her opinion of marriage to a half-breed!

Taking Alisha's arm, David turned them around and they headed back toward the village. Soon they were too far away for Black Wolf to hear the remainder of their conversation.

"Alisha, I know Black Wolf, and he'd never ask you to marry him because your father pressured him into it. If he asks you to be his wife, you can be sure it'll be because he truly loves you."

She smiled a little wistfully. "I suppose you're right." Her face suddenly aglow, she swore intensely, "Oh, David, if Black Wolf loved me, I'd marry him in a minute! Where we lived wouldn't even matter. He'd be my life; my very reason for living! I'd gladly follow him to the ends of the earth just to be at his side!"

The sound of a twig snapping in the woods caused them to whirl about. At first they didn't see Black Wolf approaching, but as his tall shape came into view, David smiled. "I'll leave you two alone."

He made his departure quickly, leaving Alisha to wait for Black Wolf.

As the powerful warrior drew closer, she started to greet him with a warm smile, but the cold scowl on his face dissuaded her.

Fuming, Black Wolf stalked to Alisha, clutched her shoulders, and jerked her against him. As he glared down into her puzzled face, he tried to make himself despise her; instead, he found himself reacting to her sensual beauty. He was perfectly aware of her opinion of him, and he should find it easy to hate her. But as his body began to respond to her closeness, he could think of nothing except for his need to take her passionately.

Baffled by his harsh treatment, Alisha attempted to free herself from his firm hold. He immediately impeded her movements by tightening his arms about her. Then his mouth swooped down on hers, and as his lips continued their stimulating attack, his hands dropped to her soft buttocks. Forcefully, he shoved her to his hardness, and even through her Indian dress and leggings, she could feel his splendid arousal.

Moving swiftly, he picked her up, turned, and carried her into the dense shrubbery. Laying her down on a thick cushion of grass, he stretched out at her side.

Although Black Wolf's kiss had left her breathless and longing for more, she was still wary of his strange mood. Timidly, she questioned, "Black Wolf, is something bothering you?"

He grinned cynically, and taking her hand, moved it down to his erection. "This is what's bothering me at the moment. Why else would I be here? When my passion demands release, why not appease it with you? After all, you're always willing."

His remarks wounded her, and it took all the will power she could exert to keep from crying. Protecting her pride, she said coolly, "Maybe I used to be willing, but now that my father has found me, I no longer have to try and please you." Lashing out, and longing to hurt him, she continued untruthfully, "I always pretended passion because I was afraid of what you might do to me if I didn't cooperate. Well, now that my family is here, I no longer fear you."

She tried to scramble to her feet, but he quickly had her trapped beneath his strong body. "Let me up!" she demanded furiously. "I don't want to make love to you! I never did! I was only faking it!"

Her tirade added more fuel to Black Wolf's already simmering anger. He believed her, for he thought her capable of such deceit. His tone was edged with fury. "I don't give a damn if you respond or not. But I intend to take you. You can remain submissive, or you can fight. It doesn't matter, because I'll still have my way with you."

She started to spout a retort, but his lips were suddenly on hers, kissing her demandingly, almost brutally. Alisha didn't want to surrender, but, as always, his kiss destroyed her defenses. Slowly, somewhat reluctantly, she wrapped her arms around his neck.

Regardless of what she had said, Black Wolf sensed that her response was real. She might consider herself better than him; but not when it came to his satisfying her passion!

Resting on his knees, he reached up under her dress and removed her leggings. The sun, shining brightly, shone down on her bare thighs. Tantalizingly he brushed his hand across her womanhood, and when his finger entered her warm depths, her hips arched in response to his erotic fondling.

"Oh, my darling!" she purred fervently. "I want you!" Caught up in their heated embrace, she let down her guard and murmured her true feelings. "Black Wolf, you mean so much to me! Please love me!"

Mistaking her declarations for lies, Black Wolf's

anger erupted. For a moment, he felt as though he did despise her! Recalling her conversation with David, the words "humiliating" and "degrading" thundered through his mind. Why did she insist on telling him lies? He knew her true opinion of him!

Now controlled by his anger, Black Wolf undid his trousers, then penetrated her so aggressively that Alisha cried out. When he began to move inside her, her discomfort dissolved as a feeling of rapture came over her.

Black Wolf drove into her vigorously, and she locked her ankles about his waist, wanting his deepest entry. His demanding strokes sent her soaring to love's tempestuous heights. Together, they soon reached the peak of their pleasure, and Alisha held tightly to the man she loved as his frame trembled with his completion.

Black Wolf immediately left her and drew up his pants. His icy stare sent a cold chill up her spine. Moving tentatively, she retrieved her leggings, and standing, she put them on. Then, turning to face him, she started to question him about his perplexing mood; but before she could, he whirled about and stalked away. His rude, heartless departure was more than she could bare. She knelt to the ground, covered her face with her hands, and cried.

Entering the tepee, Alisha looked directly at her father, who was sitting at the lodge fire with Charles and Clint. Speaking strongly, she announced, "Papa, I want to leave here at once!"

"We'll leave in the morning," he told her.

"No!" she argued. "I want to leave now, this very minute!"

Tolerantly, he explained, "But honey, you know that

Charles is waiting to talk to Black Wolf." A little threateningly, he added, "I am also waiting to speak to the man."

Raising her chin defiantly, she remarked, "Then as far as I'm concerned, you two can wait! However, I know that Mr. Smith and Johnny are camped only a few miles from here, and I intend to find them. I'll spend the night with them, for I refuse to stay in this village any longer."

Moving to his daughter, Jack asked carefully, "Did something happen between you and Black Wolf?"

"I hate him!" she said viciously. "I hope I never see him again for as long as I live!" Feeling desperate, she reached out and clutched her father's arms. "Papa, please take me away from here! Please!"

She seemed to be on the verge of hysterics; and worried, Jack replied hastily, "All right, honey. We'll leave now if you want."

"Oh, yes, Papa!" she cried.

Joining them, Clint asked his father, "But what about that talk you need to have with Black Wolf?"

Jack didn't have a chance to answer, for suddenly Black Wolf appeared. His unexpected presence drew everyone's immediate attention.

Speaking exclusively to Charles, Black Wolf remarked, "If you have no objection to Spotted Fawn coming with us, I'll go home with you for an extended visit."

Eagerly, Lansing assured him, "I have no objections. In fact, before I went to St. Louis my housekeeper quit. If Spotted Fawn wants, she can have her position."

Black Wolf nodded brusquely. Then turning to Jack, he uttered emphatically, "In response to our earlier discussion, under no circumstances will I agree to marry your daughter!" Without so much as a glance in Alisha's direction, he spun about and left the lodge.

403

Chapter Thirty-Five

The weather was chilly, and a brisk wind blew as the travelers and their horses plodded over the grassy terrain. They were now venturing out of the area known as the Black Hills and their course was mostly downhill.

Riding abreast of her father, Alisha glanced thoughtfully at Spotted Fawn's back, for the Indian woman rode in the lead beside Justin. Clint and Johnny brought up the rear. The afternoon when Alisha and her family had left Running Horse's village, Spotted Fawn had asked them to please take her with them. Alisha had wondered why Spotted Fawn didn't want to wait another day and travel with Black Wolf, Charles, and David. She had questioned Spotted Fawn, but the young woman hadn't wanted to discuss her reasons for leaving immediately, and Alisha hadn't insisted on an explanation.

While Alisha thought of Spotted Fawn, Jack too was deep in thought. He was curious as to why Alisha had been so insistent on leaving the village without delay. They had now been traveling for days, but despite his curiosity, Jack hadn't tried to pressure his daughter.

However, he now decided to pry. Clearing his voice, he began, "Honey, don't you want to tell me what happened between you and Black Wolf?"

Just the sound of Black Wolf's name sent emotional pain into her aching heart. But feigning indifference, she asked coolly, "What makes you think anything happened?"

"Wasn't he your reason for wanting to leave on the spur of the moment?"

She raised her chin. "I'd rather not discuss Black Wolf." Anger sparked in her eyes. "I hope I never see him again!"

Jack smiled tolerantly. "You'll be seeing him very soon."

Alisha sighed heavily; for she knew her father was right. They were supposed to wait for Black Wolf and his party at the old abandoned cabin at the foot of the Hills. From that point Spotted Fawn would leave her present traveling companions and join the others on the last leg of the journey. Black Wolf's party would ride to the Longhorn, while Alisha's rode to the Bar-S. Although the two spreads bordered each other, the shortest route to each ranch would take the two groups in different directions.

When Black Wolf arrives at the cabin, Alisha told herself, I'll simply ignore him. I'll also keep my composure, for I'll not let him see how much he's hurt me.

Jack disrupted her thoughts. "Alisha, if Todd still wants you to marry him, will you consider his proposal?"

"Yes, I will," she said, her resentment toward Black Wolf bringing forth such a declaration.

"Do you love Todd?" Jack asked, watching her closely.

"Papa, please don't give me the third degree!" She

405

was feeling irritable.

Speaking wisely, her father advised, "I hope you never marry for any reason other than love."

Wishing to change the subject, Alisha said briskly, "I'll be glad to see Loretta." Jack and Clint had told her everything that had happened between Loretta and Joel. "I feel so sorry for her, but I'm happy for Joel and his wife."

"You'll be good for Miss Ingalls," Jack remarked. "She needs a friend."

Clint had confided in his sister, and she was aware that he believed Jack was falling in love with Loretta. Watching her father speculatively, she murmured, "But she already has a friend in you."

He brushed aside her words. "I probably represent a father figure to Miss Ingalls. She needs a friend closer to her own age."

"Loretta needs someone to mend her broken heart. A friend can't do that." She raised an eyebrow. "But a lover could."

"Alisha!" he cried. "Are you insinuating that I . . . ?"

She laughed fondly. "Why not?"

"There's at least twenty years between us; that's reason enough." She started to continue, but Jack silenced her. "The discussion is closed!" He withdrew into his thoughts. Where did Alisha and Clint get the foolish notion that he was romantically interested in Loretta Ingalls? Why, the very idea was absurd. She was indeed a stunning woman, and he couldn't deny that he was attracted to her, but an intimate relationship between them was out of the question.

As Jack was trying to convince himself that he wasn't enamored of Loretta, Spotted Fawn turned her horse around and rode back to join Johnny. Sensing she needed to talk alone with his brother, Clint urged his mount into a gallop and moved to the front of the procession.

Johnny didn't welcome Spotted Fawn's company; after all, she had been the cause of his public humiliation. Furthermore, because of her, he had been made to appear ridiculous in front of his own family!

Johnny had been Spotted Fawn's reason for leaving with Alisha and the others. She had wanted to travel with Johnny without Black Wolf watching over her. She knew her cousin would have ordered her to stay away from Johnny. Throughout the journey, Spotted Fawn had attempted several times to persuade Johnny to talk to her, but he had always managed to avoid her. Why was he being so elusive? Had he stopped loving her? Or had he never cared about her? She had to know, for she still loved him.

"Johnny," she began apprehensively, "do you blame me?"

"For what?" he asked sharply.

"Because my father made you run the gauntlet?"

He kept his voice lowered so no one would overhear, but in spite of his quiet tone, she could detect his rage. "Spotted Fawn, you tempted me. Hell, you practically threw yourself at my feet! Then, when I succumbed to your wanton display, your father acted like I had raped you! If you ask me, it was the other way around. You seduced me!"

She was aghast. "You speak words that are not true!"

Young Stevens was so enraged that he didn't notice that Justin was now riding toward him and Spotted Fawn. Johnny's handsome face was distorted with bitterness, and forgetting to keep his voice down, he threatened, "Stay the hell away from me, you dirty squaw, before I slap you right off your horse!"

Reining in beside Johnny, the scout teased, "Now, son, don't you realize it would be a trifle painful to be

407

knocked off a horse? Here, let me show you what I mean." Justin drew back his arm so quickly that his unsuspecting victim had no chance to duck. The man's large fist hit solidly against Johnny's chin, the powerful blow knocking him from his horse and onto the ground.

"Kinda painful, ain't it?" Justin chuckled as Johnny got awkardly to his feet.

He rubbed a hand gingerly over his bruised chin. Then as anger consumed him, Johnny foolishly reached for the pistol strapped to his hip.

Justin's rifle was ensconced firmly in its scabbard, and he was unarmed except for the Bowie knife that suddenly appeared in his hand like magic.

Moving swiftly, Jack rode up alongside his youngest son, and as Johnny pulled his pistol, he kicked the gun out of his hand. Jack's face was livid. "Damn it, Johnny!"

"Why didn't you let me shoot him?" the young Stevens hollered, his eyes bulging with fury.

"You fool! You idiot!" Jack shouted. "Smith would've killed you!"

Johnny turned to Justin, and when he saw the scout slipping his knife back into its sheath, the sight made him pale. The man had grabbed the knife so incredibly fast that Johnny hadn't seen the deadly weapon materialize.

Continuing, Jack demanded, "Johnny, you owe Spotted Fawn an apology." When his son looked at him sheepishly, he explained, "We all overheard what you said."

Valuing her pride, Spotted Fawn said quickly, "Mr. Stevens, I do not want his apology." She urged her horse into a canter.

Alisha caught up to Spotted Fawn and rode beside her. She longed for a way to ease her friend's distress and embarrassment, but what could she possibly say? Alisha had never been so angry or disappointed in Johnny. She wondered why her youngest brother had no love for anyone but himself. Why was he always so selfish?

Meantime, Jack's thoughts were running along the same lines as his daughter's. But Jack knew where his son had gotten his selfishness; it was a trait Johnny had inherited from his mother.

Late afternoon shadows fell across the landscape as the weary travelers reached the abandoned cabin where they were to await the others.

Justin, eager to return home to his family, now parted company with his traveling companions and headed in the direction of Fort Laramie. Jack had asked him to keep in touch, for he had grown to like and respect the rugged scout and hoped that their friendship would continue.

The Stevenses and Spotted Fawn had been at the cabin only a short time when four men arrived on horseback. Clint grabbed his rifle and took a vigilant stance at the uncovered window as his father cracked open the door. Jack cocked his Winchester as the strangers reined in their mounts. The four horsemen had a clear view of the two rifles pointed in their direction.

"Who are you and what do you want?" Jack asked suspiciously.

One of them spoke up, and gesturing to the man mounted at his side, he said, "My name's Abe and this here is my brother Carl." He indicated his other two comrades. "These men are our friends Frank and Harvey. We ain't lookin' for trouble. We was plannin' on spendin' the night at this here cabin, but I reckon you folks beat us to it."

"I'll have to ask you to go on your way," Jack replied.

"Mister," Abe said strongly, "it's gonna be colder than a witch's tit tonight, and it looks like it's gonna rain. You got any objections to us settin' up camp in that old lean-to where you got your horses stabled? It's big enough for us and the animals too."

Jack was hesitant to give his permission and was about to decline when Johnny remarked, "Hell, Pa, why don't you let them use the lean-to? There's no reason to make them spend the night without shelter."

Unknown to Jack, Johnny had found these men's names familiar and had a reason for wanting them to remain. Through them, he hoped to get his revenge on Kicking Buffalo. As he waited expectantly for his father to decide whether or not to let them use the lean-to, a plan began to take shape in his mind.

Jack glanced at his oldest son and waited for his approval.

"Let them stay," Clint decided.

"You can use the lean-to," Stevens called to the riders.

"Much obliged," Abe replied. He and his companions headed for the structure, which was located a couple of yards from the cabin.

Johnny waited until after supper before leaving the cabin. The others took for granted that he needed to relieve himself and didn't question his departure.

Once outside, Johnny moved quickly to the lean-to. Approaching, he said clearly, "It's Johnny Stevens; and I want to talk to you."

The men knew Johnny, for last spring they had played poker with him at the Golden Horseshoe. Abe and his men were wanderers and never stayed in one place for very long; they were also shady characters and were always one jump ahead of the law.

"Stevens?" Abe exclaimed, shocked at finding the young rancher in these parts.

Entering the flimsy shelter, Johnny saw that the men were seated around a small campfire. The lean-to was open on one side, where the smoke escaped.

Stevens nodded at each man individually, then turned his attention to Abe, who he knew was their leader. "I've got a favor to ask of you."

Abe scowled. "I don't do favors."

Johnny smiled cunningly. "I think you'll want to do this one. I'm traveling with my father and brother, and we have a real pretty Indian gal with us." He omitted mentioning Alisha, for he didn't want these men to know of her presence. "I want you to abduct this gal, kill her, and then leave her on the trail."

His listeners were astonished. "Why do you want us to kill her?" The question was asked by Carl.

"I have my reasons," he muttered. "If you all do this for me, then come to Backwater, I'll pay you. I can't get my hands on a lot of money, but I can manage a couple of hundred."

"Just how are we supposed to abduct this woman without your pa or brother shootin' off our heads?" Abe said skeptically.

"I'll tell Pa that I need to talk privately with Spotted Fawn. Then, I want you to make it look like you jumped us. You can tie me up, then take off with the Indian. When Pa comes looking for us, he'll find me tied and won't suspect that I had anything to do with it."

"What's to keep your pa and brother from comin' after us?"

"You men are experienced on the trail. Pa and Clint wouldn't stand a chance of finding you if you didn't want to be found. Hell, my father and brother are

411

ranchers; they don't know how to track."

"Why do you want us to leave the woman's body where it can be found?" Abe wanted to know.

"So her death will get back to her father."

"You got somethin' against her daddy?" the one called Harvey spoke up.

"I swore to get even with the man, and this is one way to do it."

Abe got to his feet. He was a big man, and when he took a stance beside Johnny, his frame towered over the young man. He glanced over his shoulder and studied the horses belonging to Johnny's traveling party before returning his attention to the matter at hand. "In the mornin', you take that Indian gal outside, and we'll be waitin' for you. At daybreak, we'll pretend to pull out, then backtrack and watch the cabin. When we grab the woman, we'll leave you tied and gagged, but when your pa finds you, tell him you was attacked by some trappers. We don't hanker showin' up in Backwater only to have the sheriff arrestin' us because Stevens pressed charges against us for killin' a damned squaw."

Abe grinned inwardly. He was pointing out these options merely to gain Stevens's confidence; secretly he was planning not only to murder Johnny, but Clint and Jack as well.

Johnny nodded eagerly. "Don't worry, I'll do exactly as you say."

"Now you'd better get back to the cabin before your pa comes lookin' for you."

Johnny left quickly.

Abe watched until young Stevens had entered the cabin, then he turned and eyed his companions. A sly smile spread across his bearded face as he waited for their comments.

It was his brother Carl who voiced his objection. "Why in the hell did you tell Stevens we'd kill that

Indian gal? We ain't got time for no killin's. We got to get to Mexico."

The men had been in the Hills searching for gold, but their quest had been unsuccessful. Now they were heading south and planned to spend the winter in Mexico. Too much time had been spent in the Hills, and with cold weather rapidly approaching, they intended to travel straight to Mexico. Carl was dead set on making the trip without wasting time.

Abe was undisturbed by his younger brother's opposition. "Johnny Stevens wasn't totally honest with us."

"What do you mean?" Carl asked, his interest immediately piqued.

"There's two women in that there cabin," he declared.

"Why do you think that?" asked Harvey.

He gestured toward the horses belonging to the Stevens. "I count five horses, but the way Johnny talked there's only four people. Him, his brother, father and that squaw."

"Maybe the fifth one is a pack horse," Carl suggested.

"A pack horse don't need no saddle," Abe replied flatly, pointing at the five saddles that had been stored in the lean-to. A wicked, lewd glint came to his small eyes as he continued. "I reckon that fifth horse belongs to Johnny's sister. When we was at the Golden Horseshoe last spring, I overheard some cowhands talkin' about the Stevens woman. They said that she's got hair so light it's almost white. Well, I ain't never seen no woman with hair that color, and I got an urge to see her for myself."

Abe walked over and sat down at the fire. "Can you imagine how much the Comancheros would pay for a woman with white-colored hair?"

Abe and his men knew how to contact the Mexican

outlaws known as the Comancheros, for they had ridden with them on occasion.

"She'd bring a high price," Frank said enthusiastically. He was the youngest of the group.

"But is she pretty?" Harvey asked.

"Them cowhands didn't only talk about her hair, but also about her looks. They said that she was the best-lookin' woman they'd ever seen." Abe's sudden grin was lust-filled. "I wonder if she's got that same shade of blond between her thighs."

Abe's companions were wondering the same thing and were equally curious.

"What about the Indian gal?" Carl questioned. "Are we gonna kill her?"

"Johnny said that she's pretty, and if she is, we'll take her to Mexico too and sell her to the Comancheros. She won't be as valuable as the Stevens woman, but she'll bring a good price."

Harvey was the next one to speak. "What do you plan to do about the men?"

"We'll have to kill 'em. I don't want 'em chasin' us, and I sure as hell don't want 'em runnin' to the law."

"Why do you reckon they're in these parts?" Carl asked.

"Who knows? And who cares?" Rising, Abe stepped to his bedroll and placed it close to the fire. Lying down, he folded his arms beneath his head, and while gazing thoughtfully, murmured, "I ain't never seen no woman with white-colored hair coverin' her plaything, and I sure am anxious to see Miss Stevens without any clothes."

"Are you gonna poke her?" Frank questioned eagerly.

"Does a bear shit in the woods?" Abe laughed grotesquely.

Chapter Thirty-Six

"Does Chuck ever confide in you?" Charles asked David. They were riding leisurely, allowing their horses to walk at an unhurried pace.

"Chuck?" David repeated. It was hard for him to think of Black Wolf by a different name. "We're good friends, but he doesn't discuss his personal affairs with me. Why do you ask?"

Black Wolf had ridden ahead to scout the area, and Charles and David were free to speak about him. "I'm concerned about Chuck's relationship with Alisha. I think those two are in love, yet for some unexplained reason they keep avoiding each other."

David agreed. "I know what you mean. I've tried to get Black Wolf and Alisha to talk to me about their feelings, but they both clam up."

Before Charles could continue, he caught sight of Black Wolf returning. He was pushing his horse at a quick gallop. "Chuck seems to be in a hurry. I hope nothing is wrong."

They reined in and waited for Black Wolf to join them. Arriving, Black Wolf drew his stallion to such an abrupt halt that the huge animal reared back dangerously.

Black Wolf curbed the spirited steed. As he rubbed the horse's neck he said hastily, "I ran across a set of tracks. It looks like there are four riders and two pack mules. For some reason they stopped, then began backtracking. They're heading in the direction of the cabin where we're supposed to meet Spotted Fawn and the others."

"This could mean trouble," Charles pointed out.

"We'll ride in closer to the cabin, then I'll go the rest of the way on foot. There's less chance of detection if I leave my horse behind with you and David."

"What do you mean, you'll go the rest of the way on foot?" Charles exclaimed. "I might be old, but I'm not decrepit! At least, not yet!" he added, remembering his rheumatism.

Black Wolf decided not to argue with him. "All right, we'll leave the horses with David."

"I'm not staying behind!" the boy blurted out.

This time, Black Wolf was about to object, but Charles didn't give him a chance.

"We're wasting time," Lansing grumbled. "Let's get going." Slapping the reins against his horse, he took off like a bolt, leaving the others no choice but to follow.

As Johnny came awake, the bright sunlight filtering into the cabin made him aware that he had slept much later than he had planned. He sat up with a start, his eyes scanning the unfurnished room. When he saw everyone sitting by the lit fireplace, he threw off his top blanket and hurried to his feet.

Noticing that he was awake, Jack asked, "You want a cup of coffee?"

"No thanks," Johnny replied. Anxiously he wondered if Abe and his men had grown impatient and had left the area. Trying to sound mildly interested, he asked, "Did those men leave yet?"

"They were gone at daybreak," Jack answered.

Damn! Johnny cursed to himself. Dawn was hours ago! He was now certain the men had tired of waiting for him to bring Spotted Fawn outside and had gone on their way. Nonetheless, he would go through with his plan, just in case Abe and the others were still around.

"Pa, I'd like to talk to Spotted Fawn," Johnny said, sounding humbled.

Jack nodded toward the girl. She was sitting beside Alisha. "There she is; talk all you wish."

"I mean, I need to talk to her alone."

Stevens eyed his son distrustfully. "Anything you need to say to her you can say in front of the rest of us."

Spotted Fawn, hoping desperately that Johnny had had a change of heart, said quickly, "I will talk alone with him."

Turning to the girl, Johnny favored her with a charming smile. "Will you take a walk with me?"

Standing, she replied eagerly, "Yes, I will." She hurried to her robe and slipped it over her shoulders.

"Don't go too far," Jack warned them as they went to the door.

"We won't," Johnny assured him as he ushered Spotted Fawn outside.

The moment they departed, Alisha mumbled worriedly, "Why do you suppose Johnny wants to talk to Spotted Fawn?"

"I hope he intends to apologize to her," Jack remarked.

Alisha didn't believe her brother capable of such gentlemanly conduct where Spotted Fawn was concerned. However, she decided to keep her opinion to herself. Getting to her feet, she said casually, "I think I'll step outside for a moment."

Her father wasn't fooled. "You planning to keep an eye on Johnny?"

"I'm sorry, Papa, but I just don't trust him. I'm afraid he's going to take advantage of Spotted Fawn."

"Don't wander away from the cabin, and if Johnny causes any trouble, call out to me."

She assured him that she would, then flinging a buffalo robe over her shoulders, she darted outside. She had once again borrowed David's pants and shirt, and as she paused on the dilapidated porch, the cold wind whipped about the legs of her trousers. She looked around but couldn't see Johnny and Spotted Fawn. She had on a pair of high-topped moccasins, and the soft soles muffled her footsteps as she left the porch to search for the pair.

Meanwhile, Johnny had led Spotted Fawn into the dense shrubbery that surrounded the isolated cabin. As he kept their conversation sporadic, his eyes were continually scanning the immediate area, hoping that Abe and his men would make a sudden appearance.

Growing impatient with Johnny, Spotted Fawn decided to press him. She brought her steps to a halt, and when he tried to encourage her to continue their walk, she refused. "Johnny," she began firmly, "why did you want to talk to me?"

He expelled a sigh of disappointment. Apparently, the four men had given up and were no longer in the vicinity. Frowning, he said short-temperedly, "Let's go back to the cabin. I don't have anything to say."

She was perplexed. "Then why did you tell your father that you wanted to talk to me?"

He was about to give her a sarcastic answer when all at once Abe and his companions materialized from the thick vegetation. As they surrounded Johnny and Spotted Fawn, Abe mumbled irritably, "It took you long enough. We were ready to call the whole thing off and head on for Mexico."

"I slept late," Johnny explained a little reluctantly.

Feeling frightened, Spotted Fawn gasped, "Johnny, what is going on? Why are these men here?" She clutched at his arm.

Roughly he threw off her grasp. Looking at Abe, he demanded, "Hurry up and tie me, then take this squaw and get out of here."

Speaking to Harvey, Abe ordered, "Keep a lookout." Then, returning his attention to Johnny, he asked with a sneer, "Is your sister a-travelin' with you?"

Sensing a trap, Johnny reached for his holstered pistol, but in a flash Carl had stepped up behind him. As he jabbed the barrel of his pistol into Johnny's ribs, he said smoothly, "I'll take that pistol of yours." Quickly he slipped the weapon from Johnny's holster.

Now, with fear overwhelming him, Johnny asked plaintively, "You aren't planning to kill me, are you?"

Before Abe could respond, Harvey shouted, "There's someone comin', and it's a woman with white-colored hair."

A large smile spread across the leader's face. "Go grab her."

Harvey obeyed eagerly, for he was anxious to get a real close look at the Stevens woman.

"Why do you want my sister?" Johnny raged.

"Why do you think?" Abe taunted.

"You got this squaw; why don't you just take her and get the hell out of here?"

Abe looked over at Spotted Fawn. Reaching out, he grasped her robe and flung it to the ground. As his eyes discovered her inviting curves, he murmured thickly, "She sure is a pretty little Indian gal. But I ain't never had a taste for squaws, I've always had a weakness for blond women." His eyes sweeping back to Johnny, he added, "Women like your sister."

At that moment Harvey returned with Alisha. He had captured her in his strong arms and one hand was clamped over her mouth.

She fought wildly against the man holding her imprisoned, and her struggles had caused her long hair to fall down around her face.

Abe, awestruck by Alisha's flaxen tresses, stared as though he were spellbound. A few moments went by before he could find his voice. "You're just as pretty as them cowhands said you was," he said hoarsely.

Cautiously Harvey removed his hand from her mouth. "Carl's got a gun pointed in your brother's ribs, and if you scream, your brother's gonna be dead."

She nodded weakly, her eyes turned on Johnny. "Why are these men doing this?" she asked.

When Johnny didn't reply, Abe chuckled coldly. "Why don't you answer her?" he jeered.

Johnny's face was beet-red. "Damn you! I'll get even with you for this!"

"Just like you were gonna get even with this squaw's daddy?"

"What does he mean?" Alisha demanded of her brother.

Answering, Abe replied, "Stevens offered to pay us to kidnap this here Indian gal. He wanted us to kill her and leave her body where it could easily be found so her daddy would learn of her untimely death."

"Johnny, no!" Alisha cried. Her brother's evilness sent chills up her spine.

Taking slow but deliberate steps, Abe moved to Alisha. His huge hand reached over to caress a lock of her hair, and avoiding his contact, she turned to flee. Her attempt was in vain, for Harvey grabbed her waist, then flung her into Abe's awaiting arms. Pulling her against his brawny frame, he mumbled thickly, "We decided not to kill the pretty little squaw. We got better plans for her, and for you too. You gals are gonna take a trip with us to Mexico. After we get our fill, we're gonna sell you two to the Comancheros."

Frank, who had been watching the proceedings without participating, now lurched for Spotted Fawn and jerked her into his embrace. Bending his head, his lips came down on hers, and keeping her small frame pinned, he kissed her forcefully.

"We ain't got time for that stuff!" Carl yelled to Frank. When the young man released Spotted Fawn, Carl spoke to his brother. "Let's shoot the men, then get the hell out of here. We can play with the women later."

Agreeing, Abe said briskly, "Miss Stevens, I want you to call out to your father and brother. Call 'em real casual-like so they won't think anything is wrong." He looked from Harvey to Frank. "When the men step outside, shoot 'em."

"I won't call for them!" Alisha said defiantly.

Clutching a handful of her hair, Abe drew her head back painfully. Glaring down into her eyes, he sneered, "You'll do as I say or I'll . . ."

"Or you'll what?" a deep, unexpected voice suddenly sounded. Black Wolf had approached soundlessly, taking everyone by surprise.

Freeing Alisha, Abe whirled about, and the sight of the warrior standing with a rifle pointed at him caused him to gasp sharply.

Carl, intending to use Johnny as a shield, took a quick step behind his prisoner; however, as he did, a rifle barrel touched the back of his head.

Calmly, Charles warned, "Drop your gun."

As Carl obliged, Harvey and Frank reached for their holstered pistols, but the figure now emerging from the thicket gave them just cause to pause.

His Winchester cocked and ready to fire, David said

smoothly, "Draw those guns, and I'll blow you to pieces."

Black Wolf spoke to Spotted Fawn, "Gather their weapons." His blue eyes went to Alisha. "Where are your father and Clint?"

"Inside the cabin," she answered. She longed to rush into his arms, but the cold expression in his eyes dissuaded her.

"Go get them," Black Wolf ordered tersely.

She obeyed, and turning about, headed quickly for the cabin.

"What do you want to do with these guys?" Clint asked his father as he entered the cabin.

Jack, standing in front of the fireplace, was deep in thought. He had a lit cheroot, and pitching the partially smoked cigar into the hearth, he answered despondently, "Let them go free."

Although it galled Clint to do so, he refrained from arguing with his father's decision. He understood why Jack was setting Abe and his men free; if he were to press charges against them, Johnny would also go to trial, for he had been an accomplice.

Alisha and Spotted Fawn were in the cabin sitting on their bedrolls, and speaking to Clint, Alisha asked, "Where's Johnny?"

"When I last saw him, he was at the lean-to, avoiding everyone."

Jack sighed wearily. "I can hardly believe that Johnny did something so evil."

"I've always known that he could be contemptible," Clint began. "But I never dreamed he could stoop so low." Heading for the door, he continued, "I'll tell Black Wolf and Charles to release Abe and his men."

Standing, Alisha murmured uneasily, "Papa, I'm

going to talk to Johnny."

He nodded his approval. "All right, but tell him to stay away from me until my temper has had time to cool."

Grabbing her robe and slinging it over her shoulders, Alisha hurried outside. She purposefully kept her eyes turned away from Black Wolf and the others. She didn't want to see Abe or his comrades; nor did she want to look at Black Wolf. His icy attitude was more than she could bear.

When she reached the lean-to, she saw that Johnny was no longer there. Deciding to search for him, she was about to leave when, out of the corner of her eye, she caught sight of Black Wolf approaching.

He had seen Alisha heading for the lean-to and had decided to follow her. It had been an impulsive decision, one he was now wishing he hadn't made. They had nothing to discuss. Their relationship was over and done with.

Alisha waited for Black Wolf to say something, but when he merely continued to study her with an expression she couldn't discern, she mumbled hesitantly, "Have . . . have you seen Johnny?"

A hard glare came to his vivid blue eyes. "Your brother's at the back of the cabin, staying to himself. Which is for the best, because if he crosses my path . . ."

She cut in, "Black Wolf, I can understand your feelings. Spotted Fawn is your cousin and you love her. What Johnny tried to do is unforgivable, but Spotted Fawn wasn't harmed, so why don't you just let my father handle Johnny?"

He smirked. "What's he planning to do, send Johnny to bed without his supper?"

"Don't be sarcastic!" she snapped.

"Your brother and his friends should have to pay for

what they tried to do, but because Johnny is a Stevens, he's going to get off scot-free."

"What would sending him to prison accomplish?"

"Justice!" Stepping forward, he grasped her arm, and staring down into her face, he said between gritted teeth, "Keep your brother away from me, or so help me God, I'll kill him!" He released her brusquely and whirled about.

"Are you leaving?" she asked.

"Yes," he grumbled.

"When will I see you again?" The words passed her lips before she could stop them. Why did she let this man continually destroy her pride?

Black Wolf faced her. "I don't know, but if you need me, you know where to find me." He paused for a moment. Then, "Goodbye, Alisha," he said firmly.

The finality in his tone severed any last shred of hope that he might love her. "Goodbye, Black Wolf," she returned, speaking barely above a whisper.

She watched him as he walked away from the lean-to and out of her life. Refusing to give in to her tears, she found a place to sit, intending to stay there until Black Wolf and his party were gone.

David came looking for her, and they fondly embraced, promising to see each other again soon. A few minutes later, she heard Black Wolf and the others riding away, and as the sounds of hoofbeats were fading into the distance, Alisha left the lean-to. It was time to go home, and once there, she'd find a way to get over Black Wolf.

Chapter Thirty-Seven

Awaking slowly, Alisha turned to lie on her side. Intending to snuggle close to Black Wolf, she moved her arm to place it across his warm body. Finding no one next to her, she opened her eyes with a start. Where was he? Had he gone hunting again?

She sat up, and as her eyes looked about her bedroom, she came fully awake. Limply she fell back onto the bed. She wasn't in Black Wolf's lodge; she was at home. Now she missed Black Wolf so much that her heart felt as though it were breaking. How long would it take her to get used to living without him? The deep void he'd left in her life was drawing her into an endless pit of depression. She knew she had to find a way to put Black Wolf behind her and start anew. She must stop pining for this man who didn't love her; to continue to do so was not only foolish, but also self-destructive.

Telling herself that starting today she'd turn over a new leaf, she got out of bed and dressed quickly. Sitting on the stool in front of her dressing table, she brushed her blond tresses vigorously. Deciding to go downstairs for breakfast, she rose hastily and was smoothing the folds of her printed gown when suddenly she felt dizzy. She swayed unsteadily for a moment, but the spell soon passed and lending it little importance, she left her bedroom and hurried down the stairway to the dining room.

Seeing only Johnny at the table, she asked, "Where is everyone?"

He answered glumly, "Mary isn't feeling well, and Pa told her to spend the day in bed. Clint's on the range. Miss Ingalls in in the study with Pa."

Sitting, and pouring herself a cup of coffee, she queried, "Why are Loretta and Papa in the study?"

"How would I know?" he snapped. "Pa told her he wanted to talk alone with her and off they went. He doesn't confide in me."

"Johnny, it's going to take time for Papa to forgive you. Hiring those men to kill Spotted Fawn was evil and . . ."

He interrupted sharply, "For God sake, Alisha, let it rest! I can't very well undo what happened, and I don't like hearing about it over and over again!"

She agreed. Although his ploy had been cruel, it was over and done with. Talking it into the ground would solve nothing.

The table was set with covered dishes, and removing one of the lids, Alisha saw two fried eggs. She lifted the platter, intending to transfer the food onto her own plate, but as she continued to eye the eggs, her stomach churned. A feeling of nausea washed over her, and the morning fare was suddenly unappetizing. Replacing the platter, she covered the food.

"Aren't you hungry?" Johnny asked.

"I was," she answered. "But I lost my appetite. I think I'll just have coffee."

As she sipped the drink, her brother watched her thoughtfully. He wondered if her relationship with Black Wolf had ruined her life. He seriously doubted if any decent white man would want to marry her; not after she had lived with a Sioux buck! Mentally envisioning her in bed with a half-breed filled him with repulsion.

Seeing his expression, Alisha asked, "Why are you looking at me like that?"

Deciding to get his feelings out into the open, he demanded harshly, "Why in hell did you let that half-breed ruin you? Don't you realize no white man will want to marry you? You're a goddamned, disgusting white squaw!"

Alisha paled. "How dare you!"

He stood abruptly, shoving his chair backwards. "You make me sick! This whole family turns my stomach! You're all a bunch of Indian lovers!"

Rising and pushing back her own chair, she asked angrily, "If you feel so resentful toward Indians, then why did you make love to Spotted Fawn?"

"I didn't make love to her!" he spat. "I took her the same way I'd take a whore!" His mood softened somewhat, and he proceeded in a more level tone, "Alisha, you're my sister, and I feel something special for you. But you have cheapened yourself, and I can't forgive you for what you've done. Nor can I understand why Pa and Clint didn't kill Black Wolf for touching you. It has taken this to make me realize that I don't belong here. I'm going to my room to pack my clothes and move into town. As far as I'm concerned, I no longer have a family. I disown all of you."

"If you leave, how do you intend to support yourself?"

"I'm quite sure I can get a job tending bar at the Golden Horseshoe." He shrugged casually. "If not, then I'll find work elsewhere."

He spun around and stalked out of the room. Alisha didn't attempt to stop him. Maybe his leaving was for the best, for Johnny had been right, he *didn't* belong here. Slowly, she returned to her chair. She was struck with pangs of anxiety as she wondered how her father

427

would take Johnny's departure.

Meanwhile, together inside the study, Jack and Loretta remained unaware of the discussion taking place outside.

Gesturing to the chair in front of his desk, Jack asked Loretta to be seated.

Doing as he requested, she watched him as he walked around to his own chair.

His eyes, glazed with tenderness, studied her across the span of his desktop. As always, he found her extremely lovely. Her radiant auburn locks were arranged in a flattering upsweep, and her light-blue frock fit her soft curves perfectly.

As she waited for Jack to explain this private meeting, Loretta returned his gaze. She was happy that he was now back home. She had missed him more than she'd thought she would. Although her heart still ached for Joel, she couldn't deny that Jack Stevens' presence eased her pain. She was impressed with Jack, for she thought him quite handsome. He wasn't attractive in the same way as Joel. Jack's weather-beaten face and brawny build were ruggedly appealing, whereas Joel had exuded an aura of elegance.

Absently Jack ran a hand through his reddish-blond hair, as full now as it had been in his youth. "Miss Ingalls . . ." he began.

"Please call me Loretta," she said quickly.

"I'll be glad to, if you'll call me Jack."

She smiled warmly. "Yes, of course I will."

"I want to talk to you about giving a dinner party. Since Mary isn't feeling well, you'll have to handle most of the preparations. Do you think you can manage?"

"I'm sure I can. How many guests are you planning to invite?"

"Quite a few," he replied. "I'll make out a guest list, so you'll have the correct number."

"Is there a special reason for this party?"

"Yes, I want to introduce Black Wolf to the citizens of Backwater."

She arched a brow. "Isn't it Mr. Lansing's place to introduce his grandson?"

"I suppose, but I'd like to do this for him." He grinned largely. "Besides, it gives me a good excuse to have a party. This home could use a little merriment."

Watching him speculatively, Loretta questioned, "Are you by chance playing Cupid?"

He looked a trifle embarrassed. "Wh . . . what do you mean?"

She smiled teasingly. "When I make out the sitting cards for dinner, do you want me to place Black Wolf and Alisha side by side?"

"Am I that obvious?" he asked.

Laughing gaily, she answered, "Yes, you are. But I think your ploy is delightful, and I'll gladly be your conspirator." Her expression was now one of respect. "Jack, I think you're a wonderful, exceptional man."

He was flattered. "Thank you, but what did I do to deserve such praise?"

"You know how deeply your daughter loves Black Wolf, and you want to help her. Not many fathers would be so obliging, especially if their daughter was in love with a half-breed."

"I've always tried to judge a man by his worth, not by the color of his skin. Considering the way in which Black Wolf is now treating Alisha, he arouses my anger, but I still admire and respect him as a man." He became curious. "How did you know that Alisha loved Black Wolf?"

"Last night before we went to bed, Alisha and I had a long talk. She confided in me. She loves him very much."

429

"Did she say anything about Todd Miller?"

"No, why?"

"On the trip home, she told me she was considering marrying Todd. Of course if she marries him, it might prove to be the biggest mistake of her life."

"You don't have to worry about Alisha marrying Mr. Miller."

He was bemused. "What do you mean?"

"It seems Mr. Miller has fallen in love with a young lady who lives in Texas. Her name is Brenda Davis."

Jack was shocked. "Wasn't this kind of sudden?"

"You've been away so much, and then were so preoccupied with Alisha's disappearance, that you didn't keep up with Backwater's social affairs. Sheriff Davis is Brenda's uncle, and she came to town to see him. She recently lost her father. From what I understand, her father and the sheriff were brothers, and years ago they had a falling out. Apparently this bitterness between them was never resolved, although it seems that the sheriff's brother would've been willing. Sheriff Davis's brother was a wealthy man, but his riches came from the ranch he had inherited from their father. Believing his brother had a right to part of his fortune, he left him a substantial sum of money. Brenda was able to locate her uncle, and she came here to give him the money that her father had willed to him."

"How did you learn all this?"

"The new schoolteacher is Todd Miller's aunt. She and I visit each other often, and she told me everything."

"Brenda Davis and Todd fell in love?"

"Yes, from what Mr. Miller's aunt says, it was love at first sight. Brenda has returned home, and now Mr. Miller plans to sell his ranch, move to Texas, and marry Miss Davis."

Jack was overwhelmed. "It must've been the fastest

courtship in history."

Loretta smiled ruefully. "Sometimes love can happen very quickly." She had loved Joel from the first moment she had seen him.

"I wonder who Todd will find to buy his ranch?" Jack pondered vaguely. Then, setting his thoughts on a different course, he grinned at Loretta and announced, "I once told you that I intend to teach you how to ride. It's a mite chilly outside, but it's a clear, sunny day, so why don't I give you your first lesson?"

"I don't have any riding clothes," she replied.

"Borrow something to wear from Alisha."

"All right," she agreed. She was looking forward to the outing, for she enjoyed Jack's company immensely.

A knock sounded on the door, followed by Alisha's voice: "Papa, may I come in?"

"Of course," he called, and as she entered, he stood and walked around the desk. Stepping to his daughter, and noting her pallor, he asked, "Honey, are you all right?"

"Yes, I'm fine," she assured him, although she was actually feeling out of sorts. Grasping his arm, she continued urgently, "Papa, Johnny is in his room packing. He plans to move into town."

The news didn't come as a surprise to Jack. He had been expecting his youngest son's rebellion.

"Are you going to stop him?" Alisha asked.

"No," he answered. "He's a full-grown man, and if he wants to leave, then he can do so." He paused, then added solemnly, "All things considered, it's probably for the best."

Alisha didn't say anything, for her feelings were the same as her father's.

The ranch house sat in a valley bordered on all sides by small, rolling hills, their slopes interspersed with beautiful pines and spruces.

At the crest of one of these hills, Jack and Loretta pulled up their horses, and dismounting, Jack stepped quickly to his lovely companion and assisted her to the ground.

"How did I do on my first lesson?" Loretta asked pertly.

"You did exceptionally well," he replied, studying the face looking up at his. The brisk air had turned her cheeks rosy, and her eyes were shining brightly.

Mesmerized, his scrutiny deepened, and beginning to feel uncomfortable under his intense perusal, Loretta moved away. The hill overlooked Jack's house, and moving to the edge, she gazed down at it.

He watched her for a moment. The riding clothes Alisha had loaned her fit her faultlessly. The divided skirt was a soft yellow, and beneath the matching vest, she wore a long-sleeved blouse. Because it was chilly she wore a jacket, its deep brown the same color as her hat and western boots.

Jack walked up behind her, and placing his hands on her shoulders, he urged her to face him. "You look very stunning."

Blushing slightly, she murmured, "Thank you." She could feel herself responding to this rugged, attractive man, and these feelings confused her. She was still in love with Joel. Why did Jack's presence seem to revive emotions she thought had died the day Bonnie Sue had reclaimed her husband?

Jack, his heart filled with desire, was as disturbed as Loretta. He thought her too young for him; he also knew she was still longing for Joel. Losing Carson had left her vulnerable, and it would be natural for her to turn to another man in her loneliness. Did he want to be second choice? Could he love her, knowing all along that deep in her heart she wanted another man? Or did he have the power to erase Joel from her life? A small frown wrinkled his brow as he recalled the way in which Carson had coldly ignored Loretta. The moment he had learned that his wife was alive, he had forgotten Loretta's existence. Loretta deserved better than that. Carson had never given her all his love; a large part of his heart had belonged to Bonnie Sue; but Jack knew that he himself could love her exclusively. However, as the difference in their ages crossed his mind, he removed his hands from her shoulders and stepped back. Overwhelmed with desire, he had temporarily forgotten that he was too old for her.

Collecting himself, he said brusquely, "We'd better get back home. I have a lot of work to do."

Loretta was surprised when she suddenly realized that she had been hoping he would kiss her. She felt foolish. Jack Stevens didn't want to be a suitor; he merely wanted to be a friend. Trying to sound collected, she replied, "Don't forget to make out that guest list for me."

"I'll take care of it right after dinner," he promised, taking her arm and leading her back to the horses. He held the stirrup for her, and as she lifted her foot, she came close to losing her balance. As she tottered in his direction, his arms went around her supportively.

Finding Loretta in his embrace was more than Jack's will power could take, and drawing her closer, he lowered his head and pressed his lips to hers. The touch of her mouth against his sparked his passion, and turning their kiss into one of heated longing, he slipped his tongue between her teeth.

Her arms tightened about his neck as she returned his passion. When he drew her against his male hardness, she didn't resist. Her thighs next to his set fire to her need, and she clung to him, loving the feel of his stiff maleness and the strength in his firm hold.

Jack hadn't expected her to respond so freely, and knowing he would take her here and now if their embrace continued, he released her. Taking a backward step, he inhaled deeply in an effort to control himself. Jack Stevens was a virile man and a passionate one. His self-restraint could be pushed only so far, and he knew it had reached its limit.

"Loretta," he began kindly, "you're very young, and in some ways probably very innocent. I don't think you're aware of the implications involved when you kiss a man as passionately as you just kissed me."

Loretta lowered her eyes to avoid his gaze. She had never married, so naturally he would take it for granted that she was still a virgin. She wondered if she should tell him that she was no longer innocent. Would he think badly of her? Yes, she decided; he would think her cheap. Not wanting to lower his opinion of her, she didn't confess; instead she murmured hesitantly, "I'm sorry. Please forgive me."

His passion now controlled, Jack replied gently, "I'm the one who should apologize. I should be thoroughly ashamed of myself for taking advantage of a young lady."

Lady! The word tore into her conscience. If he knew the truth, would he still consider her a lady? Suddenly she questioned why this man's opinion meant so much to her. Why since Joel's departure had Jack Stevens become such a big part of her life? Why did he fill her thoughts and tear at her heart? She had no answers to these perplexing questions, and her feelings were in turmoil.

Stepping to her side, Jack once again offered to help her mount. This time, she did so without mishap. When she was seated, he went to his own horse and swung into the saddle with ease.

On the short ride back to the house, Jack kept their conversation impersonal.

Chapter Thirty-Eight

As Alisha descended the stairway, most of the guests had already arrived and the downstairs was filled with people mingling about.

Jack was standing in the foyer talking to friends, but catching sight of Alisha, he made his excuses and walked over to greet her. His eyes reflected his pride as he watched his daughter looking lovely in her lilac silk gown. The skirt was adorned with a fancy lace design, and a sash of white silk trimmed with black velvet fit the waistline, then tied into a flowing bow at the back. Alisha's dress was cut low in front, revealing the soft swell of her ivory breasts. Her jewelry consisted of a single strand of pearls with matching earrings. Her hair was drawn back on the sides and held in place with pearl-studded combs, leaving the rest of her long blond tresses to cascade gracefully past her bare shoulders.

When she paused in front of her father, he took her hand and kissed it. "Honey, you look beautiful."

"Thank you, Papa," she replied, smiling prettily. "You look very handsome yourself."

Jack wore a fawn-colored dress jacket and dark brown trousers. The clothes fit his strong frame snugly, the tight fit emphasizing his powerful physique.

Alisha, wondering if Black Wolf had arrived, glanced about as she hoped to spot him among the other guests.

Jack grinned knowingly. "He isn't here yet."

Feigning puzzlement, she stammered, "Who . . . who isn't here?"

"Black Wolf," he replied. "And don't try to deny that you weren't looking for him." Jack knew that his daughter had been apprehensive about this dinner party and had even gone so far as to ask him not to go through with it. She didn't have to tell him that Black Wolf had been the reason behind her protest. She was trying very hard to get over the man, and Jack was aware that seeing him again would be difficult for her. However, Jack still believed that Alisha and Black Wolf were in love and belonged together. He hoped that this party might help them reconcile their differences.

Taking his daughter's arm, Jack started to escort her into the parlor when he became aware that Clint had just admitted more guests. Jack and Alisha, poised at the bottom of the stairway, had a clear view of the three visitors.

As Black Wolf entered behind his grandfather, Alisha gasped softly. Her gaze swept over him with a mixture of astonishment and admiration. She had never seen him look more handsome. He was wearing a gray dinner jacket, white ruffled shirt, and charcoal-gray trousers. His black hair had been cut and was now collar-length. He exuded an air of refinement and seemed to be perfectly at ease in his new appearance.

Jack's guests were also staring at Black Wolf with amazement. They had been expecting Charles Lansing's half-breed grandson to be somewhat of a savage.

Quickly Jack ushered Alisha over to welcome their guests. As her father was greeting Charles, she turned her attention to David and thought him handsome in his dress clothes; however, unlike Black Wolf, he didn't appear to be at ease. The boy kept pulling at his black cravat as though it were choking him. Alisha smiled, and her heart filled with love as she continued to study him. She had never before fully realized how dear David was to her.

Feeling her eyes on him, David looked at her and smiled fondly. Moving to his side, she kissed him on the cheek.

Her open token of affection caused a blush to redden his face. Although he was a little embarrassed, he nonetheless was pleased that Alisha was apparently happy to see him.

"How have you been?" she asked. Alisha hadn't seen him or Black Wolf since she had parted company with them at the abandoned shack.

"I'm fine," David answered. His green eyes shone brightly as he continued, "The Longhorn is a great place to live, and I'm learning a lot about ranching." He had missed Alisha and was glad to see her again. He was suddenly struck with a pang of guilt. For the last two weeks he'd been so occupied with his life at the Longhorn that he'd let Alisha slip from his thoughts. Why hadn't he found the time to visit her? He murmured apologetically, "Alisha, I'm sorry I haven't come to see you before now."

She was about to assure him that he needn't feel bad when Charles said briskly, "Alisha, aren't you going to welcome Chuck and me?"

"Chuck?" she questioned, confused by the name.

"My grandfather prefers the name," Black Wolf explained.

The mere sound of his deep voice sent her pulse racing. I still love him! she cried inwardly. In a way she didn't want to acknowledge him, for she knew that

437

when she looked into his familiar face her heart would break. But she could hardly wait to once again gaze into his brilliant blue eyes and become mesmerized by the man she loved so hopelessly.

Carefully Alisha raised her eyes to his, and struck with mixed emotions, she somehow managed to murmur collectedly, "Hello, Black Wolf. Why didn't Spotted Fawn come with you?"

"She didn't think she'd feel at ease in this kind of gathering." Then, bowing from the waist, he took her hand and placed a light kiss upon it. "Alisha, you look ravishing," he said smoothly, his even tone concealing the powerful impact her presence had on him.

Looking on, the other guests remained astonished by Black Wolf's manners. Some were so astonished that they actually spoke their thoughts out loud.

Aware of the disturbance Black Wolf's presence was provoking, Charles hastily mumbled the conventional proprieties to Alisha, then anxious to show off his grandson, he urged him away and began introducing him to the other guests.

Alisha watched wistfully as Charles and Black Wolf mingled and conversed with everyone.

Jack was about to escort Alisha into the parlor when he caught a glimpse of Todd Miller coming in their direction.

Joining them, Todd carried on a polite conversation, but Jack soon sensed that he wanted to be alone with Alisha, so he excused himself, and taking David with him, went into the parlor.

Todd hadn't seen Alisha since her return, and now that they were alone, an awkward silence fell between them. Miller was uneasy, for he was sure that Alisha was upset with him for not coming out to the ranch and paying his respects. Jack's feeling that Todd wished to talk alone with Alisha had been correct. He didn't know if she had heard about his engagement, and because he had once proposed to her, he felt that he owed her an explanation.

"Alisha," he began hesitantly. "Did Miss Ingalls tell you about my plans to marry?"

A few days ago, Loretta had remembered to tell Alisha about Todd and Brenda.

"Yes, I know all about it." She smiled sincerely. "I wish you happiness."

Alisha's beauty hit Todd profoundly. Although he thought his fiancée pretty, in his opinion she wasn't nearly as beautiful as Alisha. His deep sigh was one of resignation coupled with disappointment. If only things had been different, then he'd be marrying Alisha instead of Brenda. Since coming into contact with Black Wolf, Todd felt that Alisha might still be pure, for even though the man was a half-breed, he was apparently well-mannered. Most likely his treatment of Alisha had been that of a gentleman. If Todd hadn't found Brenda's wealth a temptation he couldn't resist, he would've considered resuming his courtship of Alisha. However, money had his first loyalty.

"Have you sold your ranch yet?" Alisha asked.

"No, but Charles told me that he wants to talk to me about it. I'm hoping he intends to offer me a good price."

Alisha was a little surprised. "I wonder why Charles would want to own your ranch. His spread is so large that he certainly doesn't need more land."

Todd shrugged. "I don't know." Changing the subject, he inquired, "May I get you a drink? A glass of sherry, perhaps?"

"Yes, thank you," she answered warmly.

Her smile enhanced her beauty, and unable to resist her loveliness, Todd drew her gingerly into his arms. "Alisha," he murmured huskily. "May I kiss you?"

439

Reading rebuff in her eyes, he added unhesitantly, "Consider it a 'goodbye' kiss, for soon I'll be gone and we may never see each other again."

She wasn't especially eager to agree to a kiss, but not wanting to hurt his feelings, she complied. She lifted her face to his and offered him her lips.

Meanwhile, inside the parlor, Black Wolf happened to glance in their direction, and the unexpected sight of Miller kissing Alisha hit him potently. For a moment his blue eyes flashed with resentment, but he quickly took control of his anger and regained his composure. If Alisha wanted Todd Miller, then she could damned well have him!

Jack, standing close by, had also seen the couple's embrace, and stepping to Black Wolf, he uttered hastily, "Don't misinterpret that kiss. Todd Miller is engaged to a lady who lives in Texas."

Black Wolf was baffled. "But I thought he and Alisha were engaged."

"No. Although Todd once proposed to Alisha, she didn't commit herself."

Black Wolf wondered why Alisha had lied about being engaged to Todd and wanted to question Jack further, but before he could, one of Jack's friends beckoned him and he walked away.

His expression ice-cold, Black Wolf returned his gaze to Alisha. Although she was no longer kissing Todd, the pair were holding hands and talking easily to each other. As he continued to scrutinize them, Black Wolf decided that he hadn't misread their kiss. Alisha was using her feminine wiles to recapture Miller, and he was sure she'd have no problem winning back the man's affections.

Wrapping her shawl around her, Alisha stepped out

440

onto the front porch. Going to the intricately carved railing, she stood beside it and gazed into the surrounding darkness. Her thoughts wandered to dinner. The food had been delicious, and the meal had met with everyone's approval. Loretta, with Mary's assistance, had done an excellent job.

Although dinner had been very savory, actually Alisha had eaten very little. Black Wolf had been seated at her side, and his proximity coupled with his cold reserve had robbed her of her appetite. Considering how close they had once been, it seemed ironic that they could now be as impersonal as casual friends. Alisha frowned irritably, for she knew her aloofness was a pretense. She adored Black Wolf; he was the center of her heart and soul. Also, she was beginning to suspect that she might be pregnant. The last few mornings she had been plagued with nausea, and her time of the month was now weeks overdue. What would she do if she were pregnant? Could she go to Black Wolf and plead with him to marry her? Her pride balked at the idea, but her baby was more important than her pride. If she should be with child, then a marriage between herself and Black Wolf was the only solution. They must both protect the child they had conceived.

Alisha, buried in her troubled thoughts, didn't hear the front door open, nor was she aware of the man walking up quietly behind her. She was totally unaware of his presence until he whispered her name.

Startled, she whirled about and was unnerved to find herself facing Black Wolf.

"I saw you come out here," he explained.

"Why did you follow me?" she asked, praying he was about to proclaim his love, take her into his arms, and ask her to be his wife.

"Spotted Fawn wanted me to ask you if it would be

441

all right if she were to come here and visit you occasionally. She's the only woman living at the Longhorn and is lonesome for female companionship."

"Of course I don't mind. I'd love to see her," Alisha answered calmly, concealing her inner disappointment. He wasn't going to profess his love, and if she continued to hope that he would, then she'd wait in vain. He wasn't in love with her and never would be. So why couldn't she accept it and stop wishing for something that would never come about?

As Alisha was absorbed in her own unhappy musings, Black Wolf's thoughts paralleled hers; he believed that he'd never win her love. He supposed if he weren't half Sioux, she might have fallen in love with him. Remembering her conversation with David, the words "humiliating" and "degrading" swept into his thoughts. The remembrance aroused his anger.

Cold rage gleamed in his eyes, and seeing this, Alisha asked uneasily, "What are you thinking about?"

"Nothing I'd care to repeat," he grumbled. He had no intentions of letting her know that he'd overheard what she thought about being married to a half-breed.

She was perturbed. Why must he always refuse to confide in her? Raising her chin in a defiant gesture, she said coolly, "I really don't care what you're thinking about. Your thoughts are of no interest to me."

He believed her. "I've been aware of your disinterest for some time."

"Oh?" she queried. "Well, that goes both ways. You certainly couldn't care less about me. The Longhorn is only an hour's ride from the Bar-S, but you haven't bothered to come see me. If it weren't for this dinner party, you probably would've stayed away indefinitely."

"That's true," he agreed without emotion. He

wondered what kind of game she was playing. Did she wish to resume her courtship with Miller, and in the meantime carry on an affair with him? Did she plan to have Miller for a husband, and himself for a lover?

"So you don't deny that this dinner party is the only reason why you're here?" she demanded, her harsh tone masking her unhappiness.

"What other reason would I have?" he shot back testily. "I thought I already made it clear that there's nothing left between us."

"Nothing left?" she spat. "Don't flatter yourself! There was never anything between us! Our paths just happened to cross and for a time we were forced to share our lives. We were together out of necessity and for no others reason!"

Holding tenaciously to her self-respect, Alisha brushed past him and walked proudly into the house.

Mary Cummings and Alisha helped Loretta clean up after all the guests had departed. Then, as the other two women retired, Loretta went in search of Jack. Certain he was in his study, she knocked lightly on the closed door.

"Come in," he called.

Entering, she closed the door behind her and walked slowly to his desk. Jack was seated, but at her arrival her had gotten to his feet.

"Please sit back down," she said warmly.

"Only if you'll join me," he replied, gesturing to the chair in front of his desk.

Complying, she remarked, "I think the dinner went very well, don't you?"

"Yes, I do," he concurred. "You did an excellent job."

"I had a lot of help from Mary and Alisha," she

reminded him. She paused, then proceeded, "Jack, Todd Miller spoke to me before he left, and he said that Mr. Lansing offered to buy his ranch. Did you know that he was planning to do so?"

Jack was surprised. "No, I didn't. Why in the world would Charles want to own two spreads?"

"I have no idea," she replied. Standing, she went on, "I thought you might find the news interesting. Now, if you'll excuse me, I think I'll go to my room."

He also rose, and moving around the massive desk, went to her side. Appreciatively, his eyes took in her lovely appearance. She was strikingly attractive in her white satin evening gown, which was trimmed with groseille velvet and black lace.

Her beauty soon had him spellbound, and although his better judgment warned him to beware, he nonetheless drew her against him. His lips came down upon hers, and responding, she slipped her arms about his neck.

His desire burning, he held her close as he whispered in her ear, "Loretta, may I make love to you?"

She longed to cry "Yes." Joel had awakened her needs, and since he had left her, there had been no one to appease her passion.

When he didn't receive an immediate answer, Jack released her, saying contritely, "Forgive me. I don't know what got into me. I shouldn't have made such a suggestion to a lady like yourself."

"No!" she blurted without forethought. "I'm not the innocent lady that you think I am! If I were to make love to you, you wouldn't be the first!"

"Joel?" he questioned.

"Yes," she admitted, near tears.

Jack thought no less of her. Her eyes were downcast, and placing his hand beneath her chin, he tilted her face up to his. "I hope you aren't feeling ashamed. You loved Joel."

"I still love him," she stated strongly. She stepped back from his touch. Looking at him directly, she continued, "However, I cannot deny that I'm very attracted to you, nor will I deny that I want you. When I'm in your arms and you're kissing me, my response is not only real but overwhelming." Continuing her honesty, she admitted to Jack, as well as to herself, "In fact, you arouse my passion more than Joel did. I don't understand why. It's not as though I'm in love with you, although I do like you very much."

Jack grinned easily. "How can you be so sure that you're not in love with me?"

"Because I'm in love with Joel," she replied simply.

Preferring not to bed a woman who was in love with another man, Jack replied evenly, "Loretta, my suggestion to make love was a mistake. I withdraw it and ask your forgiveness. Now, I think it might be best if you go to your room and we let this matter rest."

She accepted his brusque dismissal with an outward indifference. Bidding him a pleasant good night, she held her chin high and left the study. As she closed the door behind her, she gave in to her true feelings and allowed her tears to flow. She had acted like a hussy, and Jack Stevens had very gallantly put her in her place. How could she have been so forward as to tell him that he aroused her passion? She had never before behaved so brazenly, not even with Joel!

Loretta's shame hit her with a force, causing her to sob convulsively before she fled from the door and toward the stairs.

Her deep sobs had sounded inside the study. Worried, Jack had hastened to see about her. By the time he had swung the door open, she was gone. For a moment he debated going after her but then decided against it.

To reach his own quarters, Jack had to pass Loretta's bedroom. Hesitantly, he paused at her closed door. He wondered if she was still upset. He blamed himself and wished he had handled the situation more delicately. In spite of his better judgment, he knocked at her door.

It was opened almost at once. "Jack!" Loretta exclaimed softly.

She had undressed and was now wearing a blue nightgown with a matching peignoir. The delicate material was transparent, and her provocative attire revived Jack's passion, whereupon he stepped into the room, shut and locked the door, then brought Loretta into his embrace. Casting aside his reservations, he held her firmly and moaned hoarsely, "You're so beautiful! . . . God, how much I want you!"

She practically melted into his arms, and putting her hand on the back of his neck, urged his lips down to hers. Their mouths blended together, the exchange demanding and fervent.

Lifting her into his strong arms, Jack carried her to the bed. The covers were already drawn back, and he laid her down on the cool sheets. He reached for the lamp on the bedside table and lowered the flame. Then, turning and facing Loretta, he impatiently removed his clothes.

As he disrobed, the lamp's soft glow illuminated his handsome physique. Watching, Loretta's eyes shone with passion as she admired his solid, muscular build.

Now completely unclothed, he lay at her side and drew her into his arms. She trembled as she felt his hand move under her gown, following an upward path to fondle her breasts.

Leaning over her, he lowered his mouth to hers, his lingering kiss making her head swim with longing.

It had been a long time since Jack had been intimate with a woman, and his need was building feverishly. Quickly he helped her lift off her nightwear, flinging the clothes to the carpeted floor. He moved over her, and she opened her legs, for she too was eager to consummate their union.

He entered her with one quick thrust, then as her heat engulfed him, his hips began to move circularly. A thrilling sensation filled her senses, and she purred ecstatically, "Oh Jack! . . . You feel so wonderful!"

Bolstered by her encouragement, he thrust into her uncontrollably, sending stimulating chills through Loretta's entire being. Grabbing her legs and placing them around his waist, he lunged forward and achieved even deeper penetration. Crying out with ecstasy, she clung tenaciously as her hips converged time and time again with his.

Their fulfillment merged, and clutching her slim hips, Jack pulled her thighs to his as he sought total release. Loretta gasped aloud as she too found wonderful completion.

Drained, Jack withdrew and dropped exhaustingly to lie at her side. When his breathing slowed to normal, he groaned huskily, "Loretta Ingalls, you're a wonderful lady."

Smiling, she snuggled close. "Jack Stevens, you're 'kinda' wonderful yourself."

He chuckled good-naturedly. "I'm not as spry as I used to be. In my younger days, I could've lasted longer."

Rising up on her elbow, she gazed down at him with a teasing twinkle in her eyes. "How are you the second time around?" she asked saucily.

"I always get better as I go along," he assured her, grinning wryly.

She giggled. "I hope you intend to back up your words."

"Just let me rest a minute, little darlin', and I'll be right with you."

She placed a sweet, endearing kiss on his lips. "I'm only teasing. You don't have to try again. You were man enough for me the first time."

"What do you mean, try?" he asked gruffly, but without a trace of anger. "There's no try to it. Just wait and see; I'm more man than you might be able to handle." He feigned a serious, contemplating expression. "All along I've been worried about you being younger than I am, and now I realize that a younger woman is what I need."

Suddenly, grasping her waist, he lifted her so that she was straddling him. "It'll take a young woman like yourself to keep me satisfied," he grinned complacently.

Loretta was amazed to feel that his manhood was erect and ready for penetration. Smiling a little wickedly, she eased herself down onto his hardness, and as he filled her, she moaned with pleasure.

Again he took her powerfully, completely, and their passionate union sent Loretta soaring blissfully into an erotic paradise.

Later, basking in the afterglow, Loretta was cuddled against him when he surprised her by suggesting, "Loretta, let's get married."

She was hesitant to agree. "But, Jack, you know that I love Joel."

Her declaration hurt him deeply, for it pained him to hear her admit her love for another man. However, he kept his emotions concealed and said evenly, "Carson is permanently gone from your life. In time, you'll get over him. I'm hoping that gradually you'll learn to love me."

She was silent for some time before asking, "Jack, are you in love with me?"

He answered calmly, "Yes, I am. I don't know exactly when it happened. But there's no doubt in my mind that I love you."

"I'll marry you," she decided quietly.

"Do you mind telling me why?" he responded.

"I don't want to spend the rest of my life alone. I long to be a wife and mother. Also, I think we'll have a good marriage. Although I'm not in love with you—not now, anyway—I respect you and I'm very fond of you."

He frowned slightly. "I was hoping you felt more affection for me, but at least you're honest." His expression lightened as he chose to accept things as they were. "But you're right, darlin', we'll have a good marriage. I promise I'll dedicate the rest of my life to making you happy, and maybe someday you'll find yourself in love with me."

Loretta didn't comment, for she believed she'd never love any man but Joel Carson.

Chapter Thirty-Nine

Jack and Loretta were seated at the table when Alisha and Clint came downstairs for breakfast.

Sitting, and helping herself to a cup of coffee, Alisha smiled at her good friend. She noticed that Loretta seemed a little flushed.

Jack waited for Clint to join them before announcing, "Loretta and I have some news to tell you two."

Clint grinned largely, for he was quite sure that his father was about to announce his engagement to Miss Ingalls.

Loretta was seated at Jack's side, and before continuing, he slipped his hand into hers, then glancing from his son to his daughter, he said, "Loretta and I are getting married."

Alisha was as pleased as Clint, and her face aglow, she exclaimed, "Papa, that's wonderful news! I'm so happy for you both."

"Congratulations, Pa," Clint remarked joyfully. turning to Loretta, he said, "Welcome to the family, Miss Ingalls."

"Please call me Loretta," she replied.

"When do you plan to get married?" Alisha asked.

Loretta answered, "We haven't set a date yet."

"Why don't we marry next week?" Jack suggested. She was surprised. "So soon?"

"Why not?" Jack questioned. "Last night you said you wanted to be a wife and mother, so why procrastinate? Next week, I'll make you a wife. Then if I don't soon make you a mother, it won't be from lack of trying."

Seeing Loretta's deep blush, Alisha smiled secretively. Her father was a great teaser and she knew Loretta would have to grow accustomed to his ways. Her tiny smile faded as her thoughts continued to drift. Although she was sincerely happy for Loretta, she also envied her. If only Black Wolf was as anxious to marry her as Jack was to marry Loretta! As a feeling of morning sickness washed over her, Alisha was reminded of her pregnancy. She supposed that very soon now, she and Black Wolf would also be getting married. However, she was certain that the bridegroom would be a reluctant participant.

Loretta's voice intruded on Alisha's thoughts, gaining her full attention.

"Very well, Jack. If you want, we'll be married next week."

He hugged her and kissed her lips soundly. His affectionate embrace in front of his family embarrassed her somewhat. Apparently, her future husband was a very open and demonstrative man.

Following breakfast, Jack and Clint had work to take care of and excused themselves. Remembering to kiss his love, Jack did so without hesitation. Then, before leaving with Clint, he told Loretta that he'd be late returning because he planned to go into town and see Johnny, then pay a visit to Charles.

When the men had gone, Alisha turned to Loretta. "I hope you and Papa will be happy together."

"I'm sure we will. Your father is a wonderful man, and I care very deeply for him."

Alisha watched her speculatively. "You aren't in love with Papa, are you?"

Taken off guard, Loretta stammered, "Why . . . why do you think I don't love him?"

"Carrying deeply for a man is not the same as loving him."

She saw no reason to be dishonest. "You're right, of course, I'm not in love with Jack."

"Is he in love with you?"

"He says he is."

"Papa never says anything that he doesn't mean. Does he know how you truly feel?"

"Yes, he does." Her voice took on a note of pleading. "Alisha, I can't help how I feel. I can't make myself love your father. If I could, then I would. But I'm still in love with Joel."

"Then why are you marrying Papa?"

"Joel is lost to me forever." Tears smarted in her eyes as she continued sincerely, "Alisha, I promise you that I'll be a good wife to Jack. He'll never regret that he married me."

Alisha decided not to pass judgment. "I believe you," she said warmly.

"I'll succeed," Loretta stated. "I'm looking forward to being Jack's wife. I feel more at ease with him than I've ever felt with any man, including Joel. Also, I respond more willingly and fervently to Jack than I did to Joel. I don't understand why; But for some strange reason, your father brings out a playful, spirited part of myself that I never knew existed."

Shrewdly, Alisha implied, "Maybe you're in love with Papa and don't even realize it."

Loretta disagreed. "No, I still love Joel Carson." Sadly, she added, "And I think I always will."

Alisha didn't reply, but the initial happiness she had felt for her father's marriage was now shadowed by some reservations.

Johnny tended bar at the Golden Horseshoe and was working when Jack entered the saloon. It was midday, and the establishment wasn't very crowded. He went up to the empty bar and ordered a beer.

Johnny wasn't surprised to see his father. He'd been expecting a visit from him. He was sure the man was here to plead with him to return home. As far as Johnny was concerned, his father could beg and he'd still not go back to the Bar-S. He was through with ranching, and he was finished with his family!

"How have you been, son?" Jack asked, his concern real.

"Fine," Johnny answered tersely, drawing the beer and placing the mug on the bar.

"Have you considered coming back home?"

"No," he said flatly. "And if you're here to preach to me, then save your breath."

"I had no intentions of asking you to come home. I'm here for an entirely different reason."

Johnny's curiously was aroused. "Oh?" he asked archly.

"Next week I'm getting married, and I'd like for you to attend my wedding."

Young Stevens was shocked. "Who are you marrying?"

"Loretta Ingalls."

Johnny laughed harshly. "You're actually marrying Carson's discarded goods?"

Rage flashed in Jack's eyes. "Johnny, if you insult Loretta again, I'm liable to forget you're my son! I'm warning you, damn it!"

"Don't get riled, Pa," he said quickly. "If you want to marry her, it's all right with me. But I think you're acting like an old fool. The woman has to be at least twenty years younger than you are. She's not in love with you, either. She's still in love with Carson. If you ask me, she's marrying you for your money. Everyone around here is going to draw the same conclusion. She'll make you the laughing stock of the town."

Jack slammed a coin onto the bar. His son had thoroughly disappointed him, and afraid he might say something that he'd later regret, Jack spun about and headed for the swinging doors.

As he watched his father leave, Johnny experienced a moment of contrition and almost called out an apology. But the moment was gone. Besides, he had been right. Jack Stevens was a fool to marry a woman who was not only twenty years his junior, but also in love with another man.

When Charles asked David and Black Wolf to take a ride with him, he didn't tell them their destination, nor did he tell them his reason for wanting their company.

As they rode onto Todd Miller's property, Black Wolf and David grew very curious about Charles' strange behavior. Why was he taking them to Miller's ranch?

As with the Stevens's place, Todd's house sat in a shallow valley, surrounded on all sides by small, rolling hills.

Charles was leading the way, and riding to the top of one of these hills, he reined in. Black Wolf and David drew their horses to a halt beside his, placing Charles in the middle. For a moment, the three riders gazed down upon Todd's place. The one-story ranch house was Spanish style with a front veranda and a red tile roof.

The bunk house sat on the right, and to the left were the stables and tack room. The whitewashed corral and barn were located a short distance behind the house.

"Todd's spread is impressive, don't you agree?" Charles asked, looking at David.

"Yes, sir," the boy answered. He sighed dreamily. "I hope someday I'll have a ranch as nice as this one. Naturally, I'd prefer to own a place as large as yours, but I try to keep my dreams within reason."

Charles chuckled. "Todd's ranch is more than lucrative, and it's one of the best spreads in these parts." He glanced at Black Wolf and then back to David. "Did you two know that Todd is selling it?"

Neither knew, and Charles continued, "I intend to buy it myself."

"Why do you want two spreads?" Black Wolf asked.

"I don't," he replied flatly. He smiled at David. "This ranch will belong to you, boy."

"Wh . . . what!" he exclaimed.

"Of course, it won't legally become yours until you're of age. But I'm going to leave it to you in my will in case I die before you turn twenty-one."

"Mr. Lansing," David began rapidly, "I can't accept such an expensive gift."

"It's not a gift; it's your inheritance. I've grown awfully fond of you, and I feel as though I found two grandsons at Running Horse's village. Someday, Chuck will own the Longhorn, and you'll own this spread."

Black Wolf grimaced. He wished his grandfather wouldn't take for granted that he was going to leave the Sioux and become a rancher.

David was flabbergasted. "Mr. Lansing, I don't know what to say."

"Well you can start by not calling me Mr. Lansing. My name's Charles, and I want you to start using it.

And as far as not knowing what to say, a simple 'thank you' will suffice."

Incredulous, David stammered, "I . . . I thank you, but I just can't believe all this."

Charles laughed heartily. "Believe it, son! Look around in all directions, for someday this land will be yours, and it stretches farther than the eye can see."

Doing as Charles requested, David tried to imagine the ranch as his own, but the shock had rendered him numb, and at the moment he was beyond coherent thought.

Black Wolf was impressed by his grandfather's generosity. The longer he was around the man, the more he grew to respect and love him. "Charles," he began sincerely, "I appreciate what you're doing for David. There are no words to express how I feel."

Charles looked at his grandson. Dressed in western clothes, and with his hair cut, his resemblance to the Lansings was more pronounced. Love for Abigal's son cut deeply into his heart.

Black Wolf proceeded carefully, "I wish you wouldn't just assume that I plan to remain at the Longhorn."

"I prefer to think optimistically and will continue to do so until you prove me wrong." Quickly, he returned his attention to David. "I hope to hire Miller's foreman so he can keep the ranch operating until it's time for you to take over."

"Won't controlling two spreads be too much work for you?" David asked, concerned for Charles's health.

"It won't mean extra work for me, because I plan for you and Chuck to keep this ranch prosperous. In my younger days I could've managed, but my age is slowing me down. However, you and Chuck are able-bodied men, and there's no reason why you two can't handle everything. I know you won't let me down. I'll

456

have a lot of money invested in this spread, and if I have to suffer a loss, it'll leave me financially drained. But I've got faith in you both, and I know you won't disappoint me."

Although Black Wolf knew Charles' affection for David was sincere, he suddenly realized the man could be quite devious. Apparently, his grandfather was not above using any available means to hold onto his grandson. Accepting his grandfather's ploy in good humor, a shadow of a smile teased Black Wolf's lips.

Deciding to head back home, Charles turned his horse around and took off in a gallop.

Black Wolf started to follow but was detained by David. "You know your grandfather has an ulterior motive for buying me this ranch, don't you?"

Black Wolf chuckled. "He's as sly as a fox."

"Are you mad at him?"

"Of course not. I admire him, and he makes me proud to be a Lansing."

"He's going to try to manipulate you into staying."

"I can't hold that against him. If it was the other way around, I'd probably do the same thing."

They spurred their horses into a loping trot. "I hope your grandfather gets his way," David remarked. "I don't want you to leave. I hope you stay here and marry Alisha."

"Regardless of Charles's schemes, in the spring I plan to return to my father's village."

"What about Alisha?"

"It's over between us," Black Wolf answered firmly, and before David could continue, he slapped the reins against his stallion and rode off to Charles.

As Charles poured glasses of brandy for Jack and himself, he told his good friend about his plans for

Miller's ranch. The men were closeted inside Charles' study, and as Lansing brought him his drink, Jack remarked, "I imagine David was pleased."

Jack took a seat in front of the desk, and going to his own leather chair, Charles eased into it. His rheumatism was bothering him, and a look of pain crossed his face.

Seeing his discomfort, Jack asked, "Does Chuck know about your rheumatism?"

"No . . . I don't want to worry him."

"You should tell him so he'll see to it that you start taking care of yourself."

"I'm capable of taking care of myself without anyone's help," he replied, then quickly changed the subject. "How are things at the Bar-S?"

Jack smiled expansively. "A change is about to take place at the Bar-S."

When Jask said no more, Charles prodded impatiently, "Well, go on. What's this change?"

"Loretta Ingalls and I are getting married next week."

Lansing was amazed. "No kidding?"

"I've never been more serious."

"Congratulations, Jack! I'm real happy for you." Jokingly, he taunted, "You think you're man enough to keep that young gal satisfied?" His friend's face became deeply worried, and Charles added quickly, "Hell, Jack, don't look so upset. I was only joshing."

"I know, but you unintentionally hit a sore spot. The difference in our ages has me worried. With Loretta I merely joke about it, but someday it might become a serious problem."

"Nonsense!" Charles declared. "You're still a robust, virile man and will remain so for a long time. You might think forty-nine is over the hill, but when you're my age, you'll know just how young it really is. Hell, you're in your prime. Relax and take full advantage of it."

"Not everybody's feelings are going to coincide with yours."

"For instance?"

"Johnny, for one," he answered glumly. "He thinks I'm acting like an old fool and even went so far as to accuse Loretta of marrying me for my money."

"Since when did Johnny ever say anything that merited listening to? I realize he's your son and that you love him, but he isn't worth a grain of salt. We all have our crosses to bear, and he's yours."

"This time, what he said had a ring of truth to it. I don't mean about Loretta wanting my money—I'm referring to our age difference. People will talk, and most of them will probably think I'm acting like an old fool."

"Do you love her?" Charles asked.

"Yes, I love her very much."

"Then to hell with what people say! Besides, people won't talk as much as Johnny has led you to believe. When a man's young and promiscuous, then people talk about him; but when he's forty-nine and promiscuous, he's admired!"

Jack laughed. "Charles, why do I get the feeling that you aren't taking my dilemma seriously?"

"You're about to marry a beautiful, classy young lady, and you call it a dilemma! I wish I had your dilemma. I'd take it to bed with me and keep it there until I was exhausted."

"My friend, you have most assuredly lifted my spirits. I should've come here and talked to you before visiting Johnny. And I'm going to take your advice and quit borrowing troubles."

Watching him speculatively, Charles surmised, "There's more to it than Loretta's age, isn't there?"

"Yes," he admitted. "She's still in love with Joel Carson."

"Now that does pose a serious problem. You'd better find a way to get him out of her mind, or else every time you make love to your wife, there's going to be three people in your bed."

"That's another part of my dilemma. Last night, Loretta and I made love, and I could swear that Carson was nowhere in her thoughts until it was over. If she truly loved the man, don't you think she would have thought about him while making love to me?"

"You'd think so," Charles agreed. "If I was a betting man, which I have been on occasion, I'd be willing to wager that she's no longer in love with Carson, but is in love with you."

Jack smiled, for Charles had voiced his own suspicions. "I'm beginning to suspect the same thing. The question is, how do I convince Loretta?"

Loretta was dusting the furniture in the parlor when she heard someone knocking at the front door. Putting down the feather-duster, she smoothed the folds of her gingham gown, then hurried to see who was calling.

She opened the door unhesitantly, smiling to welcome the visitor; however, the person confronting her caused the smile to disappear as her face paled with shock. Raspingly, she choked out, "Joel!"

Moving swiftly, he drew her into his arms, hugging her tightly. "Loretta," Joel murmured. "I've missed you."

She leaned into his embrace, relishing his closeness. She felt as though she were living a miracle! Joel was back in her life! It was almost more than she could grasp! However, as the reality began to sink in, she squirmed out of his embrace. Gazing into his hazel eyes

460

with disbelief, she stammered breathlessly, "Where . . . where is your wife?"

"Bonnie Sue is dead," he whispered. "She died of pneumonia. She wasn't strong enough to survive such a serious illness."

"She's dead?" Loretta cried softly, feeling as though she were living some kind of unbelievable dream.

"Let's not discuss Bonnie Sue, at least not now."

Her eyes took him in. Although he was wearing a heavy jacket, she could tell that he had lost weight, and his face was somewhat haggard; but in spite of these flaws, he was still exceptionally handsome.

Warily, she questioned with bated breath, "Joel, why did you come back?"

"I came back for you," he replied.

Chapter Forty

Black Wolf and David had ridden into Backwater to buy some supplies for the Longhorn. Before returning home, Black Wolf decided to stop in at the Golden Horseshoe.

The saloon was fairly crowded, and several men were standing at the bar. Quite a few of these customers had met Black Wolf and David, and they acknowledged the pair as they made room for them at the bar.

Black Wolf wasn't aware that Johnny was now working at the Golden Horseshoe, and as he caught sight of young Stevens, his eyes narrowed angrily.

Black Wolf was dressed as a rancher, and it took a moment for Johnny to realize who he was. Then, as recognition registered, a look of pure loathing crossed his face.

Staring coldly into Black Wolf's unwavering gaze, Johnny remarked loudly, "We don't serve Indians in here!" He glanced fleetingly at his customers, expecting them to back him up. When it became apparent that they weren't about to do so, Johnny looked back at Black Wolf. "I said we don't serve Indians! Now, get the hell out of here before I throw you out!"

Black Wolf smirked and was about to reply when

suddenly the proprietor's voice bellowed, "Stevens, you'll serve Mr. Lansing or lose your job!" The owner had been in his office, and as he had stepped out of the room, he'd overheard his employee's malicious remarks.

"But he's a damned Sioux buck!" Johnny uttered, his tone whining.

"He's Charles Lansing's grandson and he's welcome in this establishment," the proprietor said emphatically. Walking to Black Wolf, the man continued, "Mr. Lansing, please accept my apology for this unfortunate incident." The man had attended Jack's dinner party and had been greatly impressed with Black Wolf. He had managed to talk with Black Wolf during the evening and had enjoyed their discussions, and he hoped he'd decide to stay permanently at the Longhorn. In his opinion, Backwater needed good citizens like Chuck Lansing.

Sulking, Johnny mumbled, "Well, I'm not serving no dirty redskin!" Quickly, his gaze flitted over the customers. "Don't you all feel the same way I do? Surely you don't want to drink in the same room with a damned Indian!"

The patrons offered no encouragement, for the ones who had met Black Wolf liked and respected him, and the ones who weren't acquainted with him had heard enough good things about Lansing's grandson to accept him in their town as well as in their saloon.

Receiving no support, Johnny jerked off his bar apron and slung it to the floor. "You're all a bunch of Indian-lovers!" he raved. Stalking out from behind the bar, he glared at his boss and yelled furiously, "You don't have to fire me. I quit!"

Meanwhile, Black Wolf was itching to get his hands on the angry young man, but respect for Johnny's family held him back. Also, he was a lot larger than

463

Johnny and knew if he were to get into a fight with him, the match would be one-sided.

However, Johnny made a crucial mistake and stopped in front of Black Wolf, threatening, "You stay away from my sister! If I so much as catch you looking at her, I'm gonna turn you into buzzard bait!"

"Why, you stupid little idiot," Black Wolf replied, his tone more surprised than angry. He was finding it hard to believe that Johnny actually had the gall to confront a man twice his size.

Johnny's holstered pistol was strapped around his waist, and moving swiftly he drew the weapon.

Black Wolf let him draw the gun before spinning out with incredible speed and kicking the pistol out of his hand. As the gun landed on the floor, Black Wolf grabbed Johnny by the shirt and jerked him forward. "I should break your scrawny little neck!" he raged. He had to call upon all his will power to keep himself from choking Johnny. The man's scheme to have Spotted Fawn murdered still infuriated him. He released his opponent cautiously, then nodded to David. "Let's go," he mumbled tersely.

Black Wolf turned his back on Johnny and took a step toward the doors. His whole being trembled with the need to whirl about and send his fist smashing against Johnny's face. But his conscience nagged at him, telling him young Stevens wasn't worth it. Suddenly, though, an image of Spotted Fawn flashed in front of him, and his conscience no longer had control. Turning on his heel, Black Wolf said with a cold calmness that belied his intentions, "To hell with it!"

The attacker moved so unbelievably fast that Johnny had no chance to avoid the blow. Black Wolf's large fist landed viciously across Johnny's chin, sending him sprawling backwards before he fell awkwardly to the floor.

Leering down at him, Black Wolf spoke his rage quietly. "Stay away from me, or so help me God, the next time I might kill you!"

Without further words, he went to the swinging doors, pushed them aside, and darted outside. David was close on his heels.

Loretta had taken Joel into Jack's study, and as she poured him a glass of brandy, she said uneasily, "Things aren't the same as they were when you left."

"What do you mean?" he asked.

She handed him the drink. "When you and Bonnie Sue were reunited, I believed you were lost to me forever. So I put you behind me and went on with my life."

When she hesitated, he said anxiously, "What exactly are you trying to tell me?"

Taking a deep breath, she replied, "Jack and I are engaged. We're to be married next week."

Joel was astounded. "You and Jack!" he exclaimed.

His attitude provoked her. "Did you think no other man would want me?"

"Of course not," he answered at once. "I just find it hard to believe that you got over me so easily. I've only been gone for a few weeks, and you've already fallen in love with another man." He took a liberal swallow of brandy.

"I didn't say that I was in love with Jack," she specified. "I said that we're engaged."

"Then you don't love him?" he queried, his face alight with hope.

"No . . . no, I don't," she stammered, wondering why she was finding it difficult to deny her love for Jack. She wasn't in love with her fiancé, so why did she feel as though she were being dishonest with Joel? It was a perplexing question and one to which she had no answer.

Stepping to Jack's desk, Joel put down his glass, returned to Loretta, and gathered her into his arms. "My darling," he said pressingly, "break your engagement, then come with me to St. Louis."

She snuggled against him. "Why St. Louis? I thought you wanted to go to San Francisco."

"I changed my mind," he uttered quickly. "I was going there to work for Bonnie Sue's uncle, and . . . and now I think it'd be best if I don't come into contact with anyone in her family." He raced on nervously. "I mean, how can I completely forget her if I'm surrounded by her kin?"

Releasing Loretta, he began to pace back and forth. There was a look of panic on his face, and he seemed like a man possessed. "I don't want anything to do with San Francisco. . . . I want to start over again, and this time I plan to give all my love to you. Bonnie Sue is dead and . . . and I can accept that she's gone."

Loretta moved to Joel, placed a hand on his arm, and deterred his restless pacing. She was worried, for she had never before heard him ramble on in this peculiar way. "Are you all right?" she asked. She noticed that tiny beads of perspiration dotted his brow.

He coughed dry, wiped his wet forehead, then stammered shakily, "Yes . . . yes, I'm fine." He clutched her shoulders, and his fingers kneaded into her flesh. "I'm just anxious to get away from Backwater. I'd never have returned if not for you. Sweetheart, tell me you'll end your engagement and come with me to St. Louis. . . . I need you!"

She gazed deeply into his eyes and felt as though she were looking at a stranger. Instinctively, she started to pull away, but he suddenly had her clasped against him. He groaned huskily before his lips came down on hers, his kiss demanding as well as desperate.

Surrendering, Loretta leaned willingly into his embrace as she wrapped her arms around his neck. She waited anxiously for his kiss to ignite her passion and was confused when it failed to do so. She loved Joel; she always loved him! Why was his kiss leaving her cold?

Relinquishing her, he murmured feverishly, "Loretta, I have a room at the hotel. Will you pack your clothes and come with me? We'll stay at the hotel tonight, then leave tomorrow for St. Louis."

"I can't leave here without talking to Jack," she replied firmly. "I owe him an explanation."

He nodded. "Yes, of course you do." He was about to say more when the study door opened. Turning, the pair saw Jack entering the room.

Pausing, Jack exclaimed, "Joel!" His gaze swept the study. "Where's Bonnie Sue?"

"My wife is dead," Joel replied softly. "She died of pneumonia."

Jack groaned. "God, I'm sorry to hear that! When did she die?"

"Last week," Joel murmured. Stepping away from Loretta, he approached the other man. "I plan to move permanently to St. Louis."

"Then why did you come back here?" Jack asked, although he was sure he already knew the reason.

Taking a stance close to Stevens and looking him straight in the eyes, Joel replied, "I came back for Loretta."

Brushing past him, Jack went to his desk and poured himself a glass of brandy. "Bonnie Sue has only been dead a week and you're already trying to reclaim Loretta. You certainly didn't mourn very long for your wife!" With drink in hand, he whirled about and faced his rival. "Bonnie Sue deserved better!"

"I once spent months grieving for Bonnie Sue, and I saw no reason to do so a second time."

Jack arched an eyebrow. "Apparently, you can turn your feelings off and on whenever and however you please."

Carson's eyes bulged wildly. "If you're implying that I didn't love my wife, then you don't know what in hell you're talking about! . . . I loved her! . . . Do you hear me? . . . I loved her!" Perspiration continued to bead up on his brow as he once again took on the resemblance of a man possessed.

Jack didn't respond to Joel's outburst. Instead, he turned to Loretta. "Are you leaving with him?"

She couldn't look him in the eye, and lowering her gaze, she mumbled almost inaudibly, "Yes, I am. You know I've always loved Joel."

Jack's temper erupted. "Then you two can damned well have each other!" His obvious anger caused Loretta to raise her eyes. She hadn't expected him to be angry; disappointed perhaps, but certainly not riled.

He read her thoughts. "Did you think I was always mild-mannered, that I don't have the same feelings as other men?" His expression was almost predatory as he went to her and grasped her arms. "Loretta, if you leave with Carson, you'll be making the biggest mistake of your life! You don't love him, nor does he love you!" Forgetting himself he shook her roughly. "Don't you realize that I'm the man you love?" He wished he could shake the truth into her.

Forcefully, she freed herself from his violent grip.

Finding no love in the eyes that looked guiltily into his, Jack relented. "Go on, Loretta!" he thundered. "Leave with Joel!" He had seen the parked buckboard in front of the house and knew Carson had come prepared to take Loretta back with him. "I'll have

Mary pack your things and see that they're brought into town."

Joel held out his hand to her. "Come on, darling," he coaxed.

Hesitantly, she went to Joel, took his hand and left.

Moments later, as Loretta rode away from the Bar-S, she wondered why her heart was aching. She was once again with Joel! She should be ecstatic, but for some inexplicable reason, she was terribly depressed.

Riding up to the Lansing ranch, Alisha came close to turning her horse about and fleeing back to the Bar-S. She had decided to make this unexpected call on the spur of the moment and was now having second thoughts.

Alisha now knew she was pregnant and had come to the conclusion that she must confide in Black Wolf. He was the child's father and had a right to know of her condition.

Deciding to follow through with her plans, she dismounted slowly, swung the reins over the hitching rail, then walked to the front door and knocked.

It was opened by Spotted Fawn. Happy to see her friend, she exclaimed, "Alisha! Please come in."

Doing so, Alisha asked Spotted Fawn how she was feeling, then stood in the foyer for a few minutes and carried on a polite conversation. However, the reason behind her visit became pressing and she asked, "Is Black Wolf home?"

"Yes, he's in the study," Spotted Fawn answered.

"Is he alone?"

She said that he was.

Alisha removed her jacket and wide-brimmed hat and handed them to Spotted Fawn. "May I talk to him?"

"Yes, of course," she answered, taking Alisha's things and hanging the articles on the coat rack.

Spotted Fawn started to show her the way, but Alisha said hastily, "Never mind; I know where it is."

Alisha's heart beat nervously as she walked down the hall to the study. Finding the door closed, she rapped softly.

"Come in," Black Wolf called.

Taking a deep breath, she went into the study, where she found Black Wolf seated at his grandfather's desk. When she entered, he got quickly to his feet.

Alisha was dressed in riding garb, and her tan suede trousers clung temptingly to her slim hips. The top two buttons on her long-sleeved shirt were unbuttoned, exposing the slight swell of her soft breasts. In one sweeping gaze, Black Wolf's piercing regard devoured her provocative beauty.

Leaving the door ajar, Alisha moved farther inside the room and paused in front of the desk.

Alisha's unexpected visit had rendered Black Wolf speechless. He was not only astounded, but also very curious as to why she was here. Then, suddenly believing he knew the reason, he said somewhat gruffly, "I know why you're here, and I don't intend to discuss the matter with you." He was sure she was about to berate him for hitting Johnny. Obviously, young Stevens had run home to his family and told them everything, and now Alisha had come here to fight her brother's battle.

Finding him arrogant, she spat resentfully, "You're impossible!" Alisha knew nothing about Black Wolf's and Johnny's disagreement and had no idea what he was talking about.

Still referring to his and Johnny's physical altercation, Black Wolf grumbled, "Some things in life are unavoidable, and this happens to be one of them.

Although I admit that I'm partially to blame, I don't intend to take responsibility for it and do the honorable thing."

Black Wolf had been talking about a gentleman's apology; but Alisha erroneously believed that he somehow had guessed that she was pregnant and had no intentions of honorably proposing marriage. Her anger began to simmer hotly. "You beast! . . . You vile, detestable, black-hearted devil!" Her wrath now burning out of control, she spouted furiously, "I hope you go back to your father's village and stay there forever! I never want to see you again! I hate you! And when our child gets old enough to ask about his father, I'm going to tell him that you're dead!"

She swirled about and was heading for the door when Black Wolf caught her. Grabbing her arm, he turned her to where she was facing him.

"What did you mean by 'our child'?" he demanded.

"I meant exactly what I said!" Roughly, she pulled away from his firm hold. Letting her temper run amuck, she rambled, "I never dreamed that you wouldn't offer to take responsibility for your child! Whether you love me or not, I believed you would care about our baby!"

Learning she was with child took him off guard for a moment. Then, realizing she thought he'd been referring to her pregnancy instead of his fight with Johnny, Black Wolf came close to drawing her into his arms and explaining the mix-up. But the words "humiliating" and "degrading" came back once again to torture his mind. The memory still had the power to hurt deeply, causing him to lash out harshly, "Do you find being pregnant and unwed more humiliating and degrading than marriage to a half-breed? Did you decide that marrying me is the lesser of the two evils and your only alternative?" His violent anger distorted

471

his handsome face. "Have you now reconsidered and decided that marriage to me is no longer beneath your dignity?"

Alisha was so upset that his innuendos didn't even register. Retaliating, she retorted icily, "I'd find marriage to you hell on earth!"

Leaving, she swung back the partially open door and hastened into the hall, where she collided with David, who was about to enter the study. The collision knocked her off balance, but righting herself, she pushed the boy aside and went on her way.

David started to call out to her, but changed his mind and stepped into the study. Glaring at Black Wolf, he said heatedly, "As I was coming down the hall, I overheard what you said to Alisha. How could you have been so cruel?"

"You, more than anyone else, should understand my anger! However, before you start picking at my conscience, let me make it quite clear that I'll do the honorable thing and marry Alisha. Regardless of how I feel, or how Alisha feels, the child comes first."

David smiled without warmth. "I'm glad to hear that you're so noble. Now, why don't you explain why I, above anyone else, should understand your anger."

"Early on the day that Alisha and her family left the village, you took a walk with her. You remember, don't you?"

"Of course I do."

"I was close by and overheard your conversation, or at least part of it. You asked her why she'd refuse to marry me, and she told you that she'd find it too humiliating and degrading. Can you imagine how that made me feel?"

"Yes, I can," David replied. "But, Black Wolf, you misunderstood. I had asked her if she'd marry you, and she had told me that if you proposed because you loved

472

her, she'd marry you in a minute. But if you proposed because you felt obligated, or if her father had pressured you into doing so, then she'd flatly refuse. I wanted to know why. She said that she'd find a forced marriage too humiliating and degrading."

He hesitated, watching Black Wolf closely. The man was hanging on to his every word. "We started back toward the village," David continued, "and I told her that you wouldn't marry her if you didn't love her. She agreed, then swore to me that if you truly loved her, she'd follow you to the ends of the Earth just to be at your side."

Black Wolf expelled a heavy sigh. "My God!" he groaned. "How could I have been so wrong about her?"

"You had Alisha pegged from the day you met her. You're so against marrying a white woman that Alisha never stood a chance. And I think somehow you wanted her to spurn you so that you wouldn't feel forced to make a choice between your people and hers. But, you know, Alisha doesn't expect you to make that choice, for she's more than willing to marry you and live with the Sioux. She only wants to share her life with you, and she doesn't care where you both live so long as you're together."

David eyed the man shrewdly. "Black Wolf, you can no longer run away from your feelings for Alisha to avoid making that final and inevitable choice between your father's people and your mother's." He waited a moment, then asked anxiously, "Which choice will you make?"

Black Wolf didn't answer David's question. Instead, he hurried toward the door, calling over his shoulder, "I'm going after Alisha."

Chapter Forty-One

Dusk was approaching as Alisha rode away from the Lansing ranch and onto open grazing land. The radiant sun sent brilliant red streaks blazing across the horizon. Although the sunset was stunning, it completely escaped Alisha's notice. Her thoughts were too filled with Black Wolf and her unborn child.

Keeping her mount at a steady, easy gallop, Alisha gave the gelding free rein, for he was a Bar-S horse and knew his way home.

Her tears smarted, but she was determined not to cry and forcefully held them back. Black Wolf wasn't worth crying over! He was a cold, unfeeling monster, and she hoped she'd never see him again as long as she lived!

She turned her thoughts to her baby. She must find a way to protect her child. She was pregnant out of wedlock, and if she stayed here to have her baby, he would be branded a bastard. Society could be very cruel to children born under these circumstances, and Alisha was determined to save her child from such a harsh fate. She would ask her father for money, move east, pass herself off as a widow, and then after her baby was born, she'd find a way to support herself and

474

the child. She didn't try to delude herself; she knew the future would be difficult and filled with hardships, but she was willing to make any sacrifice to protect her baby.

She placed a hand on her abdomen and talked to her unborn child. "Unlike your father, I love you and I'll take care of you. I promise you faithfully that you'll always have your mother's devotion."

Suddenly, detecting sounds of advancing hoofbeats, Alisha glanced over her shoulder and was horrified to see that Black Wolf was in pursuit. Why was he following? As far as she was concerned, they had nothing left to discuss. He had said it all when he'd refused to share responsibility for their child. She might be able to accept his cold feelings for herself, but when he had forsaken their child, he had taught her how to despise him. She would hate him until the day she died!

As he drew closer, she pulled up her horse and slipped her rifle from its leather scabbard. She quickly cocked the weapon, and when he reined in beside her, she had the gun aimed at him.

Her eyes stared coldly into his. "Stay away from me or I'll blow you to Hades!"

"There's no reason to resort to violence," he replied easily.

"I'll gladly resort to murder, if that's what it'll take to keep you out of my life!"

"You don't mean that." Stealthily, he watched the rifle aimed straight at his heart.

"Yes, I do mean it!" she raged. "I hate you!"

Taking her unaware, and lurching with lightning speed, he grasped the rifle and jerked it out of her hands. Resting the gun across the front of his saddle, he said calmly, "I can talk better when I don't have a loaded rifle pointed at me."

"I don't want to talk to you!" she spat, furious with herself for letting him steal the rifle with such ease.

Moving swiftly, he reached over and grabbed her bridle reins. "There's a tack shed not far from here; we'll go there to talk."

"You bull-headed, no good, sorry excuse for a man!" she shouted. "Didn't you hear what I said? I don't want to talk to you!"

He didn't respond to her tirade; instead, he sent his stallion into a lope, and keeping a tight hold on Alisha's reins, he forced her horse to follow.

Realizing it would be useless to protest, Alisha fumed in silence during their short ride. The Longhorn was a mammoth spread, and several tack sheds were dotted across the land.

Reaching one of these storage shacks, Black Wolf pulled up, dismounted, stepped to Alisha's horse, and lifted her from the saddle and onto the ground.

Pushing out of his arms, she raved, "Don't touch me!"

Disobeying, he swept her back into his embrace. Pinning her against him, he uttered firmly, "Stop fighting me, you little wildcat."

Continuing her struggles, she cried angrily, "I hate you!"

"You don't hate me, Alisha," he murmured soothingly. "You love me, and I love you."

At first his proclamation didn't register, but as she slowly became aware of his words, she ceased fighting. "Did . . . did you say that you love me?" she stammered with disbelief.

Smiling, he held her even closer. "Yes, I love you. I love you with all my heart."

She had waited so long to hear him confess his love, and now that he finally had, the moment brought her no happiness. He might love her, but he cared nothing for their child, and she could never forgive him for that.

"Maybe you do love me," she said irritably. "But I still despise you!"

"Why do you think you despise me?" he asked, his tone gentle.

She replied sharply, "You don't want our baby!"

"But I do," he assured her.

She was hesitant to believe him. "That wasn't the impression I got when we talked earlier."

He took her hand. "It's cold out here; let's go inside the tack room."

She allowed him to lead her into the shelter, and as they entered the shed, she pulled her hand away from his. She glanced about vaguely, paying little attention to the bags of oats, saddles, bridles, and other odds and ends piled neatly in the room.

Going to a small stack of blankets, Black Wolf took one and spread it out on the wooden floor. Then, turning to Alisha, he gestured for her to sit down on the blanket. She complied, removing her hat and placing it at her side. Joining her, Black Wolf began, "After you left the study, I had a talk with David. He set me straight on a few things."

In detail, Black Wolf explained everything to Alisha, telling her about the day he had overheard part of her conversation with David, and the way in which he had misconstrued her reason for using the words "humiliating" and "degrading." He then let her know that he had thought she'd come to the Longhorn to berate him for hitting Johnny, and when he'd been referring to the fight between himself and her brother, she had mistakingly believed he was refusing to take responsibility for her pregnancy.

Finishing, he murmured, "I can hardly believe how close we came to losing each other over misunderstandings."

"Black Wolf, that's because you won't open up and talk to me. You're always so elusive."

"That was the only way I had to protect my feelings, for I was always certain that you couldn't really love a half-breed."

"My darling!" she cried, going into his arms. "You were so wrong about me!"

"I know," he admitted, drawing her snugly against his chest. "I promise you, Alisha, that from this moment forward, I'll always share my deepest feelings with you."

"And I shall share mine with you," she vowed.

His blue eyes twinkled as he remarked, "You can start sharing your feelings by telling me why you pretended to be engaged to Todd Miller."

She blushed somewhat. "Initially, I didn't want you to think that you were the only man who desired me. Later, I wanted to admit that I had fibbed, but I was afraid you'd think badly of me. I knew you had no patience with dishonesty." She looked at him pleadingly. "I'm sorry I lied to you."

Her face was raised to his, and his lips came down on hers. At first, their kiss was tender, and both were content to feel the other's touch. Soon, however, their passion began to climb, and as her lips parted, his tongue sought entrance, tasting the sweetness of her mouth.

"Alisha," he whispered ardenly, "I need you, and I want to make love to you."

"Oh yes, my darling!" she groaned, wanting him with all her heart and body.

Her movements anxious, she took off her boots as Black Wolf shed his own. Their jackets were also removed and pitched to the floor. Then, Black Wolf eased her farther down onto the blanket, and unfastening her trousers, he slipped them past her hips and down her legs. Smoothly, urgently, he peeled away her lace underwear, placing the garment aside.

His eyes relished her bare loveliness before he bent his head and placed his lips against her delectable womanhood.

Entwining her fingers in his dark hair, she encouraged his erotic fondling, and as his warm mouth continued to stimulate her passion, she felt as though she'd swoon with ecstasy.

"Darling!" she finally purred heatedly. "Take me now! . . . I want you so much!"

Gently he spread her legs, and kneeling between them, he released his trousers, shoving them past his muscular thighs. Gazing down into Alisha's flushed face, he smiled.

Although his sudden smile was sensual and impassioned, it was also filled with so much love that it sent Alisha's heart racing with joy.

Positioning himself with care, he penetrated her swiftly, his invasion making her tremble with longing.

Placing his hands under her hips, he brought her thighs up to his. "Alisha," he whispered as her ardor caused waves of desire to consume him.

Responding with unbridled rapture, Alisha arched beneath him, loving the feel of his hardness deep inside her.

His need now feverish, he pounded rapidly against her, and matching his strokes, she moaned provocatively, "Yes, Black Wolf. . . . Take me. . . . Take me, my darling."

"I love you, Alisha," he murmured. "You're mine and will always be mine."

Their need was now building ecstatically, causing Black Wolf to move against her strongly as their thrusting brought them to love's greatest bliss, where they clung tightly and were wonderfully fulfilled.

Black Wolf kissed Alisha tenderly, then drew up his trousers and left her to get another blanket, which he spread over them. The tack room was becoming quite chilly.

Cuddling close, she murmured, "It feels so heavenly to be back in your arms again."

"I know," he answered, kissing her brow. "When do you want to get married?"

She smiled. "Black Wolf, that wasn't a very romantic proposal, but I'll hold you to it just the same."

"Promise?" he murmured.

"You have my word," she responded happily. Patting her stomach, she continued, "Considering the circumstances, I think we should get married as quickly as possible."

His tone very serious, Black Wolf remarked carefully, "Your father is going to be against us returning to the Sioux."

"So you've decided to stay with Running Horse's people?"

"Did you think I wouldn't?"

She sighed deeply. "To be perfectly honest, I wish we could stay here and live at the Longhorn. However, I'm willing to make our home with the Sioux. As long as we're together, I'll be happy."

"Are you sure?" he pressed her.

"I've never been more sure of anything. I love you, Black Wolf. You're my life, my heart, my soul."

"Alisha," he groaned hoarsely, "what did I ever do to deserve a woman as loving as you are?"

She hugged him desperately. "That goes both ways, darling. Your love is as inspiring to me as mine is to you."

His lips conquered hers in a long, passionate kiss. "I love you so much," he murmured. He placed a hand on her stomach. "I also love our baby."

"Do you want a boy?"

"A son would be nice, but I'd be just as pleased with a daughter."

"When do you plan for us to return to your father's village?"

"I don't want you traveling until after the child is born."

"The baby should arrive in early June."

"In that case, we'll plan to leave in July. By then, you and the child will be strong enough to make the trip."

"Our leaving will break your grandfather's heart," she murmured sadly.

"I know," he whispered. "But it can't be helped. My place is with Running Horse."

"And my place is with you," she added, meaning it with all her heart.

Although evening shadows were darkening the study, Jack didn't leave his chair to light a lamp. Remaining seated, he stared vacantly, his gaze fixed on nothing in particular.

Losing Loretta to Joel had hurt him severely. At first he had tried to will the pain away, but it had continued to consume him until finally he had given into it.

Now, hoping brandy might make Loretta's betrayal easier to accept, he lifted the half-filled glass to his lips and took a large swallow.

He still believed that Loretta loved him and was only infatuated with Joel. If only she weren't so blindly enamored of Carson he might be able to make her see the truth.

Suddenly Jack smirked as he complained aloud to himself, "You didn't try very hard to convince her of the truth. You let her go without even putting up much of an argument, showing no gumption whatsoever!"

Impatient with himself, not to mention angry, he finished off the brandy and slammed the empty glass down on the desktop. A woman like Loretta was worth fighting for, yet he had submissively handed her over to Joel.

He frowned, mumbling, "It was as easy as taking candy from a baby, wasn't it, Carson? Well, Joel, my old friend, all's fair in love and war, and I'm not going to surrender the woman I love without first putting up one helluva stand!"

Bolstered by his decision, Jack was about to get to his feet when the study door opened. Glancing up, he saw Clint entering.

Stepping to a lamp, Clint lit it, then turned to his father. "Mary asked me to come here and let you know that she had Loretta's clothes packed." He walked over to stand beside Jack's chair. "Mary told me about Joel coming here and Loretta leaving with him. If you're sending her things into town, I'll take them to her."

"That won't be necessary," Jack said, standing. "I'll take them to her myself."

"Are you sure you want to do that, Pa?"

"You're damned right, I'm sure! I intend to have a long discussion with Loretta, and if Joel doesn't like it, then that's his problem."

"He might try to stop you," Clint warned.

"Try is all he'll do!" Jack declared forcefully. "The day that Carson can stop me from doing something I want to do will never come to pass."

Clint didn't argue, for he knew his father was right.

Joel had wanted Loretta to share his room, but she had insisted on separate quraters, leaving him no alternative but to tell the hotel clerk that he needed to rent another room.

482

Joel had escorted Loretta upstairs, then he'd left to return the rented buggy and horse to the town's livery stable.

Alone, Loretta had paced her room as she'd waited for Joel's return. She couldn't fathom why she was feeling so anxious and upset. Joel had come back into her life and she should be the happiest person on earth! So why . . . why wasn't she overflowing with joy?

When an hour passed without Joel showing up, Loretta had begun to worry. What was taking him so long? By the time two hours had gone by, she had grown gravely concerned.

Now, deciding to go look for him, Loretta hurried to the wardrobe to remove her coat, but the sudden knock on her door deterred her.

"Who's there?" she called.

"It's me, darling," Joel replied, his voice distinctively slurred.

"Come in," she called, watching closely as he stumbled into the room. Perturbed, she spat, "Joel, you're drunk!"

"No . . . no," he replied brokenly. "I'm just a little tipsy. I'll be all right as soon as I have dinner and coffee." Tottering clumsily to the bed, he managed to sit on the edge.

Loretta knew that drinking to excess was not Joel's usual style. Worried, she went over and sat beside him. His arms were resting on his knees, and his head was bowed; his shoulders slumped.

Kindly she prodded, "Joel, what's wrong? Does it have anything to do with Bonnie Sue?"

His head jerked up, and the wild glare in his eyes actually frightened her. "Don't talk about Bonnie Sue!" he snarled. "She's dead and . . . and there's nothing I can do to bring her back!" His frantic guilt coupled with his drunken condition sent him rambling incoherently. "Don't you realize if I could have a second chance, I'd not hurt her the way I did? . . . She didn't deserve the way I treated her! . . . Oh God, I hate myself! . . . But I loved her! . . . I swear that I did!"

Raspingly, she asked, "What did you do to her?" She wasn't sure she wanted to hear his answer.

"It's what I didn't do!" he exclaimed madly. "I couldn't make love to her! Everytime I tried, I'd envision that Sioux buck taking her time and time again! I'd see his large brown hands caressing her soft white flesh and . . . and then I'd see her beginning to respond. . . ."

Leaping to her feet, Loretta shouted, "Stop it! I don't want to hear anymore!"

Bolting from the bed, he gripped her shoulders tightly. "But you must hear the rest! I have to tell someone! If I continue to keep this guilt bottled up inside me, it'll drive me crazy!"

"No, Joel! Please!" she cried imploringly.

"Loretta, I'm begging you to listen! . . . God help me, I'm begging you!"

She pulled free from his uncomfortable grip, and moving away, she stepped slowly to the window. Drawing back the flimsy curtains, she gazed down at the quiet street. The fact that she no longer loved Joel hit her profoundly, and it took awhile for her to regain her composure.

"All right, Joel, if you feel that you must confess, then I'll listen. However, before you bare your soul, I want to make myself perfectly clear. I'm not going to marry you. From the moment you came back into my life, I sensed that there was something vital missing between us. Now, I know what it is: Love. We aren't in love. I think we once loved each other, but it died before it even had a chance to fully bloom."

"You don't mean that," he whispered.

Whirling about, she confronted him. "I do mean it, Joel."

"Are you going back to Jack?"

"If he'll have me, which I doubt."

He dropped limply back onto the bed. "He'll take you back. Jack's no fool."

"No, he isn't," she cried tearfully. "And I shouldn't have treated him as one."

He lifted his bloodshot eyes to hers. His face tortured, he mumbled solemnly, "It seems we've both done a good job of hurting two people who never deserved to be treated so cruelly." He shrugged. "Well, it isn't too late for you to make amends, but I'll have to live with what I did for the rest of my life."

She returned to sit at his side. "Joel, you mustn't punish yourself in this way."

"Loretta," he groaned, "I'll carry this guilt with me to my grave!" He reached over and clasped her hand in his. Quietly, and in a strained voice, he began telling Loretta the tragic events that led up to Bonnie Sue's death.

Chapter Forty-Two

As Joel's story unfolded, Loretta listened with reluctance. She didn't want to know what happened between Bonnie Sue and Joel; she felt it was too personal. However, despite her reservations, Loretta made no attempt to stop Joel. She believed him when he said that if he didn't talk to someone about his guilt, it would drive him crazy. So, regardless of her feelings, she paid close attention as Joel began to pour out his heart.

Bonnie Sue waited impatiently for her husband to come to their bedroom. He was having a drink in the hotel lobby, but before leaving, had assured her that he'd return soon. The moment he had left, Bonnie Sue had hurried to her armoire and removed the garment that she had been sewing secretively. The flowing, graceful nightgown was finished except for a few stitches at the ruffled neckline. Taking her needle and thread, she had quickly completed the final touches. Then, removing her dress and undergarments, she'd slipped into the nightgown and hastened to the mirror to study her reflection.

Bonnie Sue had looked extremely lovely and seductive in the lilac gown that she had sewn so diligently, and as she had taken each dainty stitch with precision, she'd hoped desperately that the provocative garment would revive her husband's passion.

Now, turning back the bed covers, she lay down and propped the pillows against the headboard. Carefully, she arranged the billowing folds of her gown so the material would drape gracefully along her slender body. Anxious for Joel's return, she stared at the closed door and waited for it to open.

A few minutes later, Joel returned, and his wife's seductive ploy hit him incredibly. It wasn't like Bonnie Sue to be promiscuous. She had always been a little shy when it came to the intimacies of marriage, and her shyness had met with his approval. She certainly had never initiated their love-making.

Walking farther into the room, Joel closed and locked the door. Then, when he turned back around to face his wife, a bitter frown hardened his features. He wondered if this provocative change in Bonnie Sue was somehow related to Strong Fox. Had the warrior stirred a passion in her that he himself had never aroused? Was she now tempting him because she needed someone to appease this need that Strong Fox had awakened?

Suddenly, Joel wiped such thoughts from his mind. Of course Strong Fox hadn't pleased her! She had been his victim; not his lover! What was wrong with him? Why did he keep doubting his wife's fidelity?

"Joel, what's wrong?" Bonnie Sue asked warily, wishing she could read his thoughts. She had seen his bitter frown and was anxious.

Burying his suspicions, Joel smiled. "Nothing's wrong," he answered evenly.

She held out her arms to him. "Then come here, my

darling, and hold me."

He was hesitant to do so, for he knew she wanted him to make love to her, and he was afraid he'd be impotent. If only he could stop envisioning her and Strong Fox wrapped together in amorous bliss! If he could somehow erase the picture from his mind, then maybe he could regain his virility. Telling himself that this time he'd blot out all thoughts of Strong Fox, he went to his wife's side and sat on the bed.

Gingerly, he drew her into his arms. She raised her lips to his, and his mouth descended to hers.

Bonnie Sue needed Joel desperately, and his kiss set fire to her passion. Although she had always been somewhat bashful when it came to sexually pleasing her husband, she nonetheless had thoroughly enjoyed their intimate unions. However, she believed it was now time to set aside her shyness. She would pleasure her husband as a good wife should: freely and sensually. Also, if she could arouse him to the point of ecstasy, surely he'd forget those months when they were apart and return her love to the fullest.

Throwing away her old inhibitions, Bonnie Sue grasped Joel's hand and placed it on her breast. With her lips still sealed to his, she purred, "Love me, darling."

As he kneaded her soft mound, he could feel her nipple hardening beneath the gown's delicate material.

Encouraged by her husband's response, Bonnie Sue decided to go a step further. Removing his hand from her breast, she slipped it under her nightdress, moving it slowly, temptingly, until his palm was touching her womanly core. Nibbling at his earlobe, she moaned delightfully, "Oh yes, my husband. . . . Touch me. . . . Touch me all over."

He could feel his manhood responding to his wife's seduction. "Bonnie Sue!" he murmured, easing her back onto the bed. Anxiously he lifted her gown, admiring the golden triangle between her thighs before urging her legs apart and sliding his finger into her moist depths. Soon his need to take her completely was pressing, and he was about to shed his clothes when, all at once, his vision came back to haunt him. His eyes glassy with jealous rage, he looked down at his hand pressed against her soft flesh, but he was no longer seeing his own hand, but Strong Fox's. Had Bonnie Sue also opened her legs so shamelessly for that Indian buck? Had she purred and squirmed beneath the warrior's probing finger?

Unable to cope with his suspicions, he bolted from the bed, went to the liquor cabinet, and poured himself a stiff drink of whiskey.

Now Bonnie Sue was crying; tears rolled down her face. Sitting up and straightening her gown she moaned wretchedly, "Oh Joel, what is wrong with you?"

Turning and facing her, he started to mumble an apology, but before he could, she was struck with a violent coughing seizure.

Hurrying to her side, he sat down and handed her his handkerchief. When the spell let up, he said firmly, "That cough has been hanging on for weeks. I insist that tomorrow you see one of the fort's doctors. I can't understand why you haven't done so before now." He touched her brow. "You feel a little hot. Have you been running a fever?"

She scowled at him. "If you ever bothered to touch me, you'd know the answer to that question!" Her anger and resentment flared heatedly. "But you don't want to touch me, do you? Because every time you do, you think about Strong Fox! Do you imagine him rubbing his hands all over me? My God, are you jealous of the man who held me captive? That monster who raped me time and time again?"

His insane jealousy exploded: "Yes!" Bounding to his feet, he glared at her frantically. "Did you respond to him, Bonnie Sue? Is that why you're now so passionate?" He frowned distastefully. "How could you cheapen yourself with an Indian buck? You were raised to be a southern aristocrat. You were a purebred lady. I actually had you on a pedestal!"

Bonnie Sue was shocked by his ugly accusations, and as a strange numbness came over her, she left the bed. Going to the armoire, she took out a set of clothes.

"What do you think you're doing?" Joel demanded.

"I'm going for a walk," she replied, her emotions remaining strangely calm.

"It's cold outside, and I think it's going to rain," he said shortly.

She began to dress. "I really don't care. I want to get away from you and be alone with my thoughts."

"Then you stay here, and I'll leave," he offered.

"No! I need the fresh air," she remarked, her tone adamant.

She finished dressing quickly, grabbed her cloak, and without giving her husband so much as a backward glance, left the room.

Loretta drew her hand from Joel's vise-like grip, and stepping aside, turned her back toward him and gazed blankly out the window.

Joel continued, "When it started raining, I became worried and went to look for her. By the time I found Bonnie Sue she was soaking wet and her fever was raging."

Brusquely, Loretta whirled about to face him. "Please spare me the rest of your story. I can well imagine the ending. Bonnie Sue caught pneumonia and it killed her. Now you blame yourself because if it hadn't been for your jealousy, she'd never have wandered about in the rain."

Joel's eyes gleamed hopelessly. "You have no sympathy for me whatsoever, do you?"

"I think you're pathetic!" She spouted the truth before realizing her cruelty. Who was she to pass judgment?

Leaving the bed, he went to her side. "I begged Bonnie Sue to forgive me, and she did so on her deathbed."

"Then you must learn to forgive yourself," Loretta told him kindly.

Her gentleness renewed his hope, and he grasped her hands. "I think I could find a way to forgive myself if I had you. Loretta, please marry me!"

"No, Joel!" she said firmly, pulling her hands free. "I don't love you."

"You aren't in love with Jack, are you?" he demanded.

She walked to the door and opened it. "Joel, please leave."

"Not until you answer me! Are you in love with Jack?"

Was she? When she had fallen out of love with Joel, had she fallen in love with Jack? Had the two emotions crossed so easily and subtly that she hadn't even been aware of the exchange? An image of Jack flashed before her, and the happy moments they had shared ran fleetingly through her mind. Yes, she thought, I love Jack Stevens! He's everything a woman could want in a man. He's strong, gentle, giving and compassionate.

Her unyielding gaze locked with Joel's. "I didn't realize until now just how deeply I love Jack. I fell in love with you overnight; but with Jack, it happened gradually and became stronger with each passing day." She opened the door wider. "Joel, please respect my feelings and leave."

Hesitantly, he moved across the room. "All right, Loretta, I'll do as you say. But I plan to leave on the morning stage, so you have until then to change your mind." He paused in front of her, took her hands, and squeezed them tightly. "I hope you'll have a change of heart, Loretta, for I truly do love you."

"You love me because you need me, but Jack needs me because he loves me. Can you understand the difference?"

Releasing her hands, he nodded solemnly. "Yes, I can." He leaned over and placed a light kiss on her cheek, but the touch of his lips left her cold.

It was on the tip of his tongue to plead with her to marry him, but knowing it would be useless to do so, Joel left without further comment.

Loretta closed the door, then moved back to gaze out the window. A buckboard from the Bar-S was now parked in front of the hotel, but she was too troubled to notice it. In the morning, she decided, I'll go to Jack and tell him how sorry I am.

Tears stung her eyes. Oh God, what if he doesn't forgive me? He might not even believe that I love him! How could I blame him for feeling that way? All this time, I've always sworn to him that I loved Joel, when all along I was in love with Jack! How could I have been so foolish?

A loud knock on the door disrupted her thoughts. Joel! she cried inwardly. Why did he return? I don't want to see him! Nonetheless, she gave in and called with a trace of irritation, "Come in."

She heard the visitor entering, and keeping her back turned in his direction, she said testily, "Joel, why did you come back? I told you it was all over between us.

First thing in the morning, I'm returning to the Bar-S. I'd leave now if it wasn't growing dark outside. When I see Jack, I'll even get down on my knees and beg him to forgive me if it should be necessary."

"You won't have to beg. A sincere 'I love you' will suffice."

Loretta spun around, and the sight of Jack standing in the open doorway shocked her. He was grinning happily and his arms were held out to her.

Crying aloud with joy, she flew into his embrace, and as he gathered her close, she sobbed over and over, "I love you! . . . I love you! . . . Jack, my darling, I love you with all my heart!"

Her declaration was music to his ears. "I love you too, Loretta!"

"Please forgive me!" she pleaded, tears flowing freely.

Wiping at the tears wetting her cheeks, he murmured, "Darlin', all is forgiven."

"I'm so glad you're here," she said softly.

He chuckled. "I came here to fight for you, but it seems that won't be necessary."

"You were going to fight for me?" she asked, astounded.

His eyes twinkled. "You're worth fighting for."

Wrapping her arms about him, she replied cunningly, "Will you settle for a passionate interlude instead of a fight?"

"That's a tough decision," he teased, closing the door with a solid push. Lifting her, he carried her to the bed, and as he laid her down with care, he remarked quite casually, "Later, we'll visit the parson and ask him to marry us."

Surprised, she stammered, "Do you mean . . . you want us to get married tonight?"

Lying beside her and taking her into his arms, he

asked, "Why not? I don't see any reason to wait until next week, do you?"

"No, I don't," she answered happily.

"Then it's settled. We'll get married tonight, but first, didn't you say something about a passionate interlude?"

"It seems that I did, but the memory is a little hazy," she purred playfully.

"In that case, allow me to freshen your memory," he whispered as his lips came down to possess hers.

Anxious to return to the Bar-S, Jack and his bride rose early the next morning. As she followed her husband down the stairs and out of the hotel, Loretta could hardly believe that she was now a wife. As planned, they had visited the parson and gotten married; then they had enjoyed a leisurely dinner in the hotel dining room before retiring to their room where, on their wedding night, they had found complete rapture.

Now, as they stepped out of the hotel to walk to the livery stable, the sight confronting them caused their steps to halt suddenly.

Joel and Johnny were standing in front of the Golden Horseshoe, and their gazes swept across the street to lock with Loretta's and Jack's.

It was a moment before Johnny left Joel's side to cross the street. Walking up to the couple, he looked at his father and said, "There's a rumor going around that you and Miss Ingalls got married last night."

"The rumor's true," Jack replied. He hoped his youngest son wouldn't say anything to arouse his anger.

Johnny smiled pleasantly, which surprised his

father. "Good!" he declared. "Joel's invited me to go to St. Louis with him. However, if Miss Ingalls had changed her mind about accompanying him, then I'd been left behind. So, needless to say, I'm glad you two are married. Now I can get out of this boring town and go to a lively city like St. Louis. Joel has friends there, and he's sure he can get us both jobs."

"When are you leaving?" Jack asked. He should've known his son's happiness stemmed from selfishness.

"In a couple of hours," he answered.

"You'll keep in touch?" his father wanted to know.

"Sure, Pa," he assured him, although he had no intentions of doing so. "Well, so long, and tell Clint and Alisha goodbye for me."

With that, Johnny turned about and headed back across the street. Watching, Jack almost called out to him. A parting between a father and son shouldn't be so cold and unfeeling. He longed to embrace Johnny and tell him that he loved him, that if he ever needed him not to hesitate to get in touch. But Jack didn't call out to his son, for he knew Johnny didn't want his father's affection. He had disowned his family and wanted no part of them. Sadly, he wondered if he'd ever see Johnny again. He hoped he would, praying that someday his youngest son would mature into an honorable and compassionate man.

Looking away from his son, Jack turned to Loretta. She was watching Joel with a solemn expression on her face. "Are you feeling sorry for Carson?" he asked.

"No," she murmured. "Truthfully, I was feeling sorry for Bonnie Sue. She deserved a better husband than Joel."

"Joel's weak," Jack said firmly. "Bonnie Sue may have been fragile all her life, but she was the strength in that marriage."

Tucking her arm into her husband's, Loretta smiled up at him. "Let's go to the stables. I'm eager to return home."

He returned her smile. "So am I, and Alisha and Clint will be happy to hear our news."

As they began strolling, Loretta replied, "Yes, but Alisha is going to be upset with us because she missed the ceremony."

"Talking about Alisha and Clint . . ." he remarked, catching sight of them riding into town with Black Wolf.

Seeing Jack and Loretta, they guided their horses to the side of the street and dismounted.

Hurrying to them, Alisha said hastily, "Papa! When you didn't come home last night, we were so worried that something had happened to you!"

"Something did happen," he declared, grinning. He waited for Clint and Black Wolf to join them before explaining, "Loretta and I are married!"

Alisha looked at Loretta, her face questioning.

"I love your father," Loretta said happily. "I was so wrong about loving Joel."

Hugging her, Alisha cried, "I'm so happy for you!" She then embraced her father, exclaiming, "I love you, Papa!"

Alisha waited for the others to express their good wishes, then slipping her hand into Black Wolf's, she said to her father, "We're getting married, and we plan to do so as soon as possible."

Jack smiled. "That's wonderful news. I suspected all along that you two were in love." He shook hands with Black Wolf. "Son, welcome to the family. It makes me very happy to know that although I have lost my daughter, she'll be no farther away than the Longhorn."

"I'm sorry, Mr. Stevens," Black Wolf began. "But

496

this summer, Alisha and I will be returning to my father's village."

"No!" Jack exclaimed, his tone desperate. "You can't be serious! The Black Hills is no place for Alisha! My God, you know that war between the Sioux and the cavalry is inevitable. What will happen to Alisha then? How can you claim to love her, then place her in such danger?"

"Papa, please," Alisha implored. "Black Wolf and I have discussed this in detail. I'm more than willing to live with him in his father's village."

"Mr. Stevens, when war develops, I'll bring Alisha back to the Bar-S. I have no intentions of placing her life in jeopardy."

"No!" Alisha argued. "Black Wolf, I won't leave you!"

Firmly, he said, "We won't worry about that now. We'll cross that bridge when the time comes."

"Does your grandfather know you're returning to the Sioux?" Jack asked.

"Yes. I told him last night."

"How did he take it?"

"Not very well, I'm sorry to say."

Grasping at his last chance to change Black Wolf's mind, Jack said strongly, "You owe it to Charles to remain at the Longhorn!"

"No, Mr. Stevens," Black Wolf uttered emphatically. "I owe it to my father to return. For over thirty years, I never even knew my grandfather existed. But I have loved my father all my life. Running Horse's health is failing, and I intend to spend as much time with him as possible. If it weren't for winter, I'd leave now." He purposefully omitted mentioning Alisha's condition.

However, Alisha saw no reason to omit it. "The weather isn't our main reason for waiting until summer, Papa. I'm pregnant."

Suspiciously, Jack questioned, "Is that why you two are getting married?"

Her face aglow, Alisha answered, "No, Papa. We love each other!"

Sadness shadowed Jack's face, causing Loretta to be concerned. "Darling, what's wrong?"

"I'm not only losing a daughter, but also a grand-child."

"Papa," Alisha cried, "please don't think of it like that! I love Black Wolf! Can't you be happy for me?"

He held out his arms to her, and Alisha went into her father's embrace. "I am happy for you, honey." He drew her desperately close. "But I'm going to miss you with all my heart."

Looking on, Black Wolf sympathized with Jack's feelings. He knew when the time came, it would be extremely difficult for the man to let his daughter go to the Sioux.

Glancing away from Alisha and Jack, Black Wolf sighed heavily. He almost wished he'd had the strength to hold onto his convictions to never love a white woman, for he had always known that their separate worlds might cause unhappiness. But it was now too late to think about what he should have done. He loved Alisha and was not about to lose her. They would have to find a way to be happy in spite of the sadness their leaving would bring upon Jack and Charles.

Alisha left her father's embrace and snuggled into Black Wolf's. As though some unseen force was threatening to take her away from him, he drew her as close as possible. She was his life, his whole world, and he'd never let her go!

Epilogue

The three riders were spotted before reaching Running Horse's village, and the small group of warriors who rode out to greet them was led by Kicking Buffalo.

Black Wolf, Alisha, and Spotted Fawn reined in their horses. They had crested a small hill and had a clear view of the men who were riding out to welcome them.

Recognizing her father, Spotted Fawn tensed and her heart picked up speed. Would he acknowledge her? Had his heart softened toward her during her absence?

Sensing Spotted Fawn's anxiety, Alisha turned toward her and smiled encouragingly. "Everything will be all right." She knew that Spotted Fawn was no longer infatuated with Johnny, and if she felt anything at all for him, it was probably contempt.

Smiling in return, the young Indian woman replied, "I pray that my father has forgiven me." She turned her gaze to the infant who was safely enclosed in the upright cradle strapped to Alisha's back, and reaching over, she touched the baby's hand in a gentle caress.

Soon after the child's birth, Spotted Fawn, with Black Wolf's assistance, had made the moveable cradle for the journey through the Black Hills. The cradle was made from a board two and a half feet long and one and a half feet wide. The infant rested in a brightly embroidered sack which was nailed securely to the board. The baby's covering opened in front and was laced up and down with buckskin strings. Over the arms of the infant was a wooden bow, the ends of which were firmly attached to the board, so that if the cradle should fall the child's head and face would be protected.

As the warriors arrived, Black Wolf dismounted. Grinning largely, he stepped to Kicking Buffalo, who was swinging down from his pony. The two men embraced fondly.

"Black Wolf," Kicking Buffalo began, "it is good to see you again."

"How's my father?" he asked urgently.

"Running Horse is very ill. The cold winter was hard on him. It is good that you have returned, for soon my brother will leave us to go to the spirit world."

Black Wolf grieved. "Are you sure he's dying?"

"The Medicine Woman says it is so."

The men had been speaking in their native language, but during the long winter months at the Longhorn, Black Wolf had started teaching Alisha Siouan, and she was able to understand that Running Horse was dying.

Noticing the baby strapped in the upright cradle, Kicking Buffalo asked his nephew, "Are you now a father?"

"Yes, I am," he replied, and in spite of his worry for Running Horse, a smile touched his lips, for Black Wolf utterly adored his child.

"Running Horse will be pleased to learn that he's a grandfather." The warrior paused, then inquired, "How long do you plan to stay with us?"

Alisha held her breath as she waited for Black Wolf's

reply. Although she was still willing to live permanently with the Sioux, a large part of her heart longed for them to make their home at the Longhorn.

"I'm not sure," Black Wolf answered.

Alisha relaxed. Why wasn't he sure? Was he debating returning someday to the Longhorn?

Carefully, Kicking Buffalo raised his gaze to Spotted Fawn. She met his eyes, praying desperately for his forgiveness.

Kicking Buffalo smiled tentatively. "Welcome home, daughter. You have been missed."

Joy raced through her. She knew that was her father's way of letting her know that he had forgiven her. "How is mother and Flying Hawk?"

"They are well and will be happy to see you." He turned to Black Wolf, and switching to English, said, "I thank you for taking good care of Spotted Fawn." He looked at Alisha. "I also thank you, Fallen Snow."

"You're welcome," she murmured softly. "But Spotted Fawn has been so much help to me that I don't know what I'd have done without her."

"My daughter is a good woman." Once again, his gaze went fondly to Spotted Fawn. "I am proud to be her father."

As Kicking Buffalo mounted his pony to lead them into the village, Spotted Fawn watched her father through a tearful blur, her tears a sign of her joy.

Running Horse's wife showed Black Wolf and Alisha with their child into the chief's lodge, then left so the four of them could be alone.

Alisha stood back as Black Wolf went to his father's bed and sat beside him. The man's eyes were closed and he wondered if he was asleep. Gently, Black Wolf placed his hand on Running Horse's arm. "Father?"

501

he whispered.

His eyelids fluttered, and at first he didn't realize what had awakened him. Then slowly becoming aware of Black Wolf's presence, he turned his head to the side and looked at him. Smiling feebly, the chief spoke as though his son had not been away for months, "I was dreaming about the morning you were born. I was sitting at the river and had one of my visions."

Running Horse was speaking Siouan, and even though Alisha had not yet mastered the language, she was able to grasp most of what the chief was saying.

His voice was extremely weak as he continued explaining his dream, "I dreamt of a pack of wild dogs, and among them was a cross between a dog and a wolf."

Black Wolf had heard his father describe the vision several times, but the chief seemed set on repeating it one last time, so he made no attempt to dissuade him from doing so.

However, Black Wolf had never told Alisha of his father's vision, and she listened with intense interest.

"The wolves began to move into the land belonging to the dogs, causing conflict and war to erupt. Often, at night, this half-dog and half-wolf would wander to the top of a high ridge, where he would listen to the howling of the wolves. For many years, his love for the dogs kept him from returning the wolves' constant howls, but finally his instincts took control; and one night under a full moon, he climbed up upon the ridge. He lifted his head and cried one long, baleful wail, his cry identical to that of the wolf's. Then, he turned and looked down at the pack of dogs who were the only family he had ever known. His eyes overflowed with tears, and they spilled freely, falling onto the rocky terrain and rolling down the steep hillside. These tears flowed to where his father stood watching. The dog dipped his head and licked up his son's tears, then when he returned his gaze to the high ridge, he found it empty. He knew his son had gone to live with the wolves. The tears he had licked from the ground mingled with his own, and bowing his head, he shed not only his own tears, but also those of his son."

Alisha had been so fascinated with the dream that she spoke without thinking. "What does the vision mean?" The unexpected sound of her own voice actually took her by surprise. She looked quickly to Black Wolf. Was he angry at her for speaking out of turn?

"Fallen Snow?" Running Horse called. She had blurted the question in Siouan and the chief was impressed. He tried to raise his head but was too weak.

"Yes, Father," Black Wolf said. "My wife is here with me."

"Wife?" the chief repeated, pleased. "Tell Fallen Snow to come closer. I want to talk to her."

Black Wolf motioned for her, and she went to his side and sat down. The baby was still strapped to her back and was sound asleep within the snug cradle.

Running Horse answered Alisha's inquiry without preliminaries. "The vision means that Black Wolf will leave the Sioux to live with the white man."

"Would that make you unhappy?" she asked.

"The spirits have willed it so. It is not my place to be happy or unhappy. We must all do as the spirits command."

Alisha gave her husband a sidelong glance, but his face was inscrutable, and she couldn't read his thoughts. Before marriage, they had discussed the white man's religion, as well as the Sioux's. They had both agreed that, regardless of the names given to Him, there was only one god. Where the Sioux referred to spirits, the white man would probably use the term

"Fate." The Indians believed in a high and all-powerful Spirit; the white man called him God.

The infant, awakening, began to whimper. Hearing the baby's soft cry, Running Horse's face lit up with joy. "Black Wolf, do you have a child?"

Quickly Black Wolf helped Alisha take off the upright cradle, then removing the infant from its portable bed, he showed the child to Running Horse.

A smile crossed the chief's pallid face. "The child is beautiful. Have I been blessed with a grandson or a granddaughter?"

"A granddaughter," Black Wolf answered.

Alisha hoped Running Horse wouldn't be disappointed that the baby wasn't a boy. But the prideful gleam that shone in the chief's eyes told her that he was delighted.

"Does she have a name?"

"We named her Abigal," Black Wolf replied.

"When I go to the spirit world, I will tell your mother that you chose her name for your daughter. She will be pleased." His expression became questioning. "Her Sioux name?"

"We haven't given her one. We decided to let you name her."

"I am honored," he replied. "Unwrap her so I can have a good look."

Carefully Black Wolf removed the light blanket, then lifting the infant, he held her so that Running Horse could see her clearly.

The chief studied the baby thoughtfully. Her hair was as black as her father's, but her eyes were going to be brown like her mother's. At four weeks, she was a chubby, healthy baby, and now, growing uncomfortable, she let out a demanding wail.

Her strong cry caused Running Horse to smile, and as Black Wolf handed the child to Alisha, he said with

504

deep feeling, "My heart is thankful that my grand-daughter is healthy and full of vigor. Black Wolf, you must keep her that way. Return to Charles Lansing's ranch where your daughter can grow up with plenty of food and good care. Hunger and tribulations will soon befall the Sioux. I beg you, do not let little Abigal suffer these hardships."

Although Black Wolf avoided discussing the issue, deep in his heart he knew his destiny would not be altered. "Have you thought of a name yet?"

"Yes. She will be called Summer Sun, for like the sun in summer, she will bring warmth into the lives of those who love her. The spirits tell me that Summer Sun will feel much compassion for all mankind and will have a heart which overflows with kindness."

Alisha cuddled her daughter close. The baby had fallen back asleep and her little face was serene. Would Running Horse's prediction come to pass? Would her child possess an abundance of compassion and kindness?

Reading Alisha's thoughts, Running Horse said readily, "My prophecies always come true."

Pleased, Alisha smiled and placed a loving kiss on her daughter's brow.

Black Wolf thought he had prepared himself for Running Horse's death, yet when the chief died, the loss of his father hit Black Wolf very hard. With the help of Alisha's love and understanding, he came to grips with his grief and put it behind him. But Black Wolf had loved both of his parents and knew his memories of them would stay with him for a lifetime.

Running Horse had been gone for over a month when Kicking Buffalo found Black Wolf sitting alone at the riverbank. He approached his nephew hesitantly, for he dreaded telling him the news he was about to deliver. Without speaking, he sat down and joined him.

Black Wolf knew that his uncle had been in a conference with the council, a meeting to which he himself hadn't been invited. Sensing Kicking Buffalo's reluctance to talk, Black Wolf tried to put him at ease. "I know why I wasn't invited to attend the conference. The council has decided on a new chief, and they didn't want me to be there because I was the main topic of conversation. And what they had to say about me wasn't especially commendable."

"Black Wolf," Kicking Buffalo began hastily, "your father's people love you, even the old men who make up the council."

"Why do you refer to everyone as my father's people? Aren't they also mine? Does my white blood completely alienate me?"

"No, of course not. However, the council has decided that our chief should be a full-blooded Sioux. They are afraid that your mixed heritage might make you prejudiced toward your mother's people."

Black Wolf concurred. "My mixed loyalties would pull me in two different directions." He smiled warmly. "Are you the new chief?"

"Yes, I am," he answered.

"The council made a wise decision."

Kicking Buffalo spoke uneasily. "Running Horse knew that you wouldn't be made chief. Somehow, he knew that the council wouldn't appoint you. He admitted this to me, and he also said that he agreed." He looked carefully at his nephew. "Your father believed, and so do I, that the spirits want you to leave the Sioux. Your fate was foretold on the morning you were born." He paused, then added somberly, "My nephew, the time has come for you to fulfill your father's prophecy."

"Are you ordering me to leave this village?"

"No," he answered quickly. "This is your home, we are your people. You are my brother's only child and I love you. If you refuse to follow your destiny, you may stay with us for the rest of your life. But I must warn you that when the time comes, I will proclaim war against the Bluecoats and all whites who try to take away our land. If you remain, you will have to fight your mother's people. Your good friends Major Landon and Justin Smith will become our enemy." He watched him closely. "If you found yourself facing either of them on the field of battle, could you kill them?"

Sudden perspiration beaded his brow as he envisioned himself in physical conflict against the two men whom he loved as brothers. "No, I couldn't kill either of them," he admitted truthfully.

"Black Wolf," the new chief murmured sadly, "you must do as the spirits have willed. Charles Lansing is a rich man and owns a lot of cattle. Many of the Sioux will choose peace and move to reservations. The white chiefs in Washington will not worry if their stomachs are empty, but you and your grandfather will have the means to feed them and the money to buy needed supplies. You can do more good for the Sioux by taking your place in the white man's life. Do not be selfish and think only of yourself and this determination you have to remain loyal to your father's people."

Kicking Buffalo stood and without further words walked away, leaving Black Wolf alone with his deep thoughts.

One night weeks after Black Wolf's and Kicking Buffalo's discussion at the riverbank, the setting sun cast a golden hue across the Longhorn.

The four people seated on the front porch watched as the last light of day faded over the horizon.

Loretta, heavy with child, said to Charles, "Maybe I should go to the kitchen and help Edna with dinner."

Upon Spotted Fawn's departure, a new housekeeper had been hired. "That's not necessary," Charles answered. "I'm sure Edna can manage just fine."

"By the way," Jack began, speaking to his good friend. "Thanks for inviting us to dinner."

"You're more than welcome," Charles replied. "Since Chuck and Alisha left, this place seems so lonely." He grinned at David, who was sitting sideways on the stalwart railing. "I'm just glad I have David to keep me company."

The boy sighed despondently. "I sure miss them," he mumbled, referring to Black Wolf and Alisha.

"I wonder how they are," Loretta pondered softly.

"I'm sure they're fine," Jack murmured, missing them so much that his heart ached for their return.

Charles was seated in a rocker, and rocking the chair with a slow, smoothing motion, he said solemnly, "I wish they'd come back. But I'm probably wishing in vain, for Chuck seemed determined to make his home with the Sioux."

David, staring thoughtfully at the darkening horizon, noticed two riders approaching. They were too far away for him to recognize them. "Someone's comin'," he uttered, somewhat disinterested.

"A couple of your cowhands?" Jack asked Charles.

"No, they're all at the bunkhouse."

As the visitors drew closer, David tensed. His eyes widened with disbelief as he suddenly realized who they were. Excited, he exclaimed, "It's Black Wolf and Alisha!"

His announcement sent the other three bounding to their feet. They hurried to the edge of the porch so that they could get a better view.

"It *is* them!" Charles cried exultantly.

The four raced down the steps, and as Black Wolf and Alisha arrived, they were greeted jubilantly.

Following hugs, kisses, and zealous welcomes, a semblance of order came over the reunion.

They had all returned to the porch. Jack held his granddaughter as though he intended never to let her go; then he asked Black Wolf, "Son, why did you return?"

"There are several reasons why I decided to come back, but my father's death was the most important one. My love for Running Horse was the main reason that I had to return to the Sioux."

"I understand," Jack replied. "Love is a very strong bond."

"Yes, it is," Black Wolf agreed, his eyes meeting Alisha's. He could see her happiness. If he had decided to stay with the Sioux, he knew his wife wouldn't have complained, even though her heart had longed to return to the Longhorn. Turning to Charles, he said with sincerity, "It's good to be home."

Holding back his tears unsuccessfully, Lansing stepped to Black Wolf and embraced him firmly. His voice quivered with emotion. "Chuck, you'll never know how much it means to me to hear you say that. All those years when I was building this spread, there was some unknown force driving me. Now I know that it was all for you. All the hard work, disappointments, and frustrations that it took to make this ranch were well worth it."

At that moment, the housekeeper stepped out onto the porch. "Dinner is ready," she announced.

Releasing his grandson, Charles remarked, "Set two more places at the table." His gaze sweeping from Black Wolf to Alisha, he added with feeling, "My family has come home!"

Jack and Loretta were sitting on the porch swing, and handing Abigal to Alisha, Jack helped his wife to her feet.

"Isn't the baby due next month?" Alisha asked Loretta, noticing her heavy pregnancy.

"Yes, and I'm so anxious."

"It's hard to imagine that Abigal will have an uncle or an aunt younger than she is." Alisha looked at her father. "Speaking of uncles, how's Clint?"

"He's fine."

"Have you heard from Johnny?"

"No, not a word."

Charles said flatly, "You'll hear from him, just as soon as he needs something."

Escorting Loretta into the house, Jack agreed, "I'm sure you're right."

Charles started to follow the couple, but pausing, his gaze fell upon the others. His eyes grew misty as he studied Black Wolf, Alisha, his great-granddaughter Abigal, and David. Smiling, he said movingly, "You could never imagine how wonderful the sight of my family is to these old eyes of mine. I thank God for each and every one of you."

Slipping into bed beside her husband, Alisha snuggled close. "Black Wolf, are you sure you aren't regretting your decision to come back?"

"No," he assured her. "This is now home to me." He smiled. "You know the old saying. 'Home is where the heart is.' My heart's at the Longhorn with Charles, David, Abigal and you."

"But a part of your heart will always be with the Sioux."

"Kicking Buffalo was right, though, when he said

that I can be more help to them here at the ranch. When the time comes, and it most assuredly will, I'll see to it personally that the people on the reservations receive food and supplies."

"You can't help them all," she reminded him. "There will be too many reservations, and some of them will be too far from here."

"I know," he sighed sadly. "But if I can help a selected few, it will save future generations."

"The future?" she mused aloud. "I wonder what it holds for us?"

"I know what the immediate future holds for you," he replied seductively, leaning over her.

"I can hardly wait," she purred teasingly.

His lips sought hers in a long, love-filled exchange. They were nude, and as their flesh touched, passion sparked between them.

Expertly, Black Wolf aroused his wife's need to an ecstatic pitch before drawing her thighs to his and penetrating her swiftly.

Alisha responded to her husband's exciting thrusts, and they soon became totally engulfed in their ardent joining. Together, they soared to love's highest plane before drifting blissfully back to earth.

Black Wolf kissed her endearingly, then moved to lie at her side.

They remained silent for a time, both at peace with their own thoughts. Gradually, Alisha's musings turned to David, and she murmured, "I wonder what the future has in store for David?"

"He'll own Miller's ranch."

She smiled affectionately. "Darling, that sounds so cut-and-dried. Now that you're a married man, have you no romance in your blood? David is so extremely handsome, and he's smart, brave, and daring. What kind of woman will it take to win his heart? She will have to be very special, don't you think?"

Black Wolf chuckled. "Alisha, my lovely romantic, we'll just have to wait for the future to become the present before learning what kind of woman will conquer David's heart."

Cuddling intimately, she whispered sweetly, "Black Wolf, I love you."

"I love you more," he returned playfully.

"Impossible," she murmured, rising up and moving over him.

As his wife's soft, supple body aroused his passion, he said thickly, "Why is it impossible?"

"Because my love for you cannot be surpassed," she toyed, nibbling at his earlobe.

"In that case, will you settle for a tie and agree that we love each other equally?"

"That all depends," she breathed.

"On what?" Her provocative ministrations were stirring his desire.

"On what happens next," she responded invitingly.

Grasping her around the waist, he pinned her beneath him. Recalling the first time they had made love, he repeated the words he had spoken to her on that special occasion.

"Beautiful lady, you're about to get more than you bargained for."